Praise for

RACHEL LEE

"A suspenseful, edge-of-the-seat read."
—*Publishers Weekly* on *Before I Sleep*

"*Shadows of Myth* is a fantastic fantasy....
Rachel Lee, known for her terrific romantic suspense tales,
provides a wonderful good vs. evil fantasy."
—*The Best Reviews*

"Rachel Lee deserves much acclaim for her
exciting tales of romantic suspense."
—*Midwest Book Review*

"Lee crafts a heartrending saga."
—*Publishers Weekly* on *Snow in September*

RACHEL LEE

SHADOWS of PROPHECY

LUNA™

www.LUNA-Books.com

LUNA™

First edition January 2006

SHADOWS OF PROPHECY

ISBN 0-373-80219-6

www.LUNA-Books.com

Printed in U.S.A.

For the rays of light in our lives:
our four children and our editors and our agent,
who have shown infinite patience in this year of Job.

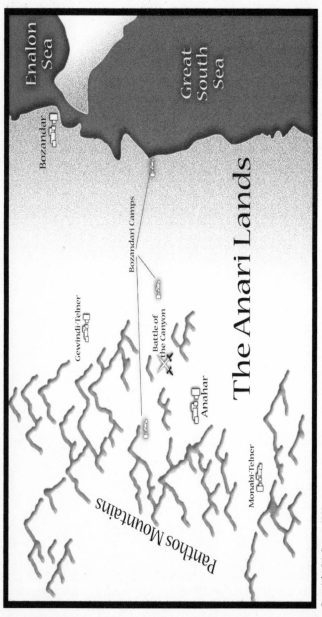

The Anari Lands

Enalon Sea

Great South Sea

Bozandar

Bozandari Camps

Gewindi-Telner

Battle of the Canyon

Anahar

Monabi-Telner

Panthos Mountains

Copyright Cris Brown, 2005

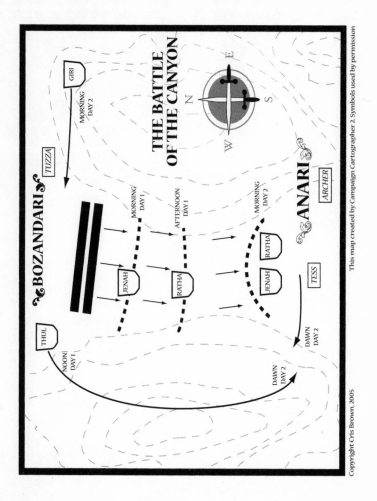

THE BATTLE
OF THE CANYON

BOZANDARI

ANARI

TUZZA

GIRI

MORNING
DAY 2

MORNING
DAY 1

AFTERNOON
DAY 1

MORNING
DAY 2

ARCHER

JENAH

RATHA

RATHA

JENAH

THUL

TESS

NOON
DAY 1

DAWN
DAY 2

DAWN
DAY 2

N
W
E
S

1

Giri Monabi crept silently over the sand, his dark eyes focused on the patrol below. Across the steep valley, his brother Ratha moved with equal silence, invisible in the dark night. It was not the homecoming the brothers had imagined.

The Bozandari patrol moved with the casual arrogance born of power, twenty-four men in two columns walked the road, swords sheathed, shields slung over their backs, helmets hanging from sword hilts, equipment clanking with each step. Their voices were loud against the stillness of night, the voices of men who did not anticipate trouble and believed they would be trouble's master if it arose.

The hatred of three generations of servitude burned in Giri's heart as he watched the soldiers. Almost without thought, his hand moved to his sword, fingers tightening in anticipation of dealing quick and ugly death. But he knew that, despite their casual manner, these men were skilled soldiers, and easily a match for Giri and his companions. There would be another time to wreak vengeance.

He began to slither backward, knowing that Ratha would

be doing likewise at this very moment, having reached the same conclusion. Even an alert guard would have been hard-pressed to see the movement, and these Bozandari were hardly alert. Giri and Ratha had shadowed them for nearly two hours now and knew that the patrol leader had not even taken the most basic of security measures. There were no advance or flank guards to scout the route or surrounding terrain. It was as if they were walking down the streets of Bozandar itself.

Giri had moved perhaps ten yards when he felt the prick of the sword against his side. He froze and heard the almost silent warning.

"Annomendi."

Tess Birdsong sat beside the fire, staring into the flames as the bitter wind blew down from the north. Three of her fellow travelers, Archer Blackcloak and his two black-skinned Anari companions, had vanished into the desert to keep guard. A strange desert, dotted with strange plants that grew out of sandy soil, creating eerie shapes among the tumbled boulders.

There was much in this world, she thought, to keep guard against—at least in the weeks since she had awoken in the midst of a slaughtered caravan with no memory of who she was or how she had come to be there. Indeed, she wasn't sure if the name she was using was truly hers. All she knew was that it had felt right somehow when she had been asked her name.

Other than that, all she knew about herself was that on her ankle there was a tattoo of a white rose. Sometimes she looked at it, wondering what clue to her past it might contain. But to-night it was too cold for such musings, and too much threat had pursued them from Lorense, where they had slain a mage.

Something hooted, echoing in the silent forest. One of her companions? Or some beast that had not fled with all its fellows?

She knew not, and the shiver that passed through her came not only from the bite of the wind.

Across the fire, Tom Downey slept the sleep of untroubled youth. He alone of the party had been spared the need to kill back in Lorense, when they had defeated the mage Lantav Glassidor. Tom had seen many ugly things, but he bore none of them on his conscience.

Unlike herself. Tess looked down at her hand, at the healing scar there. Those were memories best left in the dark recesses of the mind until they were needed.

Nearer to her sat her friend Sara Deepwell, an innkeeper's daughter who was proving to be one of the legendary magical women known as Ilduin. As was Tess herself, though she still rebelled emotionally at the idea.

Sara slept rarely now. Her mind and heart were too burdened with grief.

With a sigh, Tess stirred the coals of the fire, watching pinpricks of burning ash rise to the darkened sky. They were headed to war, yet she doubted that either she or Sara was ready for such a thing. Horror behind them, horror ahead of them.

Suddenly Tom sat up, instantly awake and alert. "Something is happening," he whispered.

But around them the desert remained silent.

"Annomendi."
Announce yourself, spoken in the clipped, northern Anari dialect. Giri, still frozen, replied carefully with the formal address of greeting.

"Giri an Monabi-Tel, ahnorren tir al sarlohse il Anari gelehsahnen." Giri of the Monabi Clan, returning of free will to the service of the Anari.

"What have you seen?" the man demanded, prodding Giri with the sword.

"Of you and your companions, I have seen nothing," Giri replied. "Of these men below, I have seen much—and much to despise."

"How many are you?"

"My brother is across the valley, and my friends await us behind the bend of the road. We are returning to help, to fight for our freedom."

The man let out a satisfied grunt. "Well, a fight there will be. And if you and your friends are true to your words, it shall begin for you tonight."

Giri spread his fingers in the Anari gesture of peace. "May I roll over and know into whose service I have come?"

The sword moved away, and Giri slowly rolled onto his side, looking up into midnight-black eyes. The man was definitely northern Anari, his features slightly rounded, his skin that fraction of a degree paler.

"Jenah of the Gewindi Clan," the man said. "Now rise and lead me to these friends of yours. One ambush would be more than sufficient for this night."

Jenah extended a hand, and Giri grasped it, allowing himself to be pulled to his feet. With a low whistle, Jenah signaled whatever companions might be nearby, then walked at Giri's side as they made their way back along the road. Within minutes, Giri heard Ratha's almost silent hiss, echoed a moment later by Archer.

"Be in peace," Giri said, keeping his voice low. "I come with Jenah of the Gewindi Clan."

Archer and Ratha rose from behind rocks, seeming to materialize only an arm's length away. Archer's eyes were hard and cold. "By what right do you capture my companion and friend?"

"By the right of a warrior who dislikes surprises in the night," Jenah said. Even in this dim light, Giri could see Jenah's face harden as he looked at Archer and took in his much lighter skin. "And any companion and friend of your kind is hateful to mine."

Giri didn't know whether Archer would detect the deadly threat in Jenah's choice of words. He spoke quickly. "I am grateful that you slew me not, Jenah Gewindi. Now slay not my friends, for you know naught of them, naught of their motives, and I dare say naught of greater forces that placed us in this chance encounter tonight."

Before Jenah could respond, Giri drew his sword and held it by the blade, with an infinitesimal dip of his head. "On pain of *Keh-Bal*, I place myself and my friends in your service."

"On pain of *Keh-Bal* shall you serve," Jenah replied, taking the sword by the hilt and turning it around before offering it back to Giri. "Come quickly now. There is dark work to be done."

"I must first let the rest of my company know where we are going," Archer said. "By Giri's oath, I will return."

"Can he be trusted?" Jenah asked.

"With more than your life," Giri replied. His tone left no room for doubt or argument.

Tom Downey peered into the darkness, trying to make out a shape to go with the approaching sound, a sound that was too deliberately noisy to seem like a threat. "Who goes there?"

"'Tis only me," Archer said, appearing out of the night. "We are discovered."

Behind Tom, Sara Deepwell and Tess Birdsong stiffened.

"Is there trouble?" Sara asked.

"Aye, there will be soon," Archer said. "Giri was met by another Anari, who apparently intends to ambush the Bozandari patrol we've been shadowing. He has pledged us to the fight, as well."

Tess looked up with almost hollow eyes. "We knew there would be more fighting. But so soon?"

Archer shook his head. "Milady, I cannot choose the time and manner of the Anari rebellion. Giri and Ratha are committed to its cause, and a noble cause it is. We have already sworn to help them. Apparently that begins tonight."

"We follow you, Archer Blackcloak," Sara said, drawing her sword. "Where you lead, we will go."

Archer's long black cloak was tossed on the night wind, a fold blowing back over his shoulder to reveal the gleaming hilt of his long sword. For an instant, just an instant, Tess thought she saw a shimmer about him, the ghost of a younger, happier man. Then the shimmer vanished and he was once again the hardened warrior.

"The three of you must stay here," he said flatly. "The horses must be protected, and I need you, Sara and Tom, to guard the Lady Tess. I sense her part in matters to come will be of extreme importance. Regardless, we cannot risk two Ilduin needlessly."

Both Sara and Tom seemed about to voice a protest, but then nodded. "Very well," Sara said, sheathing her sword once more. "Mayhap we can do more as healers this night."

"Of that," Archer said, "I have no doubt. But should we three fall, you three must return to Whitewater."

Tess abruptly rose to her feet. "Don't fail," she ordered.

A low chuckle escaped Archer, and he bowed. "I shall do my very best, Lady."

Then, this time moving with silent stealth, he disappeared back into the shadows among the rocks, lost to view.

Tom looked at Sara and Tess. "I think we should follow him."

But before anyone could respond, the shadows moved again, and they found themselves looking at the drawn swords of five dark-skinned Anari. They were surrounded.

"You will stay here," one of them announced, "until your companions have proved themselves to be true."

Tess sighed and dropped back down beside the small fire.

"They're true enough," she muttered. "Truer than this night is cold."

Tom squatted beside her, as did Sara, holding their hands out to the warmth.

"Truer," Tom answered beneath his breath, "than one among our captors, I fear."

Sara nodded. Tess remained motionless, feeling the tingle and burning begin in the palms of her hand. Something built within her, and for the first time she had an inkling of what it was. Slipping her hand within her cloak, she grasped at the bag of twelve colored stones nestled between her breasts.

"Aye," she said presently. "Evil is near."

Archer, Giri and Ratha climbed the ridge alongside the northern Anari. Soon they reached its ragged, bare top and peered over once again at the column of soldiers marching so arrogantly down the darkened road.

Jenah spoke to them. "We will attack in three groups after they enter the defile ahead. One group will attack the column's head, another its rear. The third group will be archers, firing from above." He eyed Archer's quiver. "You will be with the third group. Ratha and Giri will divide among the others."

Ratha spoke. "My brother and I always fight together."

Jenah's face hardened. "Not this time. I do not yet trust you fully."

"A fine way to treat an oath of *Keh-Bal*."

"The oath is meaningless if the witness to it is dead."

Ratha and Giri both stiffened, but before they could respond to the insult, Archer waved them to silence.

He turned to Jenah. "Have you searched any farther, or have you followed only this column?"

"This column," Jenah said. "As have you."

Archer gave a short nod, acknowledging that the Anari force

had been aware of his party for quite some time. "Yes, and since darkfall, their behavior has been troubling."

Jenah frowned. "How so? They are behaving exactly as they did all day."

"That is what concerns me."

Jenah eyed him narrowly. "Why would they be baiting a trap? They know nothing of my group."

"Perhaps not," Archer replied. "But perhaps caution is the order of the evening."

"Gewindi-Tel has committed to this attack," Jenah said. "It was decided among the elders six days ago. I will not shame my Tel by cowardice, and your companion has sworn himself to my side. We attack."

Archer nodded. "The oath is sworn and will be met. However, there is evil afoot in this night. My companions and I have faced much, braved much, endured much. If we are to die this night, let us die together."

After a long, silent stare, Jenah nodded. "Very well. You will join the rear attack force. And *Keh-Bal* upon you if your deeds match not your words."

As the moon settled on the far mountains, Ratha watched the Bozandari patrol reach the head of the defile through which they had been marching, break ranks and prepare to make camp. "Not long now," he whispered.

"Aye," Archer said. "Jenah is a wise leader. He will wait until they are settled, then fall upon them. I only pray that he has not been led into a trap."

Ratha studied Archer's eyes for a long moment, then nodded slowly. In the past six years, he had seen much in those eyes. Never had those eyes led him astray, and oft had they kept him from danger. Yet even after all of that, Ratha's cultural memories were strong, and it seemed odd to be standing beside a white man as his brothers prepared to do battle against white men. The man Ratha had been would not trust a man like Archer in such a battle. The man he had become could not imagine a more worthy companion.

Below him, the Bozandari had settled. Ratha knew that Jenah and his men were moving silently into the valley like a red adder stalking a desert hare, slipping from rock to rock, shadow to shadow, preparing to strike their prey. Even as the thought crossed his mind, he saw the other Anari around him rise into low crouches. He rose with them, moving with patient, deadly purpose to close the rear of the trap.

With a shrill, trilling cry, Jenah signaled the attack, and forty Anari rose from the rocks to fall upon their nearly sleeping enemy. Ratha spotted a wide-eyed Bozandari soldier reaching for a sword. No sooner had his hand closed around the hilt than a blade flickered out of the night and severed his head, sending him into eternity with that same wide-eyed stare.

Now the rear force was upon the enemy, as well, and Ratha, Giri and Archer took up their familiar close battle tactic, blades flashing in synchronized efficiency, parrying and killing in a relentless rhythm of destruction. Archer's world narrowed to the space immediately in front of him, Bozandari blades flashing in the cold blue moonlight, his breath smooth and even as he matched strides and movements with his companions, the three of them a single entity with but one awful purpose.

Suddenly, in the distance, a sputtering fire arced into the air, lighting the valley in an eerie red hue. Three more flares burst upward, trailing a graceful tail of sparks, before bursting into flame high overhead. Cries of horror told the rest of the tale.

"It's an ambush," Archer hissed.

"Yes," Ratha replied. "We have been led into a trap."

Dozens of Bozandari seemed to materialize beyond the mouth of the defile, falling upon the Anari with the same sudden savagery that only recently had engulfed the members of their patrol.

Off to Ratha's right, Jenah screamed commands above the din of battle, trying to reorient his men to the new threat, but too many were still engaged with the Bozandari in the patrol. Blood flowed all but invisible in the red light of the flares, evident only as glistening geysers erupting from throats, bellies and the stumps of freshly hewn limbs. Screams of pain and rage mixed with the clang of metal upon metal, drowning out any attempt to restore order to the shattered Anari.

"Massacre," Ratha muttered, still hacking his way forward with his companions. "They will all die."

"We must echelon right," Archer said. "We will move toward Jenah. He must know that Giri has kept his oath."

"Aye," Ratha said. He glanced over to Giri. "Echelon right, on Lord Archer's command."

Giri nodded and, at a single word from Archer, the three men pivoted an eighth-turn in perfect unison. Step by step, slain foe by slain foe, they angled across the melee toward the Anari leader. Ratha stepped into the belly of a still-thrashing Bozandari soldier, noticing the dying man only to the extent necessary to keep his own balance and stay with his companions.

Soon they could see Jenah's back, almost within reach, as the tall, broad man tried in vain to protect two of his wounded brothers from another wave of Bozandari soldiers. The Bozandari fought with patient intensity, shoulder to shoulder, shields nearly overlapped, save only for enough space to deliver a scything thrust with each step. Anari courage and honor stood no chance against such training and discipline. It was only a matter of time.

Ratha and his companions reached Jenah at the same instant as the Bozandari wave.

"Jenah!" Archer cried. "Fall in behind us!"

Jenah shook his head. "I must die with my Tel."

"Then you are a fool!" Ratha said, breathing heavily as his sword whirled against the Bozandari ranks. "What profit is your death except to our enslavers? You are betrayed, and to find the betrayer is now your honor."

"My honor is my Tel!" Jenah cried, thrusting at an enemy at the very moment that his foot slid across a blood-slicked rock.

Jenah slipped to his knees, his sword lowered for just long enough to allow a Bozandari blade to slash across his back. The blade would have cleaved his spine, had he not risen up to thrust his own sword through the attacker's throat. But Ratha knew the wound was crippling.

"Blood have you shed for your brothers," Ratha said. "Your honor is fulfilled. Now fulfill its greater burden and fall in behind us. Revenge for Gewindi-Tel you will have, but not on this treacherous night."

Fury warred with sorrow in Jenah's eyes, but after a moment he nodded and circled behind them. Archer gave the command to withdraw, and the three began to step backward over the bodies of Bozandari and Anari, their feet and legs sticky with blood, arms and swords still swirling, keeping their opponents at bay.

Finally they reached the confines of the defile, where the greater Bozandari numbers could not be brought to bear. Recognizing this, and satisfied with the carnage they had wrought, the Bozandari withdrew into the darkness, leaving Ratha and his companions drawing huge gulps of dry air as they finally lowered their swords.

Ratha heard a cry behind him and turned as Jenah slumped to the ground on hands and knees, his head hanging limply, blood dripping from his chin.

"Come," Archer said. "Let us take him to Lady Tess. Perhaps she can give him aid."

Ratha nodded, bile rising in his throat as he looked out at

the carnage in the dying light of the setting moon. "But she cannot aid them all, Lord Archer. By the gods, she cannot aid them all."

me castrated in the dying light of the setting sun. Tess saw
water, an immense hill, and a figure. As the sun... she cannot
was it.

Surrounded by armed men, the small group at the fire could
do and say little. Tess felt Sara's hand steal within hers, grasping warmly. She looked at the young woman and saw not fear,
but determination to weather this somehow. Tom, too, looked
determined, but he was staring into the fire as if he saw something there other than the leaping flames.

"Tom?" she called quietly.

For long moments he neither moved nor answered. Finally
he said, "Patience. Evil will betray itself."

The counsel to patience was their only option. It wasn't as
if the three of them were in any position to fight five armed warriors. But Tess felt there was more in Tom's statement. He did
that every so often, making a remark that sounded more like
formal prayer than mere speech. At such moments, Tess expected to look over into the face of a wizened old man and not
one who had barely reached adulthood.

"It is a gift," Sara whispered, as if reading Tess's thoughts. "He
is a prophet. A seer."

Tess was startled. True, she remembered little enough of this
world. But she couldn't forebear asking, "Do such exist?"

"Aye," Sara answered. "Few they are, rarer than glazengold. One of the greatest is in Bozandar. Tales told at my father's inn say that when foreknowledge overtakes him, he cannot even see the present, speaking only of the future. Oft his words cannot be understood except in hindsight."

"Hmm," Tess said, feeling an inexplicable skepticism. "Very useful. So easy to predict the past."

Sara's eyebrow arched, and then she shrugged. "'Tis like our powers, Tess. They terrify me. I know not what I do, or how I do it. Do you?"

Tess shook her head. "It feels like riding an untamed horse. It goes where it wills, and I but follow."

Sara nodded. "But for all that, we cannot deny that it is real. At times, I think it is our curse."

They both fell silent as they remembered the mage Lantav Glassidor, burning alive as each drop of Sara's blood touched him as Tess ordered him cleansed. As evil as the hive-master was, neither of them was comfortable with the way in which he had died...even if he had kidnapped and tortured Sara's mother these past six years.

Tess was troubled, too, by the scar on her palm. Somehow she had stopped Tom's sword in midair as he went to kill Lantav, but she had not touched the instrument. Yet afterward this reddened scar had appeared on her palm, as if she *had* reached out and grasped the blade. It was beginning to fade, but it raised questions about what she had done and how. And why her action had affected her physically.

Tess turned her hand over and showed it to Sara. "I did not touch Tom's blade."

Sara nodded and turned over her hand. It bore an identical scar. From her palm had dripped the blood that had burned Lantav. "Maybe we Ilduin share each other's ills."

Tess stared at Sara's scar, and a chill crept down her spine.

What was going on here? How tightly were the Ilduin bound? And in what ways? She closed her fist. "I do not know what to think."

"Nor I. Perhaps we share the scar because we shared the experience."

"Perhaps." After all, Tess thought, it had been she who had told Sara to cleanse Glassidor.

And little enough they had accomplished in the end, for as they had traveled south to the Anari lands, they had heard rumors of other hive-masters like Lantav, mages who melded the minds of many into one mind.

And worse, they had glimpsed the dark power behind Lantav. Something not of this world, Tess thought. Something greater than any power in this world. Something she doubted she and Sara were strong enough to face.

Tom seemed to draw his attention back from the fire. "Sorry," he said, shaking his head. "I was daydreaming."

"We're all exhausted," Sara said reassuringly. "I wish I could lie down and sleep."

Tom smiled faintly. "Not with all those swords pointed at us."

Tess returned his smile, then twisted to look at the encircling Anari. Giri and Ratha had predisposed her to like their kind, but someone or something among these men filled her with a dark sense of cold, oily evil. One among them belonged to the enemy. One among them was a traitor to his kind.

She wished she could tell which one, but that sight was denied her. Instead she was gifted only with the amorphous ugly feeling.

Suddenly the night sky filled with a red flare to the south of them. All of them gaped, never having seen such before.

Then Tess felt something else. Her head bowed, and her heart ached. "Many are dying," she said. "Too many."

Sara gripped her hand and squeezed it. "I feel it, too," she said in a hushed voice. "The battle has begun."

Two hours felt like two days as they waited for the return of their companions. Tess's thoughts kept returning to Acher, leader and friend, a man with strength to lean on. A man who still distrusted her, yet protected her. She closed her eyes, willing his safe return along with Giri and Ratha.

Eventually the sound of heavy, uneven footfalls could be heard approaching across the rocky terrain. The three immediately rose to their feet, and their captors turned their attention and their swords to the sounds.

Moments later, as if born of the very darkness itself, Archer appeared. Giri and Ratha followed, between them holding yet another Anari, who appeared to have trouble keeping his feet. Farther yet behind them came another handful of dark men. Then no more.

"We were the ones ambushed," Archer announced. "Most of Gewindi-Tel were slaughtered."

The man being steadied by Ratha and Giri lifted his head suddenly, and the heat of anger blazed from him, almost palpable in the night. "We were betrayed!" Jenah spat. "Betrayed by one of our own."

Tess hurried toward him. "You are injured!"

"Aye, Lady," Giri said. "A sword gashed his back as he fought to defend his brothers. Let no one question his valor on this night."

"Let me see."

But Jenah straightened himself and shook off the support of Ratha and Giri. "I need no white healer. I need a sword. I want to know who betrayed us!" Then, his last dregs of strength used up, he crumpled to his knees.

"Lady," said Giri urgently, as he, Ratha and Archer formed a protective triangle around the fallen leader, swords drawn.

Tom and Sara drew their weapons, as well, and stood back to back.

Tess needed no further encouragement. She ran forward to the fallen Anari, hoping against hope that she could find in herself whatever it was that had saved a young lad in Derda who had been all but dead from cold and starvation. She had no idea what she had done then, but everyone had been sure she had been the cure.

Now she knelt and laid her hands on the fallen man's back, against the hot, wet blood, feeling the slash beneath her palms. She closed her eyes, imagining as vividly as she could that the wound beneath her hands was knitting together, muscle to muscle, skin to skin. Her palms grew hot, as if they were aflame, and she nearly cried out.

Moments later, the world faded into blackness.

A healer such as the world hadn't seen since the White Lady, Theriel, Archer thought, as he watched over the unconscious Tess and the steadily improving Jenah. With his own eyes he had seen flesh heal beneath her hands. Now there was nothing but a scar left across Jenah's back.

But the cost to Tess had been great. As the sun began to rise, painting the red desert in a myriad of fiery colors, he cradled her head in his lap and waited for her to awaken.

All the other Anari, both those who had been in battle and those who had stood guard here, had put away their swords and sat, waiting. Tom and Sara watched Tess with worried eyes. Ratha and Giri alone remained on guard, ready to protect their company and Jenah.

Tess stirred, a murmur escaping her. At once Archer stroked her golden tresses. "Be still," he said. "You are safe."

For a fleeting instant a smile fluttered over her lips, then vanished. He had seen her smile so rarely, he realized. But none of them smiled nearly enough these days. The savagery of their time in Lorense, and the horrors of the deaths of thousands of refugees in Derda, had left a deep mark on all of them.

Tess's eyes fluttered open and met his, blue meeting gray for an electric instant. Her mouth formed a surprised O; then she abruptly sat up. At once she raised a hand to her head.

"Who hit me with the hammer?" she asked.

"'Twas the healing," Archer reminded her.

Recalled to what had passed, she looked toward Jenah and appeared as stunned as any of them by what she saw. "Oh!"

At that moment, Jenah rolled over onto his back with a groan. His eyes opened suddenly, taking in the dawning day, and Giri and Ratha standing guard. "What happened?" he demanded.

"Sit up and see," Giri said. "The Lady Tess healed you."

Jenah pushed himself up gingerly, as if he did not believe what he was told. But upon discovering he no longer hurt, he leapt to his feet and looked around.

"Thank you," he said, bowing to Tess. "And please forgive my words, Lady. My people are not used to such kindnesses from yours."

"You were in pain," Tess said, smiling. "People oft say things they do not mean. Think nothing more of it."

But then his gaze returned to his fellows.

"So this is all that remains of Gewindi-Tel, the proudest of the northern clans." His voice was already sparking with anger again. "A handful of stalwarts and a traitor."

The men who had fought beside Jenah last night stirred not at all. Their faces were as impassive as if they had been carved from the stone the Anari worked with such unparalleled skill. The five who had remained to guard the campsite were not quite as impassive, however. Though they betrayed little except by the flicker of their eyes, it was obvious that they knew suspicion fell upon them.

"You have nothing to say?" Jenah asked.

"I wish only that I had died in my brother's place," one of the men said. "First came he from my mother's womb, but only by the moments it took for me slip out after him. I spent my life chasing him. If now I must follow him into death, then so be it."

Jenah seemed to weigh the man's words for a long moment, then nodded. "Be at peace, Jahar Gewindi. Your brother died at my side, valiant to the last. Let not your mother lose two sons on this day. Already too many mothers will bear that burden."

Archer watched as Jenah interrogated each of the men, one by one. As long as he had spent in the company of Ratha and Giri, he could not yet read the faces of Anari except in the most obvious of moments. What Jenah sought, and whether he was seeing it, Archer had no idea.

"It is not safe to remain here," Tom said, quietly. "Master Jenah, I know you are angry, and that one thought alone burns in your mind. But we are not far removed from the Bozandari who killed your kinsmen last night. There will be time enough to sort this out once we have found a suitable resting place."

"And what of a resting place for my brothers?" Jenah asked. "Am I to leave them in the sand, to be picked over by the vultures, their bleached bones to be swallowed up into the vast, empty memory of the desert?"

"We cannot bear them with us," Archer said. "And the lad is right. It is too dangerous for us to remain here. The gods will embrace the spirits of your fallen, whatever may befall their bodies."

"Anari never leave their dead behind," Jenah said.

"There is much that Anari have never done," Archer said. "But I fear you will need to learn to do most of it before this war is over. Come, let us away, for the safety of those who remain in your Tel, lest all your mothers weep in vain."

* * *

Tom walked beside Sara, occasionally reaching over to grasp her hand. The sun was nearing its zenith, and even in the middle of winter, faint shimmers of heat rose from the red sands. Their horses walked beside them, pausing from time to time to graze from the occasional bunches of pale green grass or the leaves of the bushes that dotted the landscape.

"This is a beautiful land," Tom said. "But a hard land, as well."

"Yes," Sara said. "It is a land to make one's heart weep—with beauty and with pain."

"That feeling I know well," Tom said, giving her hand another squeeze. "I feel it every time I look at you."

"Now, now," Sara said, suppressing a smile. "Speak not every word that is in your heart, Tom Downey, lest I come to long for the days when you spoke none at all."

"I'm sorry," he said, quickly looking away.

"No!" Sara replied. "Tom, you really must learn to recognize when I jest. I like your words. So many nights I lay in bed, wishing that you would voice your thoughts, afraid I was mistaken when I read your eyes. Now I have no such doubts, and that lightens the burden of my heart."

"Then let me lighten it more," Tom said. "For in all the world, there is no soul with such sparkle, no other face that I would wake to, no other voice that I would carry into my dreams. Please do not ache for the past, Sara Deepwell. Whatever you have done, you have done for the love of all that is good and right in this world."

"I would that your words were enough, Tom. But I bear the stain of my blood, the stain of my heritage, it seems. When I heard tales of the Ilduin in my father's inn, they were tales of lightness and beauty, hope and joy. Never did I imagine that I would be one of them. And never did I imagine that Ilduin blood would be so dark."

He could hear the aching loss in her words, and he knew she was once again seeing the dead and dying forms of her mother and the dark mage Glassidor. If only Lady Tess had not stilled his blade, he would have spared Sara this burden. Instead he had stood mutely by as the final act was played out in soul-chilling screams.

"You are of love, Sara Deepwell," he whispered. "That is all I know of such things. But it is enough."

Near the front of the small column, Tess rode beside Jenah, whom she had insisted take Archer's mount. She rode at Archer's demand, for he was not sure she was yet strong enough to walk. And, she thought, he might well be right. A deep, aching fatigue seemed to press through every muscle and sinew in her body. She longed for sleep but could not bring herself to relax.

"You should rest, Lady," Jenah said quietly. "Your body cries for it."

"As does yours," Tess replied. "And yet you also hold yourself awake. So we are both stubborn."

Jenah laughed, and for an instant Tess saw once again the infinite beauty of the Anari people. She had seen it in the fleeting moments when Ratha and Giri joked amongst themselves. They were a people who, when the cares of the world could be set aside, seemed to glow with an inner joy that shimmered in the iridescent blues of their black skin. They were, she thought, the most beautiful people she had ever seen.

"What?" Jenah asked.

"Oh," Tess replied, "I was just thinking how lovely your people are to behold. If the finest gold were spun into human form, it would not approach the Anari."

"You mock me," Jenah said, though the warmth in his eyes belied the accusation. "We are but humble desert stonemasons."

"And I but a simple blond woman," she said. "Take good

words where you find them, Jenah Gewindi. I fear you have heard too few."

"That much is true," he said, smiling. "And thank you, White Lady, for your kindness. Someday, perhaps, you will tell me by what grace of the gods you were sent to me in my time of need."

"I do not know whether it be a grace of the gods or a curse of men," Tess said. "Perhaps some of both. The road to this place has been long and filled with heartache. But here we are, and on we go."

"Tell me of your journey?" he asked. "Perhaps it will distract me from the ache in my back. While you have saved my life, I still feel the pain of the blow."

"I am sorry that my healing was not more complete," Tess said. "But of my journey, there is both too little and too much to tell. I awoke in the wreckage of a slaughtered trade caravan, far to the north, with no memory of who I was or whence I came. Archer and his Anari companions came upon me and took me to Whitewater, where we met Tom and Sara. Then we set out together to learn who had murdered the caravan, and that led us eventually into the city of Lorense, where we confronted the dark mage Lantav Glassidor and slew him.

"After that, we came south, for Ratha and Giri had heard of the uprising here and wanted to lend their swords to the cause. We skirted the edge of the Deder Desert, dodging Bozandari patrols, until we reached the borders of the Anari lands and came upon you last night. And that, my friend, is my journey."

Jenah studied her for a moment and nodded. "There is much that you do not tell me, Lady Tess. I accept that, for I can see in your face that what you tell me is true. And your friends certainly bore true their oath last night. Perhaps in time I will learn more of you and your story. For now, however, I accept that you are here of free will and with pure heart."

"I thank you for your trust, Lord Jenah."

He laughed and shook his head. "I am hardly a lord, my Lady. I was simply chosen by my Tel for this mission. Chosen, it seems, to lead my brothers to their deaths."

"Bear not that burden alone," Tess said. "From what Archer has told me, you did all that could be asked for, and more besides. Your brothers' blood is not on your hands, but on the hands of he who betrayed you. And in time, we will know who that is."

"That time will be soon now," he said, looking up at a jagged ridgeline. "Beyond that rise lie the villages of Gewindi-Tel. And there the truth will out."

At the top of the rise, Giri looked out at the village below and paused for a long moment. Tess came up beside him and saw the glistening in his eyes.

"What is it?" she asked.

"I've waited a long time to see a telner, m'Lady. I thought I would never see one again."

"Gewindi-Telner," Jenah announced with a sweep of his arm. "Home of Gewindi-Tel, my clan."

Tess at once noticed the odd configuration of the village: a large, round central building surrounded by a plaza that seemed to mimic flames spreading out from the sun. From there radiated three winding paths that led to smaller round buildings, each of which was set amidst even smaller stone buildings and fallow fields.

"All Anari villages are constructed in this form," Giri said. "It symbolizes the end of the First Age."

"What does it mean?"

Giri's eyes clouded with sorrow. "In the end," he said quietly, "the gods were so angry with the Firstborn that they tore the world asunder. It is a reminder that the world today is but a small part of what it once was."

Tess looked down on the village with new appreciation, then realized they had been spotted. Even from this distance she could see the villagers beginning to gather, facing in their direction.

Jenah sighed heavily, but when he spoke, his voice was taut with anger. "Let me ride ahead and tell the story, lest the lady and her party be misunderstood."

Giri nodded. "A good idea, cousin. I will ride with you as a token of our good faith."

Jenah nodded. Giri turned, and in one sleek movement he swung into his saddle. "Wait here," he said to Tess. "I'll come when it is time."

Tess was surprisingly ready to dismount and just rest for a few minutes, even though she had been dreaming of the comforts of civilization for these many hours past. She had hardly begun to dismount when strong hands clasped her waist and aided her.

Archer. She turned and managed a wan smile. "Thank you."

He gave a slight bow of his head. "Let us make a small fire and eat something. Perhaps Lady Sara will be good enough to create one of her stews. You need to regain your energy, my Lady."

Since events in Lorense and the discovery that Sara, the innkeeper's daughter, was one of the fabled Ilduin, she had become Lady Sara. Tess herself had been referred to as such much longer, but she was still finding it difficult to accept the obvious implication: that she was set apart from her fellows.

She turned her gaze from Archer and looked down the long slope. Jenah and Giri were riding slowly, as if they dreaded delivering the message they bore. And in the town below, new stillness seemed to indicate that the people guessed what that message would be.

Sara and Tom seemed only too glad for the distraction of preparing a meal. Ratha gathered some wood and laid the fire before returning to his position against a rock. It was clear he was still on guard, though now it was against the traitor among the Anari. The remaining Anari, a group of less than twenty, merely sat stone-faced, awaiting their moment to return home…and their moment to be judged.

While the horses grazed among the sparse vegetation, Tess sat crosslegged on the brow of the ridge, looking down on the valley spread before her. Archer settled beside her, one knee raised, leaning back on his arm.

"The flower of the Gewindi Clan is mostly gone," he said soberly.

"What did they hope to accomplish by attacking that patrol?"

"Exactly what came to befall them." He sighed. "You dozed for a few minutes during the ride, and I spoke with Jenah. He said that Bozandari patrol was on its way to the Telnah, to take more slaves. Most of the men who died last night would have been taken. And some of the women, as well. They chose to fight instead, to preserve their Tel. From stories they have heard, the slave patrols have lately been killing many of those they don't take, or burning the villages' food supplies and leaving the Tels to starve."

"Why in the world would they do that?"

Archer made a small movement, suggestive of a shrug. "The Bozandari have always been a hard people. Long it was a hardness born of necessity. Their home city has always been a way station and trade center, but the Bozandari themselves had little to sell. So they learned to exact the greatest possible profit from their location. Traders coming to Bozandar are taxed, and the market keepers also take tax in kind on all goods brought for sale. It was how the Bozandari learned to survive."

He paused a moment. "In times gone by, this was naught but a means of feeding themselves and their people. But taking from all whom they encountered became a way of life. And as their wealth grew, they could afford larger armies with which to intimidate or conquer their neighbors. For a people accustomed to providing for themselves from other people's labors, conquest and plunder were but a small step."

"But whyever do they turn these people into slaves?"

"It began because the Anari are such great workers of stone. The Bozandari wanted their cities to shine with the same beauty and skill, so they collected the best of the Anari stoneworkers and took them to Bozandar. But beyond that, why work a market oneself when one can make a slave do the work? Why cook one's own meals when a slave can do that? Again, for a people whose history lies in surviving on the work of others, 'tis but a small step."

Tess shook her head. "There are no limits to the cruelty of men."

"It seems not." His face grew shadowed, as if he were remembering things best forgotten.

For his sake, she tried to change the subject. "How is it the Ilduin came to have such power? If Sara and I are to be useful as Ilduin, it would seem that we ought to know who we are and how our powers work."

He was silent for a moment, as if drawing himself out of a dark pit. "You speak of the Mysteries."

"The Mysteries?"

"Aye. The secrets of the Ilduin. The Ilduin of old may have known. 'Twas said their powers were gifts from the gods. But whatever they knew, they kept to themselves. 'Tis said that at the end of the First Age, when horror and destruction lay all around, the Ilduin oversaw the building of the Anari temples and concealed all the Mysteries within those temples. If that be true, none has ever found the answers, though many have tried over the centuries."

The stew was soon ready. Sara had an amazing way of throwing a few things into a pot and in a short while producing a savory meal. Tess ate with a hunger that surprised even herself, as if she had not eaten in weeks. Almost as soon as the food hit her belly, she could feel herself strengthening.

By the time Sara and Tom had finished cleaning up and were about to put out the cook fire, Giri began to ride up the slope toward them. He came fast, but not fast enough to cause alarm.

When he reached them, his face was grave and full of sorrow. "Let us go down to Gewindi-Telner. They have offered us lodging at Telnertah, the village temple."

He looked past them at the other Anari. "You will follow us."

From times past, Archer recognized a few of the older Gewindi, and they him. His travels had taken him over most of the known world in his time, and taken him more than once. A few nods greeted him as he and Tess led the procession into town, but beyond nods, the greetings were nonexistent. The usually warm and outgoing Anari had become cautious of strangers over the three generations of their enslavement, and with the day's bad news, they were even less inclined to warmth. Most faces were stoic, but on some tears coursed down.

Giri led them straight to the temple and into the guesthouse, made of stone and roofed over with a perfectly carved vault of granite.

"Stay here," he told the party. "There is to be a judgment, and outsiders will not be welcome."

He stayed to help unload the horses, then guided their mounts away to a stable. The rest of the party remained in the comfortably large round room that was somehow ensconced in the temple. There was a door that led into the temple proper, but Tom soon discovered it was locked.

"We can't go in there?" he asked.

Ratha shook his head. "Not without invitation."

In a corner was a small fountain with water gushing up from it, probably from some underground spring. There was a hearth on which wood for a fire had already been laid, though not lit. And there were a half dozen elevated stone pallets that could serve either as chairs or beds.

Windows beneath shades of animal skin that could be rolled up or down gave a view onto the sun-shaped plaza and beyond, to one of the curving paths that led between leafless trees to another section of the village.

Tess found herself drawn to the window and stood there for minutes uncounted, feeling as if she stood on some kind of brink.

"What is it, Tess?" Sara asked, coming to her elbow. "What do you see?"

"'Tis not what I see but what I feel."

Sara nodded and remained beside her, staring out the window. More minutes passed, then a soft sigh escaped her. "It speaks to us."

"Yes. But I don't understand."

"Nor I."

Together they continued to stare out at the sun-drenched plaza and the winding stone path, so carefully laid out by long ago masons.

"This work is amazing," Tom said, peering closely at a wall. "The stones are seamless."

He pulled a hair from his head and attempted to slide it into the almost invisible crack between two stones. "I can't...and the joints aren't even square. See how each rock is cut in a different shape, yet each fits exactly into the others?"

"That is one of the many wonders of Anari stonework," Archer said. "The stones are locked together so that nothing can dislodge them. But wait until you see the other things they create from stone. Items of such beauty and intricacy that no one else can mimic them."

"Our blessing and our bane both," Ratha said. "But that is about to end."

With those words, he reminded them all that they had come to join a revolution.

Tess turned back to the window, Sara at her side, and resumed her study of the view, unable to escape the feeling that it was speaking to her.

The sun was sinking low in the west when at last Jenah returned. He was followed by a group of young men and women who bore stone platters of food for the guests and, surprisingly, flowers for Tess.

She accepted them with a smile and an expression of gratitude, but felt uncomfortable at being singled out in this fashion. After all, Archer, Ratha and Giri had fought beside the men of Gewindi Tel and certainly deserved more thanks than she did.

"Eat," said Jenah. "Then we have a favor to ask of Lady Tess."

That news was enough to destroy Tess's appetite, but out of courtesy she tasted the food…and found it to be too wonderful to pass up.

Giri came to sit beside her around the feast and said reassuringly, "Fear not, Lady. All will be well."

"Guests are treated royally by the Anari," Archer added. "Among the desert peoples, to deny succor to a stranger is a mortal sin. Now that they are sure we are not agents of Bozandar, the old ways resume."

"Aye," Ratha agreed, with a laugh. "Wait until you taste the hospitality of Monabi-Tel."

Giri joined his brother's laugh. "Indeed. Monabi-Tel must exceed Gewindi-Tel."

"Of course," Ratha said.

His voice broke into song, a melody that sat low in his chest and seemed to rumble with the memories of the mountains themselves.

Monabi-Tel an leekehnen
Monabi lohrisie
Zar Tel mim Torsah seekehnen
Monabi lohr
Monabi fohr
Monabi-Tel wohbie.

Tess found herself laughing, despite having no idea what the words meant. Somehow the melody made her want to clap her hands as gleefully as a child. Finally she asked, "Of what do you sing, Ratha?"

"It is a children's song," he replied with a grin. "The words do not work well in your language, but it is something like this: Monabi-Tel live decently, Monabi people say. Our Tel craves wisdom peacefully. Monabi are good. Monabi are strong. Just ask Monabi-Tel."

"As you can see," Giri said, joining in the mirth, "we are raised to be a proud people."

"And yet you make fun of yourselves at the same time," Tess said.

"But of course, m'Lady," Giri said. "To be proud and not make fun of oneself is arrogance. To make fun of oneself and not be proud is self-loathing. But to be proud and still make fun of oneself, that is wisdom."

"Monabi-Tel were always our bards and tricksters," Jenah said with an almost imperceptible wink. "Take naught that they say seriously."

"And Gewindi-Tel were always our solemn and hardworking mentors," Giri replied. "Look not to them for joy, but only for labor."

"How much of any of this should I take seriously?" Tess asked with a playful smile.

"Very little," Archer said, chuckling. "The play among Tels has been thus for time out of mind. From the smallest grain of truth they will build a mountain of playful lies about each other."

"Aye," Giri said. "It is why we have never made war amongst ourselves. You might say we celebrate our common differences."

"That is well-spoken," Jenah said. Turning to Tess, he added, "That which divides us is but a fraction of that which unites us. And thus have we played and laughed and worked together from the First Age."

He paused for a moment, shifting forward in his seat. "But not all is play and laughter, m'Lady. As I said, we have a favor to ask of you. And the Lady Sara, if she would not mind."

"I will do what I can," Tess said, uncertainty and dread growing within her heart. "I fear I know too little to be of much use."

"And I," Sara added. "I pray that you do not expect too much, lest I disappoint you."

"What they ask is naught but a small thing," Jenah said, smiling. "Our Telneren ask. They will explain."

4

Jenah led Tess and Sara out of the guest room and through the larger circular entrance room by which they had come. He paused a moment to orient them.

"Each Anari Tel consists of three family groups. This room is my family's entrance to the temple." He pointed through a window at one of the serpentine paths that led to another round building surrounded by smaller houses. "That is my family's dwelling place. My people always come to the temple along that path and through this door. This demonstrates our awareness that we are part of a larger whole, yet each must follow his own path within the whole."

"It's beautiful," Tess said, looking around her at the glyphs on the walls. "I can see why people believe the Ilduin secrets lie within your temples. These walls sing with meaning and yet hover out of reach, like forgotten dreams."

"Like forgotten dreams," Sara echoed, nodding. "Yes."

"Come," Jenah said, indicating a door on the inner wall. "The Telneren await."

They stepped through the door into another large circular room, obviously at the center of the temple. The walls and ceiling offered a panoply of glyphs and recessed reliefs that drew the attention from one to the next as if by a magnetic force. In the center, a round altar stood with three lighted candles. Around the altar sat six Anari women, their eyes closed, mouths moving silently and yet in unison. Jenah touched a finger to his lips and waited with them as the women completed their prayer.

When they finished the prayer, the six women opened their eyes simultaneously and turned to Jenah. The oldest of the women spoke quietly.

"These are the Ilduin?"

"Yes, mother," Jenah said. "I present Lady Tess Birdsong and Lady Sara Deepwell, of Whitewater, in the northern lands. Upon my honor, they come with pure hearts and of free will in the service of the Anari."

"Upon your honor, with pure hearts and of free will, we accept their service," the woman said. Then she broke into a smile and offered a slight bow, instantly mirrored by the others. "Welcome to Gewindi-Telner, my Ladies. We are honored to be blessed with Ilduin presence."

"The honor is ours," Tess said, repeating the bow and the words Jenah had taught her, the ritual greetings of the Anari. "My hosts bless me with their hospitality."

"My name is Eiehsa of Gewindi-Tel," the woman said, now stepping closer. "My son has told me of your meeting, and the courage of your companions. I would thank you for saving my son's life, and know that I feel such in my heart, but a formal recitation would neglect the souls of those whom you could not save and the mothers who grieve them. I fear you have come to our land in perilous times, and yet we ask your blessing."

"My blessing?" Tess asked, surprised to learn that Eiesha was Jenah's mother. "I don't understand."

"Ilduin were they who taught us to shape these walls

such," Eiehsa said, "and Ilduin are the spirits that move within Anari hands as they shape the stone. It is the custom of our people that children receive an Ilduin blessing as soon as they leave their mothers' breasts, but our only Ilduin was taken as a slave four years past, and many are the unblessed children. On behalf of my Tel, I entreat that you would bless these young souls, that their future may be brighter than their past."

"I do not know what to do," Tess said. "Sara and I are of Ilduin blood, yes, but we have not yet learned even a fraction of what that means."

The woman smiled. "It is not what you may know that would bless our children, Lady Tess. It is the essence of the goodness that lies within you which carries the grace of blessing."

Tess remembered the horrors of Lorense and wondered if there was indeed goodness in her Ilduin heritage. Would she bless these people—or damn them? She could see the same thoughts echoed in Sara's eyes.

"I fear the Ladies doubt themselves, Mother," Jenah said. "Much pain have they suffered in their journey here, and I sense there is much they regret. Little has Lady Tess told me, but in the spaces between her words there are volumes to be read."

The woman nodded and held out a hand to each of them, palms up. The warmth in the woman's eyes completed the invitation, and Tess and Sara each placed a hand in hers. The woman's eyes closed, and her lips moved again in a silent prayer. Although her back was to the other Telneren, they, too, closed their eyes and mouthed the prayer in unison.

"These are hands of soft hearts," Eiehsa said, her eyes still closed. "For only soft hearts could grieve so. May Adis guide their grieving hearts into safe harbor and his cleansing waters carry their stains into the abyss."

"May Adis guide their grieving hearts into safe harbor and

his cleansing waters carry their stains into the abyss," the other women echoed in unison.

Tess had closed her eyes almost on impulse, but now she opened them as she felt water pouring over her hand. Two of the other women had approached them with shallow, stone pitchers from which the water flowed.

Eiehsa smiled and gave their hands a squeeze. "What Adis has taken into the abyss, you must release, lest you be taken into the abyss with it. Bear your burdens no longer, noble Ilduin."

Tess's thoughts warred against each other. On one side was the impulse to accept that what was past was past and embrace her future. On the other lay doubt, the urge to dismiss the woman's words as so much mystical refuse. Only when she saw the tears flowing down Sara's face did she know to which impulse she would yield. There was naught to be gained and much to be lost in continuing to flay herself for what had happened.

"I accept the forgiveness of Adis," Sara whispered through her tears.

"I accept the forgiveness of Adis," Tess repeated, now feeling her own tears begin to flow. "Let us go forward together, Sara, in the good that we know to be."

"Yes, Lady Tess," Sara said, reaching over to squeeze her hand. "In the good that we know to be."

A wide smile lighted Eiehsa's face and, it seemed, the entire room. "And now, you will bless our children?"

The children filed in through the three great entryways, accompanied by mothers who appeared both anxious and proud. All the children were very young, some infants in arms, others certainly no more than five summers. At the altar, the three lines merged and began to move in a circle around Tess and Sara so that each child would be blessed by both.

As she touched each soft head and absorbed each smile,

Tess felt beauty growing within her, a lightness and warmth that she was sure she had never felt before. Her lips murmured gentle words of blessing, but it was as if she was the one being blessed. She had no idea how many children she might have blessed…a hundred? But she was transported by the experience until, at its very end, she lifted her eyes to the dome of rock above her head and stared into its very heart.

It was as if the symbols drew her, lifting her, until she felt light on her feet, as if she could soar above. Surely all the blessings she had given and the warmth she had received in turn had gone to her head.

"Tess?" Sara's touch was gentle, but it brought her back to earth. Tess realized they were alone in the temple now; even the clan mothers had disappeared.

"I'm sorry," she said, trying to gather herself.

"Did you see something? The mothers thought you were communing and left you to be in peace."

"I don't know." Tess tilted her head again and looked upward, but this time the symbols on the ceiling merely looked like a foreign language and tugged at her not at all. "I felt something, but…" She shrugged. "I don't know. Perhaps I'm simply tired."

"We should go back to our room, then. It's time for a meal, and it's growing chillier even in here."

Tess nodded and began to follow Sara out of the temple and through the nave. A carving caught her eye in the nave, however, and drew her immediately to it.

"What is it?" Sara asked. "Do you recognize it?"

"I don't…" Tess shook her head, trying to find a way to describe what she was feeling. "I don't remember it, exactly. But it's familiar somehow, as if I *should* remember it." Hesitantly she reached out to touch the symbol and run her hand over it. At once it was as if she could hear music.

She snatched her hand back sharply.

"Tess?"

"Touch it, Sara, and tell me if you sense anything."

Sara's brow knitted, but she obeyed, placing her fingertips on the lines that delineated the symbol, drawing them gently over it as Tess had. Then she, too, yanked her hand back.

"Music," she breathed.

"Aye," murmured Tess.

"But what does it mean?"

"I know not." Then a thought struck her, and with it a sense of wonderment. "It is as if they are trying to speak to us."

Sara's mouth opened with awe, and slowly she placed her hand on the symbol again. "Aye," she whispered. "Aye. It plays the same notes again."

Lowering her hand, she looked at Tess. "What shall we do?"

"I think perhaps we should ask the Telneren if they hear the music, too."

"And what if they don't?"

"Then we may have found the means of the transmission of the Mysteries."

"Oh!" Sara's eyes grew huge.

"It would be wonderful if we could understand it."

Sara surprised her with a little giggle. "Aye, there is that, isn't there? What good is an answer if you cannot understand it?"

The war councils had already begun. When Tess and Sara returned to the guest lodging, they found that all the men, except Tom, had gone.

"They're meeting somewhere," Tom told them. "To discuss strategy for an Anari uprising. Gewindi-Tel is too weak now to act alone, but there are other Tels, many of them, and there are thousands living in the great Anari city of Anahar. So they are discussing how best to get started."

Sara at once sat beside him. The fire was blazing brightly, and more food had replaced the earlier repast, spread atop one of the stone pallets. "Why aren't you with them?"

"Archer wanted me to stay here to look after the two of you." He looked as if he felt a little dismayed by that order.

"Well, I am glad you are here to be our champion," Sara said stoutly. "I would have missed you."

Tom brightened, and Tess turned away to hide her smile. She was, she realized, still ravenous, so she picked up a small stone bowl and began to fill it with tantalizing tidbits. "I wonder," she said, "that they can afford to feed us so well."

"Apparently the evil winter didn't strike early here as it did up north," Tom answered. "I was talking with Jenah about that. He had heard of what was happening but had no idea it was as severe as it was, especially around Derda."

Just as Tess began to feel replete with food and was considering stretching out on her bedroll, which someone had kindly spread for her, Archer entered the lodging, along with a blast of winter's breath.

"We must pack and leave at once," he said.

Tess leaped to her feet. "What's wrong?"

"The entire village is making ready to leave. Bozandari revenge is about to arrive."

Archer sat astride his mount, watching the line of villagers as they made their way up into the crags of the mountains above the town. It was a moonless night, but somehow the cliff faces reflected enough starlight to make the path visible.

It was also a terrible night to be exposed to the elements. The bitter, icy wind rushed down from the north, bringing with it the smell of snow soon to fall. Men and women alike carried the younger children in their arms, even though they also bore heavy packs on their backs. Every single member of Gewindi-Tel had tried to bring enough to get them as far as Anahar.

Archer doubted they had succeeded. Even with his party's packhorses loaded as fully as they could be, no one could carry enough. They would have to hope they would be given food as they passed through other villages.

And that they would grow this small seed of an army.

There were no elderly among the Anari. They did not age as did other men. Created at the hands of the Ilduin, they had been gifted with long life and extraordinary health. Aye, they could die from illness and injury, but illness seldom befell them. They grew older, more mature, and were less likely to want adventure than the younger members of the group, but until the day they died they worked the fields and the stones as strongly as anyone.

The reduction in their numbers, the shrinking of the clans, had come about only because of the Bozandari and their rapacious ways.

The long lives of the Anari, Archer thought, should have warned the Bozandari that eventually trouble would come. For among even this band of Anari, probably a third of them could still remember the times before the slavers had come and conquered them. These elders helped keep the flame of freedom alive in the hearts of their people.

Bowed but not broken, he thought. The Bozandari would never understand.

As the last members of the column passed him, he turned his mount and began to follow. When he reached a promontory, he paused to look back. He could see the torches of the approaching Bozandari army to the northeast, but they were yet a long way from the village.

This group would escape. Satisfied, he spurred after them.

Giri emerged from the night a short time later and fell in beside him. "We'll be well away by first light."

"Aye."

Another icy gust of wind blew down the funnel of the mountains and into their faces. For an instant Archer felt the sting of sleet. Then it was gone.

"What I do not understand," Giri said, when the wind would no longer snatch away his words, "is why the Bozandari have suddenly become...worse. 'Twas bad enough when they could come into the *telners,* taking the strongest and best to make into slaves or whores, but never before did it seem that they wanted to rid the world of all Anari. After all, we have been their garden of new slaves."

Archer rode silently for a minute or two, thinking over how much he should tell his friend. He did not wish to dishearten Giri, but on the other hand…

"There is a worse evil afoot in this world, my friend, than Bozandar and its armies. I fear this evil is using the Bozandari as he used Lantav Glassidor and his minions."

"What is this evil?"

"Some name him Chaos. Others call him the Enemy."

Giri stiffened but questioned no further. Apparently the memory of the Anari was not as short as other races, who had long since forgotten such tales or abandoned them as fantasies.

Archer sighed and lifted his head to the heavens, noting that the stars were beginning to blur behind wisps of clouds.

The tight, cold knot that had never quite eased over the countless years seemed to be growing in his chest until it would consume him.

Thus it begins again.

The first glow of dawn found them well away from Gewindi-Telner, hidden in the wild reaches of mountains only the Anari knew well enough to traverse. Even here, far out from civilization, there were signs that some rock had spoken to a mason and been harvested.

But the Anari also knew that some of the mountains and rock bound evil in their depths, an evil as old as the world itself. Here they passed quietly, as unobtrusive as might be. Remembering the fire creature they had fought in the Adasen basin, Tom could well understand the caution he saw in those around him.

But at other times there was apparently no evil to concern them, and the pace quickened and conversation resumed.

Eventually, before the canyons and ravines in the mountains had felt the sun's touch, Jenah called a halt.

"It is safe here," Jenah told Archer and the rest of his party. "Long have Anari camped safely in the embrace of these rocks."

Embrace was a good word, Tom thought, looking around them, for it seemed as if they had entered a circle of level ground created by the stones themselves. Dismounting, he helped as much as he could, lifting packs from the tired shoulders of Anari mothers and fathers who carried children now awakening and famished. He helped build cook fires with a strange black rock that burned and seemed to be in abundance here, and carried buckets of water from the waterfall hidden behind the rocks.

Soon tantalizing smells filled the camp, and, not long after that, hungry children were being fed before their elders dipped in.

He was glad finally to rejoin his own little group: Archer, Ratha, Giri, Tess and Sara. Most especially Sara. Any weariness he might have felt was banished when she smiled at him and squeezed his hand as he sat beside her.

She passed him a bowl of the stew she had made, and he tucked in with great delight.

"You are sure it is he?" Ratha asked Archer.

"Aye. His ugly touch is all over the world right now. After Lorense, there can be no doubt."

Tom leaned forward. "Who are you talking about?"

Archer looked at the lad gravely. "Have you heard the tales about Chaos?"

Tom felt his heart skip a beat. "He who would destroy the world?"

"Aye, lad. The same."

"But I thought…" Tom's voice trailed off as he looked inward and realized that what he had once thought to be a fairy tale for children was no such thing after all. He had sensed it ever since Lorense and what he had seen that day as Sara and Tess had battled Lantav Glassidor. The mage, skilled though he was, had been possessed by something darker and uglier, and Tom had seen it.

He looked at Archer once again. "Glassidor," he said. "He was but a doorway."

"Exactly," Archer replied. Even in the warmth of the rising sun, the day remained cold, and Archer was wrapped deeply in his cloak. For a man who could look like vengeance on two feet when they faced trouble, he appeared singularly inoffensive at the moment.

"But not the only one," Tom said, though he was hoping he was wrong.

"Not the only one," Archer agreed, his voice heavy. "We have heard of other hives. You know that. But there is more afoot."

Tess, who had been drawing in the dust at her feet with a twig, spoke. "There is a larger doorway open now." She sounded almost as if she were in a trance. "Can't you feel it?"

Tom felt a shivering within, an unpleasant sensation, not unlike when he feared he might fall from a great height. He closed his eyes, trying to deal with the feeling, trying to find his well of courage. But instead of courage, he found words that insisted on being spoken, though he had little idea what they meant.

"When the three approach, the Twelve must guard the unbound Enemy."

His eyes popped open, and he found everyone staring at him.

"Well," said Archer, "that's clear enough. Would you could tell us the outcome, Tom."

Tom merely shook his head, wondering at these times when he felt compelled to speak words that did not seem to be of his own design.

"I will tell you," Archer said slowly, tossing yet another small coal on the fire, "that the Enemy has grown since last he and I crossed paths. In those days he could not have done what I saw him do in Lorense. Nor what I suspect he does with the weather. It will indeed take the Twelve to save us."

As if his words had drawn the fury of the heavens down on them, the skies swiftly clouded over and the wind became a gale of sleet. From around the entire camp came cries of surprise as everyone hunkered down within cloaks and blankets.

Tom edged closer to the fire. Tess alone seemed oblivious but continued her tracings in the dust of the ages.

As quickly as the gale had arrived, it vanished, as if the peaks around them had swallowed it up. Above, the sky remained clouded but appeared benign enough otherwise.

"That was strange," Tom muttered.

Ratha placed a hand on his shoulder. "Eat up, lad. Matters will get stranger yet."

Tom turned to look the Anari in the eye. "If you seek to comfort me, that is an unusual way to do it."

Ratha laughed, a sound that seemed to drive back the edges of evil. "I was just assuring you that you have much adventure to look forward to."

It was hard now for Tom to remember that only a few short weeks ago he had been living with his family in the small town of Whitewater and dreaming of great adventures rather than the humdrum life of a gatekeeper's son. Thinking back on it, he sighed. "I think, Ratha, that I have encountered more adventure than a lifetime needs."

Ratha leaned close. "Aye, lad, you have. We all have. Unfortunately there seems to be no end in sight."

Archer had taken note of Tess's writing in the sand. "What do you seek, Lady?"

Slowly Tess looked up. "It is a symbol I saw in the temple at Gewindi-Telnah. I keep feeling that I should know what it means."

Archer left the stone on which he had been sitting and went

to crouch beside her. "Show me," he said. "I have some command of the Old Tongue."

Carefully she traced the flow and curve of the intricate symbol, trying as best she could to get it to resemble exactly what she had seen on the wall.

Archer nodded slowly. "It says, *One who blazes with the light of the gods.*"

"I wonder why it seems so familiar," she said.

Sara leaned over. "You forgot part of it, Tess." Taking the stick from the other woman's hand, she drew a rounded triangle around the letters. "Does that mean anything?"

Archer's expression now looked as stony as any Anari's. "The enclosure means that it holds within a name. The name in this case is…Theriel."

"The White Lady," Tom breathed. "She of the legends."

Reaching out suddenly, Archer rubbed away the symbol with his gloved hand. Then, without a word, he strode away from them.

Tess stared after him. "I upset him."

"Much about the past upsets him, Lady," Ratha said bracingly. "Especially when the present is but another maw of the past."

"What does that mean?" Tom asked.

Ratha cocked his head to one side, as if considering his words with care. "We fight an old battle, Tom. What is to come has already been."

The fleeing villagers rested only long enough to see to their needs and catch a few hours of sleep. By midday they were on their way again, following a path that would have been invisible to all but the initiated.

Everywhere there seemed to be a recognition that they were leaving behind the familiar forever. That at the end of this march, one way or another, the world would change eternally.

* * *

Sara found herself walking among the *Telneren,* with Tom at her side. The women sang in an easy, lilting rhythm that matched their strides, and although Sara could not understand the words, the melodies and harmonies seemed to reach into her soul. She squeezed Tom's hand and glanced over to him. The look on his face gave her pause.

"Is something wrong?" she asked.

"They sing with such joy," he said. "I can't find any joy in this journey."

She favored him with a smile. "Not even with me, Tom Downey?"

"Of course," he said, his voice faltering. "I didn't mean…it's just…so much…and so much more…."

"Don't lose courage, Tom," she said, giving his hand another squeeze. "They sing with the joy of courage. The joy of those who know their cause is just, who know they will overcome."

"If the last two days are a portent," Tom said, "the Bozandari can stamp them out Tel by Tel until there are none left."

"And if they allowed themselves to stand Tel by Tel, that might happen. But this is why we march to Anahar. I suspect Gewindi-Tel are not the only Anari with this idea." She pointed ahead. "Look at how Ratha and Giri and Jenah have fallen in as one. Bonds of kinship are strong among the Anari, just as they are in Whitewater. When trouble befalls any, all respond. The Bozandari will regret having burned the tail of this great desert adder."

"Do you miss home?" he said. "At the mere sound of the word—Whitewater—I see my mother bringing a bowl of stew to my father, then sitting by the fireplace with her knitting. And my heart weeps. I wonder how they are surviving this winter, and whether we shall go home to a ghost town."

"Now, Tom, you know Whitewater folk better than to say

such a thing. Why, look at us. Much hardship have we seen on this journey, and yet we walk on. Why would you think our kinsmen capable of any less? Whitewater presses its shoulder to the mountains. Our people are good beasts of burden. When the load is heavy, we pull together. Let us not fear for them."

"Your Lady speaks the truth," Eiehsa said, during a pause in the singing. "Fret not about what you cannot affect, Lord Thomas. The sun will rise and the sun will set, but the heart beats during light or darkness."

"Lord Thomas," Tom said, chuckling. "I am quite certain I do not merit that title. I am merely Tom Downey, of the village of Whitewater, son of a gatekeeper."

"Lady Sara is a noble Ilduin," Eiehsa said with a deep smile. "I am sure her eye would not fall fair on one less noble than she."

"She's right," Sara said. "You are the son of a gatekeeper, yes, and a noble thing indeed is that alone. But you are more than that, Tom, and you know this to be true. Much do you speak that a young man would not see, and when you do, I hear the voice of ages on the wind. You are a prophet, Tom Downey. Mark my words."

"A master of the obvious, perhaps," Tom said.

"Now, lad," Eiehsa said, "I suspect the Lady will be for tanning your hide if you continue to speak thus. You wonder if you are worthy of her. But that is your wonder, Tom, not hers. Her eyes say she has no such doubts."

"Not even the least," Sara said, giving him a playful smack on the bottom. "So either you are indeed worthy, or I am a blind and stupid girl. I'll thank you not to imply the latter."

"Are you going to let her spank you like that?" Archer said with a deep, grumbling laugh, having suddenly appeared at their side.

"Um…yes?" Tom asked.

"Smart lad," Archer said, winking at Sara. "He knows what

is good for him. And I know what is good for me, and for all of us, if I may prevail upon Mother Eiehsa and her sisters for another song to lighten our steps."

"Very well," Eiehsa said. "In the presence of such nobility as Lord Archer and his companions, perhaps our oldest and most beautiful song is in order. We sing it but rarely, yet it is the song that binds our souls as can none other. Sisters, let us sing."

Their voices rose together, and even Archer sang along, translating the words for the rest.

> *Our roots lie deep in mountain stone,*
> *On desert sand we stand, alone,*
> *But not alone, not e'er are we,*
> *For graced by blessings each are we.*
>
> *The rising sun and setting moon,*
> *Bring rhythm to the heart's own tune,*
> *The summer warmth and winter rain,*
> *Renew our strength to stand again.*
>
> *We live as one, in joy and peace,*
> *And know we all, when labors cease,*
> *That in the arms of gods we sleep,*
> *Our souls forever theirs to keep.*
>
> *Weep not, Anari, tall and proud,*
> *Let not thy burdened back be bowed,*
> *Created one by Twelve are ye,*
> *Live long in honor, brave and free.*

Sara found herself singing along, her voice dancing with those of the Anari as if born of a strength beyond her own. If the Twelve had indeed created the Anari, then that grace must surely wash away any stain. For in the lilt of their voices, and hers, she found a peace like none she could remember.

Finally even Tom sang beside her, their voices rising like the dreams of lovers not yet met as if to play among the stars. Long had she wished for this, to hear his voice unite in song with hers. If it took a horrific flight through all the world to hear his voice thus, then every horror was paid in this moment.

"I do love thee, Tom Downey," she said, leaning in to kiss his cheek.

In the instant that her lips tasted his sweetness, a brief, flitting whisper sounded. And then the arrow lodged in his side.

"By Elanor!" Tom cried, sinking to the ground.

Archer heard the cry, but his eyes were already on the ridge to their left, looking at the rainbow of arrows arcing through the air toward them.

"Cover!" he cried.

The words were unnecessary, as already the Anari were going to ground amidst the rocks, mothers clutching children to their breasts, men unslinging their own bows and nocking arrows.

Archer reached down and lifted Tom with one arm, the other gently pushing Sara aside. "Let us get him safe from further wounds first, m'Lady. Then you can tend to these."

She nodded, her face white as a midnight moon, and scrabbled alongside Archer into the lee of a rock. The clatter of arrows on rock lasted another few seconds that seemed like an eternity, then stopped.

"Why do they show mercy?" she asked.

"It's not mercy," Archer said. "They have no easy targets and waste not the work of their fletchers. This is but a brief respite, and then they will fall upon us with all their fury."

Tom let out a long, low groan, and Archer rested a hand on

his shoulder. "Breathe easy, my friend. The wound hurts worse than it is. Your Lady Sara can tend it beyond any notice. I promise you."

Tom nodded weakly, his eyes screwed closed, and Archer glanced at Sara's face. She saw the truth as plainly as did Archer. The arrow had entered Tom's side, just below the ribs, the tip protruding from his belly. He would indeed need Ilduin magick.

"I'll get Lady Tess," he whispered in her ear, so that Tom would not hear it. "And try to organize our defense."

Sara nodded, and cradled Tom's head in her arms, murmuring an entreaty to Elanor, the goddess of healing.

Archer slipped from rock to gully to rock, taking the faces of shaken Anari in his hands and explaining what he needed of them. In moments, their shock was replaced by a cold determination. Finally he reached the head of the column, where Jenah had already recalled the advance guards and was issuing instructions. Tess was tending the wound of an Anari whose calf had been pierced through, and Archer waited for her to finish before speaking.

"It's Tom," he said. "Midway back in the column. He is shot through the belly."

"Damn them," she swore, Ilduin fire flashing in her eyes. "I will go to him."

"Quickly, please," Archer said.

"They will attack soon," Jenah said, after Tess had left. "They follow us like a hunter after wounded prey."

"Yes," Archer said. "And when this is over, we must consider why that is. But that is for later. For now, we fight."

No sooner had the words left his lips than a cry arose on the ridge, and two hundred Bozandari rose from their positions and began to descend upon the Anari. These were not seasoned troops, for they came on too fast, and soon were stumbling amidst the loose shale and talus on the slope. Now the Anari added their arrows to the hardships of the advance, and within minutes the ridge was a roiling mass of screaming forms, comrades stepping on comrades in an attempt to press the attack, trying vainly to form battle order, lest they emerge onto the valley floor as a vulnerable rabble.

"Hold fast!" Archer bellowed, the order echoing down the line as a few Anari rose to advance.

To meet the enemy on the slope would be madness, for their descending mass would shatter any line. But once they reached the base of the slope, those in front would suffer from the headlong rush of those behind. Then they could be struck with effect—if only the Anari would be patient.

"Steady!" Jenah yelled, his deep voice seeming to carry the weight of the mountain itself as it boomed and echoed through the valley. "Steady!"

Arrows continued to thin the Bozandari ranks, but Archer could see that too many were making it through the deadly hail. "Ratha! Giri! To me!"

"We are already here, m'Lord," Giri said. "Where else would you find us in a fight?"

"Hiding under a rock, perhaps," Ratha said, dark humor swimming in his words.

"Speak for yourself, brother," Giri said, grinning.

"On my word, we advance," Archer called, ignoring their verbal horseplay, his eyes sweeping up and down the line. "Jenah, can you flank them?"

"Aye, Lord Archer," Jenah responded. "Doubt not our valor, nor our skill."

"I doubt not," Archer said, feeling his muscles tense for the spring. "I doubt not. Advance!"

Anari men and women rose and moved on the enemy, fire in their eyes, fury in their bellies. Archer had had but a few minutes to teach them the old fighting ways, and many were the mistakes. But many things were done correctly, as well, and soon the deadly swirl of swords began to bite flesh. The eyes of the Bozandari were wide with terror, for this was not the helpless prey they had imagined. Still, they fought with the skill borne of countless hours of drilling, managing to form a ragged line in the chaos.

If fury be the fuel of battle, then the Anari burned bright in its cauldron. They fought with the fury of men and women who had lost too much, endured too much, buried too many and grieved their last breaths. The Bozandari fell before them like blood-drenched sheaves of desert rye, yet still held their line.

With a deep cry that seemed to emanate from the depths of the earth, Jenah ordered his flanking force into the attack, and now the issue was fully decided as panic swept down the Bozandari line. For Archer, minutes stretched into hours, his mind blurred against the carnage at his feet, the clang of metal on metal and the screams of the dying. Killing had become an all too familiar routine, and his body performed almost without need of his mind. It was better this way, he decided. Better not to be there when he and those around him did such things. Better to simply let muscle and steel and nature take their course.

Tess looked up to watch the final carnage with a grim satisfaction, then returned her attention to Tom. Words she did not remember having known flitted through her mind: *sepsis, peritonitis.* The wound was indeed grave, and her hands worked with almost mechanical precision to extract the arrow. The cry that rose from Tom's throat as she drew the shaft out was beyond human, and Sara sobbed beside her.

"Find water," Tess said, looking into Sara's eyes. "And those herbs you keep in your pouch. Find them now, Sara. I need your help. Do you hear me?"

Sara nodded numbly, and Tess reached up to squeeze her

shoulder with a blood-smeared hand. "Sara! Listen. I need you to help me. Get water and your herbs. Now."

"Yes, m'Lady," Sara said.

As she left, Tom's hand moved to Tess's thigh, gripping it so tightly that she could feel the bruises forming. She met his eyes and kept her voice steady and even.

"I have the arrow out, Tom. I need to clean the wounds as best I can, and put a poultice on them. Stay with me, Tom. Look at my face and stay with me."

"Ohhhhhhhh Elanor," he moaned. "My sins are grave."

"He says the prayer of the dying," Eiehsa said, kneeling beside her.

"Stop that!" Tess said, fury in her voice. "You are not going to die, Tom Downey, Prophet of the Prophecy. You are not going to die in this place. By the power of the Twelve, I forbid it!"

The sky seemed to crack with a thousand peals of thunder, halting even the last of the Bozandari in their tracks. Tess seemed to shimmer from a sun within, light blazing from her eyes.

"I forbid it!" she cried again. "You may not take him!"

The pouch between her breasts seemed to burn like fire, and she yanked it off, allowing the stones to spill over Tom's belly. The stones flared like golden fire, dancing over his wounds. He cried as blood hissed into steam and the stones sank into his flesh, but she held his arms pinned as she looked up to the heavens.

"Ilduin tessuh nah elah! Ilduin mees lahrohn nah elah! Tessuh nah elah!"

Fury swept out of the sky, flaming hail sizzling on the dead, dying and fleeing Bozandari, igniting their bodies and reigniting their screams. An inhuman howl rose through the valley, a howl to chill the blood of the gods themselves, and with a final pealing boom, the sky seemed to expel its own rage. In the echoing silence that rode its wake, only Tom's low whimper could be heard.

"My Lady Sara," he moaned. "I love you."

"And I love you, too," Sara said, appearing beside Tess with a pitcher of water and her pouch of herbs. "I have loved you from the moment I was old enough to know what love is, Tom Downey. And I will not lose you this day, nor any other. My soul is bound to yours forever."

"I love you," he whispered, eyes fluttering closed. "I love you always, dear Sara Deepwell. Always."

And he was still.

Tess remained filled with the power. It shot about her body like lightning and made her blond hair flow as if in a gale. Her eyes seemed to shoot sparks. All who could see her began to back away in terror, except Sara, who fell across Tom's lifeless body and wailed.

Archer ran toward them, consternation on his face. "Lady Tess," he said sharply. "My Lady Tess, cease!"

She turned toward him, her face unearthly as it seemed to glow from within. For an instant it appeared she might lash out at him. Then, with a soft cry, she closed her eyes and sagged. An instant later she lay in an unconscious heap.

"Tom!" Sara cried. "Oh, Tom, I cannot bear to lose you!" She looked up at Archer, her face stained with tears. "Why could she not heal him?"

Eiehsa knelt beside her and gripped her shoulders, drawing her into a tight embrace. "Hush, my lady, hush. It is in grief that we are born, and into grief we all must come."

Archer knelt beside Tess, taking a quick survey. She was once again in that deep sleep that followed her attempts at healing. Then, not doubting the powers she had called on, he bent forward until his ear was next to Tom's mouth and nose.

"He breathes," he told Sara. "He lives."

Then he strode away to find Jenah and the other clan elders.

The power that Tess had called upon here would not go unnoticed. They needed to move again as swiftly as possible, before worse trouble came their way.

Whether she knew it or not, Tess had drawn the attention of someone even worse than the Bozandari, for the Enemy would not fail to detect such a huge use of power.

Their party was truly hunted now.

The clan elders moved swiftly, comprehending the threat as well as Archer, for they, unlike the races of men, understood such powers. Stoically the Anari swiftly buried their dead and tended the wounded. Stretchers were made for Tom and some of the other wounded, creating even greater burdens for the fleeing villagers, but none complained.

Ratha, Giri and Jenah, now riding Tom's horse, rode out ahead to scout. As the fleeing villagers began their trek once more, with Tom in their midst and Sara riding beside his stretcher, Archer came to claim Tess.

As he had expected, she was still unconscious, but now her hands clasped the twelve stones he had glimpsed only briefly in the past. Carefully prying them from her fingers, he stashed them in the leather pouch that lay beside her on the ground and slipped the cord around her neck.

Then, swiftly, he mounted his own steed, and two Anari helped lift her onto the saddle before him. With his arms tight around her, keeping her safe, they followed the rest of the villagers.

He had much to think on. Perhaps too much. Tess had put them all at risk; he would have to warn her to use her powers sparingly. Now trouble would lie around every twist of the path ahead.

"She spoke the Old Tongue."

Eiehsa had come up beside him, riding one of Gewindi-Tel's few horses. He looked at her, then nodded. Tess's head bobbed a little against his shoulder, and he adjusted his hold on her, trying to keep her comfortable as well as safe.

"Few know the Old Tongue," Eiehsa said. "I myself have only a smattering. Where did she learn it?"

"I know not. Perhaps in the days before she lost her memory someone tutored her."

"Mayhap, although I know of none but yourself with a complete command of the language." She paused and sighed heavily. "My Lord, did you hear what she spoke?"

Archer shook his head.

"She told the gods that the she forbade them to take Tom. And then she said, 'Sisters, help me now. Sisters, rally your strength to me now. Help me now.'"

His head turned sharply toward her, and the tightening in his chest grew worse. "Are you sure?"

Eiehsa shrugged. "Nearly. As I said, my command of the Old Tongue is lacking. But…I am fairly certain that is what the Lady said. And in response, fire rained from the heavens, but only upon the Bozandari."

Archer looked down at the small woman in his arms, finding it almost impossible to believe now what he had seen with his own eyes: that she had challenged the gods. Even more troubling, however, were the words she had spoken.

The last prayer of Theriel.

Once again the refugees began to move, although not without increased security. Jenah sent roving patrols deep into the surrounding mountains. Meanwhile, women at the rear of the column swept away any trace of their passage. Archer doubted that such efforts would be of much effect. The Enemy that tracked them was not relying on footprints in the desert sand. Still, if these arrangements made the Anari more aware of the danger and more alert to any sight or sound, then perhaps there was value in them after all.

By midafternoon, they had climbed higher into the mountains and begun to pass networks of caves. Archer had heard of such a redoubt but had never seen it. Now, at a silent command from Jenah, the Anari began to file into one of the cave entrances. As he joined them, Archer saw that the cave was well-selected. It and its side chambers were easily large enough to give shelter to all, and it offered excellent sightlines over any approach.

"Once," Eiehsa said to Archer, "years ago, Gewindi-Tel came here to escape the slavers. When we returned, our village had been laid to waste. We never again fled our village, lest we deprive our heirs of their rich history. Long ago, we swore to the

Ilduin that we would defend the Telnertah. Now, it seems, that oath must be broken."

Archer, who still held the unconscious Tess with her head on his shoulder, answered in heavy tones. "It may be that the time to preserve the temples has passed."

Eiehsa looked at him, her eyes unreadable, and finally nodded. "It may be that the temples have come to life."

Archer looked down at the woman he held, still unsure what he thought of her and what she had done. "That may be," he agreed. "May the gods save us all."

"The gods," said Eiehsa, with a mixture of bitterness and sarcasm, "are to blame for this all. Delude yourself not, Master Archer. 'Twas not simply the Enemy and his brother who brought the evil upon the world, nor the love and fury of the Ilduin. The gods themselves created such a power among men, then turned their backs and let that power take its own course. Once the Ilduin had made their awful choice, then the gods proclaimed their wrath and rent the world asunder, as if they could never have foreseen such an event. Mayhap it will be the Ilduin who save us from the gods, Lord Archer."

Archer looked sharply at her, trying to read the knowledge that lay behind her words, but could find nothing more than what she had said. Nor did she seem inclined to add to it. Instead she turned and began to tend to the children. A gust of wind blew down from the glacier that ever topped this mountain, driving a chill down inside his cloak. Archer at once shrugged it higher on his shoulders and wrapped more of it around Tess.

His arms ached with the effort of holding her these many miles, yet he did not begrudge the ache. He begrudged no pain that life brought him, for penance and suffering were his adjudged lot. Nor did he feel sorry for himself. Atonement was his burden, and his alone. He walked to the entrance of the cave and looked out at the roiling black clouds. The Enemy sought them.

With a shake of his head, he turned and began to look for a safe place to lay Tess. The cavern was cold and dank, but the Anari were already building a large central fire, and a natural chimney somewhere above sucked the smoke away, while drawing in fresh air from the cave's mouth.

Archer soon found Tom and Sara, and was pleased to note that Tom seemed to be stirring. Ratha and Giri appeared as if from nowhere to help him lay Tess upon her spread-out bed-roll. For an instant she appeared lifeless; then, to Archer's vast relief, she rolled onto her side and curled up.

"How is Tom?" he asked Sara.

She looked up, her face much calmer now, and with perhaps even the hint of a smile. "He improves. He is dreaming, and from time to time he murmurs. His wounds appear healed." But then she looked at Tess, and her face saddened. "But what it cost her!"

"I think it cost you, as well," Archer said, squatting down to take her chin in his hand and turn her face so he could better see it. "No Ilduin has ever called such force from the sky without the aid of her sisters. Whether you knew or not, she drew on your power at that moment."

Sara shook her head. "That is fine. What does it signify if I tire? Tom is alive."

Archer merely nodded, then rose, feeling suddenly very old and very tired. "Keep an eye on Tess, I pray you. I need to speak to the elders."

Then he strode away across the cavern floor toward the fire, where the Gewindi elders were gathering. Women all, they were the lifeblood of the clan, the keepers of knowledge and the arbiters of all problems.

They warmly invited him to sit with them, making space near the comforting flames. For a while they spoke little, as if gathering their resources and thoughts. At a second fire nearby, the cooking had already begun, and the smells of food hung in the air.

Eiehsa finally spoke, her voice deep with the knowledge of many years. "The prophesied times are upon us," she announced.

Five other heads bobbed in agreement.

"For the first time in our lives, we have seen the true power of the Ilduin unleashed. This can mean but one thing."

"Ardebal," one of the women said.

"Yes," Eiehsa agreed, seeming to stare into Archer's soul. "Ardebal has awakened. And he stalks Gewindi-Tel."

It had been two generations of men since Archer had heard the Anari name for the Enemy. And something in the old woman's face said she knew far more than any was meant to know.

"Yes," Archer said. "I believe he looks for Tess and Sara. Earlier on our journey, Lady Tess said that she felt what seemed like an oily presence trying to crawl into her mind. I had thought this was perhaps the hive mind of Lantav Glassidor, whom she slew in Lorense. But during that fray, and at times since, I have sensed the presence of the old Enemy. I think perhaps it was he who tried to crawl into the Lady's mind, and he still who seeks to capture her."

"Well might that be," Eiehsa said. "But you know more of this than you have said. You know far too much of the Enemy to be merely a passing mortal. Long are the legends of your life, Master Archer, even counted in the days of the Anari. It is not merely Ladies Tess and Sara whom the Enemy seeks. He seeks you, too, does he not?"

Archer paused for a long moment, then finally nodded. "Yes, Mother. It may be that he does."

"And do you know why?" Eiehsa pressed. "It behooves us all to know exactly where we stand in this morass, lest we step onto what we think be firm rock and instead sink into a quicksand."

For long moments Archer stared into the leaping flames of

the fire. Around his heart, an ancient carapace began to crack, and into the cracks seeped a pain nearly as old as the world. Along with the pain came a harsh certainty. He turned his head to look once again at Eiehsa.

"I am," he said, his words weighted as if with lead, "Annuvil."

"The elder brother," Eiehsa said. "Beloved of Theriel, against whom Ardred made the war that ended the First Age."

"Aye, Mother," Archer said. "It was my brother and I that destroyed the world."

"Nonsense," the woman said. "Unless the old tales be twisted by the mists of time, it was your brother whose selfishness and jealousy led to the founding of Dederand. It was your brother who raised an army against the people of Samarand, and kidnapped and murdered Theriel on your wedding night. It was your brother who inflamed the rage of the Ilduin and brought down the rain of fire. Bear ye not the weight of his ill deeds, Lord Annuvil. It profits you nothing and costs you much."

"I bear only the weight of my own deeds," Archer said. "But that weight enough is heavy for a soul. Offer me not the blessing prayer of Adis, for I cannot turn from who I am, or what I have done. But let us speak no more of this, I beseech you. The present times are dark enough without the darkness of the past laid also upon them."

Eiehsa and the other Anari closed their eyes in the same instant, and their lips began moving, mouthing words Archer could not discern. For a long moment it was as if every sound had been sucked from the cave; the fire itself seemed to stand still between them. Then, as one, their eyes opened.

"The pain of Annuvil and the Ilduin stands among us," Eiehsa said, rising, her voice carrying throughout the caves. "Born of the jealousy of Ardebal, simmered in his hate, seared by his rage. Good stood as evil threatened, yet the soot of the evil still blackened the sky."

All talk among the Anari had ceased; every eye in the cavern was upon the old woman, who spoke with a rolling resonance that seemed to draw strength from the rocks themselves.

"Now," she continued, "in the darkness, good stands once more, and once more the scent of black hate hangs in the air. Our people are enslaved, our Tel-mates murdered and our telner turned to ash. Silent were the Anari in the last days of the First Age, standing apart and claiming no side in the madness. But silent are we no more. If it be Ardebal whose evil darkens our lives, let it be Annuvil and the Ilduin whose goodness leads us into the light."

Try as he might to find words with which to interrupt, Archer could but sit and listen, knowing what was to come, knowing the awful price that would come with it. A part of his soul rebelled against the thought, for he wished to add no more death to the tally in his account. Yet he knew that could not be. Death had stalked him through the ages, and now it stood up behind him once more.

Eiehsa's voice rose to a crescendo. "Lord Archer, Lady Tess, Lady Sara, into your hands I deliver the heart and might of Gewindi-Tel. And, I dare say, the heart and might of all my people. We shall go to Anahar and there make firm our pledge to your service. For it is in your service that we shall find our delivery."

She bowed her head slightly, then extended her hands. "I beseech Elanor to grant us healing through these brave souls who have journeyed here to join us. And upon *Keh-Bal*, I swear to their service the fealty of Gewindi-Tel. Let any who dissent speak now, or be bound by my oath."

The silence in the cavern seemed to thunder in Archer's ears. None spoke. None saved himself from what Archer knew was to come.

"We are thine, Lord Archer," Eiehsa said, offering her clasped hands. "Our wisdom, our dreams, our blood, we put into your hands. Honor us by accepting this oath."

Seconds seemed to drag into hours as Archer weighed his decision. To refuse the oath would be an act of unspeakable rudeness among the Anari. To accept it might well be their death sentence. He felt a presence and was astonished to see Tess conscious and at his side, with Sara, Giri and Ratha close behind. They too looked to him for guidance, and had throughout this long journey. It was as if the weight of all hope rested on his shoulders and his alone.

Then a look passed between Tess and Sara, and Archer realized in that moment that he was assuming too much. They, too, as Ilduin, would bear the weight and worry of the Anari oath. And, he realized, they, too, had gifts to offer and a prize after which the Enemy lusted.

Tess nodded silently.

Archer turned and clasped Eiehsa's hands. "I accept your oath, Mother. And I pray that I and my companions will be worthy of your service."

After a meal that was almost a feast, as if the Anari were celebrating having bound their fate to Archer, Eiehsa and the other clan mothers began to relate stories of the First Age.

Archer slipped away to stand guard at the cave mouth, perhaps because he couldn't bear the recitation yet again of past horrors. Except, thought Tess as she settled in to listen, he had shared those tales himself, almost as if he felt a need to remind his listeners of the dangers of arrogance and jealousy.

It amazed her, however, to realize that he was the Annuvil of the story he told, the elder brother who had won the love of Theriel, only to find himself caught up in a war, a widower almost before he was wed.

She wished she might reach out to him in some way to ease

a pain that must have ridden him hard these many years, but he had taken himself away somewhere. Besides, she doubted any words she might speak could heal a wound so old and deep.

"The Firstborn," Eiehsa said, her voice carrying to all ears that cared to listen, "were immortal, created by the gods to fill the world with beauty and song. But they were also created in the image of the gods, and with that came less than perfection, for the gods themselves are not perfect."

Immortal? Tess's mind couldn't seem to grasp the idea that Archer was immortal. In fact, thinking about it, she could only consider immortality to be a curse. The joys of life were ever so much sweeter when the days were numbered.

But even the notion of immortality paled beside the prospect that the gods were imperfect and had made their creations with the same imperfections.

She tucked that nugget away for later consideration, for she sensed that therein lay a very important bit of information.

Important enough, perhaps, to save the Anari from their persecutors.

The clan mothers began to sing together again, this time with a rhythm and melody that seemed to creep along the spine and seize the mind in a spell.

Then Eiehsa flung a handful of sparkling sand upon the fire, and out of the flames a figure grew.

All sound in the cavern vanished except for the singing of the clan mothers. Even the flames, leaping higher, seemed to dance. The reddish glow from the fire caught on the stalactites, making it seem that bloody teeth surrounded them, ready to bite.

The figure continued to grow out of the flames, yet it was not of the flames. It was the figure of a young woman, dressed in white. A beautiful woman with cascading blond hair and eyes the color of a midsummer sky. Taller she grew, until she towered over them gracefully, so that all in the cavern might see her.

The hem of her long dress appeared to ruffle on a breeze not borne of the fire from which she sprang. In her hands she held a small bouquet of white roses, and on her lips was the soft smile of love.

She reached out one hand and clasped another's, a figure that coalesced beside her. He was tall, taller than she, and his face was marked with both love and youth. Long dark hair he had, and an innocence about him that made the heart ache.

He drew closer to the lady, and their lips met, sealing a kiss that whispered of eternity.

Then another appeared, a fair and beautiful man whose face

also shone with youth, and overshadowed the dark man. But on his face there was no love, only lust and anger.

An instant later the fair and beautiful young man wrested the woman away from the darker one. She struggled against him, but only briefly, for he killed her with a savage blow of his sword before she could defend herself.

Then the images from the fire became ugly and dark, a quickening kaleidoscope of war, of death. At the head of an army the dark man sought vengeance, his sword raised high. He was met on the field of battle by the beautiful golden man and another army.

The view changed again, filled with fallen bodies, and weeping men and women. A city burned.

Then a circle of eleven appeared, eleven women who joined hands and began to sing together.

A new vision, of fire raining from the sky, of a city blasted until nothing was left but a plain of black glass as far as the eye could see.

Then back to the circle of women, who stood tearfully, with their heads bowed. Then, one by one, they dropped each other's hands and looked around as if waking from a dreadful dream.

As one, they crumpled to the ground in despair, as if they hated what they had done.

And one by one they were gently carried away by the Anari.

Finally a huge temple began to rise from the flames, carved by Anari hands, guided in every detail by the women from the circle, women who now looked haunted and full of grief.

"Anahar," said Eiehsa, her voice rising above the other mothers. "The temple that was given to all of us to keep the knowledge alive. The temple of atonement. The temple we guard with our lives."

Turning, she cast her gaze upon Sara and Tess. "You have

been sent to learn the mysteries. We have showed you the tale behind them."

Her voice rose, reaching even the farthest recesses of the cavern. "We have been chosen. We are the Guardians. Our lives are but grains of sand in the river of time, but the temple is eternal. It will be our salvation. Hearten yourselves, my brothers and sisters, for the fight for our freedom will be but the first step on the long road to defeat our ultimate enemy."

She pointed to fire again, flinging yet another small puff of sparkling dust, and the image of the fair and beautiful man rose again, now with his face twisted by hate. "Never forget he would see us all dead, for he has nothing to live for except power. Keep him in mind. He ended the First Age and would gladly end the second. He comes cloaked in beauty, with his heart full of death. He is Ardebal, Lord of Chaos!"

For an instant the figure loomed over them all, threatening; then, in an eyeblink, everything returned to its natural state.

The clan mothers sat, appearing exhausted; the fire settled back into its pit. Only the angry red teeth of the cave remained to remind them of what they had just seen.

Tess felt a hand steal into hers and turned to see Sara. She squeezed the younger woman's chilled fingers, hoping the gesture was reassuring. But in Sara's eyes she read the same feeling that filled her own heart: *How were the two of them supposed to do this impossible task that had just been set for them?*

Sara returned to find Tom still asleep on his pallet. For a moment his eyes flickered open, and it almost appeared as if they glowed orange, though she knew it was only the reflection of the fire's glow. Still, his face was pale, and weakness was evident in his limbs.

Acting on an impulse almost beyond her understanding, she cradled his head in her arms and opened her bodice, tucking his lips to her nipple. His response was equally instinctive, as he began to suckle in his sleep. Sara caught her breath, both from the pleasure of the touch and from the realization that she could feel liquid emerging from her breast, flowing into his mouth. For a moment she wondered how this could be, for she had never been with child and certainly never delivered one. Yet the moment seemed to fit with her heart's call, and she closed her eyes and hummed a quiet tune as he nursed.

"I have heard the tales of Ilduin succor, saved only for the lady's mate and children," Eiehsa whispered.

Sara opened her eyes with a start, then caught her cry before it emerged as she looked into the old woman's kind face.

"Forgive me, Lady Sara," Eiehsa said. "I did not mean to startle you. But not often does one witness a miracle, though many have my eyes beheld these past days. Still, this seems to me the greatest of all, for the love of the Ilduin was deep in legend, and their milk is said to heal even the most shattered soul."

"I know not why I did this," Sara said, stroking Tom's hair as he now slept at her breast. "I knew only that I must do it."

"That is often the way of love, Lady Sara. To ponder the reasons is often to miss the moment in its passing. You gave yourself into that moment, and even now color is returning to the young lad's face. It was your love that he needed, Lady. Your love and the milk of your kindness. And that you gave. I would that we all gave so freely."

Sara smiled and bowed her head. "Thank you, Mother. Though I fear I am not worthy of such praise. It is neither effort nor sorrow to care for one I love so dearly. But can I carry that same burden for the world at large? For that is the burden which seems placed upon me, and upon Lady Tess. We are unskilled and can act only on the calling of the moment. I fear we shall need much more than that if we hope to prevail."

"Now, now," Eiehsa said, reaching out to stroke her shoulder. "Tomorrow will be upon us soon enough, and in its coming it will bring troubles of its own. Fret not for those, my child. Simply care for Tom in this moment and trust your Ilduin blood to guide you in the next."

Sara felt Tom sag into a deeper sleep, and she gently fixed her bodice and lowered him to the pallet. Then she turned to Eiehsa, tears glistening in her eyes.

"I fear I would slay a thousand souls to save him, Mother. As I watched the legend in the fire and recalled how I felt when Tom was wounded, I knew all too well why my sisters came together to mete such destruction. Love is a great thing, Mother. But it can also be a curse."

"That it can, Lady Sara," Eiehsa said. "And it is upon each of us to choose which it will be. Ardebal's love created the fire, Lady Sara. Your love creates healing."

"But also have I bled fire, Mother. When my own mother was murdered before my eyes, I bled Ilduin fire upon her killer and tormented him into his last moments. I am no goddess of life, and I know that. I pray that I also am no goddess of death."

"Your young heart carries a heavy load," Eiehsa said, squeezing her hand. "The past and the future can crush you in their vice if you permit it. Perhaps the best that you can do is to banish both and live in the kindness of each moment. That is all any of us can do."

Sara sighed. "In this moment, then, I long for sleep. If you will pardon me?"

"Of course, Lady," Eiehsa said. "I too need rest, as do we all. Let us pray for a sleep that carries us into the heart of Elanor and heals our pain."

"Or," Sara said, "for a sleep that carries me into the heart of my darling Tom and nestles him forever in mine."

"Ahh," Eiehsa cried softly, a wide smile breaking over her

face. "To be young and in love again. It warms my old bones, child. Thank you."

With that, she left for the circle of her companions, and Sara slid in next to Tom, holding him to her, praying that his dreams would find her heart, as well.

As others were falling asleep in the cavern, Tess made her way outside to find Archer. He proved to be but one of several who were standing guard over the cave and its occupants, but he stood apart. He always stood apart, she realized. In some indefinable way, he was separate.

The thought of that loneliness filled her heart with a sorrowful ache as she approached him. He didn't turn his head, didn't take his eyes from the mountains and valleys he watched so intently, but he knew it was she.

"Why do you not sleep with the others, Lady?"

She paused, still six paces behind him. "Sleep eludes me," she said finally, then crossed the distance to his side.

He gave a brief nod but still failed to look at her. She watched his face, chiseled harsh by the starlight, cast in secrecy by the deep shadows around his eyes. He looked like a figure out of myth—or nightmare. Sometimes she found she wasn't sure which. Nor did she care. The sight of him always struck a chord deep within her.

"So," he said, "you have seen the story of the end of the First Age."

"Aye." She turned her gaze from him to look out over the shadowy rills of the mountains. "'Twas much as you told it."

"There is only one tale. It can be told in many forms, but there is only one tale."

She nodded, neither knowing nor caring whether he saw. "I find," she said slowly, "that much as I thought I was confused and frightened when I awoke amidst the carnage of the caravan without memory, I grow more confused with each passing day, not more enlightened."

"'Tis always that way when one realizes that much is demanded of one...but exactly what that might be remains a mystery."

"Aye." She sighed. "I'm also frightened. I'm frightened that I might fail when so much hope is placed in me." Her fingers rose to caress the bag of stones around her neck.

"We all share the same fear, my Lady," he said, his voice a deep, quiet rumble. "This time was foretold for centuries, but foretold or not, I think none of us is prepared."

Tess might have laughed at that, except for the lock that dread held on her heart. "I fear for Tom."

Now he *did* glance at her. "Why? He appears to be recovering."

She gripped the stones tightly. "How did I get the stones back? I saw with my own two eyes as they sank into his flesh and sealed his wounds."

Archer shook his head. "I know not. I found them in your hands when you were unconscious after the healing. I returned them to the bag, and the bag to your neck."

"Did you see what they did to him?"

Archer hesitated. "In all honesty, my Lady, I was distracted by the rain of fire from the sky."

Would she could laugh, for somehow his response was so understated it seemed to cry out for humor. But laughter had deserted her, at least for now.

"I don't know how that happened, either."

"You spoke the last prayer of Theriel." Now he turned toward her, facing her, his posture almost accusing. "If you cannot remember anything before the caravan was slaughtered, how is it you recall a prayer that has not been spoken in centuries?"

Tess shook her head, feeling even more frightened, and now frustrated, as well. "I do not recall my words."

"I do. They were spoken with Theriel's dying breath, calling her sisters to her, to help her. The result was the utter destruction of Dederand."

"The plain of glass," she said, remembering the visions in the fire.

"Aye, that was the result. Such power was never before unleashed, nor since. Until you."

"But…" Her throat clogged, and she could not speak in her own defense.

He surprised her then, by reaching out to touch her shoulder. "I am not saying you cast down the rain of fire. I am saying only that you spoke Theriel's last prayer, and your sisters, wherever they may be, answered and saved us from the Bozandari."

Her mind reeling, Tess spread her hands helplessly. "I know nothing of this. For the sake of everyone, I must somehow learn! I want to see no more blasted cities, even in tales told around a fire."

His arm moved around her, drawing her close to his side, within the shelter of his cape. The warmth was welcome, the comfort even more so.

"That is why we go to Anahar, my Lady," he said, his words soft enough that they reached only her ears. "There at the main temple, all the secrets of the Ilduin are inscribed. 'Tis said that the adept can learn merely by walking through it and pondering the story's many meanings. It is, I am told, a story that tells itself across the ages, through time, a key to the powers of the Ilduin."

"And then what?" she asked, a bitterness near tears filling her.

"Then we do what we must."

"I don't wish to create any more ugliness!"

"At times, Lady," he said his voice laden with pain, "we are given no choice. We cannot let Ardred rule. You saw him through Lantav. You have brushed against his evil. He would turn this entire world and all in it to dust to satisfy his lust for power and revenge."

Remembering the moments of which Archer spoke, Tess shuddered. Finally, in a wisp of a voice, she replied, "No. We cannot let him succeed. But what did I do to Tom when I healed him?"

"That I cannot say. It is the first time I have ever seen cleansing Ilduin fire heal. He took that fire within him and was healed." He repeated it as if it still amazed him. "Many are the ways of Ilduin healing, but never before has it been by fire."

"I fear it."

Archer nodded slowly and drew her even closer. "I suspect Tom will not be the same. But he must be one of the purest beings ever to have walked this earth to have survived your fire. Take heart in that, my Lady."

There was little enough to take heart in, she thought. Once again her fingers tightened around the bag of stones, a burden growing heavier with each passing day.

All of a sudden, a voice called from the cave. "My Lord? My Lady? Lady Sara begs you to come. Tom Downey has awakened."

Tom sat up, leaning against a boulder that Sara had padded with a blanket for his comfort. His eyes remained closed as he ate the spoonfuls of gruel she fed him. The rest of the cavern was quiet as the Anari slept, and the fire was beginning to burn lower, though its warmth lingered in the huge cave.

Tess knelt opposite Sara and reached out to touch the young man's forehead. "How do you feel, Tom?"

Between mouthfuls he answered, "Achy, but apparently much better than I was, from what Sara has told me."

Archer, too, settled beside Tom, close to his feet. "You were all but dead, lad."

"I am certainly not dead now." He waved aside the gruel, his eyes still closed. "I actually feel fairly well, considering. Not quite ready to lift a boulder, but I might manage to lift Sara."

The words brought a smile to Sara's lips. A smile so full of love and longing and relief that the two who saw it felt the same in their hearts.

"However," Tom continued, "I cannot open my eyes. The light is too bright."

Sara caught her breath. The cavern was dim, even the fangs

hanging from the ceiling barely reflecting the ruddy glow now. "Can you see at all?"

"Yes, but…it's almost as if I'm trying to look into the sun."

Carefully Tess leaned forward and touched his eyelid. "Brace yourself, Tom. I am going to look."

He nodded. "I'm ready."

She lifted his eyelid and felt a bolt of shock that ran the length of her spine. His irises appeared to have become colorless—almost, but not quite, like panes of glass. Certainly at a glance it might appear that he had no iris at all, only pupil. And somewhere in the depths of that dark pupil, she caught a glimpse of the fire that had saved him.

Jerking her hand back, she let his lid fall. After a moment, she steadied herself enough to speak. "We must find a way to deal with this so you can see, Tom."

"I would be grateful, Lady Tess. I am useless enough without being blind."

Archer squeezed his ankle. "You have never for a moment been useless, lad. And I suspect this change in your vision will prove in some way to be a benefit."

Tom laughed, but it was an unsteady sound. "As long as I do not need someone to guide me every step of the way, I shall not complain."

Sara touched his cheek. "My love, if I must guide you every step for the rest of your days, I shall only give thanks that you are with me still."

Tess felt the prick of tears behind her lids and turned to Archer. "I need a strip of leather about this wide." She indicated the measurement with her fingers. "And it must be long enough to tie around Tom's head."

Archer nodded. "I'll see what I can do."

"I will also need an awl, Sara, if you have one. I have seen you mending clothes. But it will need to be sturdy enough to pierce leather."

"I do not have one," Sara said. "But perhaps one of the Anari…"

"I'll get one," Ratha said, having been awakened by the quiet discussion. "Ours are fashioned from the hardest of stones and will certainly suffice for your needs."

"Thank you," Tess said.

"My beautiful Sara," Tom said, his eyes still closed, reaching up to take her hand. "I feared that never again would I hear your voice. And yet, in my dreams, I knew you had not been harmed."

"My only pain was that of thinking you might not survive," Sara said. "And that was greater than the worst pain I have ever felt."

He squeezed her hand. "Sing for me, please? Sing me a song of home?"

"Yes, my love," Sara said.

And when Sara began to sing, Tess could almost feel the warmth of the Deepwell Inn in its best days.

A day, a day of harvest time
A night of warmth and ale
A day, a day of harvest time
And gentle with the tale.

Come bring the sheaves of barley now
And pelts from forest deep
Come sing the joy of harvest time
And gentle into sleep.

Oh harvest night! Oh fire bright!
Beside you we around
Oh harvest song, we sing nigh long

And gentle with the sound.

A day, a day of harvest time
And family gathered near
The toils and spoils of harvest time
And gentle with the year.

By the time Sara had finished, Anari children had stirred from their beds and gathered around her, their eyes and smiles wide with wonder. Tess did not know whether the children could understand the words, but so rich was Sara's voice that, even without the words, one would have felt the meaning of the song.

"Home," Tom said, a wistful smile on his face. "I never thought it could be so beautiful."

"Oft we miss what too oft we see, lad," Archer said, having returned with the strip of leather. "But I think you will see Whitewater again, as if for the first time."

"And when you do return home," Tess said, taking the proffered strip of leather, then the awl from Ratha's hand, "I want you to bring your bride with you. And then, what a harvest festival Whitewater will see!"

Archer looked at her, as if reading her thoughts. In truth, she feared that Tom and Sara would never see their home again. But this was not the time to dwell on fears. Her hands working as if by a memory all their own, she held the strip over Tom's face for a moment, then began boring a pattern of tiny holes in the leather.

"Try this," she said, placing the strap over his eyes. "The holes shouldn't let in too much light. Can you see?"

"I can," Tom said, tying the strap behind his head. "Thank you, Lady Tess. At least now it doesn't hurt to look at Sara."

He let the sentence hang for a moment, then broke into a wry smile. "Of course, it never hurts to look at Sara."

"It had better not," Sara said, nudging him. "Because you're going to be looking at me for a long, long time."

"Do you promise?" he asked.

"Be it a promise or a threat," she replied, smiling, "I mean what I say."

"Be careful what you wish for, Tom," Ratha said, his smile gleaming in the firelight. "The love of a woman is not to be trifled with. And Lady Sara has the pledge of Gewindi-Tel at her service. You had best keep her happy."

"I thank the gods that I shall now have more days, many I hope, to devote to my lady's happiness," Tom said. Clasping Sara's hand, he carried it to his lips. "Now, will one of you please tell me what has happened since the battle in the rift?"

Ratha, a born storyteller, recounted the day's events in a manner bound to be engraved in oral history as long as the Anari existed. Those who had wakened to Sara's song hung on his every word as if they had not lived through the events themselves.

When he fell silent, the cave, too, fell silent, seeming to swallow even the crackle of the flames in the firepit. A stillness deeper than sleep filled them all, as if they hung suspended over a brink of some kind.

"These times were foretold," Tom said slowly, his voice altered as if by something greater than himself. "The prophecies are coming to pass."

Another moment of silence, then his voice grew stronger and adopted a rhythmic cadence.

> *When Weaver comes, to all she brings*
> *A Foundling found and sword that sings*
> *Destroyer old be bitter, bold*
> *His vengeance cold*
> *Winter burns with icy breath*
> *Bringing many to their deaths*

> *But all must hope or hope will fail*
> *Then Firstborn King will pierce the veil.*

Tom sat abruptly bolt upright, staring across the cavern past Tess as if he could see something that wasn't there. And one name whispered across his lips.

"Theriel."

A moment later he slumped back against the stone, and his head rolled to one side as he lost consciousness.

Sara gave a cry and reached out to cradle him. Tess immediately felt for the pulse in his throat.

"He's all right," she assured the others. "He must have worn himself out."

"This lad," said Ratha heavily, "needs someone to help him properly cultivate his prophetic talent. Someone who can teach him to use it wisely."

Archer nodded. "Erkiah Nebu."

"Nebu?" Ratha's face creased with concern. "But he is in Sedestano."

"We will send for him when we get to Anahar. He will come."

Ratha nodded, apparently harboring not the least doubt that Nebu would come if Archer summoned him.

With that Archer rose and vanished into the shadows at the mouth of the cave.

Whatever might come toward them, it seemed, would have to pass through him first.

Tom wasn't the only one who needed help with his powers, Tess thought as she curled up on her bedroll nearby. The scattered bits of memory that remained from the earlier battle both plagued and frightened her. How could she have caused such a thing? Yet apparently she had.

She closed her eyes, and finally sleep began to take her; exhaustion would not be denied. For the first time in several weeks, she began to dream, and the dreams were fitful and disturbing. She felt as if she wanted to wake up but could not as the dreams took her.

Once again she dreamed of awaking amidst the slaughtered caravan, but those images held little terror for her now, as she had relived those hours repeatedly. But the dream did not stop there....

A wooded hillside, beneath which was a fenced field. A woman riding a horse, head tossed back, smiling in delight at the beautiful day. Tess ran toward her, the word "Mother" on her lips, but it seemed no matter how hard she ran, she could not reach the woman on the horse....

Then it was as if the entire image juddered, fracturing into pieces of stained glass, before once again settling into a picture of a field, a horse, a hill...and no woman.

Grief pierced Tess's heart until she cried out, "Mother!" and began to sob.

"Tess?" Sara's voice woke her, the young woman's hand shaking her shoulder. "Tess, are you all right?"

Tess blinked, then sat up quickly, trying to shake off the dream. Her cheeks were wet, she realized, and she quickly wiped them dry on her sleeve.

"Tess?"

"I dreamed," she answered.

Sara's face reflected deep concern. "Just a dream?"

Slowly Tess shook her head. "I think...I think I was remembering my mother."

"You're getting your memory back!" Sara sounded thrilled. "That's wonderful."

But as Tess sat there feeling cold to the bone, she sorted through her impressions of the dream and found nothing good at all. Slowly she shook her head.

"What?" Sara asked.

"We have something in common, it seems. My mother disappeared when I was a child."

As soon as she spoke the words, she knew they were true, and remembering the horror that Sara's mother had undergone, and the horrors of her discovery, Tess felt lead settle into her heart.

Sara leaned closer, her voice a whisper. "Do you think she was taken the same way my mother was?"

"Maybe. It feels...bad." Tess closed her eyes and bowed her head. "I fear...I fear I was taken the same way."

Sara gasped, then argued, "But you're *here*."

"Aye, I'm here. And I don't think that was intended."

Sara huddled closer to her. "What are you saying?"

"I'm saying that Archer is right. I'm a danger to this party. Evil seeks me."

10

At the first weak light of dawn, the refugees left the shelter of their cave and resumed their trek south toward Anahar.

Ratha, Giri and Archer rode out together, working their way up the treacherous talus of a steep slope to gain a view to the east and Bozandar. Other scouts spread out in other directions.

Ratha was in surprisingly good spirits, all things considered, and he put that down to their increasing nearness to Anahar.

Anahar. The mere name made his heart lift with joy. Anahar was hearth and home to the Anari people, however far they might spread over the world. Anahar the beautiful, ever calling her children home.

The temple itself was a towering feat of stonemasonry and artistry, its beauties changing with the movement of sun, moon and stars, revealing different aspects as the light changed. The smaller village temples were mere copies of the great temple, each showing but a portion of the edifice in Anahar.

The temple had survived the last Bozandari invasion, and Ratha hoped it would survive this coming rebellion. Little else in the Anari lands had survived the Bozandari invasion. Nearly everything that existed now had been built in the three generations of their enslavement.

And worse, all that was new had been built without the benefit of the best Anari skills. It was a small silent rebellion, not to use the best and highest of their skills when forced to build for Bozandar, but it was one necessary to the Anari people—the only expression of independence left to them.

But the temple... Ah, the temple!

Smiling inwardly, he breathed deeply of the fresh morning air. Even the present danger could not dampen his spirits this morning. In his entire life, which was a goodly span, he and his fellows had never spent a day without thinking of rising up from beneath the heel of Bozandar. Now it had begun. Fire filled his veins, and the thought of freedom was a heady brew.

Somehow the appointed hour had come. He wasn't sure why, after all these years, every Anari seemed to accept that *this* was the time long awaited. It just was.

And with two Ilduin at their side, perhaps there was true hope of success.

He glanced over at Archer and wondered what his friend was thinking. Always he seemed to carry a heavy burden, but this morning the burden appeared to nearly bow him. But before Ratha could speak a comforting word, Archer lifted an arm and pointed.

"There."

A cloud of dust had arisen in the east. The Bozandari army was coming for them once again.

Archer gathered together the clan mothers, and Jenah and his immediate lieutenants, about fifteen persons in all.

"This time," he said, "they must not catch us unprepared. It is a larger force than we met yesterday."

Eiesha shook her head. "How can they keep finding us?"

Archer's gray eyes seemed to darken. "I suspect they are receiving assistance in that."

After brief reflection, Eiesha nodded. "So it must be. It was written once that wherever an Ilduin stood, the golden warp and woof of reality bent around her. There was a time when the clan mothers could sense this, but no longer."

Archer nodded. "Such powers have steadily diminished since the First Age. But, Mother Eiesha, we dare not count upon having two Ilduin among us. Both are untutored in their powers. Instead we must fight for ourselves."

"Of course." The woman snorted. "Ever have the Anari stood for themselves and for others in need. *That* has not changed since the First Age. But I have an idea."

"Aye?" Archer listened respectfully.

"The Bozandari sought to steal our stoneworking skills, but there are secrets we never revealed to them, secrets handed down from father to son. Among Gewindi-Tel, there are several who know these secrets and guard them. I will call upon their expertise."

"To do what, Mother?"

Eiesha smiled. "To build a wall."

Tom sat outside the cave entrance, trying to adjust to his new world as viewed through the pinpricks in the leather band across his eyes. Tess had done well, he thought. The holes were placed so that he could look to either side or straight ahead. Some head-turning was still required, but that was beginning to feel natural.

And he could see. Already once this morning he had attempted to remove the leather strip and had discovered that the light was too painful to be borne. Part of him wanted to indulge in a bout of self-pity, but a stronger self refused to let him. He might have been completely blind. Instead, he could see well enough through the mask. He would not need to spend the rest of his days hanging on to someone's shoulder.

Sara hovered over him as if he were a nursling. It didn't irritate him. After the words and touches they had shared last night, her care for him could never be a source of anything but joy.

Except that he was sitting here thinking how little he deserved her. This quasiblindness hadn't improved his sense of worthiness one whit. She deserved so much more than he would ever be able to give her, especially now.

But even as that weight clung to his heart, he knew now was not the time to indulge in such thoughts. Either one of them might be dead within a matter of hours. Facing the war, absolutely nothing was certain.

But a small sigh escaped him anyway as he forced himself to walk around the rocky ground, learning to use his strange new vision. It was clear he would never be a swordsman now.

Sara joined him, carrying yet another bowl of gruel. "How does it go?" she asked him.

He accepted the bowl and remained standing as he quaffed it. When he was done, he wiped his mouth on his sleeve and passed the bowl back to her. "It goes well, actually," he told her, trying to sound positive. "Thank you for the gruel."

"It was nothing. Do you hurt anywhere?"

He instinctively put a hand to his stomach. "Amazingly not. But I do wonder what happened to my eyes."

"Eiesha said that you are the first ever to be cured by Ilduin fire."

He stared directly at a rock face ahead of him. "I suppose the answer lies somewhere therein," he said.

"Is it too terrible?"

"'Tis annoying," he admitted. "But at least I can see."

She touched his arm gently and turned him to face her. "I

thank the gods you are still alive, my Tom. For you were dead for certain had not Tess intervened."

He nodded slowly, accepting her judgment. "But that doesn't make me feel any less annoyed at the moment," he told her, forcing a hint of humor into his voice.

"Certainly not." Then she smiled at him, a sun shining through an emotionally gray day. "But would you like to hear the news?"

"Aye."

"Here." She led him to a boulder, and they sat side by side. "We do not march today because the Bozandari are coming our way. But guess what the Anari are going to do."

He shook his head.

"Mother Eiesha says they have stone-working talents that they have kept secret these many years. She has sent masters of the stone out to build a wall to protect us."

"Oh, I would like to see that!"

"As would I."

"But…" He frowned. "Can't the Bozandari simply mount a wall?"

"I suspect," Sara said, "that this will be no ordinary wall."

In that she was right. Archer, Giri and Ratha rode out with the masons to act as their protection should scouts from the Bozandari column come upon them.

The place chosen was in the midst of a huge defile, the only one nearby through which an army could hope to pass and, Jenah said, the one by which the slavers most often came to Anahar. Years of being used as a path had cleared the way and flattened the earth almost to a roadlike surface.

"Not for long," Jenah said. He was one of the stonemasters himself, and when they had decided on the spot, he joined them, pressing his hands to the side of the defile and closing his eyes.

Ratha moved close to Archer and murmured, "I am sure, my lord, that you know the rock lives."

"I have heard it said."

"'Tis a living thing, the stone. And the stonemasters must choose rock that is willing to cooperate. Never do we force our will on living stone."

Archer nodded, watching intently as the Anari masons continued to press their palms to the stone, eyes closed, bodies motionless.

From his position above the defile, he could also see the approaching cloud of dust. An hour, maybe a little more. He hoped the rock would leap into this task with verve, although such a thing was nearly beyond his imagining. The Anari seldom let an outsider see them work with the stone.

The wind suddenly picked up, cutting angrily through clothes and nipping at exposed skin. Archer lifted his head and try to sense anything that might be borne on the breeze. What he felt disturbed him mightily.

"We need to be done soon," he told Ratha and Giri. "We are not unwatched."

But just then the stonemasters seemed to have found their answer. They started to climb the defile with a skill belonging to those who frequented these mountains and soon joined Archer's party.

"We need to be away from here," Jenah said. He cocked his head to the west. "We can watch from over there, safe and out of sight."

Archer gestured to the defile. "The wall?"

Jenah grinned between his teeth. "Oh, aye, there will be a wall, Lord Archer. But the Bozandari will be beneath it."

Then Jenah and his fellow masters mounted their horses and led the way to their place of concealment.

Conveniently out of sight, there was a place for their mounts to graze contentedly, though they had to be hobbled against the coming landslide.

The party clambered back up over steep rocks until they could peer between sharp teeth of granite at the defile, now safely in the distance. The soldiers were getting closer now. A keen eye could just about pick out the individuals amidst the sudden, sharp bursts of light reflecting off their shields.

"They expect to be met," Archer murmured.

"Aye," Jenah agreed. "They carry their shields before them."

Giri chuckled quietly. "This is not the meeting they expect."

Archer nodded agreement, but in his heart he knew sorrow. Would that it did not always come to this killing. Yet it always had, sooner or later. And like it or not, he was going to have to help train the Anari and forge them into an army for the first time in their history. After that…

The wind snaked into his cowl and down his neck. After that there was an even bigger battle awaiting them. He felt it on the breeze. He tasted it on the air. And wishing it were not so changed nothing.

War was on the wind. Death was on the wind. The future of the world hung in the balance.

Just then he felt the ground beneath him shudder. 'Twas but a small shudder, but it felt as if the mountain were waking from sleep.

The soldiers were closer now, the first of them beginning to enter the defile. It wasn't a huge column. Maybe two hundred. At their head rode an officer in gleaming armor, a blood-red feather in his helmet. His horse pranced slightly sideways, as if it would prefer not to enter the gorge. The beasts of the world had always been more sensitive than the men.

Scouts appeared at the top of the gorge walls, sent ahead to ensure no attack awaited the column. The riders signaled with their spears, and the column quickened its pace, moving forward as if they hoped they could hurry through fast enough to escape any ambush.

Indeed, the gorge was an ideal place for an ambush, but the soldiers were unprepared for the one that came their way.

At first it seemed merely to be a loose boulder that fell toward them. The sound of it breaking free warned those below so they could scatter away from the point of impact. For a while the column was disordered while the officer worked at regrouping them. When he finally had his column reformed, he looked up again at his scouts, positioned at the very lip of the defile. Again they signaled that all was clear.

The unit marched forward at a double-time pace once again. And then they were at the very middle of the defile.

Archer felt the ground beneath him shudder yet again, but this time with more ferocity, yielding a growl from deep within. Great power coiled in the rock, like a waking beast, and he felt a moment's pity for the soldiers in the gorge.

Then it happened. Defying every belief in the solid immobility of stone, the mountains to either side of the gorge screamed with stress and embraced the entire unit, reaching out with huge fingers of stone to block any escape. The scouts atop the ravine walls yelled as the ground beneath them collapsed with a roar and they were swept down to join their fellows. The confounded troops broke formation and began to run in every direction, but wherever they ran, sheer stone walls met them.

Then, with a groan almost too deep to be heard, the walls of the defile reformed until they covered the whole, sealing themselves together.

The groan faded away. The world became eerily silent as if the forces just unleashed had sapped even sound from the air.

The ravine was gone as if it had never been. Above it lay a tumble of rocks that appeared to have been there for ages.

And, somewhere beneath, an entire unit of soldiers lay buried.

11

The strange silence lasted for a long time. It seemed as if the entire world fell quiet before the power of what had just happened, even the stonemasters themselves.

Archer barely moved a muscle as he stared at the place that had once been a ravine and now appeared to be an extension of the mountains to either side. In his life he had seen many great magicks, but this surely was the greatest. The earth had swallowed up two hundred men and left no sign of their passing. It was not what he had expected, and the prickle at the base of his neck warned him that it had not gone unnoticed.

Jenah finally flopped over onto his back, his eyes closed. He appeared exhausted, as did his fellow stonemasters. When he spoke, his voice was heavy and hollow. "I do not think we can ask that again of the stone. We had best hurry to Anahar."

"Aye," Archer answered, "for we are not being pursued by the Bozandari alone. I have no doubt that other eyes have seen what just passed."

Jenah's eyes opened, blazing with anger, as he looked at Archer. "Do you realize how this twists us? What it makes of us? In times past, no master would ever have dreamed of asking the stone to kill."

"I know." Archer's answer was simplicity itself.

"For countless centuries, since our creation, we have always cooperated with the stone, helping it become something even more beautiful. The stonemasters and the stone worked together, creating a wonderful harmony that enhanced both. And as long as we did that, the stone was willing to be cut from its moorings and reshaped into the very essence of its own soul."

Archer nodded, then gripped the other man's shoulder in understanding.

"We did not ask the stone to kill them," Jenah said, his mouth drawn into a tight line. "We asked only that they not be allowed to pass. The stone has done this thing. Good stone, not the evil stone, of which we are always wary."

Finally Jenah shook himself and sat up. "It saddens me. This war will make beasts of us all, yet I can no longer tolerate what is being done to my people."

"It is the sad truth of war," Archer agreed. "I would that it were not necessary. Unfortunately I fear your rebellion is but the first step on a longer, darker road to amend errors of the past. *His* rank smell is on the wind now. He plays with us as he would play with toys, and when at last he grows impatient with his amusements, he will move to slay us all."

Jenah's brow creased. "How can he have so much power, Lord Archer? He was merely of the Firstborn."

"He was merely the favorite of one of the gods, Sarduk, else he would even now be dead at the end of his brother's sword." Bitterness laced the words, along with haunting loss.

Jenah reached out and briefly gripped Archer's forearm. "Why should a god have favored him?"

"Because Elanor favored the Ilduin. It seems those who created the world are little better than those they created to inhabit it."

"Then," Jenah said, "we must find a way to be better than even the gods."

"Such purity existed once."

"Theriel." Jenah breathed the name. "Oft have the mothers told us of her. They have promised that another would come in her stead."

"The Weaver." Archer's jaw tightened. "Let us hope she comes in time for you, for it is already too late for me."

Jenah's expression was questioning, but Archer spoke no more. Instead they mounted and rode back to the others, bearing a tale that would both gladden and sadden hearts.

The next two days brought an arduous trek, for the city of Anahar was hidden in the most rugged of the mountains. They were not attacked again, but the sense of being watched grew with each passing hour. Archer began to scan the skies almost ceaselessly, and Tess noted it.

"What do you think is up there?" she asked, falling in beside him as they rode.

"I do not know," he answered.

"Perhaps the oily thing that keeps creeping around the edges of my brain and along my spine?"

He lowered his gaze and took her in. She looked exhausted, but exhausted from something more than the trek. There was something weary within her deep blue eyes, something wary and frightened.

He summoned a faint smile. "I doubt I would find anything oily in the skies."

She shrugged. "We are being followed. You feel it, too."

"Aye. Although in my case there is nothing oily about it. It is rather more like a prickle at the base of my neck."

She surprised him with a smile of her own. "It's not after *you*."

"If that is so, it is only because it has not realized I am here. Our enmity goes far back."

"It wants me." She said it simply, but her tone indicated that she had come to a grim acceptance. "I do not even know who I am, or where I came from a few weeks ago, but it wants me. I am beginning to wonder if that caravan was slaughtered because of me."

He reached out and laid a gloved hand on her arm. "Think not that way, my Lady. You did not force anyone's hand to commit such an atrocity. Blame those who committed the act."

She looked straight at him then. "How do you know I didn't do that? You saw what I was capable of after Tom was hurt. Can you be truly sure of me? I can't."

His hand fell from her shoulder, and they rode a while in silence amidst the cacophony of many quietly talking voices, the crying of young children, the jingle of harness, and even, from time to time, the sound of men and women laughing.

"At first I distrusted you," Archer admitted after a while. "I do not feel quite so inclined since you faced Lantav."

"Since I met Lantav, I feel even more inclined to distrust myself. Do you know what I bade Sara do to him? I am a woman without a past riding into a future I know nothing about, in a world I cannot remember. At this moment, Archer, I am quite terrified of myself. And mostly I am terrified because something is clinging to my mind, trying to draw me to it. I don't care to be someone's weapon. I don't ever want to call down fire from the sky again!"

At that moment, his face hardened. "Lady, we are not always granted choices about what we will do. Sometimes we must do what is necessary for the greatest good. And sometimes what we do will be ugly. But if we do not fight *him*, there will be ugliness and suffering beyond your imagination. What was done to Lantav and those soldiers will fall upon the innocent, even to the newborn babes. The Bozandari are but a pale shadow of the Enemy, yet even they will come into an Anari telner and, taking a fancy to a woman, dash her nursling child to the stones and carry her screaming away. That is *men's* evil, and yet it is a bare shadow of the evil the Enemy will cause."

Tess rode on in silence for a while, sensing that there was much the man beside her was not saying, yet sensing also that his strength and wisdom would protect her.

"I feel terrible about what I did to poor Tom's eyes."

Archer grunted. "You saved his life, Lady Tess. I doubt either he or Sara would have it otherwise."

"Perhaps not, but it would certainly be nice if I could avoid unintended consequences of my actions."

He chuckled deep in his throat. "Don't we all feel so?"

"I don't understand why that should have happened. I was trying to heal his wounds."

"Perhaps you healed more than you knew."

"You mean what has happened to his eyes was a healing? I cannot believe that."

Archer seemed to shrug within the dark folds of his cloak. "It may be that our Tom will now see more clearly than he ever has. Time will tell."

All of a sudden, he said, "Follow me, my Lady. I have something to show you that you will not see from the path we take." Then he spurred his horse off to the left.

Tess followed him, leaving the column of refugees behind as she went with Archer up a narrow trail into the trees. Here the vegetation was far more lush than up north. Soon her nose and mouth no longer were full of dust and grit, but instead filled with the scent of pine and some kind of flowery perfume.

The slope was steep, the trail full of switchbacks. As they

climbed, the air grew cooler, until the horses were snorting clouds of steam.

The trail opened from time to time, giving breathtaking views of valleys and rivers far below. The peaks of the mountains, as far as the eye could see, already wore wintry cloaks of white. Occasionally, in a deeply shadowed place, their horses trod through snow.

But it was around a tight turn in the trail that the view opened out upon a breathtakingly beautiful city, visible in a valley some distance away.

"Anahar," Archer said simply.

Tess caught and held her breath, astonished that the city appeared to be a larger version of the village they had fled. Much larger. But she was even more astonished that stone could appear to be so golden, so shining, at once seeming to reflect the sun and to hold the sun within it.

Below her the city lay spread out, the round central temple rising high above all other buildings. The streets, of which there were many, all much longer than in the village, curved, following a winding path, as had the shorter ones at Gewindi-Tel. Clearly could she see that the village had been a smaller copy of the great city.

But where the one had been charming, this was breathtaking. No wonder the Bozandari had wanted Anari builders. The city of Anahar was not only built from living stone, but the stone continued to live in its new shape.

"Words fail," she finally whispered to Archer.

"Once the cities of the Firstborn had such beauty," he said, "but now they are dust. Anahar lives on, a bulwark, a memory, a tale, a promise. When we arrive there, our journey truly begins. There we will build the army that will throw off the yoke of Bozandar. And there you will follow the temple mazes until you have learned who you are."

"It will tell me who I am?"

"It may give you no names and bring back no memories, but it will tutor you in your powers if only you find a key. And keys are there to be found."

Tess found herself reluctant to turn from the view and follow Archer back down to the party of refugees. The reluctance arose not so much from the burden that awaited her—and Sara, of course—in Anahar, but simply from the fact that the city was so beautiful from up here, one of the most beautiful things she had ever seen.

She hoped desperately that her sojourn there would not forever turn it into an ugly memory.

12

As Tess turned away from the view, the Presence within her simmered with anger and rage. Anahar stood for everything that had been stolen from him. At the end of the First Age, the Anari were the only race whom the gods had permitted to live on in their original state, and their city was a monument to the secrets of that age. In it he saw not beauty, but betrayal.

Betrayal by his own brother. Over the centuries, the world had come to look upon Ardred as the Enemy, due to the lies of his brother. He was no enemy. He was Ardred the Fair, second son of the Firstborn King, a king in his own right. Annuvil was the evil one, the one who had stolen Theriel and then had demolished Ardred's kingdom of Dederand.

Soon all that would be set right.

As Tess rode down the slope after the man called Archer, Ardred withdrew into a small corner of her mind so that she would not feel his presence for a while. He wished he could reveal himself to her, show her his love and admiration for her. He wished he could tell her how he had searched across the ages and the sundered world for her and her alone, the woman who was the equal of Theriel, the woman whose purity of heart could make him weep for joy. He wished he could tell her how he had tried to bring her to himself, only to discover his efforts had somehow been interrupted, leaving her memoryless in this ugly world.

But it was not yet time. First he had to deal with the mess Annuvil had made of things. First he had to deal with the corrupt Ilduin, who had abused their power after his attempt to save Theriel from Annuvil had resulted in her death.

His hatred simmered like a stew not quite ready to be served, but Ardred was patient. An immortal could afford to be patient, and this was not yet the time to correct the wrongs his brother had inflicted upon the world. But that time was approaching, and with each passing day, as the world faded even more from the heights of its ancient glories, it drew closer.

Soon he would emerge. Soon Tess would stand at his side as his bride. The three worlds would be reunited, with him as the rightful king.

All would be as it should have been in the First Age.

Gently he eased himself from Tess's mind, careful not to make her aware of him as he did so. There was much he needed to prepare, and for now he could safely let Tess and the Anari move forward unimpeded.

The Anari. They would be punished for their crimes of indifference in the First Age. And Annuvil and the Ilduin would be punished for their crimes, as well. It was only a matter of time.

Tess felt somehow lightened as she and Archer returned to the Anari. The refugees still wound their way through the mountains, but Anahar was within reach before nightfall.

As they rejoined the column, it seemed that everyone shared Tess's lightening of heart. A group of men and women were singing a cheerful harmony, tossing the verses of the song back and forth. Children, too, felt the excitement, even those too young to truly understand. They were laughing, running in and out of the column. Burdens seemed to have grown lighter, and steps had quickened.

Anahar.

Tess shivered a little as the name whispered in her mind, but then she realized it was not the inky voice she had heard in the past but something lighter. Something that almost seemed to be part of herself, yet not.

Anahar. The whisper came again, and Tess grasped the leathern bag of stones that hung around her neck.

The voice whispered again, *Come to me, sister, and we will learn together....* And then it was gone.

Tess clung to the stones for a while longer, trying to feel these sisters she had felt before, pondering the voice and its words. With sudden certainty, she knew that there was another Ilduin in Anahar. Perhaps at last she would get some answers.

In Anahar there was no difficulty in finding places to stay. As a place of pilgrimage, the city was prepared for large numbers of visitors, and lodgings were maintained near the temple for all who might come.

But as the Anari began to settle in, Sara and Tess chose to walk up the winding street to the temple.

"The city is every bit as beautiful on the streets as it was from the mountaintop," Tess remarked. Indeed, every stone seemed to glow with a rainbow hue.

"It inspires awe in me," Sara said almost reverently. "I never dreamed of such."

"Nor I," Tess agreed. She was struck, too, by the friendliness of everyone they passed, when they might well have been mistrusted because they looked like pale Bozandari. But here, in the heart and hearth of the Anari people, it seemed generosity ruled.

Sara paused at a corner and closed her eyes. Reaching out with her senses, she at last found what it was she had been feeling since they had passed through the gates. "This is an eternal city," she murmured. "Do you feel it, Tess? This city will fall only if the mountains fall, and within its walls there is such a sense of serenity and peace."

She looked at Tess to find the older woman nodding. "This is holy ground," Tess agreed. "Yes, I can feel it. How could anyone not? It permeates everything."

"Then perhaps we really *will* learn to use our powers here. And perhaps tomorrow we should bring Tom...." Her voice trailed away, and she averted her face.

"Oh, Sara," Tess said, reaching out to embrace her friend. "I'm sorry. I'm so, so sorry. I knew not what I was doing. It was as if the force took me over. I never meant to hurt Tom in any way."

Sara blinked and looked up. Her lower lashes sparkled with tears. "You saved his life," she whispered fiercely. "Never think I blame you for anything."

"His eyes..."

"Yes, his eyes." Sara gave her a squeeze. "'Tis discomforting, but he is not dead. And it may be that having been kissed by Ilduin fire he will now come to be all that he was meant to be. For I know one thing for certain, Tess Birdsong."

"And that is?"

"That my Tom was never meant to be a gatekeeper like his father. He was born to other things. Why he was left in the snow in the woods—"

"Wait a minute. What do you mean?"

"Tom was an orphan. Jem Downey and his wife found him as a babe and raised him. Everyone in Whitewater knows of this, but I forget sometimes that you are not from Whitewater."

Tess smiled, gave Sara another quick hug and stepped back. "Since I can remember no other place from which my life started, I would be proud to call Whitewater home…if you have no objection."

"Now why ever would I mind?" Sara asked with a smile, and looped her arm through Tess's. "When you come to know Whitewater better, you will understand why such a question is folly." She giggled a moment, then added, "Besides, we have become sisters. If you're very nice to me, I will even share my father with you."

At that Tess laughed, and the laughter seemed to fill her with light. The sound even brought smiles from passersby.

At last they stood in the plaza before the temple. Its dome rose higher than anything around, towering as if it were a mountain itself. It had the exact shape of the temple at Gewindi-Telner, but its vast size hinted at the much larger mysteries within.

Slowly they approached a closed door.

"Do you suppose," Sara said, "that we will break some rule if we enter uninvited?"

"I do not know. But have we not been told that the temple was built to preserve the secrets of the Ilduin? And are we not Ilduin?"

"I would rather not have to prove that to an angry crowd."

Sara turned, looking for assistance. Finally she spied a woman who was striding down the street with a bow and quiver on her back.

"Pardon me," Sara called out. "Can you help us?"

At once the woman changed direction and came toward them. "Are you lost?"

"No," Sara said. "We have arrived with Gewindi-Tel. We wish to enter the temple. Is that permitted?"

The woman smiled at them, her teeth white against her dark, iridescent skin. "Well, travelers, I will tell you what every Anari knows, since clearly you are not Anari."

"Neither are we Bozandari," Sara hastened to explain. "We come from the village of Whitewater, far to the north, on the caravan route over the mountains to the western lands."

"I have heard of that village. Welcome to Anahar." The woman bowed briefly. "Now I will tell you. The temple is opened only for festivals and important meetings. Apart from such times, only a few guardians are allowed to enter to maintain it and clean it."

"Oh." Sara's face fell.

The dark woman leaned a little closer. "There is one other way in, however."

"Yes?"

Again the beautiful smile. "The doors are always open to an Ilduin."

Tess reached out and lightly touched the woman's upper arm. "You, too, are Ilduin blood."

The woman studied them for a moment, then nodded. "Aye, I am. My name is Cilla of Monabi-Tel."

"I'm Sara Deepwell, and this is Tess Birdsong," Sara answered. "We are very happy to meet you."

But Cilla was looking at Tess, and finally reached out to touch her lightly. "I have heard your call."

"And I yours."

Cilla nodded. "It is good. I have been wondering how we would meet."

Tess paused a moment as she recalled what Cilla had said. "You are of Monabi-Tel. Do you know the brothers Ratha and Giri?"

A wide smile graced Cilla's face. "Indeed I do! They are my cousins. I thought they were dead, or lost forever in slavery. Where are they?"

"They came along with Gewindi-Tel," Sara told her. "They were freed long ago by our friend Archer and have been traveling with him since."

"Oh, thank the gods! In our childhood, we three were the worst rapscallions in the Tel. Many stories are still told of our mischief. I must see them. But first I will take you into the temple."

She gave a little bow and gestured for them to follow her. "In these days, great trouble stirs on a bitter wind. Long have we sisters been isolated and ignorant. Now that at least we three are no longer isolated, perhaps we can learn that which we will need to defeat that bitter wind."

"How many of us are there?" Sara asked.

Cilla shook her head. "I wish I knew for certain. I feel them out there, but I have met no others besides you. Some, I sense, have been perverted, and for that reason I feared to delve too deeply when I would stand alone."

There was a stone bench in the plaza, not far from the door they approached, and Sara sank abruptly onto it, quivering with sobs too strong to be contained. Her heart was breaking in so many ways that she wondered if she would ever be able to put all the splinters back together. But one thing she knew for certain: the innkeeper's daughter was a thing of the past.

"I'm sorry," she said, biting her lip. "I'm sorry."

"Is she ill?" Cilla asked.

"No," Tess answered, "but she has suffered much. When you spoke of our sisters being perverted… Her mother was taken by a servant of the Enemy, long years ago. A few weeks past we found her, twisted and tortured so that the enemy's servant could control his evil hive."

"I have heard of those hives," Cilla said, her voice dropping. "Is an Ilduin at the center of each?"

"I do not know," Tess answered candidly. "I only know that we found Sara's poor mother in the worst straits imaginable, and we were unable to save her."

"My poor sister," Cilla said, her sympathy quick and real. At once she sat beside Sara and took her hand.

"I'll be all right," Sara said, her voice wobbly. "Truly I will. It's just that so much has happened…and sometimes I realize that I have not truly comprehended it all yet."

"There has been very little time to grieve," Tess said kindly. Then she briefly described all that had happened since their departure from Whitewater.

With each word, the sorrow reflected on Cilla's face deepened. "We have heard that matters are bad up north, but as yet we know very little of them. In any event, we are scarcely able to post what is left of our boundaries for fear of being set upon by the Bozandari. We must rely on travelers such as yourself."

Sara dashed at her eyes. "Gewindi-Tel has come to join a rebellion."

Cilla nodded. "It is that for which I am preparing also. Many of us are. We must be free of this boot on our necks and on our lives."

"We want to help," Sara told her. "But as yet we know very little about what we can do."

Cilla nodded. "None of us has discovered all the secrets of our heritage. Few have even tried as yet. But come, let the three of us enter the temple. I will guide you along the path. The three of us can learn together. But first let us beseech Dalenar for guidance."

"I do not remember the prayers," Tess said, "if ever I knew them."

Cilla smiled. "Then simply join your hand in mine. Lady Sara and I shall say them, for I know an Ilduin mother would have taught her such things in earliest childhood."

Sara felt her heart clench yet again, for Cilla spoke the truth. Oft had they sat in the kitchen, looking into the cooking fire, softly repeating rhymes together to pass what few idle moments there were. It had always been a quiet time for just the two of them, sometimes the only private time they could squeeze into a busy day. Now, she realized, those moments had been like tiny diamonds found among the dust of life, treasures to be cherished forever.

She smiled as she took Cilla's hand. "It has been many years, but the words have not left me. Aye, let us say them together."

Oh Dalenar of rising light,
Wisdom gained with gaining sight,
Hope of seeing in the night,
Guide our journey to the right.

13

Once they had seen to accommodations for their companions, in lodgings among the people of Gewindi-Tel, Ratha and Giri bade their leave and went to find their own kinsmen.

For Ratha, the journey through the winding streets of Anahar was one of both joy and trepidation. To be once again in this most holy of places was a dream he had thought would never come true. And yet he could not forget how he and his brother had been taken.

Or perhaps given.

Unlike the other Anari Tels, the Monabi had always been nomads. While they, too, had a telner, it was buried deep in a remote mountain valley, and it served mainly as a base from which to wander among the jagged, crystal-laden boulders that sang a constant and irresistible melody as old as the stones themselves. The barren, stony terrain south and west of Anahar provided little for a would-be farmer but offered a life-sustaining bounty to those who listened to and followed after that ancient song.

Thus had Ratha's kinsmen been better able to avoid the plundering Bozandari, and for many years his Tel had been able to maintain a stable existence, bringing jewels into Anahar on occasion and following the music of the stones otherwise. That wandering existence had given rise to the Monabi talent for wit and tale, skills that had come to be valued among the other Anari as much as the gems the Monabi offered at the yearly rites of sharing. Many were the nights he had sat around a campfire, listening to the elders fashion stories around the music that filled their hearts, his muscles quivering with the pleasant burn of a day spent in travel and good work.

All of that had ended twelve summers ago, when he and Giri had been sitting in the temple at Anahar, listening to the final sharing rites. A cousin had whispered to them, talking of a hunt that many of the young men were about to undertake.

"They are going to kill a boar for the evening feast," his cousin had said. "That has to be more fun than sitting here listening to the Mothers drone on and on."

Ratha and Giri had been of an age where such a proposition was indeed enticing. Moreover, there was Tel honor to be had, for the Tel that brought down the first feast night boar would be celebrated for the coming year. So they had slipped out of the temple and joined the other young men, the most skillful hunters from each Tel, and set out into the night. They had barely left the city when they were set upon and captured.

Ratha had noted at the time that the cousin who had invited them to the hunt had not been among the hunting party. In the time since, he had not lost the bitter taste of that night, or the feeling that he and the other Anari had been led into a trap. For years, there had been whispered rumors of Anari who were delivering their kinsmen into slavery for the Bozandari. But they had been merely whispered rumors, for to speak of such things openly would be a mortal offense to Anari honor.

As he was led in chains toward Bozandar, Ratha had found himself wishing that Anari honor could bear such accusations openly. For he had no doubt—then or now—that he had been betrayed. While Lord Archer had freed him and his brother, too many others remained in bondage.

Thus was his mood darkened by the memory of his last visit to Anahar, and while its glories could still awe him, his thoughts continually returned to what had happened and whether that cousin would be found among the Monabi-Tel who lived in the city.

"He probably is here," Giri said quietly, his thoughts evidently running along the same line. "A traitor among our kin, traveling with them among the hills, would be too soon discovered. But in a city, where there are always opportunities to slip away to a meeting in a quiet alley, such a man could long stay hidden and secure."

"No more," Ratha said. "If he is here, I will find him. And when I do..."

He didn't have to finish the sentence. There would be no gathering of the Mothers to hear the case, no defense to flow from a tongue long accustomed to treachery and deceit. The man would die on Ratha's sword, or Giri's.

"We are changed, my brother," Giri said, sadness in his voice. "In past times, when we lived among our own, such thoughts would have flown as quickly as they arose. Now..."

"Now we are soldiers," Ratha said. "For better or for worse, we have faced death and dealt death. A part of my soul is sickened by the thought that it gets easier each time, but only because that part of my soul dies a little each time. What remains..."

"Is the soul of a soldier," Giri agreed. "It is a soul that some must have so that others need not. I regret that many more will need to find that soul for our people to be free. But it is not a war we chose, for an enslaved soul bears greater scars than ours."

They walked on in silence, each carrying the weight of his

own thoughts and the scars of his own soul, until they reached the streets of their kin.

We have come home, Ratha thought. *We have come home to kill.*

The temple seemed to embrace them as they entered. There was no other way to describe it, Tess realized. In stepping through the temple doors, they had stepped into an embrace as powerful and tender, as warm and boundlessly joyful, as the arms of a mother with newborn a child. It was as if the walls whispered, *Welcome to the world, little one.*

As if in greeting, torches sprang to blazing life on all the walls, illuminating the sanctuary, adding to the sense of welcome.

Almost as if echoing the feeling, Cilla said quietly, "This is the womb of the Ilduin, the place where each sister is truly born. The mysteries are many, and so far none of us has learned more than bits of what the first Ilduin knew."

Tess nodded and moved slowly to the center of the circle of high stone walls beneath the huge dome. Everywhere her eyes fell, even in such flickering light, there seemed to be symbols and drawings and carvings.

Then she noticed the statues, twelve of them, circling the edges of the sanctuary, appearing to move as the torchlight danced.

"These are the Twelve," Cilla explained. "The eleven who cursed Dederand, and the same eleven who built this temple to preserve the mysteries for the times when they would once again be needed. And there," she added, pointing, "is Theriel, the Twelfth and the First among them. When she was killed by Ardred, the remaining eleven rained fire upon the city he ruled. Some say it was necessary. Those of us who share the Ilduin blood, however..."

Sara spoke in a hushed voice. "We feel the stain."

"Aye," said Cilla. "Theriel was pure of heart, the gift of the gods. It was she who helped bring the Anari into being, so that a better people might occupy this world. We are no better, of course. And then she was killed."

"Out of jealousy," Sara said, whispering what she had learned from the old tales.

"Not only," Tess said, surprising them by speaking. "Not only out of jealousy. She lost the protection the goddess Elanor had given her when she dared to midwife the creation of a new race. She overstepped."

Cilla and Sara both stared at her. "How do you know this?" Cilla asked. "I have never before heard it."

Tess blinked, almost as if waking. "I…know not how I learned this. I just know it."

After a moment, Cilla nodded. "'Tis said this place can awaken memories that reside in the blood."

"Perhaps." Slowly Tess walked toward the statue of Theriel, the woman around whom so much of the history of this world seemed to revolve, even centuries after her death. "Why was she so special?"

Cilla shrugged. "I know only that she was. She seemed to be at the crux of many matters in her time. It may have been her power. Or it may have been because of her protector, Elanor. None now know the answers to these questions."

"But they may be found within these walls."

"So it is said."

Tess drew a sharp breath and felt as if the floor tilted beneath her. Reaching out, she touched the item that the statue held in her hands: a white rose.

"What is this?" she asked, her voice thick.

"The white rose. 'Tis the symbol of Theriel."

The world tilted even more, and Tess sank to the floor, trying to hold herself up on one hand. "The white rose," she murmured.

Then Sara gasped, too.

"What is it?" Cilla demanded. "What is wrong?"

Mutely Sara knelt by Tess and tugged the soft leather of the boot down Tess's leg until the tattoo was revealed. A white rose.

Cilla fell to her knees, too. "By the gods, where did you get that, Tess?"

"I have no memory." The words were squeezed out.

But the tattoo was identical to the rose in the statue's hand, and all the three women could do was stare.

Finally Tess spoke, yanking the boot up to cover the tattoo once more. "I have been marked," she said tautly. "Branded. And I fear it means no good."

Word of Archer's arrival in Anahar spread on the wind, almost faster than feet could travel. The Anari knew him and knew of him, and his arrival spurred the hopes of those who would rebel against Bozandar.

Almost before Gewindi-Tel had finished settling into their compound and started cooking a meal for the children, a messenger appeared, begging him to attend a meeting with the Sharwahi-Tel.

The Sharwahi were warriors of old; their clan had been the leaders of the fight to resist the Bozandari invasion these generations past. Sadly the Sharwahi transformation from stoneworkers to warriors had not come soon enough to make them into a true fighting force. Now, with rebellion on the wind and upon every tongue, they were called again to perform a task for which they were ill-trained, with numbers horribly decimated by the earlier war and subsequent slave raids.

Archer was perhaps the most reluctant of all to engage in warfare. This coming battle might have the appearance of pitting the Anari against the Bozandari, but Archer knew better. He would once again be making war on his brother. He had no doubt that this war with his brother would be as ugly the last had been. But he also knew where his duty lay. For much he must atone, and this was but the beginning.

He followed the messenger willingly through the slowly darkening streets. Twilight came early in the mountains, and with it cold winds from the snowfields high up. Jenah strode beside him, designated by Eiehsa to represent Gewindi-Tel.

"Mother would gladly have sent you alone, Lord Archer," Jenah said. "Gewindi-Tel is pledged to you."

"It would not be my place," Archer said. "Your pledge honors the Ilduin, and me, but it remains that among the other Tel there are decisions to be made, and those must be made by Anari, for Anari. For me to speak at this council would be a grave mistake."

Jenah nodded. "You are wise as well as brave."

Archer laughed bitterly. "Wise? Would that I had handled this better when it happened in the First Times. Had I but known how my brother had grown warped by his jealousy, I would have surrendered my birthright without a second thought. There would have been no first war, and no war now to weigh upon our thoughts. Instead…"

"Bear not the stain of your brother," Jenah said. "It was he who started the war that ended the First Age."

"So the stories tell," Archer said. "As with many events, the truth is less clear than the telling of it."

"What have the tales left out?" Jenah asked.

"Only that I loved my brother," Archer said. "And that is everything."

He looked around at the sweeping curves and arches of Anahar, hewn by permission from ancient stone. Something about this city brought out the subtle memories of the old days, memories he usually could ignore. But not here.

"My brother was a great man," Archer said. "As boys, we

were the best of friends. Many were the days that we laughed as only brothers can laugh at the mischief of our youth and the missteps of our elders. I was the Firstborn, but only by a moment, for we were twins. My mother used to say that we were inseparable even in the womb, for when I emerged, Ardred's fingers were tight about my ankle, as if he could not bear that I might leave him. For many years was it thus. Where one went, the other followed, as if breath itself were something to be shared."

"No one has spoken of him thus," Jenah said.

"No one would," Archer said. "None who would have told the tale knew him as I knew him. He was called Ardred the Fair, and well deserved. Lovely in face and feature, and lovely in mind and heart. I have often wondered if he would have handled things better had I been the one to rebel. I suspect he would have, for he was the wiser of us. And yet, by accident of birth, I was the one destined to rule. It shames him not that he thought this unfair. Many were the days I thought it unfair, as well."

"En shar shirneh sen, shir an sharnet sahng."

Archer nodded agreement. "Oh foul can fairness be, and fair the foulest fate. It is a wise saying that your people do well to remember. I wish my brother and I had known of it. Much blood might have been spared."

"You were young," Jenah said.

"Yes," Archer said. "That we were. But as we grew older, I should have seen the twisting of his heart. Like all brothers, we had our petty squabbles. I did not see that this was more than that until it was too late. I did not see the torment of his mind. I did not see…that he had come to hate me. I, too, was blinded by Ardred the Fair. And unlike those who left with him to found Dederand, I should have known better. We had shared my mother's womb, yet I could not see how the fate of our births had sickened his soul. I stood by while he sank into madness."

"You love him still," Jenah said.

And that was the bitterest truth of all, Archer thought. "Yes, brother. I do. Even as I prepare to make war against him, I love him still."

"Then great indeed is your wisdom," Jenah said. "A lesser man would have given way to hate. That you cannot, that is true wisdom."

"Perhaps," Archer said. "And perhaps I am still blinded by Ardred the Fair, longing for a time that can never come again, where two brothers dip their toes in the Enalon Sea and watch the sun say good-night."

"Wish for that, Lord Archer," Jenah said. "That wish may be the salvation of us all."

14

With each step she took, Sara felt as if she were being drawn deeper into the womb of the Ilduin. Beyond the nave where they had seen the statues, the temple flowed into a second, widening anteroom. As before, torches sprang to life upon their approach, the flames pure and smokeless, with nary a flicker. The hues ranged from deep red to warm amber, to greens and blues that brought to mind the sweetest springtime fields and skies that Whitewater had ever seen. The effect of the whole was a glow that seemed to suffuse her soul with lightness and joy.

"All the beauty in the world," Sara whispered.

"Yes," Tess said.

"It has never been thus before," Cilla said. "Many times have I stood here, yet this is new to me."

Sara drew a slow breath, allowing the feelings to flow through her. "When I look into the flames, it is almost as if I can sense every happy moment in my life. I cannot see them. But I can feel them. When my mother sang to me…"

"When my mother rocked me to sleep," Cilla added, nodding.

"When my mother played pat-a-cake," Tess said. She caught

her breath. The words that followed came out in a lilting, child-hood rhythm. "Pat-a-cake, pat-a-cake, baker man. Bake me a cake as fast as you can. Mix it and pat it and roll it with glee, then toss it in the oven for baby and me."

"I do not know this game," Cilla said, looking at Sara. "But our mothers have others like it."

"As do ours," Sara said. "Lady Tess, does this help you to remember your people?"

Tess shook her head. "Sadly, no. But it helps me to remember my mother, and that is enough to cherish. Perhaps we shall all remember more as we walk these rooms. But it is enough to know that my mother played with me, and that she smiled."

"We all feel our mothers," Sara said. "It is as if this room is rich with the warmth of a mother's love."

The other two women nodded. They stood in silence for a long time, as if bathing in warm memories. The silence seemed to deepen around them, save only for a muffled, rhythmic sound. Sara let her mind drift to that sound, and soon it was as if the flames were brightening, ever so faintly, with each low *oosh-woosh*. She placed a hand to her breast, almost without thinking, and felt her own heart matching the sound around her. There was no doubt in her mind. It was a heartbeat. She saw that Cilla and Tess had also placed their hands to their breasts.

"The womb of the Ilduin," Cilla said softly. "My mother told me stories of it, but I have never felt it like this."

"This temple is not a building," Tess said. "It is a living body. The living body of our bloodline."

"Yes!" Sara said, excitement growing within her. "The mysteries of the Ilduin lie not in the statues or symbols. Thus have so many missed them. It is as if the temple has been waiting to awaken."

"It has," Cilla said, looking at Tess. "It has been waiting for you."

* * *

The lodgings of Sharwahi-Tel were not far from the Gewindi section. They were, however, occupied by many more people, bustling with life, many carrying weapons of one kind or another, apparently readying for the conflict to come.

As Archer and Jenah passed through the curving streets of Sharwahi compound, Archer was recognized. Many bowed to him, but none called him by any name except Lord Archer. Long ago he had forbidden the use of his real name, so long ago that many here did not even recall it except from tales and legends they had heard. Most of those who bowed were probably simply mimicking what they had seen their elders do for generations.

Regardless, he was uncomfortable with the attention and felt undeserving of the bows. He inclined his head in response but in no way encouraged the attention.

It made no difference.

At the center of the Sharwahi compound was a round building. This one was not like the village temples, but because the great temple of Anahar lay only a sort distance away, this building was intended only for meetings of the clan mothers.

Inside, a fire pit burned brightly, and the six mothers of Sharwahi sat around it. A space was opened for Archer and Jenah to sit on a bench. In the background, behind the mothers, stood armed men.

The most senior of the clan mothers stood, a tall, proud, beautiful woman of indeterminate age. The iridescence of her dark skin reflected the fire's glow. "I am Gelinna Sharwahi," she said, bowing to Archer. "First Mother of the Tel. And these are my sisters. We are honored by your presence, Lord Archer."

He returned her bow. "I am honored to be in your presence, Mother Gelinna. Please tell me how I may serve you."

"Sit," the woman said smiling. "Jenah, you, too. It has been too long since I set eyes on your handsome face."

Jenah chuckled. "You know where my Tel resides."

"Brash young man. It is *you* who should visit your elders."

Laughter rippled through the room.

"My daughter," Gelinna continued, "has been sighing your name since last you were in Anahar two years since. 'Tis a pity she is still too young, or I'd give her over to you just to get the sound of your name out of my ears."

Again more laughter. Jenah squirmed a little on the bench. "I am waiting," he said. "Sulah just will not grow up fast enough."

Gelinna laughed loudest of all. But then laughter faded, and gloom seemed to enter the brightly lit room.

"Fell things are afoot," Gelinna said. "All the Anari know it. We have heard terrible tales from the north, and they have nothing to do with the heel of Bozandar. But it is Bozandar that most immediately concerns us, Lord Archer."

He nodded, remaining silent.

"We can do nothing about the early winter that has begun to encroach even here, in the south. Our days are yet warm, but, as you will shortly feel, our nights have begun to carry an unnatural chill. Whatever lies behind these changes and the horrors to the north remains beyond our reach so long as we are decimated by slave raids, so long as our people must abandon their homes every few months to escape the Bozandari troops. We are a people weakened by constant loss."

Archer nodded. "I have seen."

"So we must throw off the yoke. We can wait no longer. My sisters and I sense that it is urgent for us to break free now in order to be ready for what lies ahead. But!"

She held up a finger and cocked her head to one side. "But. It is to the Sharwahi that all Anari look for guidance in this, because we fought in the past. But I tell you, Lord Archer, there are not enough of us. Nor are we well-enough trained for battle such as must come. So it is to you we turn. We ask you to teach us, so that we may teach all Anari, so that we may become an army."

For long moments there was no sound save the crackle of the fire. When Archer at last spoke, his voice was heavy. "I am sorry it has come to this, Mother Gelinna. The Anari have always been a people of peace."

"We cannot afford to be peaceful now."

"No."

He bowed his head, staring into the flames as if he might find something there, but his answer was already decided. There was none other to give.

"I will train you and anyone else who cares to join in the war to come. And I will fight beside you."

"Thank you," Gelinna said gravely. "I know how this must pain you."

"It pains us all," he answered with equal gravity. "I will serve the Anari however I can. But it is to Jenah you should speak now, for he speaks for Gewindi-Tel. He can tell you what they have so far seen and done. As for me…" He rose and bowed. "I await your orders."

Then, turning, he strode from the building into the chilly twilight.

Gradually the temple's heartbeat slowed, leaving in its wake only serene silence. The women who had been so enthralled gradually returned to normalcy and an awareness of things beyond the temple.

"There is more here," Tess murmured.

"But it will take time," Sara replied. "I cannot begin to imagine what it was we just experienced, or how it might teach us."

"Nor I," agreed Cilla. "Let us three return in the morning when we are fresh and see what else we may discover. Now I must return to my Tel, for I am sure Ratha and Giri will be there...." Her voice caught. "I have missed them so. Will you come with me?"

Tess and Sara exchanged looks. "Of course," Tess said. "We would be delighted to meet Monabi-Tel."

"And Monabi-Tel will be delighted to meet you," Cilla answered with a smile.

In Anahar, all Tel lodgings were equidistant from the temple, so the journey to Monabi-Tel was no longer than the journey from Gewindi lodgings to the temple. Beyond the compounds, dating back to the original building of the city, spread businesses, and beyond that, in the mountain valley, were the fields and grazing lands, now lying fallow for the winter.

But the walk along a winding path this time took on an even more breathtaking beauty. The flash and ripple of color Tess had seen by daylight only became more beautiful as the day darkened.

"This city," she remarked, "is a beacon."

"So it was intended," Cilla answered with a smile. "When the Eleven Ilduin of the First Age came to us and asked us to build a temple and a city to recall all that was lost, we searched out stone of a very special and rare kind. All stone is alive, but this stone is alive with color and light, and it takes joy in expressing its beauty. Sometimes...sometimes it even sings."

Tess paused and looked at Cilla. "It *sings?*" Her voice was hushed.

"Aye. Rarely, I'm sorry to say. I have never heard it, but the clan mothers teach us the story of how the city sings upon rare occasion, a song that defies description to any who have not heard the voices of these rocks. My own mother heard it once and said it was almost like the ringing of glass bells, yet more beautiful still."

"I heard something once," Tess said slowly. "When I touched the wall of the Gewindi Telnertah."

"Then perhaps you will hear the voice of Anahar while you are here." Cilla smiled. "I would so like to hear it myself. I have been hoping since earliest childhood to hear even the smallest song from these walls."

Sara spoke. "Ratha said that Monabi-Tel hears the songs of the rocks and seeks out the most beautiful. That hearing the songs is what sets your Tel apart."

"Aye, we hear the songs of individual rocks, 'tis true," Cilla agreed. "But the song of Anahar is something much more. It is as if, joined together, all the stones of this city become one voice, a voice that can be heard by all Anari, not just Monabi, no matter how far they roam. It is said Anahar only sings to call all Anari together here. And it is said that all these voices joined together create a song so beautiful it nearly breaks the heart." She released a small sigh. "But Anahar sings by its own choosing, so it may be that I will never hear its song."

Monabi-Tel was in the middle of a huge party when they arrived, a celebration of the return of Ratha and Giri. Most of the Monabi were away, searching the mountains for the choicest of crystals, but there were enough of them in Anahar, including the clan mothers, to create quite a spectacle. Ale flowed freely, along with huge amounts of food, and with everyone in the central plaza dancing and singing and talking, the festivities were difficult to miss.

A few wary eyes were turned on Sara and Tess as they followed Cilla, but the wariness soon passed as people realized the two pale women were Cilla's guests.

Suddenly Cilla let out a cry and darted forward. "Ratha!" Moments later she was in the big man's arms, hugging him as if she would never let go. Sara and Tess stood back, smiling.

"Oh, Ratha," Cilla said, "I thought I had lost you forever."

"You are not so fortunate, cousin," Ratha answered with a laugh as he lifted her off her feet and swung her in a circle. "Nor have you lost Giri. He is here somewhere, regaling pretty girls with tales of our adventures."

"Cilla!" At that moment Giri appeared out of the crowd and snatched his cousin from his brother's arms. Cilla's head was thrown back in sheer joy as she laughed and clung to Giri's shoulders.

When he set her on her feet, he was still smiling, but Tess thought she saw something unnaturally hard in Giri's eyes. Her senses prickled to full alert.

"And your brother Nagari," Giri said, "where is he? I have looked for him all evening. Does he no longer reside here in the city?"

"He has gone back to the telner on a mission for the mothers, but he should return in a few days. He will be thrilled to see you."

"Perhaps." Giri lifted her off her feet once more and squeezed her until she laughed and begged to be put down. "Come," he said, including Tess and Sara in his invitation, "let us find a quieter spot to eat, drink and share the news."

There was a place just off the central plaza, sheltered beneath a tree with a delicate lacework of leaves that allowed the last of the evening light to shine through. There they found a table and some benches, and before long Ratha and Giri had brought planks laden with food and drink for them all. Gathered around the table, they began to dine and talk.

Cilla insisted that Ratha and Giri share their tales first, so they explained how they had been captured and sold into slavery, and how after a few years Archer had found them and set them free. How they had ridden with him ever since, freely sworn to his service.

"The years," Giri said, "have not been without peril and loneliness. At any time Lord Archer would have let us come home, but we chose not to leave his side."

Cilla nodded. "I would have done the same."

"We have seen most of the known world," Ratha added. "There is, or was, much that was good there, especially once we were away from the Bozandar Empire. We crossed the northern mountains many times on the caravan trail and saw the great cities there. But our last journey that way was not a happy one."

He nodded to Tess. "We found Lady Tess carrying a child away from a slaughtered caravan. When we learned that the caravan had been attacked by servants of Lantav Glassidor, we set out to hunt them down. Since then…" He shrugged.

Giri picked up the thread. "We saw thousands die in Derda from the winter. The Adasen Basin is empty of life now, the farms ruined, the farmers dead. On our way to Lorense, Earth's Root erupted…"

"Yes," Cilla said swiftly. "That is when the clan mothers became truly concerned. Especially when they heard a fire demon had escaped."

Giri shook his head. "We met with the demon. He came after us."

Cilla drew a sharp breath. "But you are still here!"

Ratha gave Giri an elbow and chuckled. "We, uh, doused the flame, you could say. Do not upset our cousin, Giri."

Cilla sniffed. "And do not treat me like a child. I am a woman now, preparing for war."

Ratha sighed. "Aye. As we all prepare."

"So," Cilla said, shifting the subject back, "where did you go after you killed the fire demon?"

"To Lorense, to confront the hive master Lantav Glassidor. Our ladies here killed him while we fought with his minions. 'Twas an ugly affair, and we have been pursued ever since."

Cilla nodded slowly. "I have heard of these hives. Are they really of one mind?"

"It would seem so, from what we saw."

Cilla looked at Tess and Sara, who nodded agreement.

"At least at this time," Sara said. "For we sensed another power behind Glassidor."

Tess nodded slowly. "Indeed we did. And that is the power we must fear most."

"It is," said Sara quietly, "the power we will eventually have to confront."

A shadow seemed to fall over the group, and the evening's chill deepened further. Tess shivered.

"Well," said Giri, breaking the pall of silence, "tonight is not a night for such unhappy thoughts. We are back with our Tel and, more importantly, with our cousin." He raised his mug of ale toward Cilla.

"To Cilla, who was ever a scamp and now is beautiful besides!"

All mugs were lifted while Cilla laughed, but again Tess caught Giri's eye, and what she saw there made her shiver yet again, but not from cold. Something ugly had taken root in his heart, and it terrified her.

15

Sara and Tess walked back to Gewindi-Tel's lodgings by themselves. Cilla had offered to accompany them, but it was clear that she wished to stay with Ratha and Giri, and the two men would have been rude to leave the celebration being held in their honor. Tess had been quick to assure Cilla that they could find their way.

No one thought there might be any danger in the streets of Anahar.

The light flashing and twinkling within the stones themselves was enough to guide their steps. Cilla had pointed out a path that would take them directly to Gewindi's area, but Sara and Tess discussed whether to go by way of the temple.

"I want to see if I can feel anything more," Tess said.

Sara agreed. "It was…well, it was unlike anything in my experience. It would comfort me to know I have not imagined it. But…I want to get back to Tom, also. I have not seen him in hours, and he is still adjusting to his new…sight."

Tess lowered her head. "I am so sorry about that. Let us straight away to Gewindi, then. The temple can wait for morning."

Sara touched her shoulder. "No, no, Tess. It will take us

only a short time longer to go by way of the temple. We can make a brief visit. If you wish to stay longer, I shall simply return by myself."

But Tess shook her head. "No, I shall walk with you back to Gewindi. You have been away far longer than you intended, and Tom may be worrying about you, as well. Say no more."

The city was built in concentric circles around the central plaza, and while the path they took curved often around trees and buildings, it reached Gewindi-Tel's compound in about half the distance it would have taken them to go by way of the temple plaza.

They found Tom in their lodgings, not, as Sara had feared, alone, but instead with Archer, who was amusing the young man with tales of past adventures. From Tom's laughter, it was plain that the tales were humorous.

But when the women entered the room, both Tom and Archer looked their way.

"I am sorry I was gone so long," Sara said, hurrying to Tom's side. "We meant only to stay briefly at the temple, but then we met Cilla, a cousin of Ratha's and Giri's, and when all was said and done, we went back to Monabi-Tel with her and found there a big celebration."

"I warrant," Archer said, "that Monabi is glad to see Giri and Ratha."

"Aye," Tess answered, smiling. "'Twas a big party."

Tom turned his hand over and clasped Sara's. "You need not apologize, Sara. You can hardly be with me every moment, nor should you. There are important matters afoot, and you are Ilduin. Besides," he added with a crooked smile, "thanks to Lady Tess's bandage for my eyes, I can see almost as well as I could before, although not with the same breadth."

Sara nodded, as if she accepted what he said, but her face remained troubled.

"Also," Tom added, "Master Archer tells me that the seer Erkiah Nebu has been sent for."

"Aye," said Archer. "A messenger has gone to bring him here. He will train Tom's talent, I believe. A talent that will be invaluable in days to come."

"If he cannot train me," Tom said wryly, "at least he will be here to guide us."

"How can anyone guide us through the days to come?" Sara asked. "The end is not fixed."

"No," Tom answered, "but there are often better paths to choose. Perhaps Erkiah Nebu will be able to see them."

"Or perhaps *you* will," Sara answered softly. "You have already seen things that helped us."

"Aye," agreed Archer. "And your heart is true, else the Ilduin fire would not have saved you."

Tom turned his head suddenly. "As is yours."

"Now wait, lad," Archer said, shaking his head.

But Tom interrupted. "For the arrow to fly straight, first the bow must bend."

Silence filled the room as the words, seemingly so prophetic, hung in the air. Then Archer rose abruptly and strode forth. Tess followed him at once, leaving Tom and Sara to their privacy.

She found Archer beneath one of the lacy trees in a small garden not far from the door of their lodging.

"Archer?" she called softly.

He didn't answer immediately. He stood still, a large man who, it seemed, carried a larger burden.

She reached him and dared to touch his arm. He didn't pull away, but he remained stiff and silent.

"Are you all right?"

"As right as I will ever be," he replied flatly.

"Will you tell me?"

He didn't answer. The night breeze had begun to stir, ruffling the feathery leaves above them. It was growing cold, and Tess could already feel the chill on her face. She sighed and slipped her arm through his.

"Why did Tom's words upset you?" she asked, seeking another approach.

"Because I am the bow, and I am bending once again. I have no taste for this war that is coming. I have no taste at all for war. But I can see no other course."

"I know." She, too, fell silent, wishing she had any words of comfort to offer. "It seems we have no choice but to defeat the Bozandar Empire. We will need allies in the battle against *him*."

"It is always thus," he said bitterly. "Ardred sets man against man, brother against brother, so that we may all do his ugly work for him. But I can see no other way. The Anari must be free, or there will soon be so few of them that they will not count for anything in the balance of the good versus the evil. The slave raids are becoming more frequent. The acts of annihilation by the Bozandari army are happening more often. This cannot long be sustained."

"Aye," Tess agreed.

"But still," he said, turning his head to look at her, "but still I have no taste for another war. I have spent my life trying to find a way to avoid such, and instead I am once again thrust into the very heart of it."

He stepped away from her and bowed. "Excuse me, my lady. I need to be alone."

She let him go. Then, as a gust of chill wind blew over her again, she decided to go to the temple by herself. If the answers to this mess lay anywhere, perhaps it was there.

Tom and Sara had disappeared from the front room of the lodging, where a fire burned on the hearth, casting light and heat and cozy comfort, so Tess was able to go to her own room unseen and collect the heavy wool cloak she had doffed earlier in the day. Wrapping it snugly about her and pulling up the hood, she left for the temple, determined to learn all she could before it was too late.

The night's chill had apparently driven everyone indoors, for the streets were empty, though the hour was not terribly late. The rainbow light dancing in the stones was just enough to illuminate her way, although the light was at times deceptive, creating shadows that moved.

She reached the temple quickly enough, and the instant her hand touched the door, it swung open before her. When she stepped inside, the door closed on its own, and she was surrounded by warmth, silence and the light of the torches that sprang to life at her approach.

She stood in the antechamber for several minutes, allowing the peace of the building to fill her and ease her heart. Gradually the tension that had never seemed to completely leave her since she had awakened among the slaughtered caravan without any memory, eased its grip and let go.

Only then did she step into the next chamber. Again the torches sprang to life at her approach, welcoming her, letting her know she belonged here. The statues of the twelve Ilduin seemed to look benignly at her, almost seemed to whisper, *Welcome, sister.*

Slowly she walked around the outer edge of the room, stopping before each statue and looking into its face, as if she might find some kind of answer there. Some kind of recognition. Once or twice she thought she might have felt a flicker, but she put it down to wishfulness.

When she reached the statue of Theriel, she halted and stared long into the woman's face. All of a sudden, she realized that while Theriel's representation appeared to be as serene as the others, that was only a superficial impression. Somehow the sculptor had also managed to convey a feeling of sorrow and loss, a sense of immeasurable grief behind those composed features.

In an instinctive response to the recognition of grief, Tess reached out to touch the statue. The instant her hand connected with the cool stone, she felt an electric tingle fill her body and heard a voice say, "You have come at last, my daughter."

Stunned, Tess yanked her hand away from the statue and backed up several steps. Everything appeared to be as it had been all along. A shaky sigh escaped her, and she backed up another few steps, wondering if she were losing her mind as she had lost her memory. But the pull of the statue drew her back, and she placed her hand on the statue once more, this time on the face.

A song whispered through her mind, a song about not letting the sun go down and a man seeking himself.

The music sounded alien now, yet Tess knew it had once been more familiar to her than any song she had heard or sung in these past months. Images flooded in. Bitter tears. Sitting in the street, her mother's head in her lap, that song wafting from the open door of a nearby shop. Her mother's face horribly distorted, even in the sleep of death. Young Tess trying to wipe the blood from her mother's face, to comb it from her golden blond hair with slender fingers. Trying to will her mother back to life, yet knowing the effort was beyond hopeless.

The sun had gone down on Tess's life that day. She had stood in the rain at a gravesite, her fingers clutching a strong hand that quivered as much as her own. Her father's grief. No sounds of laughter from the kitchen. No more arguments over schoolwork. No more evenings disappearing into endless conversation and laughter. Emotional night, as black as the bottom of an inkwell.

Tears streamed down Tess's face as she held her hand to the statue. The weight of what she had forgotten crashed upon her like a rock slide, and her soul felt bruised and torn. The fringes of the memories were blurry, and she could not place where her home had been. But she now knew more than she had just moments before, and what she knew filled her with an empty, aching sadness.

"Yes, my beautiful daughter," a voice whispered. *"I know your pain. I felt it in every sliver of my soul and feel it still. But I needed you. Life needed you."*

Tess heard her own sobs as if from a distance, her attention focused on the voice. It was her mother's voice, and yet not. Different in some inexplicable way, yet so close as to pull at every fiber of her heart. An ugly truth began to worm into her mind.

"Why...my...mother?" Tess asked, her voice shuddering with fear, anger building in her belly.

"This you will learn, my daughter. Here. You will know and understand."

"You killed her!" Tess screamed. "You! Killed! Her!"

Tess beat her fists on the statue, small crackles of bone lost in a flurry of anguish beyond measure. Finally she stopped and saw the statue was flecked with blood. Her blood, now bursting into pure white flame. She looked down at her hands and only then felt the pain of fractured bones and torn flesh.

"Touch me," the voice whispered. *"I will make you whole."*

"No!" Tess screamed. "I would rather bear the pain than be healed by you!"

"If there had been another way..."

"Don't tell me your ends justify the means. You killed my mother!"

"Tess," the voice whispered, yet not a whisper this time. Now it seemed to echo with a thunder that shook her to her bones. *"Theresa Elizabeth Birdsong. Listen to me."*

"No!"

"Listen to me!"

Tess looked up.

"*She* asked *me to do it!*"

The world seemed to spin. And then it went black.

The party had faded into sleep for most of Monabi-Tel. Even Giri had finally given way to sleep. Only Ratha and Cilla remained, sitting together close to the dying embers of the celebratory fire pit, huddled against the chilly nighttime air.

"I never thought I would see you again," Cilla said. "We hear about what happens in Bozandar, what our people suffer."

"What you hear is barely half of what is true," Ratha said. "If Lord Archer had not wandered past the market that day…"

"But he did," Cilla said. "And you are here now."

"What remains of me is here, my cousin. But what remains is a shadow of the man you knew."

"What do you mean?" Cilla asked.

"I have done too much," Ratha said, staring into the embers as if searching for meaning in the flicker of the coals. "I am hardly Anari anymore."

"You will always be Anari, Ratha. That is your birthright."

"Anari do not kill," Ratha said. "At the very least, Anari do not kill without remorse. We were created thus, to be a race who could show men another way. Instead I have become…"

"What?" Cilla asked, her voice sharp. "Just what have you become? Other Anari have borne swords, Ratha Monabi. I and many like me will be bearing them in the days to come. Do you challenge their birthrights, also?"

Ratha shook his head, trying to find the words for what he wanted to say. He had come here planning to kill her brother. When he let the thought simmer and the old anger rose again, he still planned to kill her brother. Not in the heat of battle, but in cold blood. And he knew he was capable of such a thing. Something no Anari would so much as consider.

Yet this woman seemed determined to find in him some goodness that he knew was no longer there to be found. As if by her smile and the soft glow of her eyes she could impart to him the purity of her own heart. Perhaps once his heart had been so pure. But no more.

"I have cleaved a man in two," he said, "and seen the look of disbelief in his eyes as his belly spilled upon the ground. And I have done that without so much as a flicker of feeling, save only the satisfaction of a well-aimed thrust and the relief that there was one less enemy before me. I have stepped in his gore to get to the next of his kind and thrust again. And again. Your heart is as white as the moon, Cilla, with not a single stain upon it. I can feel it. Anyone who knows you can feel it. But mine is not. I am stained, and stained forever."

"Perhaps that is true," Cilla said. "Though I know that my heart is not as pure as you believe. If so pure a heart ever existed, it has not for a long time, save for that of a newborn baby who has not yet known pain or loss, anger or jealousy or regret."

She paused for a moment, as if waiting for him to respond, but he said nothing. She turned his face to hers and continued.

"There are others in this city who have killed. I have heard them tell tales of ambushing Bozandari, and the glee with which they describe their exploits. And I have heard their sobs in the night, when they thought no one could hear and the weight of their deeds came upon them. I cannot imagine that any sane man would bear that weight without sorrow, and I despair that any must bear it at all.

"But some *must,* Ratha. Some must, or we would be but mindless sheep under the staff of the most ruthless among us. Even the *Keh-Bal* councils know this. And when they banish someone into the sands, they kill him as surely as if they drove a sword into his belly."

"The *Keh-Bal* council acts according to the law," Ratha said.

"And its members act as a group. No one of them carries the full responsibility. It is different."

"I sat on a council," Cilla said. He looked up, ready to reply, but she gave him no chance. "They say that *Keh-Bal* erases an Anari from memory, as if he had never lived. It's not true. I remember. I remember the look in his eyes as we passed judgment, the look in his eyes as he dismounted his horse in the desert and we rode away. The old ones told us not to look back, but I did. I saw his face, Ratha Monabi, and that face will never leave me. *I* killed him. Not the council. Not the law. Me. So do not mock me with words about a heart as white as the moon. You bear scars, Ratha. But you are not alone in bearing them, unless you choose to be alone."

"Perhaps I *do* choose to be alone," he said, angry at her rebuke, the more so because he knew it to be just. "If I choose to carry my burdens alone, what right have you to challenge that?"

She rose. "None at all, Ratha. None save this, that a man who carries his burdens alone cannot be loved. And I would that you could be."

She turned and walked away without another word, leaving him with nothing but the dying embers and the echoes of her words. Neither brought warmth to the cold night. There was no warmth to be had.

10

Sara slumbered fully clothed beside Tom, beneath mounds of down-filled blankets. For some reason the cold seemed worse here in Anahar than it had at home in the Whitewater Inn. Perhaps, she had thought as she fell asleep, it was because the walls were made of stone, not wood.

But with Tom next to her and the down over her, she had grown warm enough to sleep comfortably. She was dreaming of standing in the kitchen next to her father, making bread as was the day's custom, when suddenly a dark shadow fell across her dream, a shadow full of terror and stark grief.

Instantly awakened, she sat up in the darkness, her heart hammering loudly. What…?

Then she knew: *Tess!*

Scrambling from the bed, trying not to disturb Tom with her urgency, she found her boots and shoved her feet into them. In the front room, she grabbed her cloak from where she had draped it over a chair back, then whipped it around her shoulders as she stepped into the cold night.

The temperature had fallen dramatically. Even with warmth

still permeating her garments, she shivered and felt her cheeks begin to ache almost instantly. Her hood provided little protection from the bite of a wind that refused to acknowledge any barrier.

She hesitated on the path, trying to hear Tess's call, mentally calling out to her, but there was nothing. If Tess still lived, she was summoning no one's help. But the shadow of trouble still lurked threateningly, and Sara could not ignore it.

Finally she began to run toward the temple. If Tess had gone somewhere freely, that would be the place.

The path to the temple was not that long, but its every curve made Sara want rage at its indirect nature, which slowed her progress.

But finally, panting, her lungs aching from the cold air, she burst into the temple plaza. There a door stood open as if it beckoned her. Without thought for her own safety, Sara ran up the two steps and into the anteroom.

No one was there, though the torches sprang to life at her arrival. Perhaps this was the wrong place?

Yet something drew her forward into the chamber of statues. For an instant she noticed only that the torches there were out and did not spring to life for her. Then she noticed the glow from a heap on the floor.

Tess. It was as if she were surrounded by a pale green glow that moved gently over her. She was clearly unconscious, and Sara caught her breath when she saw dark spots that could only be blood.

"Tess?" She spoke quietly, uncertainly. If someone had attacked Tess, that person might still be there, for the door to the temple stood open.

Sara listened, straining her ears, but heard nothing move. "Tess?" she asked, more boldly this time. She moved closer. "Tess?"

A groan answered her. At once Sara flew to Tess's side and knelt. "Oh, Tess!"

The green light still covered Tess's form, but somehow it did not frighten Sara. She reached right through it to cradle Tess's head. "Tess, can you hear me?"

Another groan answered her; then Tess mumbled, "She killed my mother."

Horror froze Sara. For long moments she could neither speak nor move. "Who?" she said finally, her voice a bare whisper. "Who killed your mother?"

"Her. Theriel."

Sara's shock deepened. "But…Theriel has been dead these many centuries, Tess. It cannot have been her. She was said to be of purest heart and would hurt none. It must be someone other…."

Tess moaned again and slowly sat up. "Touch the statue," she said hoarsely. "Touch the statue of Theriel." Then she looked at her hands, turning them over as if amazed they were still whole. "I was bleeding…my bones were broken…."

Sara, now seriously worried for Tess's mental state, could think of nothing to do but touch the statue herself and prove to Tess that she must have dreamed the horror of which she spoke.

Rising, she stepped toward the cold white statue of Theriel.

"Be careful," Tess said, her voice strengthening. "You may find something there you do not like. As I did."

Sara nodded, but she could scarce believe she would find anything at all. Theriel had been dead for centuries, and the statue was merely stone.

Reaching out, she touched her fingertips to the statue's face.

"Time is out of joint," Tess said from behind her. She sounded almost as if she spoke from some kind of trance.

Before Sara could respond, she felt an electric tingle race

from her fingertips through the rest of her body. Something about the statue…

"Look!" Tess said. "Behind you."

Sara turned and gasped. The green light that had a little while ago surrounded Tess now formed upright in the middle of the room. It swirled as if it were alive and gradually formed into the vague shape of a woman.

Then a voice spoke, whether aloud or in her mind, Sara could not tell. "I am Elanor," the voice said. "My daughters, welcome. As I once gave my protection to Theriel, I shall give my protection to both of you. You have many lessons yet to learn. The first of these is that your mothers did not die in vain, nor did they die against their will. When you have accepted that, return here for your next lesson."

Then the green glow vanished in an instant, and the torches sprang to life. *Elanor* herself? And what did she mean, that her mother and Tess's mother had voluntarily sacrificed themselves?

"By the gods," breathed Sara, stunned.

"She killed my mother," Tess said, struggling to her feet, every muscle quivering with shock and rage. "And now she wants me to follow her direction?"

She faced Sara. "Never."

Morning returned warmth to Anahar, a reminder that this city lay in the south, where the climate was welcoming year-round. Cloaks and other outerwear were soon shed for cooler and more comfortable clothing in keeping with the natural season.

The streets bustled with light and life, but there was a grimness underlying the superficial normalcy, for the shadow of war had already fallen.

Outside town, both men and women were gathering to learn the art of war from Archer, Ratha and Giri. Little by little, as those willing and able to fight headed out to the training field, the traffic on the streets began to thin.

It was through this thinning traffic that Tess and Sara walked toward the temple to meet Cilla. Tess was still filled with so much anger that Sara was sure the air around her must crackle with it. Tess's jaw was set, and her lips formed a tight line.

Finally Sara could hold her silence no longer. "Tess, if you feel this way, why do you go to the temple?"

"Because I can learn in spite of *her.*"

"Elanor?"

"Who else?"

"The gods work in mysterious ways," Sara said sympathetically. "Oft their reasons are not apparent to mortals."

Tess faced her fiercely. "I held my mother's dying body in my arms. I saw the light fade from her eyes."

For a moment Sara seemed unable to speak. Finally she said quietly, "As did I."

Tess froze. Then, slowly, she sagged. "I'm sorry, Sara."

"No need. The wound is fresh for you now. I understand your feelings. I have felt them myself."

"I know you have." Tess looked shamed. "I am being selfish."

"Aye," Sara said with a small smile. "And you are entitled— for a little while, at least. But there will be much loss and much grief in the days to come, and you and I and Cilla must learn everything we can so that we might prevent needless suffering. At the very least, we must extend our powers of healing."

Tess sighed and looked down at her toes. "I'm sorry," she said yet again. "It's just that…to truly remember my mother for the first time, and to remember her dying in my arms…"

Sara stepped closer and linked her hands with Tess's. "I understand. To find my mother after so many years, and to find her thus…" She shook her head.

They shared a look of deep understanding, then slowly resumed their walk to the temple.

"It is to the future we must look," Sara said firmly. "We cannot change the past."

Tess nodded but did not speak. They came around a curve, and the temple Plaza opened before them. Very few people were about, and Cilla was awaiting them by the door.

"I am torn," Cilla said by way of greeting. "I should be training with the others, yet I feel I must do this, as well."

"If we learn," Sara replied, "the hand of an Ilduin may yet do more than a sword."

"It already has," Tess said, remembering. "It already has."

Before they could enter the temple, however, a clear crystal note sounded, followed by a ripple of equally clear tones. Then, from all twelve paths leading to the temple, lines of women began to appear, each leader carrying before her an ornate rack of crystal bells, which she gently shook.

At once Cilla drew Sara and Tess away from the door. "I did not know," she murmured, "that all the clan mothers had been summoned."

"What does it mean?" Tess asked.

"They are gathering to decide matters that will affect all the clans." She looked at Sara and Tess. "I believe they will be deciding whether we go to war."

"I thought that was already decided," Tess said.

"By some clans, yes. But Sharwahi-Tel is not going to fight by itself, nor would the Gewindi or Monabi. All clans must agree. But I did not know they were going to do this by convocation."

"Is that special?" Sara asked.

"It is wholly binding. Once a decision is made, it can be broken only on pain of death. That is why convocations are so rare."

One by one, lines of clan mothers mounted the steps and entered the temple, taking their crystal bells with them. When the last had entered, the door closed behind them.

Cilla spoke. "Now no one may enter the temple, not even us. Not until they have reached their decision."

Tess suddenly looked up at the surrounding hills and shivered with foreboding. "If the Bozandari attack now…"

She left the thought incomplete, but Cilla was already dashing off, calling back over her shoulder, "I'm going to the training field."

Left to themselves, Sara and Tess exchanged looks.

Finally Tess spoke. "I don't know why I thought of that."

"I do," Sara answered. "I feel the same…uneasiness."

"Let's get our horses. Now."

Archer saw Tess and Sara riding toward him from the city along the south road. Nearby, Ratha and Giri were busy organizing the Anari who had thus far volunteered to become part of the army. At the moment there were several hundred; soon there would be many more. It was important for training as well as fighting purposes that units be formed. The units created today would be the kernels of a larger force. Command structure would already be in place.

For now, he mostly watched. He was willing to fight beside the Anari, to give them advice and even to die beside them, but he had sworn never again to lead an army, and he was not about to break that oath.

Turning, leaving Ratha and Giri to a task they were well prepared to handle, he wheeled his mount toward the approaching women. There was little doubt in his mind that they brought word of trouble.

He met them at a point well-removed from the hearing of those practicing for war. At once he noted the dried blood on

Tess's hands and tunic, and his heart squeezed. "My Lady! Why do you bleed?"

"'Tis nothing," Tess said dismissively, apparently eager to plunge ahead with what she had to say, but Sara forestalled her with a wry smile.

"She had a disagreement with Elanor, I believe. But she is healed, and only the blood remains."

"Elanor?" Archer could scarce believe his ears. "She abandoned the world when…when Theriel vanished."

"Apparently not," Tess said tautly. "From what she told me, she has been meddling all along. To no good, it would seem."

From Tess's expression, Archer could see that no disagreement would be tolerated. Nor did he have any basis for one, other than his belief that if Elanor had cared for Theriel, then as a god she must have some redeeming graces.

"But what brings you racing out here?" he asked, determined to find steadier ground in this conversation.

"A feeling," Tess said, glancing at the mountain peaks around them. "The clan mothers have gathered. Can you think of a better time for an attack?"

He certainly could not. He was also annoyed that no one had told him about the convocation. "That creates serious security problems. Someone should have told me."

"Apparently the clan mothers are accustomed to keeping their own counsel," Tess said. "Even Cilla was surprised by their arrival."

"Cilla?"

"Ratha and Giri's cousin."

He nodded, his memory jogged. It had been years now since either Ratha or Giri had mentioned her, but once they had spoken of her freely, indicating a longing neither of them had been prepared to admit at the time.

"We have sentinels at lookouts around Anahar," he said,

more to reassure himself than anything. But looking up at the frigid, glacier-covered peaks and remembering that Anahar had not been built as a fortress but as a place of gathering, he saw many possible problems.

"A word of warning would have been welcome earlier," he said irritably. "Be that as it may, we must deal with the possibilities now."

But even as he spoke, the warmth of the day vanished as if a cloud had covered the sun. A frigid wind, coming out of nowhere, howled across the valley. With its arrival, all the Anari froze in place, stunned by the viciousness of the cold.

Archer bowed his head, allowing his cowl to fall over his face for a few moments. When he looked up again, his voice was weary. "It seems he has found us again."

Tess spoke, her tone pained. "Did he ever lose us?"

Archer merely shook his head. "Ladies, I pray you return to Gewindi-Tel lodgings. Whatever approaches, I would prefer not to have to worry about you, for if you fall into the enemy's hands, I doubt we can survive the days to come."

Tess looked as if she would argue, then bowed her own head and turned her mount back toward town. Sara followed, giving him a quick glance of understanding over her shoulder.

Then the wind bit again, like a ravening beast, blowing open cloaks and shoving back hoods, leaving the hundreds in the valley unprotected.

Grimly Archer rode toward Giri and Ratha, trying to restore order among the shivering Anari before the storm broke fully.

Ardred had Ilduin; that was certain. But how many? And could these few that Archer had learn enough, fast enough?

There was little hope in his heart as his horse's hooves crunched on grass that was already beginning to freeze.

17

Back in their lodgings, Tess and Sara huddled with Tom near a blazing fire. Someone had brought food, an elaborate collection of meats and fruits and vegetables that graced the table like a work of art. All of them ate, but mostly out of necessity, as they listened to the wind rage without.

"No one can stay outdoors in this," Sara remarked. "The Anari are not accustomed to such cold. They don't even have the proper clothing for this."

"Does anyone?" Tess asked. As she stared into the fire and nibbled at a piece of sweet fruit, she realized she was feeling that darkling presence at the back of her mind again. So far it seemed to be just a hint, but she feared that through her it was collecting information. In the past it had felt as if it were claiming her, but now it seemed content to bide and perhaps watch.

The tattoo on her ankle almost seemed to burn, as if it were a brand to remind her of something. She only wished she could remember.

Reaching for the pouch around her neck, she grasped the

stones and felt them begin to warm. As they grew hot, the oily darkness in her mind dimmed even more.

With a sense of relief, she tipped the stones into her palm and studied them. Some glowed with great brightness, but others seemed dulled by comparison.

"Do you suppose," she asked, "that these darker stones are the stones of the Ilduin the Enemy has corrupted?"

Sara leaned over to look. "They do not appear as bright." She lifted her eyes to Tess's. "That is nearly half of them."

"I know."

Tess continued to study them. "I wonder if I should put them elsewhere, away from the stones that are still bright."

"I don't know. But…it wasn't so long ago that most of them glowed brightly, was it?"

"No." The word conveyed all the worry she was feeling. "He makes progress in his plans."

The wind howled with sudden outrage, as if in answer.

"If," Tom said slowly, "evil can rage, then cannot good stop it?"

"How?" Tess asked, slipping the colored stones back into the pouch and tucking it once again within her tunic. "For the most part, the times Sara and I used our powers were…accidental."

"Except for the cleansing of Lantav Glassidor," Sara said with a shudder, remembering the way the man's flesh had burned as her blood had fallen on it. "But that time it was as if I was guided from without."

Tess nodded. "I felt the same. Something came over me."

"The same happened at the Eshkar, the broken statues of the gods. I have only a vague memory of what I did."

Tom spoke. "You appeared to be filled with lightning, Sara. Blue lightning. Your hair even stood away from your body. And when you said 'Be gone from this place,' the attackers actually vanished." He shook his head. "I have seen wonders I thought could never be. And yet they have happened. The rules we have always abided by have changed somehow. The limits of our world have shifted."

Tess closed her eyes, fruit forgotten in her lap. With conscious effort, she sought out the oily dark presence at the back of her mind and pushed it back even further, squeezing it down in size and shape. She gasped as a pain seemed to lance through her head but never ceased her effort. The darkling presence continued to shrink, even as she began to perspire heavily from the effort.

Heat seemed to fill her body, all of it directed against that cold spot of darkness, as if it would burn it away. Even her brain seemed to grow hot, and distantly she was aware that she was gasping.

But the darkness continued to shrink, growing smaller and smaller until, with a small sound, it vanished.

"Tess? Tess, what's wrong?"

She opened her eyes and found both Tom and Sara bent over her. The world seemed to swim a bit, and she realized all of a sudden that her hands were aching from her death grip on the arms of chair. Finger by finger, she forced herself to let go.

"Tess?" Sara's face was close, twisted with fear and concern. "Tess, are you all right?"

"Aye…." It was little more than a sigh. "I got rid of him."

"Who? Who did you get rid of?"

"The presence."

Sara gasped and dropped to her knees beside Tess's chair. "How did you do it?"

"I shrank him until he was gone."

"But how did you know how to do that?"

Tess shook her head. "I don't know. I wish I did." Her thoughts turned toward what had happened in the temple and her encounter with Elanor. Perhaps the goddess had imparted some knowledge to her.

Looking down at her hands, she saw that not only were they healed, but the scars were gone, as well. She turned them slowly, looking at them from every angle.

Deep within, she knew with utter certainty that some kind of knowledge had been passed to her in the temple. But what? And how was she to use it?

Her tutelage was far from over.

Just then, as if coming from a long distance, crystalline music began to approach, nearer and nearer, until it filled the air and drowned out even the bitter wind. Sara ran to the door and opened it, heedless of the cold.

She looked out, then turned to Tess and Tom. "Come," she said, an awed smile on her face. "Come. Anahar sings."

And sing she did. The top-most melody only barely dipped within the range of Tom's hearing, yet as he turned his head, he could see the Anari in the streets swaying to the city's song. Beneath that melody, a trio of perfect voices weaved and danced with each other. More voices joined, some rumbling so deeply that Tom could only feel them in his bones, others sighing and sparkling throughout the middle, until it seemed the air was alive with song and light.

And oh, the light! Tom watched as reds and violets, blues and greens, danced with yellows and other colors yet to be named, for he had no doubt that never had they been seen before this day. The sky was alive with pinpoints of light that grew into balls, then receded to make room for others, the whole a perfectly choreographed tapestry that filled his heart with joy.

"Can you see it?" he yelled to Sara.

"See what?" she yelled back, and only then did Tom realize how loud the sound around them had become.

"The lights in the sky," he replied, pointing. "Every color of the rainbow, and many that no rainbow has ever dared to dream, dancing in the sky."

"I'm sorry, my love," Sara said, shaking her head as she looked up. "I do not see it."

"Nor I," Tess said. She looked at her hands, watching her fingers flick in a pattern that matched the music, as if she were forming it herself. "But I feel it."

Cilla ran up to them, her arms wrapped around her chest as if she were hugging herself, her face almost split open by a transcendent smile.

"I have heard it!" she exclaimed. "I have heard the song of Anahar!"

Tom watched as Sara and Tess hugged her, then introduced her to him. Her eyes lit on the leather across his face for only a moment; then she opened her arms and hugged *him,* too.

"You are the man who brings joy to the heart of my sister," Cilla said. "For that, you are my brother."

"I am honored to meet you, as well," Tom said, unsure of how else to respond. Glancing over Cilla's shoulder at Sara, he awkwardly returned the hug. When Sara merely smiled, he gave way to the joy of the moment and hugged Cilla tightly. "And if you are Lady Sara's sister, then you are my sister, as well."

"You must come with me," Cilla said, stepping away. "There is so much more to hear. For when Anahar sings, every Tel plays its own song. I want to hear them all! Come! Hurry!"

She skipped away, leaving them in her wake, but they quickly caught up. As they entered the neighborhood of Sharwahi-Tel, the song indeed changed. The colors in the sky were more muted, and rusty tans and greens seemed to dominate the spectrum. This was no song of celebration, but instead a song of strength and power, of struggle and conflict, and the promise of ultimate victory.

"Sharwahi-Tel is the closest to Bozandar," Cilla said, her

smile dimming. "Long have they suffered under the boot of the slavers, and long have they struggled. Anahar sings for them of more fighting. And yet…"

"Yes," Tom said. "And yet she promises them freedom if they persevere."

"Exactly," Cilla replied, her smile returning. "I had heard that Anahar sang differently to each Tel, but I did not know that each received a message and a promise. Now I *must* hear them all!"

Tel by Tel, they made their way through the city. In some, the songs seemed almost as a loving mother's tender scold, urging them to join with their kinsmen. In others, the city sang of their proud history and their duty to preserve those rich traditions. Finally, for she had saved her own Tel for last, they approached the Monabi dwellings.

They sensed it at the same moment, their smiles dropping as one, their bodies halting almost as if they had blindly walked into a wall.

For Monabi-Tel, Anahar wept.

The song was that of an old woman whose husband lies gravely ill, or a man burying his brother. As Tom looked up, he saw the barren colors of the desert, burned out by the harsh sun, fading toward a twilight almost devoid of hope for the morrow. Only one crystalline voice, one pinpoint of light, spoke of joy, and even that was a joy dimmed by sorrow.

But not sorrow. For as Tom focused on that single voice and the harmonies that surrounded it, he saw at the fringes not sorrow, but anger. A deep anger that stretched to the soul's very quick, seething within and against itself.

He felt Sara move beside him and turned to see her take Cilla in her arms, watched as the heavy tears rolled down the Anari woman's face.

"I have finally heard Anahar sing," Cilla said softly. "And for my kinsmen, she sings of grief."

"Aye," Tom said. "Grief and betrayal."

"Yes," Tess said, as if his words had crystallized her own thoughts. "Betrayal."

"What have I done?" Cilla cried out, as if hoping the song would answer her. "Has Monabi-Tel not served the hope and joy of the Anari with its every breath? Have we not sojourned among the stones, answering their call whene'er we felt it? Why do you judge us, oh Anahar? Why?"

"Two wolves stalk the one," Tom said, the words forming in the deepest echoes of his heart. "For the one wolf stalks them all."

Archer watched as the Anari rose to the music that seemed to roll out of the city like waves on the sea from a distant storm. Some were exultant, while others seemed to straighten their backs with a newfound pride. Only Ratha and Giri seemed immune to the spirit stirring among their kinsmen.

"Anahar sings," Archer said to them. "I have not heard her song in age beyond age. She calls your brothers and sisters to your side."

"That she does," Giri said, his face impassive as the stone upon which he sat. "She calls them to die."

"Come, now," Archer said. "Despair does not an army make nor a battle win. Even the bitter cold has been washed away by her song. Unless I be deaf to the portents of this world, the song of Anahar brings hope where we had naught but a wish when the sun rose this morning."

"Hope?" Giri said, turning to Archer with anger in his eyes. "Will hope train the thousands who will soon arrive? Will hope arm them? Will hope feed them on the march? I pray thee, my Lord, speak not of hope where Anari sweat and blood must soon flow in rivers. This is not a time for hope. This is a time to kill."

Giri rose and stalked away, his fists clenched. Archer turned to Ratha, concern creasing his brow. "Your brother has never spoken thus, my friend. There is an ice in his eyes that concerns me."

"Yes," Ratha said. "There is. And if you see not that same ice in my own eyes, then you know nothing of us. You have taught us to fight, my Lord. You have taught us to be brave and cold and hard. Our lives you have saved, but our souls you could not. For what we have become, what we must make of our people in this time, is alien to the Anari. Surely you should know this. You made us thus."

Archer studied Ratha's face, words warring within him as he sought a response. Yes, the Anari had been created a race of peace. And yes, he had played a role in that. He and the Ilduin had overstepped themselves, taking for their own conceit a power reserved to the gods. Yet what they had created was a beauty, and a blessing to this world.

"You speak the truth, my friend," Archer said. "I was there in the time of creating your people. The Ilduin and I wished to grace this world with a gift beyond measure, a people of such beauty and purity that all could aspire to their model. Our sin was pride, Ratha, and greatly have we paid for that. But that beauty—your beauty—endures."

"That *beauty* has made us sheep among lions," Ratha said. "Because we lacked the will to shed blood, our daughters have been made into whores and our sons into beasts of burden. Oh, great *beauty* have you created, my Lord. A *beauty* so great that we are bought and sold as trinkets and cattle."

"How long have you hated me thus?" Archer asked, the anger rising in his belly like a white flame.

"I do not hate you," Ratha said. His eyes fell, and his shoulders slumped. "I do not hate you. I am sorry, Lord Archer. My heart is heavy, and war reigns within me. I ought not to make war on the one who has given my brother and me our freedom. I spoke in anger, my Lord. Please forgive me."

Archer looked at him and saw the rippling knots in his shoulders. Ratha and his brother had not started this war for freedom, but their training and experience had set them apart in this time of preparation. Chosen among their people, they bore the yoke of leadership, and it hung heavy and awkward upon them. It was, he realized, a yoke for which he had not prepared them.

"There is nothing to forgive," Archer said, extending his hand. "Save this. It grieves me that you call me your Lord and not your friend."

Ratha managed a grim smile as he took Archer's hand. "I would that I could call you a friend, and I am honored that you see me thus. But right now, Lord Archer, I have no friends. For I can be no friend when too many for whom my heart would rejoice are soon to fall. A foot soldier can ill afford friends and a commander even less. The business upon us is a hard one, and Giri and I must harden ourselves to it. We owe our people no less."

"Then I pray that your heart will soften," Archer said, shaking his head. "For there is no comfort in iron, and a cold heart cannot find joy."

Ratha released his hand and turned to follow his brother. But for a moment, he looked back at Archer.

"If a cold heart cannot find joy," he said, "at least it cannot grieve."

Archer watched Ratha hurry after Giri. A sadness beyond words settled upon his heart. And, for the first time in a river of years, he felt tears sting his eyes. His friend had spoken bitter truth. He and the Ilduin had not created beauty but sheep for the slaughter. And in order to become more than that, they had to give up the very essence of what they had been.

How foolish, that he had thought himself ready to take the mantle of the gods and shape a race of men. So much of this war was due to his own failures. So much blood on his hands.

Perhaps Ratha was right. Perhaps a cold heart was better. For his own heart felt only grief and shame.

18

The song of Anahar pealed throughout the day and into the night. All activity stopped as the Anari listened to the call, for call it was. The clan mothers had decided, and Anahar had approved. During the next days, the ranks of the Anari army swelled as men and women answered the summons, some even having escaped from slavery.

The song had driven back the bitter winter from the valley, so that those who could not find shelter within the city, for the numbers were so great, made camp around the edges of the town. At night the valley twinkled with countless fires and was filled with the songs of those who had come to fight.

Not since the days when the temple had been built had so many gathered here in common purpose.

Among them was Nagari, brother of Cilla. He had no more been able to resist the call than any of his brothers, but his purpose in answering it was different.

He crept among the camps, listening to the talk of war, and began to anticipate the coins he would receive from Bozandar for this information.

Finally, finding a fire far from anyone who knew him, he settled down to share a little ale with a group of men who were laughing with excitement, apparently having no notion of the horror that lay ahead.

Nagari knew. He had seen what the Bonzandar army could do. He had seen villages laid to waste and the hacked bodies of those who had sought to resist. More, he had lately glimpsed something dark and ugly that lay behind the armies of Bozandar. Something that made them stronger and more fearsome—and utterly merciless.

He had no desire to cast himself on a Bozandari sword any more than he would offer himself into slavery.

He had found a way to survive the conquest of his people, and though Anahar, most sacred of cities, might call him to join his kindred, he knew there was no future in that direction.

Shivering against an odd chill, he scooted close to the fire and tried to remain deaf to the men around him, who would soon be wanting to know his clan and why he was not with them.

But even this was only a temporary escape. Sooner or later he would have to visit Monabi-Tel and see his sister. If he failed to do so and someone had recognized him as he wandered this encampment, questions would be raised.

But for now he quaffed another mug of ale to quiet his tumbling, unhappy thoughts. To force himself to remember that he would gain by what he had learned tonight. To remind himself that Cilla was safe, although she did not know it, only because of him.

For Cilla was a beautiful woman, and the slave traders would have seized her long since except for the invisible protection of Bozandar that Nagari had won for her.

He was, he told himself as the ale calmed his anxiety, a good man who had done only what was necessary to protect his sister and himself and their parents. He had sacrificed much and would never be recognized for the good man he was.

Sighing, he drained his mug and tossed a few silver coins to the men who had shared their fire and ale with him.

"I must go to my Tel now," he said. "Many thanks."

They bade him good-night with the smiles of those who thought war was going to be both exciting and good. Nagari knew otherwise but could see no point in arguing. After all, Anahar had summoned them.

Anahar. As he approached the city proper, he felt a shiver of awe. The Bozandari had more than once attempted to eradicate this city. Each time the populace melted away and the old city remained indestructible. Newer buildings could be felled, but not the heart of Anahar.

The Anari claimed that the art of building the city had been lost and hence they could build nothing so indestructible for Bozandar, though they still worked great beauties in stone for their new masters.

But Anahar, O Anahar… There was naught like the heart of Anahar in the entire world.

Nagari suspected the secrets of its building were not as lost as the master stoneworkers claimed, but of this he said nothing to his masters. The secrets that had gone into the building of the heart of Anahar were also the heart of the Anari, and this Nagari would never betray.

He was just approaching Monabi-Tel's quarters in the city when he heard his name called.

"Nagari Monabi."

Something prickled along his spine and made him quicken his step as if he had not heard.

"Nagari Monabi!"

The voice was closer now, and all of a sudden a hand gripped his arm in an iron vice, halting him in his tracks.

"Do you not recognize me, cousin?"

Slowly Nagari turned to look at his captor. At first the face was as strange to him as if he had never seen it before. "I do not…" Then the years seemed to melt away, and ice filled his heart. "Ratha?"

"Aye," Ratha answered. "And my brother Giri, as well."

Giri stepped out of the shadows, and the expression on his face was enough to freeze Nagari to his very core. Some portion of his brain scrabbled for a way to speak, looking for something sensible and safe to say.

"You escaped!" Nagari gasped.

"We didn't escape," Ratha answered grimly. "We were sold for a third time, and on that third occasion our new master set us free. Have you any thought, cousin, for the degradation we suffered?"

"It…it must have been terrible."

Ratha leaned even closer. "It was worse than terrible. You can have no idea what slavery does to the soul. For you have escaped it all these years, have you not?"

"I…I've been fortunate."

"Hmm." Ratha's grip slipped from Nagari's arm to the front of his tunic and lifted him slightly from his feet. "We have been thinking for many years, my brother and I, about how we were first captured. About who it was who suggested that a small group of us leave the ceremony to hunt the boar and surprise everyone. And who did not accompany us for the hunt."

Nagari felt his jaw drop. How could they have guessed? "I was delayed! You had left already!"

"Lies!" Ratha hissed, shoving and releasing him at the same moment, so that he fell against the wall. "How many others of us have you sold into slavery? How many times have you betrayed your own kin? *How many?*"

Nagari wanted to argue with him, to claim innocence, to

deny every possible suggestion that he had betrayed his kind and his kin. But the words would not come. It was as if for once in his life no lie would pass his lips.

"Come," said Ratha, pulling his sword and pointing the tip straight at Nagari's heart. "Tell us the truth. Surely you can speak the truth for once. Tell us how many of your kinsmen you made into pack horses and party whores. Tell us how many families grieve because of you. *Speak!*"

Nagari opened his mouth, his gaze fixed on the sword. He had to deny it. He must deny it, for surely there was no way Ratha or Giri could be certain of their suspicions.

But the words that tumbled out were not the lies he wanted to tell. They were the pain of a heart too long constricted by its own fell deeds.

"I did it to protect Cilla!"

"Pah!"

"I did! Have you no idea what the Bozandari would have done to such a beautiful girl? Can you not imagine the horror she would have faced?"

"I need not imagine," Ratha said bitterly, "for I saw other Anari daughters in bondage. I saw the welts on their thighs and the shame in their eyes. I saw their bellies begin to swell, and the terror in their faces, knowing that soon they would disappear into the night, to be butchered before their babies could shame the honor of a nobleman. Because of you, Nagari! Because of *you!*"

The struggle on Ratha's face was apparent and fierce, but gradually he lowered his sword. At that moment Cilla materialized from the shadows.

Slowly she moved toward her brother, who had struggled to his knees. When she stood over him, she stared down at him impassively.

"Cilla?" he said plaintively. "I did it to save you."

In answer, she spat in his face. The shame in his eyes

turned to anger, and his hand shot out, slapping her cheek. "How dare you?"

He was dead before his last words had faded into the night—indeed before he felt the blow that killed him.

Tom awoke to a warmth stirring beside him and realized it was Sara moving in her sleep. Sleep was a luxury in which she had not indulged much of late. While he had lain resting from his injury, she had nursed him, fretted over him, in a way that left him both grateful and ashamed. She was a strong White-water lass, his Sara, and for that he was grateful. She was stronger than he, and for that he loathed himself.

Slipping an arm around her, he made quiet shushing sounds, hoping to lull her back into the sleep she so desperately needed. He felt her hand settle over his, her skin somehow both tough and delicate, her fingertips slowly trailing along the length of his fingers. His body reacted without conscious thought, warmth growing in his loins and in his heart, and he shifted closer to her. Perhaps she was still dreaming, and if so, he dared not wake her, but the slow movement of her fingers against his sparkled through him like the lights he had seen above Anahar. His shushing sounds faded into slower, deeper breaths, and only then did he hear her soft half-giggle, half-sigh.

For a moment, he froze. But then she whispered, so soft that he would never know whether he had thought or imagined it.

"Don't be frightened, my darling. Lie with me."

His member seemed to react to her words as if with a will of its own, and the reaction was not dimmed as she pressed her buttocks against him. Her hand guided his to her breast, massaging herself with his fingers as if directing him in the caresses she most needed. He felt her breathing deepen and match pace with his, and would not have been surprised if even their heart-beats had fallen into unison, for in this moment he felt more one with her than he could ever have imagined in his boyhood fantasies.

"Aye, my love," she whispered again. "Aye."

Now almost painfully engorged, his shaft sought her as a snake seeks its burrow, answering to a primal instinct that transcended thought. Her thighs and hips shifted, and soon he felt the caress of her wetness against him, calling to him, welcoming him. Their moans rose in unison as he slipped into her and their hips began a dance as old as time itself.

Quiet it began, and patient, for even in his heat he realized that a moment such as this was not to be rushed. Small whimpers that might have been pain or pleasure escaped her lips, and she pressed his fingertips together against her nipple. The dance quickened and slowed to her sighs and shudders, for he was in the thrall of her every breath, her every sound, her every moment. He pushed her hair aside with his cheek and kissed her nape, the first curve of her strong shoulder, the soft flesh behind her ear, tasting the faint salty tang that glistened on her skin, drinking in her scent, her warmth, until he felt as if the world would be complete only if their bodies were joined and their hearts wrapped together, never again to be separate beings, forever one life, one hope, one dream, one thought.

She arched her back the tiniest bit, and he felt as if he had fallen into her, as if she were pulling him deeper with every movement, until he was wholly submersed in her love. His jaw quivered, and now one of her hands slid down to hold him in place as he fought the urge to thrust. His need cried out for satisfaction, but he held it back, still wrapped in the spell of the woman with whom he lay, trying to think her every thought, to feel her every sensation, to make of himself what would most fulfill her, for a woman such as this deserved no less and much more.

Her breathing grew ragged, and, in the dim predawn light,

he watched her lips tremble as her fingers released him and her shuddering whisper emerged.

"Now, my darling. Now."

He plunged deeper, the world losing focus, all that remained was the warmth of her, the breath of her, the taste of her—the love of her. The sparkles began again, this time starting in his toes and dancing up his clenching thighs until they reached his loins and exploded deep within her. The world seemed to grow and recede in waves of joy, fluttering within and cries without confirming her completeness, fanning the warmth in his heart until he would have sworn it shone with a white glow.

One by one, he felt his muscles flutter and then go soft, his body slowly sliding down from the peak into the pillowy depths below. It was if he were riding on a puffy cloud, mist tingling against his skin, her womanhood still embracing him, their fingers still entwined, their breath slowing, until the world began once again to reveal itself before their eyes.

"Oh, Sara," he said, the first words he had spoken since he awoke. He could find no more to follow.

"Aye," she replied, and it was not a question.

He realized he could find no more words because there were no more to be found. Her name alone spoke every thought.

"Sara," he whispered, his head settling to the pillow, his face bathed by her hair. "Sara."

She squeezed his hand and clutched it between her breasts. "Aye," she whispered. "Aye."

In the next room, Tess had listened to the muted sounds, a soft smile on her face. She would never embarrass her sister by speaking of what she had heard, but within her grew a joy that, she knew, was only the barest hint of Sara's bliss. For the briefest moment, having awakened to their stirring, she had felt the caresses on her skin, the ache in her loins. Had she been awake enough to consider it, it might have startled her. Instead, in her still half-asleep state, it had seemed only natural that she could feel Sara's sensations. And only proper to close that door and give her sister privacy in this most intimate of moments.

Now, lying in the growing dawn, she found that she could reopen that door and feel the pleasant satisfaction coursing through every nerve, the warm trickle between her thighs, the comfort of an embrace. For a moment she thought to close the door once again, but the novelty of the sensation prickled her curiosity. Even more, she realized, it was as if the door wanted to be open.

Sara felt the rhythm of Tom's breathing slide back into sleep, leaving her alone with her thoughts. Yet not alone. As if she were watching herself in a mirror, she realized she could feel Tess feeling her. There was no threat in Tess's presence, no hint of shame. She had felt the flicker of that presence earlier, then felt it withdraw, and she knew her sister had stepped back so that she could be alone with Tom. But now Tess had edged closer, drawn by curiosity, restrained by the fear that she might not be welcome.

Sara opened herself with a silent inner smile.

He is such a lovely man, Tess thought.

Yes, Sara thought in reply. *He is all that I could ever hope for.*

And yet he fears he is not enough for you.

I know, Sara thought with a pang of sadness. *If only he and I could talk like this. He would know my heart.*

It is not your heart he doubts, Tess replied, *but his own. The whispers of your soul could not assuage him.*

How long have you known this?

About Tom?

No, sister, Sara thought, stifling a giggle lest she awaken him. *About…this?*

Only just now, Tess thought, compressing her lips. *I'm sorry, Sara. I didn't mean to…*

No! Sara thought. *There is no reason to apologize. In fact…it pleases me that we can share this. I would have wanted to share it somehow, for what I feel is…*

I can tell, Tess thought, laughing quietly.

Aye, Sara thought, once again suppressing laughter. *You can. Oh, Tess, I never imagined I could feel this way. Whatever beauty there be in this world is found in love.*

So true, Tess thought. *Someday…*

I know, sister, Sara thought. *And aye, someday…he will realize.*

So you have already chosen someone for me? Tess thought, a smile creasing her face.

You cannot tell me that you do not know, Sara thought. *Surely you must see it in his eyes.*

His eyes long for one who is gone, Tess thought. *Not for me.*

Perhaps, Sara thought. *Perhaps not.*

Suddenly a thought crossed their minds in the same instant. *Do you realize what this means?*

Aye, Tess began. *If this be so, perhaps…*

…our enemy's advantage is lost, Sara completed. *If this be so…*

…there is hope after all.

"By the gods!" Giri swore. "Ratha…."

Ratha pulled his sword from Nagari's corpse and turned to his brother, every line of his face defiant. "He attacked Cilla. He was vermin."

"He was all that you say and more," Giri said. "He died more swiftly than he deserved. But the law…"

Cilla stepped forward as Ratha wiped the blood from his blade onto Nagari's breeches. Taking his hand in hers, she spoke in a chilling tone. "I am a Monabi judge. I judge that you acted in my defense. Get this…filth…out of our city."

"Yes," Giri said. "Filth."

"Take no joy in this, Giri Monabi," she cautioned. "There is a gulf between that which is necessary and that which is good."

Then she faced Ratha again, studying his face closely. "There is something in you that you need to dispel, cousin. Something dark that will not aid us in the days to come. Take the body out into the mountains and bury it, then remain there and fast until you have purified yourself of this darkness."

"I'll go with you," Giri said at once.

"No," Cilla said. "No. Ratha must do this himself, or he will ever be weak before the darkness."

She looked into her cousin Ratha's face, her own a mirror of sorrow. "You are strong. I know you can do this. Then come back to us, Ratha. Soon."

Stretching a little, she pressed her cheek to his, whispering, "May Elanor guide you and protect you."

Ratha nodded. While his face remained like stone unhewn, his eyes now reflected a troubled sorrow. When he spoke, his voice had grown low and lost all its anger. "My thanks, cousin." Then he clasped hands with Giri, and the two brothers exchanged long looks.

Finally Giri spoke. "I will help you remove the body from town."

There was too much light from the stones in most streets to hide such an act, so the brothers perforce wrapped the body in a bundle of rugs that were sometimes used to make tents. With this they merely appeared to be new arrivals looking for a place to make camp.

Cilla watched them ride away, her heart still hammering from what had passed, but her spirit certain that she had acted rightly. These were no ordinary times. A spy and traitor must be removed before he could cause more harm.

Even if he was her brother.

She had loved Nagari all her life, and she sank slowly against the wall where he had died and let silent tears flow for the brother who had always watched over her, even in earliest childhood. His death, however justified, rent her heart.

But she was Ilduin, and as she was learning however reluctantly, being Ilduin carried a responsibility that sometimes required one to be hard.

She was still weeping when Sara and Tess found her a short while later.

* * *

Both Sara and Tess had been jolted out of slumber by a sudden vision of death followed hard by a searing, aching grief. At once they saw that Ratha had killed a man and understood this man was related to Cilla.

Then both heard her silent cries, "Why, brother? Oh, why?" They nearly collided in the main room of their lodging as they hurried from warm slumber to the aid of their Ilduin sister. A look passed between them, an understanding. Wrapping themselves in their cloaks, they hurried toward the silent cries, toward Monabi-Tel. As their feet flew along the paths, they learned that Cilla had sent Ratha into temporary exile to banish his demons, and that Giri would help him only so far before he must return.

At some level it amazed Tess that Cilla's orders had been so readily obeyed by the brothers. She had never seen them defer to anyone save Archer. But Cilla was more than their cousin, she realized. Cilla was a Monabi judge.

The full meaning of that was not clear to her, but Cilla's grief was as clear as if it were her own. Another glance at Sara told her that the younger woman felt it just as strongly.

Cilla's silent grief led them straight to her, on a street not far from Monabi-Tel's gateway. They found her huddled against a wall, silent tears running down her face.

At once they squatted and gathered around her, supporting her with their presence and caring.

When she looked up, her eyes swollen and reddened, her iridescent black skin wet with tears, there was a kind of wonder in her face. "You heard me," she said.

Tess and Sara nodded. "Can you not hear us?"

Cilla closed her eyes for a few moments, then nodded. "Aye. Then you know what has passed."

"As well as we can."

"My brother betrayed the Tel. More, he betrayed all Anari. He was an instrument of the Bozandari." Her voice broke, and Tess nodded encouragingly.

"He sold my cousins into slavery, and many others, as well. And…and he said he did it for *me*."

Tess suddenly grasped the true well of Cilla's grief, and it was only partly caused by her brother's death. The betrayal was terrible, being made to feel responsible for it, more terrible still.

She reached out for Cilla and hugged her. "You have no responsibility for what your brother chose to do. None. If you had known, you would have stopped him."

Cilla drew back and met Tess's gaze. *You read my heart so well.* Tess nodded. *As now you read ours.*

Cilla bowed her head for a few minutes, as if gathering to herself all the impressions she could of Sara and Tess, of this new and amazing link between them. Then she lifted her head and looked at them both.

This does indeed offer us hope!

Suddenly the three of them were smiling at each other. They had crossed another threshold and could begin to see its possibilities. Grief still hung heavy around them, however, and when Cilla pushed herself to her feet, they were not surprised by what she said.

"I need us to go somewhere together," she said. "Some place where I can talk freely about my brother. None among the Anari must know, but…"

Tess understood. "Come to our lodging. Tom is there, but Tom is not Anari, and he understands the need for secrets."

"Aye," Sara agreed. "He has a way of seeing to the heart of things."

Back at their lodgings in Gewindi-Tel's area, Tess built up the fire on the hearth, and Sara brewed a soothing tea. Cilla wept quietly for a while, but gradually calmed and began to speak of her childhood with Nagari and how she had worshipped him. And then how betrayed she had felt when she learned he had been working for the Bozandari and claimed he had done it to protect her.

"My life," she said, her voice raw with pain, "is worth no more than any other's."

"Nor," said Sara gently, "do I think he did it only to protect *you*. That may have been his excuse, but it was not his only reason."

Cilla sighed and sipped her tea, allowing its warmth to calm her. "I did something tonight of which I am not proud, although it was my right. I stood witness to a murder and let the killer go. Indeed, I told him to hide the body. As a judge, I had the right to declare that Ratha had done no wrong. But I had no right to conceal the deed."

"These are difficult times," Tess said. "I think we will more than once be required to do things of which we are not proud."

Sara nodded, sharing the memory of what she had done to Lantav Glassidor. The sight of her blood burning the man like molten fire was not one she would ever be comfortable with.

Cilla nodded as she saw the scene in her own mind. "My poor sisters," she said at last, and sighed yet again.

"We must look forward," Tess insisted. "We will have the rest of our lives to look back and grieve for what we have done, but for now, for the sake of all Anari, we must look forward."

"Aye," Cilla agreed sadly. "Aye. 'Tis our duty."

But duty was cold comfort indeed.

With the first touch of dawn's chill light, Erkiah Nebu arrived in Anahar. Old and lame, and largely ignored by the Bozandari, he was nonetheless the greatest prophet of his times. A few of the things he had prophesied had quickly put him out of favor, which was much to his own liking. It was enough to write down what he saw and trust that those who cared would take what they needed from it.

But the summons from Archer Blackcloak—Annuvil, as Erkiah knew but kept secret in his own heart—had excited him. He had hired a wagon and two horses to make the trip as swiftly as he could to Anahar, trusting his second sight to keep him safe.

As it happened, he had twice needed to dodge patrols that might have made what was left of his life extremely painful, but he had also gleaned information he was anxious to share.

As a younger man he had come to Anahar several times to drink its wonders and stand within the embrace of its temple walls when the mothers allowed it. He thought of this place as the heart of the world, and as he entered its rainbow-hued streets, he felt the incredible love there. He did not know if that love came from the stones themselves, or from the long ago masons who had shaped them. Nor did it seem to matter. Anahar's beauty went to its very soul.

He remembered the location of Gewindi-Tel with no difficulty, and found his way to Archer's lodgings within easily, for, as he stepped through the gate, he felt the shift in the warp and woof of reality that indicated the great power of Ilduin.

He paused, astonished, for it had been a long, long time since he had sensed even a small touch of such power, but now it seemed great almost beyond description. Near where he stood, the very fabric of reality had been altered, and he could sense it as if some spark made the hair on his arms rise.

He thanked the gods that he had lived to experience such. Perhaps the end of exile was at hand. Perhaps they were nearing the restoration of the First Age. He hoped he might live long enough to see it.

Then, turning his cart over to a pleasant Gewindi girl, he climbed down. He gave the girl a coin and received a warm smile in return.

He hobbled directly toward a door that seemed to call to him. At his knock, it was opened at once by a young woman who appeared, to his inner eye, to glow with a blue aura.

"My lord Annuvil has summoned me," he said. "I am Erkiah Nebu, my lady."

At once he was ushered inside and immediately knew that he stood in the presence of three Ilduin. The one with the blue aura, the one with the amber aura, who said she was Cilla, and the one with the white aura, who called herself Tess.

"Tess," he said, and his heart leaped a little. "'Tis but a temporary name for one much older."

She looked perplexed, but he chose not to say more. To reveal too much could be an evil thing. Time and the gods had their own pace for revelation.

Then a young man with a leather strip over his eyes appeared in a nearby doorway. At once shock rippled through Erkiah, and he clutched at his heart.

"Thank the gods I have seen this day!"

No one questioned him. Instead, the women hurried to settle him into a comfortable chair, and to offer him tea and bread. They seemed to understand that an old man might have found the journey from Bozandar to be exceedingly wearying, but fatigue had left his old bones the moment he set eyes on the youth.

"Wonder of wonders," he murmured as he accepted the tea and bread with thanks. "Wonder of wonders."

Sara, with the beautiful blue aura, sat close by and encouraged him to drink the strengthening tea. "It is so good of you to travel such a long distance," she said.

He nodded, but his attention was riveted to the young man. "I have lived to see it," he said, his voice cracking with awe. "I have seen him who was prophesied. The Foundling. The prophet who was foretold."

"Yes," the woman who called herself Tess replied. "This is a time of portents aroused."

"Your full name is *Trey-sah*," Erkiah said.

"Yes," Tess answered, surprised because even she had only remembered her full name in the presence of the statue of Theriel. "Theresa."

"It may be that in your world," Erkiah replied. "But you know what it means in this one."

Tess thought back to her first hours at the caravan massacre and the first words she had learned. The young girl she had clutched to her bosom, fighting vainly to save her life. The girl who had soon been…*trey-sah*.

"Dead," Tess replied.

"And yet not," Erkiah said, looking at her. "For the name you choose to be called is *Teh-su*."

The girl had whispered those words as the bane poison spread through her body. *Teh-su. Teh-su.*

"That means 'help me.'"

"Yes," said Erkiah.

"She that was dead, come to help," Tom said, his face frozen. "It means, *The White Lady returns.*"

Erkiah nodded and placed a hand on Tom's shoulder. "Yes, my son. And that is your lesson for today. Never see so far that you miss what is right before you."

But Tess barely heard his words to Tom as shock and something very like horror filled her. The White Lady returns? Theriel returns? Did that mean she was Theriel? Or merely like Theriel? Her mind reeled as she tried to absorb this news even as she wanted to reject it.

Erkiah turned to the Ilduin. "You have much to do, and this is not the place to do it. Be at ease, Lady Sara. I will care for him. You must learn the ways of the army."

"But we…" Tess began. Her mind had become mired in the

single question of her identity, something she had increasingly managed to put aside these past weeks, focusing instead on the now and the immediate future.

"You are all that stands between brave Anari and death," Erkiah said. "For bravery is poor, if it have not eyes to guide it."

"I do not understand," Tess said. Indeed, she began to think she understood nothing at all.

"Oh, I do," Cilla said, nodding as she looked into Erkiah's eyes. "Come, sisters. We are needed."

20

"How far?" Archer asked, looking at the three Ilduin who stood with him on a bluff.

In the valley below, groups of Anari tried to step, turn and swing their swords in unison. The training was slow, frustrating work. But Jenah and Giri had set themselves to the task, and now each moved from one group to another, their voices sharp as they barked corrections.

"We do not know," Cilla said. "But they heard my heart from halfway across the city. Perhaps, with further training and practice…"

"Yes," Archer agreed. He turned to Tess. "When did you know of this?"

"Only this morning," Tess answered, looking at Sara. For the sake of her sisters' privacy, there was much she could not say. "Perhaps had I not been half-asleep when first I felt it, I might have questioned it and, in that questioning, denied it. But I know it to be true."

"And think of what it could mean for our army," Cilla urged. "The commanders…"

"Could coordinate their maneuvers," Archer said, clearly seeing the potential in this new knowledge. But the dark hive of Lantav Glassidor nagged at his mind. "It is true that this would benefit us. But we cannot become what we seek to destroy. There was evil in the hive, and not simply in the one who controlled it."

Sara looked up as a flock of birds wheeled on the wing, following an impulse that only they could detect. "Look, Lord Archer. They fly as one, yet they cause no evil."

"And we are not a hive," Tess said. "I do not wish to bend my sisters' will to my own, nor they to bend mine to theirs. Each of us has within her a door to close if she wishes, and each of us respects that. What we offer, we offer freely, both to each other and to you. We would have it no less."

"Erkiah has seen it," Cilla said. "It bodes ill to balk at the words of a prophet."

He nodded. He had been pleased to hear that Erkiah had answered his summons and come to Anahar. Even now, he was sure, young Tom was knocking eagerly at the door of wisdom. A door Erkiah would open for him, guiding him through the corridors beyond. Archer had known the old prophet for years beyond counting and knew his heart was true. If he had seen this…

But Archer had once before placed his hopes in the combined strength of the Ilduin, and of that had come the holocaust of Dederand. They, too, had been good women, faithful in service and true of heart. Like the three who stood before him, they, too, had offered their aid in time of need. But what they had wrought…

"I must think on this," he said. "I know we do not have the luxury of time, but on this matter I cannot act in haste. I have done so before, and my haste brought great destruction."

Cilla drew a breath as if to object, but Tess stilled her with a hand on her arm. "Aye, you have told me a little of it. Be assured that we stand ready to act at your command."

With that, she nodded to Sara and Cilla. "Come, sisters. He needs time to decide."

They nodded and followed her, leaving Archer with his own thoughts. He watched the growing army below him, now in the thousands, and knew how ponderous such a body could be.

Fate was among the greatest enemies in war. A horse lamed by stepping into a hole. A wagon wheel come free, the cargo spilled across the path. Over such mishaps did every commander fret, for they were certain to occur, though none could say when or where, and could stall a thousand men on the march, leaving them disordered and easy prey.

Beside such Fate stood its brother, Ignorance. Many a battle had been lost because the commander knew not where the enemy, or his own army, might be. A trail unseen, a path unmarked, an army fighting vainly with one wing as another wandered lost for hours, trying to find the field. Precious hours.

And behind Fate and Ignorance stood their father, Time. A human enemy could be defeated or outwitted, but Time marched onward, implacable, unceasing. Oft had a general wept for just one more day to prepare, just one more hour for a rider to carry his message. But Time cared not for such tears of regret, nor did it heed such pleas. It must be met, or missed, for it would not change course.

If what these three women offered was true, then the Anari could confront those three great enemies—Fate, Ignorance and Time—on more equal ground. Not fully equal, to be sure, for any and all could outwit even the greatest plan.

But the Bozandari faced those enemies, as well, and Archer had no doubt that numbered among their ranks were Ilduin-bound servants of the Enemy, aiding their commanders in their deadly intentions. For the Anari to march forth without such aid would be folly, and certain death.

Once again, Archer realized, he must trust in the Ilduin. Once again, he must reap both the benefits and the consequences of their power. The prophecies could not be put aside. The time was now.

He summoned a young Anari to him. "Go to the temple and find the three Ilduin. Tell them they must learn well, for great will be our need."

"Yes, Lord Archer," the boy said. "I will run like the desert wind."

As the boy scampered away, Archer felt the hollow in the pit of his stomach, the empty hole of pride humbled. Ratha had been right. Watching the boy disappear among the rocks, Archer realized that if he and the Ilduin had created beauty, it was a beauty to which they now owed a heavy debt.

The time had come to repay it.

Tess was barely aware that Cilla went to the door of the temple in answer to a knock and had a brief conversation with an Anari lad. She was nearly transported beyond awareness of the world around her.

The more time she spent in the temple, the more reality seemed to shift, as if it were a fluid thing. Or as if it were an overlapping picture of some sort. It not only made her feel that things were out of joint, but she also sensed that somehow it was within her power to focus the fuzzy image of reality.

But how, she did not know.

She moved slowly through the winding corridors, stopping at each new image to contemplate it, to touch it. And when she touched it, very often she would hear distant music. Distant yet not distant, for while it sounded far away, it seemed to spring from some deep well within *her*. A communication of some sort, but in a language she did not understand.

The only thing she knew for certain was that each hour in the temple transformed her in some way beneath the conscious level. She felt increasingly…different.

But the difference did not frighten her. Somehow it managed to make her feel comfortable with the internal earthquakes that were altering her forever.

Her only concern was that, lacking memory, she might not have the wisdom to handle what was happening to her.

Yet she moved on, taking the next step, needing the next change as if the building blocks of her being were somehow being replaced in their correct order, her Ilduin sisters coming behind her.

Sometimes the music nearly made her weep. Other times it filled her with joy and wonder. Each step was taken with both hesitation and excitement. For while she was called Tess, she had learned her real name. Theresa. *Teh-suh. Help. Trey-sah. Dead.*

It means more than that, Tess heard someone think. The voice of the thought was neither Sara's nor Cilla's, though both looked at her immediately. They heard the thought also. Nor was this the voice of Elanor, who had not deigned to speak to Tess since her startling revelation days earlier. This was a voice that Tess had heard in her dreams for the past fifteen years. It was the voice of her mother.

Yes, my love, the voice said. *It has been far too long for you, but only a moment for me.*

But you're…

Yes, I am, Tess. Beyond a veil that not even the gods dare to rend. And yet, they did. For you.

What do you…?

First a mere pinprick, her mother continued, *on the night you were conceived. A tiny opening through which your true essence*

could be passed on, from your earliest moment. And then…another
tear. To bring you here.

Tess could hardly hear the words, for she was focused on the
sound of her mother's voice. The touch of her spirit once again.
Childhood memories scrolled by so rapidly that she could not
grasp them, yet still the pieces of her life began to take form.

There will be time for that later, Tess, her mother said, in that
firm voice Tess had heard so often in childhood. The voice of
displeasure with a child distracted from the task at hand. *There
is much for you to learn, and not much time in which to learn it.
You cannot look to the past, for you are needed in the present.*

But I feel so…lost, Tess thought.

*Of course you do, dear. For you are lost. Caught between a past
you cannot remember and a future you cannot foresee. But you
know where you are now.*

In the temple at Anahar, Tess thought, an edge of childhood
sarcasm in her tone.

You say it as if knowing that means little, her mother replied.
*Yet it means more than you realize. The more completely you know
a single moment of your life, the more completely you know life
itself.*

Why did you…? Tess's thought began, but her mother did not
wait for her to finish.

*The past again, my dear. It was necessary. And while you never
knew it, the touch of your hands on my face in that moment made
it easier to be ushered through that veil. I went freely, Tess. And I went
certain of your love. Certain of your heart. Certain of your goodness.*

You left me, Tess said, her anger building again.

Yes, I did. To complete you.

To complete me? How?

Ilduin blood must be unchained, her mother said. *The daughter's gifts cannot fully emerge if the mother still lives. That is why
it most often skips a generation. From the moment of that first pin-*

*prick in the veil, I knew you. And from that moment I knew I would
have to leave you, and leave you far too soon. In that first instant
of your life, I knew, and I asked only that I might have time to see
the woman you would become, and that my leaving would come
without warning.*

It had been a freak accident, Tess now remembered. One moment they were walking. Then Tess had dropped a parcel and stopped to pick it up. Her mother had not noticed and had stepped on ahead. The truck had seemed to come out of nowhere, and Tess had known the truth from the first, sickening thud. She had turned to see her mother lying limp on the road, her head at an impossible angle.

I did not feel anything, her mother thought. There was no pain, dear. I was numb from the first moment, and yet I heard your voice, felt the touch of your hands, felt your grief, felt the purity of your soul. Had I voice to speak, I would have told you how much I loved you. But I could not, and that was my only regret. That was the price I paid for not wanting to know when it would happen. When it did, I didn't have time to say goodbye.

Tears welled in Tess's eyes, for now she experienced that moment through her mother's heart. *I'm sorry.*

It is I who should be sorry, Tess. Sorry I was too afraid to face what would happen, sorry I had extracted a promise that it would happen without warning, and instantly. Sorry that I thought of myself and my own pain, rather than of you and yours.

I couldn't have…

Perhaps not, dear. But I had to. And my only regret is that, knowing I would have to, I did not choose to do it better. For you.

Oh…mom…

Tess sobbed, shaking, and felt the steadying arms of Cilla and Sara slip around her, even as their thoughts wrapped her spirit in a comfort that, if not enough, was more than she could have imagined before this day.

And then she felt her mother's hug, as real as if she were standing there. Tess fought the urge to open her eyes, lest she see her.

I have always been with you, my dear. Always. Even from beyond this veil, I could see you and send my heart to you. You know you felt it.

Yes, she had felt it. So many times. The night her first lover had left her and she had wept into her pillow, her mother had been there. The day she had enlisted in the Army, so frightened of what lay ahead, her mother had been there. The first time she had treated a wounded man, his eyes filled with terror, as she took his hand, her mother had been there to ease her own terror, so that she could comfort him. Again and again, her mother's spirit had come to her, quieting her fears, celebrating her joys, soothing her pains.

Yes, my dear. And those were only the times you felt me. There were so many others. I wanted to be with you every moment, to feel with you every moment. But in the way of things, it would have been selfish of me. I had to stand at a distance, just beyond your perception, to let you grow and think and learn on your own.

A day ago, Tess would not have understood. But this morning, with Sara, she, too, had stepped back. Yes, her mother would have done the same. Painful as it would have been, she would have done it. A thought niggled at the fringes of her mind until she remembered her mother's first words.

What did you mean…'it means more than that'?

Finally, her mother thought, *you come back to the present.*

Mother…

Tess heard her mother's laugh, if only for an instant. Then her mother's thoughts darkened.

Trey-sah not only means dead, but also death.

You mean…?

I mean, dear, that the spirit within you has enormous power. The choice will be yours, moment by moment, which you will bring.

Help. Or death.

21

Erkiah and Tom sat before the fire in the main room of the lodging. Both sipped on mugs of Anari ale, potent and delightful on the tongue, although, Tom thought, nowhere near Bandylegs Deepwell's ale. A shaft of homesickness speared him, and he wished he and Sara were at home, sitting in the public room of Sara's father's inn, drinking his ale and listening to the tall stories that wiled the winter away.

But he was here, in Anahar, far from home and among strangers. Wishing it were not so would change nothing. And, he thought, when they did return to Whitewater, what tales they could tell.

"Losing your sight is not such a bad thing," Erkiah said, dragging Tom back to the present. "Many a prophet has been misguided by his eyes. No, you will turn inward to where the truth lies."

"What truth?" Tom demanded. Anger over his condition was bubbling like a slow-cooking pot. He knew he would be dead without Tess's intervention, but the price had been a high one. Sara might still love him now, but he was certain that with time she would grow weary of his disability.

"The truth you were born to speak," Erkiah answered simply. "A prophet's lot is never an easy one, lad. Never. But no one's lot will be easy in the coming days. War and worse broods on the horizon."

"And only by passing through it will we find ourselves."

Erkiah cocked one white bushy eyebrow at him. "You prophesy even now."

Tom shook his head and set his mug on the stone table beside him. "Anyone could have said that."

Erkiah snorted.

"What is the importance of the Foundling?" Tom asked. He hoped that somewhere in the morass his life had become, he could see some thread of purpose other than his love for Sara.

"The Foundling is the harbinger. Your arrival marks the beginning of the fulfillment of the old prophecies. But there is more than that, Tom. The words that you speak will guide those who must fight the evil that faces us."

Erkiah must have seen the distress on Tom's face, for he reached out and touched the young man's arm. "Fear not, Tom. Yours will not be the only wisdom. There are others. But in the most essential moments, they will turn to you, a blind man, to help them see. That is the prophecy of the Foundling."

This was far from the adventure Tom had always dreamed of, far removed from his untutored visions of battle. What he had seen of battle had been supreme horror and ugliness. Perhaps he was lucky that would not be his role, even if he felt he was letting down his friends.

"You are sure?" he asked Erkiah.

"I am sure of who you are, aye," Erkiah answered. "Now close your eyes and look inward, for there you will find your truth."

Behind the leather mask Lady Tess had given him, Tom obediently closed his eyes. At first he could think only of how life had betrayed him, leaving him virtually blind in the act of saving him. But gradually his anger eased. He was not one to pity himself, and only a few mental steps away from his anger was the realization that he had been saved by Ilduin power from certain death. And that he was fortunate Lady Tess had known how to make it possible for him to see. It was not the hawkeye vision he had once enjoyed, but he *could* see whatever he looked directly at without the light hurting his eyes.

And at night, by starlight, he could see as well as any predator.

But he was not to be a predator. Oddly his thoughts drifted to the snow wolf that had come to bow to the Lady Tess, and he wondered if that wolf and its kin were still in the northern woods. Or if the unnatural coldness of the winter had forced them farther south in order to eat.

Thinking of the wolf's eyes, he felt almost as if he were falling into those golden orbs, so not human, yet so strangely expressive. He had never seen the like. Few humans ever saw the snow wolves, for they were shy of people and hid deep in the forests.

But this one had bowed to Tess, an act that flew in the face of everything Tom thought he knew. And those golden eyes, so strangely intelligent...

He was falling toward them in his mind, and as he fell, he seemed to be passing through a door.

Tess sat on the floor with Cilla and Sara huddled around her, trying to comfort her. Although it was odd, even as grief tore at her, she felt little need of comfort. It was as if she needed to let herself shatter with the pain in order to find peace with who she was.

For she knew now that she came not from this world. Cilla and Sara had seen her world with her. She had been a healer.

She had come from a very different place, where carriages didn't need horses and armies fought with weapons this world could not imagine.

But this world, too, had weapons and threats, ones she had never dreamed of as a child. And somehow, somewhere, there must be a link, because she was *here*.

Shaking, she remembered her mother's warning not to look into the past, and bit by bit she understood why. The things she knew about her birth world were of little use here. Worse, memory would have made her initial transition all the harder. Now *this* world seemed the more real to her.

And deep within, she understood that she had been *hidden* in that world until it was time for her to come here.

Finally her shaking stopped. For the first time she realized that huge tears had tumbled down her cheeks and dampened her tunic. At last she could feel the loving comfort her sisters offered her.

Sniffling, she wiped away her tears with her sleeve. "I'm sorry," she began to say, but was interrupted.

"I don't know how I would have borne such news," Cilla said. "Please don't apologize."

"You heard?"

"All of it," Sara said. "Including that you are not from this world, and that the veil was rent between life and death to allow you to pass. You must be important, Tess."

Tess shook her head, wiping away another tear. "No more important than either of you. It is together that we become a force."

"But the decision your mother had to make..." Cilla said. "This was planned."

Tess looked at her. "How are we to know that the same plan wasn't made for you? For *all* of us?"

Sara's eyes clouded. "It was made for me, Tess. But not by any force of Theriel. My mother, too, had to die so I could emerge."

"Oh..." Tess said, further words dying in her throat. She had not even considered how her mother's revelation would affect Sara. "Oh, my sister Ilduin..."

"It is a cruel gift," Sara said, "that requires mother and daughter to be torn apart for the gift to be opened. If the choice had been offered me, I would have rejected it."

"But it was not offered," Cilla said. "To any of us. My mother's passing was twelve years ago. After Ratha and Giri were taken, Monabi-Tel set off as one in their wake. It was our first, and to now our last, experience of battle. We came upon a Bozandari force near the coast, and they fell upon us with brutal skill that none among us had the knowledge to match. We knew the fight was hopeless almost from the start. Many of our kinsmen died that day, and greatly diminished was the soul of our Tel. For in the last group fighting, as the rest were drawing away, was my mother. And there she fell, the victim of her own son's betrayal."

"Oh, Cilla," Tess said, reaching out to squeeze her hand. "I am so sorry."

"It is but a memory now," Cilla said. "I have shed my tears for her. And I have seen her death avenged."

"Your brother?" Sara asked.

"Slain," Cilla said, an icy hardness in her voice. "Last night. Do not ask me to speak more of it, for I cannot. But his death was just."

They sat in silence for a moment, their thoughts clouded and cloaked, each in her own grief. Finally Tess spoke.

"So we have all suffered, and for the plans of the same Enemy. For have no doubt, Cilla, it is he that we face as we ride off to battle Bozandar."

Cilla nodded. "We truly are one."

"Not entirely," Sara said. "The snow wolf didn't bow to *me*."

Cilla picked up the images immediately from Sara's mind.

"My word," she breathed. "That is…a portent. In legend, the snow wolves bowed only to Theriel."

As soon as the name was spoken, the walls of the temple began to dance with light and a quiet tone sounded.

"The name has power," Sara murmured.

"Yes," Cilla said. "But never has the temple answered to her name before."

Cilla closed her eyes and tried to remember every word her mother had ever spoken about the temple. There was a song, a song her mother had sung to her only once, on the day her womanhood had begun. The memories of the day were vivid, for the women of her Tel had gathered her into their midst, each passing along some secret known only among the adult women. Some of those secrets had made her smile. Others had made her blush. All had been important, in one way or another, in her life.

But the song her mother had sung, that alone had grown dusty in her memory, for never before had she heard it, and never again since. How had it begun? She tried to float back to that day, to her mother's comforting scent beside her, the lilt of her voice, the touch of her hand….

> *Elehoheh Tehrel onandar, am dahnen ahnommen*
> *Al Tehrel dahnen Anahar, ir sahn geloreten.*
> *Elehoheh Tehrel onandar, am noyen farloteeg*
> *An Tehrel dahnen Anahar, ir shahtellan ahseeg.*

She opened her eyes and realized she had sung the words. But not she alone. The temple had sung them with her, for she could still hear the echoes of its voice in the silence.

"What was that?" Tess asked, her eyes wide.

"I do not know its name," Cilla said. "It is a song of the Anari, though I heard it only once. My mother sang it to me on my blessing day…the day I became a woman. We have a ritual for such things. The older women pass on the elder secrets then. This was the secret my mother passed to me. I had forgotten it until this moment."

"What does it mean?" Sara asked. "I fear that, despite our sojourn with Gewindi-Tel, I have learned only the barest few words of your language."

"The translation is poor in your speech," Cilla said. "Great mother Theriel's heart, given in her name, Theriel's gift to Anahar, residing within us. Great mother Theriel's heart, her life renewed, Theriel's gift to Anahar, victory in her struggle."

"The temple sings to her name," Sara said, "because she has returned."

"Yes," Cilla said, turning to Tess. "'Great mother Theriel's heart, her life renewed.' That was the pinprick of which your mother spoke. Theriel's heart, given to you, at the moment you were conceived."

"If the legends are true," Tess said, shaking her head, "the world was torn apart over Theriel's heart. And now the Enemy seeks it once more. I carry the heart of a dead princess into a land that was destroyed for her love. I cannot bear this weight."

"My mother's sister, the mother of Ratha and Giri, also whispered a secret to me on that day."

"Yes?" Tess asked, looking at her.

Cilla took her hand. "Sometimes the weight of life asks not if we are able but only if we are willing. For it is in the will that our ability lies."

Tess let out a bitter laugh. "We had a similar thought in my world, though we expressed it with less beauty than in yours. Ruck up, suck up and press on."

"I do not understand the words," Cilla said, "but the meaning is clear enough."

"Yes," Tess said. "But saying it makes it no easier to do."

"If it helps," Sara said, squeezing Tess's hand, "you do not walk alone. We will…how did you say?…ruck up, suck up and press on with you."

Tess gave her a bleak smile.

"And that may be all the hope we have."

22

Three days had passed since Archer had sent the young Anari lad to Tess with word of his decision. The boy had returned that same day to tell Archer he had delivered the message as promised. But Archer had not seen Tess or her Ilduin sisters since. Even at night, when he had returned to the city to rest, he had found her chambers empty. Tom said that the women had gone to the temple, and there they had stayed. For three days.

Time, he thought, looking at the map spread on a table before him. If the map was accurate, and he had no cause to doubt the Anari scouts who had drawn it, his greatest enemy was time. He had no way to know whether Bozandari patrols had heard the song of Anahar, nor whether they would understand its import. Hour by hour, day by day, the ranks of the Anari in the valley below him swelled as more Tels answered the call. Eleven of the twelve Tels were here already, and runners from the twelfth had said they would arrive tomorrow.

How long had it been since the twelve houses of the Anari came together like this? Even on feast days, only a relative handful from each Tel came to Anahar for the celebrations. The rest were needed at their telners to care for children, tend to crops and see to the other day-to-day matters of life. This was a time beyond all memory, even a memory that stretched as far as Archer's.

"We will number perhaps eight thousand in our ranks," Archer said, looking up from the map. "We must keep many behind, to protect the children and our trains. And the temple."

"Fear not for the temple, Lord Archer," Giri said. "She can protect herself."

"Aye," Jenah nodded in agreement. "Still, there are many who are too young, too old or too injured to fight in the ranks. They can protect each other and our supplies. Our needs will not be great, so we can keep our trains small."

"No," Archer said, shaking his head. "We know not what our needs will be in full. It is better to have and not need than to need and not have. When the hour of decision falls upon us, I do not want our people scattered in the hills, searching for food.

"Our advantage," he continued, "lies in the Bozandari not knowing our numbers. Never have they encountered more than a few hundred of us. They take us for sheep who will not band together as wolves, and thus their forces are but a fraction of what we could face. A dozen legions guard the realm of Bozandar. But that realm is vast."

He pointed to the map. "Only two legions are near the Anari lands, and but one of those actively in our midst. A Bozandari legion numbers six thousand strong. And this one is broken into four camps—now three, if they have abandoned the one near Gewindi-Tel. Six thousand men are the boot of Bozandar on the neck of the Anari. They have been enough."

"But no more," Jenah said. "Now we have the greater numbers."

"Numbers, yes, for the moment," Archer agreed. "But we have not yet their skills. And our numbers will only be the greater until Bozandar realizes that we have united. If we cannot secure our border by then, this other legion will march south. And another after that. And yet another after that. We must crush those within our lands and make ourselves secure before they can bring the full weight of Bozandar upon us. We battle not Bozandar but time."

"Aye," Giri agreed, his dark eyes seeming to create living stone from the markings on the map. "Time indeed. The enemy may speak to each other through their captive Ilduin, but they cannot transport their numbers by thought alone. As soon as we fall upon one camp in strength, the others will know, as will their masters in Bozandar. The hourglass is then turned against us."

Jenah nodded. "We must choose our line of advance carefully. The other two camps will rally toward the one we strike. We must be sure we lure them onto ground that favors us and limits them."

They studied the Bozandari dispositions in silence, each weighing the same strengths and weaknesses. Archer knew the import of this decision and found himself wishing there were some other wisdom upon which he could lean. Giri and Jenah would accede to his decision, and on that decision would rest the fate of their people. A people created for peace, now bound for war.

"Here," he said, pointing again to the map, "in the Terami Hills. It is neither the largest nor the smallest of their forces. It lies between the others, yes, but to converge upon us they must follow these two passes, here and here. And they must meet in this valley, less than a day's march from our first target. They will need two days to reach it. If we can subdue the first camp quickly, we can turn and be ready as they emerge from the passes."

"We cannot strike first at the coast," Jenah agreed. "The hills are our home, and their ships can bring support too quickly. And to strike in the mountains would leave us too long and difficult a march to meet their response."

"Yes," Giri said, nodding, tracing lines through the symbols. "And they have many routes along which they could fall upon us as we come down from the mountains. Lord Archer has chosen wisely. Our victory lies in the Terami Hills. So it will be."

"So it will be," Jenah echoed.

"So it will be," Archer agreed, the weight of each word a boulder upon his back.

Time. They were at war with time.

The purification did not take as long as Ratha had expected. Digging his cousin's grave in rocky soil had in itself proved a lesson. Now that he had filled it in and covered it with boulders to protect it from scavengers, he was able to sit wearily on a rock and contemplate the amazing truth of mortality.

It wasn't that he hadn't seen others die, for he had. It wasn't that he hadn't killed others, for most certainly he had killed many.

What struck him now was the very fragility of life. Men had been endowed with the ability to snatch it away with a single blow but not to restore it once taken.

His people had always been peaceful, treasuring life in themselves and others, but now, in the reflection of his cousin's death, Ratha saw how far he had diverged from the path of the Anari.

It was then, in his sorrow for what he had done and how far he had strayed, that he realized how the darkness had overtaken him. He saw clearly what had concerned Cilla.

A true Anari would have taken Nagari before the judges. A true Anari would not have reacted as he had. A true Anari would have stayed his murderous hand.

Sitting in the twilight, staring at his hands, filthy now with the soil he had dug, filthy now with the murder of his own cousin, Ratha felt shame so deep he thought it would rend him.

But that shame was his salvation, for it wrenched him from

the darkness that had been clouding his mind since he had realized he was going to avenge Nagari's betrayal.

He wept for hours, the painful, spasmodic weeping of a man who had not allowed himself to shed a tear since childhood. With each tear the shame drove deeper into his soul, pushing out the darkness that had nearly become part of him. With each tear he called to mind the face of someone he had slain.

Only in the wee hours, when the constellation called the Boat of Vellux rode high in the sky, did his tears cease. And with their passing came a cleansed heart and a new determination.

Rising, he picked up the few items he had brought with him and began the ride back to Anahar.

War lay ahead of him, he knew. But he also knew that he would fight it for the right reasons. No longer would he swing his sword for personal vengeance. Now he would swing it only in the defense of his people.

It was a small difference, for the horrors would be the same, but it was all the difference in the world.

Tom, under Erkiah's tutelage, had discovered inner spaces that he had always hitherto ignored. In his life as Tom Downey, gatekeeper's son, he had always been too busy assisting his father or hunting or doing the many other things the lads his age did.

He had never taken the time, nor made the effort, to look inside himself. His life had not encouraged such thinking.

But now he looked and discovered unbounded spaces, larger than his life had ever been or might ever be. Images and sounds flitted across his awareness there, often disconnected and meaningless, but somehow as real as the reality he called his life.

It was a little like dreaming, yet at the same time not like dreaming at all. It had the same fractured feeling to it, as if he had gathered images that didn't fit together in terms of what he thought of as reality, yet he could not doubt they were real. And the music he heard in snatches…he was certain he had never heard anything of the sort in his life.

Little by little he grew comfortable in that space, and as he did, the visions gradually became more coherent.

So he sat for hours, smiling, taking joy from the existence of a whole new world.

Tess, Cilla and Sara had spent the last two days within the temple walls, wandering through winding corridors, touching images on the walls, seeking the knowledge that seemed to fill them with each new step. It was odd, however, that none of them seemed fully aware of what exactly was changing within them.

Finally, on the third day, they gathered in a small chamber where the carved reliefs on the walls seemed to hum with life. Settling cross-legged on the floor, they held hands for a while, eyes closed, listening to the hum and trying to feel within themselves what they had learned.

Finally Tess opened her eyes and spoke. "It seems the learning is not yet ready to be birthed."

The other two looked at her and nodded.

"I don't know whether to be upset," Tess continued, her voice a mere whisper that seemed to join the ceaseless hum and become part of it. "Have we learned enough to help the Anari army? I don't know. Perhaps it is not yet the time."

Cilla sighed. "Or perhaps we are wise enough to know the dangers in what we learn. You have heard of Dederand?"

Tess and Sara nodded.

"I have seen it," Cilla said. "An immense plain of black glass, rippled as if it were once liquid. There nothing grows. To cross it is to risk one's life and limb. If the Ilduin could do such, then we need ever be on guard against ourselves."

"I agree," Tess said. "I agree. But…we will be opposed by

some of our sisters." So saying, she took the pouch from around her neck and scattered the twelve colored stones on the floor.

At once the humming in the room intensified, as if in response. They exchanged glances, then looked at the stones.

"Here," said Tess, "is Sara's stone." She passed the blue one to Sara. Its depths were clear and glistening. "And yours, Cilla." She passed the yellow stone. It too glistened as if lit from within, seeming to cast a light of its own, as did Sara's.

The white stone glistened as brightly, and Sara pushed it to Tess. "Yours, my Lady," she said softly. "For you are she who was reborn."

Tess found herself reluctant to touch the stone. "I must tell you," she said to her friends, "that I am not at all comfortable with that idea."

Sara surprised them all by laughing. "Who is ever comfortable with the machinations of the gods? For whatever reason, my Lady Tess, you are chosen, and chosen for something special."

Tess suddenly looked wry. "I would prefer not to have an exciting future."

The other two laughed, and their laughter seemed to lighten the humming around them.

"But these others," Sara said, returning everyone's attention to the stones. "We must…learn something about them before we go to war."

"Aye," Tess agreed.

Cilla reached out a dark hand. "See this?" she said pointing to a purple stone. "It is opaque. Clouded. I would not trust it."

"Aye," Tess agreed again. "But to whom is it beholden? My sisters, we must remember that there are two forces afoot in this world that work for evil. We cannot look at these clouded stones and say which work for Bozandar and which work for the Enemy through his hive masters."

"They *all* work for the Enemy," Cilla said grimly. "I will not speak his name." She made a warding sign with her hand. "To me it seems Bozandar has always been his minion. At least since they decided upon conquest and slavery. Before that, for a long, long time, this world lived in relative peace. Then the Bozandari decided they wanted to rule the world and have their work performed by slaves. And we, bred for peace, gave them little enough resistance."

She held her stone up, watching it glow golden. "I shall watch this always, to be sure I am not falling from the path into *his* grasp. We must all do likewise."

Sara and Tess nodded. "But what of these other stones?" Tess asked. "Not all are clouded. There are a few more than we to stand against darkness."

"Only if we find them," Sara argued. "Mayhap we should attempt to call them to us."

Tess immediately shook her head. "Pardon, Sara, but I do not think it would be wise at this time to use our powers so obviously. I caused enough trouble during the battle in the mountains."

Sara nodded reluctantly. "Then let us hope they find us. In the meantime, perhaps we can learn a way to track those whose stones are clouded? To listen in to their intent?"

Again Tess shook her head, and this time Cilla made the same gesture.

Cilla spoke. "The time has not yet come for us to unleash ourselves. When it does, we will know."

Tess smiled mirthlessly. "If we know how. I hope that our powers are concealed from us only until we need them."

In silence, they stared for a while at the stones. The humming around them gradually eased into a quiet song, as if to say they had taken what lessons they could from this room.

All would have felt better had they known what the lessons were.

23

The Anari army was set to march. As far as anyone could tell, the Bozandari had no idea that an organized, military revolt was occurring. Scouts reported that nothing had changed, that the border legion maintained its three camps and no other legions had marched to join them.

It seemed too good to be true.

Their last night in Anahar, the traveling companions gathered in their front room with Jenah and Erkiah, discussing the next day's march. Archer fretted over the timing.

"We must move swiftly," he said for the third time. "*Swiftly*. Jenah, Giri, you must make certain that everyone understands. Each hour we spend in movement brings us closer to discovery, and I would have us meet the Bozandari on ground of *our* choosing. It will give us an incalculable advantage."

Both Giri and Jenah nodded.

"And where the devil is Ratha?"

Giri looked down. "He will return soon, Lord Archer. He is still in the mountains where the judge sent him to purify himself."

"There is no purity in war."

"Mayhap not," Giri agreed, raising his head and meeting Archer's gray eyes directly. "Certainly I have seen enough of the ugliness of man slaying man. But there was in Ratha a shadow that might have turned against him and us. The judge charged him not to return until he has purged it."

Archer sighed and looked down at his hands, his fingertips resting on the edge of the table on which the carefully drawn map was spread out. Finally he said, "Far be it from me to argue with that. The gods know the shadow has consumed me at times. But without Ratha, I feel I have only half my right hand."

Giri smiled faintly at the sideways compliment. "I am sure the missing half of your hand will return soon. If not, Jenah and I will make up for the loss."

Archer raised his head, looking from Giri to Jenah. "I meant no disrespect, Jenah."

Jenah waved away the apology. "I understand, my Lord. I am new to these matters. I am sure Ratha will be a far abler lieutenant than I."

"Not so," said Giri. "Lord Archer will soon have *three* right hands."

Archer smiled, allowing himself to relax a shade. In the corner, the three Ilduin were listening intently, along with Erkiah and Tom. "Cilla, if it please you, accompany Giri on the morrow."

"I will gladly do so," Cilla answered.

"Sara, will you go with Jenah?"

"Of course."

"And Tess, you must stay with me."

Tess nodded.

Tom rose. "I go also."

Sara immediately objected. "Tom, no. You must stay here...."

He turned to her, his eyes hidden behind his mask. "I cannot be coddled like a baby or I will be useless to all." Then he faced Archer again. "I will travel with you, Lord Archer. Thus, if I see anything…"

Archer nodded. "My thanks, Tom. Your vision has helped us many times."

Archer pointed to the map again. "It is three days' march to the pass. The following morn we attack."

At that moment Tom astonished them all by reaching out and gripping Archer's arm. His voice took on a distant tone, as if coming from far away.

"Regardless when you arrive," he said, "do not attack until the snow wolf bows once again to Lady Tess."

Archer's eyes narrowed. "The snow wolves are far up north."

Tom's only answer was to repeat himself. "Do not attack until the snow wolf bows once again to Lady Tess. That will be your sign."

Erkiah spoke from his chair close to the fire's warmth. "Ill befalls him who would ignore a prophet."

"Then so be it." Archer shook his head and straightened. "It is a time of omens and warnings that we have entered. The gods play with us once again." He lifted his gaze and looked at each person in the room with him. "I beg you, do not be misled. There will be great temptations in the days ahead. Listen to that which is good in your hearts and do only what is necessary to achieve the freedom of the Anari people."

"Aye," said Tom. "The time will come when we will meet the true darkness. For now, we will meet only its minions. In their own way, they are as much enslaved as the Anari they have captured."

The truth seemed to hang on the air among them, and when they all finally departed for their beds, it was with a heavy sense of dread.

* * *

The morning dawned dry and clear, the wind snapping the pennants of each Tel as it marched out. For hours, it seemed, a dark river of armed men and women poured forth from the valley into the hidden passes that would lead them to their destination. Atop the brow of a ridge, Tess sat astride her horse beside Archer, watching as the army gradually attained movement to its farthest end.

Then Archer said, "Come, my Lady," and they moved forward alongside the marching troops, faster than the men and women could walk, seeking the head of the seemingly endless column.

The usually cheerful Anari were silent this morning. No song broke out among the ranks; no conversation broke the monotony. In every face was an awareness of what they had set out to do, and among them, none were proud of it.

Their feet, too, were nearly silent. An army this size should have made a thunderous noise merely from the tramp of feet, but the Anari were surprisingly light of foot, almost silent as they ascended into the mountains.

Looking over them, Tess believed that only the very young and the very old had remained behind, that every able-bodied Anari had gathered for this task.

But of course. Anahar had sung. Anahar had called her own, this time to battle.

"Tell me," she said, "of the creation of the Anari. How was it done? And why?"

For long moments he remained silent, his jaw as firm as granite. Finally, in a tone that revealed little, he said, "They were created through the magic of the Ilduin and the arrogance of the Firstborn. We may have been blind in many ways, but we were not blind to our own failings. We sought to create a better race than we, a race that would not fall prey to pettiness and rivalries. A race that would not war."

"Until now, the Anari have not had a war," she reminded him.

He shrugged. "As you can see, that is not necessarily a good thing, my Lady Tess. They could not even defend themselves against conquest and slavery."

"They are now."

"Aye. They have been changed. They are no longer what we wrought. But that is the way of all life. It changes. The gods diminished the Firstborn survivors for their sins, and once their life spans were shortened, they became something… Well, look at what the Bozandari have done. Look at the mages with their ugly hives. That is what the Firstborn came to when they were diminished."

"And you?" Tess asked, looking directly at him. "Why were you not diminished?"

His hands tightened momentarily on his reins, and his lips drew thin. "Perhaps I have been. I certainly know that I am cursed."

He spurred ahead before Tess could press him further, but the questions still roiled in her mind. She had gathered by this time that Archer, as son of the Firstborn King, brother to Ardred the Evil One, was still immortal, as his original race had been. But why would he be exempted from the diminishment? To face his brother yet again?

Perhaps.

Reaching inward, she sought for the voices that had begun to come to her in the temple at Anahar, the voices that both informed and promised to guide. But this time all she heard was, *Patience, little sister. You will understand in due time.*

The mountains sang that night. All around the many Anari encampments, spread throughout passes and over slopes, many bodies that soon would make up a crushing whole, the mountains sang. They were cheerless camps, without fire, with only dried meat and tough biscuits for food, remaining as silent as the dead so that no scout would detect them.

And then the mountains began to sing. The song was for Anari ears only, though the Ilduin could hear some of it, too. It surrounded those it loved, the stoneworkers and masons who had given new beauty to the stone they carried away. It sang as a mother would sing to a child, as a father would offer reassurance after a nightmare. It told them that all was well and they would be watched over by magicks as old as the world itself. Older than the Firstborn, as old as the gods.

Tess shivered and pulled her blanket tighter around her shoulders as she sat on a cheerless rocky slope, a hard piece of biscuit in her hand, a skin of water beside her. Nearby, Tom slept deeply. If he heard the song, it did not wake him.

But she could hear the song and sense the promises within it, though she knew she could not hear as clearly as the Anari, for whom the song was meant.

She had heard the Anari speak many times of the living rock, but only now did she fully grasp just how alive the rock was. Older than old, with a different sense of time, it nonetheless grasped the importance of this small period in the river of years, and sought to reassure those who had clambered its slopes and carved its boulders with love.

"Lady Tess," a voice hissed from the darkness, and Tess twisted to look.

With nothing but starlight to see by, she made out the familiar shape of Ratha approaching quietly. "Ratha." She, too, whispered, aware of how far a sound could carry at night…although it was perhaps possible that the singing of the mountains would prevent such.

He crept forward, allowed to pass by the two men who had been set to watch over her and Tom, and sat cross-legged beside her on the hard rock. "Where is Lord Archer?"

"He went off a short while ago to look into something. He should be back soon."

Ratha nodded and lowered his head. Tess could feel a change in him, a deep change. It was as if an anger that had burned in him for so long had gone out, leaving only determination in its place. "Was your retreat useful?" she asked finally.

He lifted his head, and in the starlight she caught a glimpse of the gleam of white teeth. "Aye. I wonder if we all have caves within us where we dare not look for fear we will learn of the ugliness within us."

Tess thought about it. "I am certain we do, Ratha. All of us. Mine, however, seems to have been lost with my memory."

Another flash of a smile. "Perhaps you have none. For in you I have sensed a core of pure white steel."

Tess immediately grew uncomfortable. "Put me on no pedestals, Ratha Monabi. I am flawed, like everyone else."

"That is not what I mean. Besides, my Lady, our flaws are gifts that make us interesting and keep us from boredom."

"Then what *do* you mean?"

"That I sense you have already been tempered like the finest sword from the forge. You will know what you must do when the time is ripe, and you will do it unflinchingly. And the shadow will hold no sway over you."

Tess again pulled the blanket closer around her and suppressed a shiver that came not from the cold. "I wish I could be certain."

"You will be when you need to be." He sighed and pulled a biscuit from his own pack, biting into it with a crack. "This biscuit could cost a man his teeth."

"I pour water on mine."

He nodded. "I have tried that. I would rather risk my teeth."

A small quiet laugh escaped her.

"Do you hear the mountains?" he asked her curiously.

"Aye. Not completely, but I hear them. I hear they will protect the Anari this night."

Ratha lifted his head higher and looked at the towering peaks above them, many mantled in snow. "This is a great magick. A great moment. Our history does not record that the mountains ever sang."

"But I thought you could hear the rocks."

"Small rocks, yes. It is what my Tel does best. We seek out stones by their song. But never before have all the mountains sung like this. We are truly protected. If any Bozandari scout comes near, he is likely to find his way shut off. Or twisted. Worse, he may find a rock slide waiting for him."

Tess looked at the mountains with renewed respect and in doing so felt the tingle of their magick along her nerve-endings. Holding her hands up as she felt them begin to burn a little, she saw little blue crackles of light around them.

"What did you do?" Ratha breathed, staring at her hands.

"I don't know. I was thinking of the magick in the mountains and then…" Her voice trailed off as the song of the mountains seemed to grow louder in her ears and something deep within her shifted. Then the blue lightning faded from around her hands. A moment later, the world returned to normal.

"It was the mountains," Ratha said. "Did you not hear?"

"I heard something."

"The mountains recognized you. They welcomed you."

Tess looked at her hands, then up at the peaks. "Why?"

"I have no answer. But it seems they know you. And the blue fire…sometimes one sees it when two rocks strike. It is the life force of the mountains. And it touched your hands."

Tess sat on long into the night, staring at the mountains, wondering what had just been done to her.

And why.

24

By the end of the third day of the march, they were poised to attack the Bozandari camp. They spent another cold, fireless night, while just over the hilltops they could see the glow of the enemy's campfires.

The Anari army had been split into three wings, leagues apart, each with a designated role in the attack. Jenah's wing had gone west, blocking the passes that might offer both reinforcement and escape for the Bozandari below. Giri's wing was to the east, ready to fall upon the camp beneath them at first light. Archer's wing would wait until the Bozandari were engaged with Giri, then strike their flank and rear.

Men and women who had never fought, and whose training had been all too brief, fingered their weapons nervously and wondered what the morrow would bring. Most did not fear death; there were far worse things to fear. But all were edgy and scared.

The scouts ranged round them, alert to any movement from the enemy, to any encroachment by Bozandari scouts, but none came. It seemed the enemy was confident in his safety and numbers, and unafraid that anyone might trouble him.

"Such confidence," Archer muttered, "serves them ill."

Tess, who straddled her horse beside him and looked through the trees at the brightly lit camp below, nodded. She dreaded the coming day, even though her heart told her that some battles must be fought.

Archer turned to her. In the dim light, his face appeared carved from wood. "Can you sense your sisters?"

"Aye. I feel them strongly. The bond is there. They, too, are ready for the morn."

"Good." He waved a hand toward the encampment below, so brightly lit with fires it was doubtful a man there would have been able to see shadows moving in the night. "What can you sense of them?"

Tess was at first surprised by the request; never had he asked such a thing of her. Then she remembered he was accustomed to the Ilduin of the past, Ilduin who could with their powers create a whole new race of beings. Why would he not think she would be able to search among the army below for information?

She looked at him for a long time, however, reluctant to use her abilities to spy, even if she could, yet struggling with the notion that it was necessary. She wondered what it must be like to have lived so long alone, every friend you might ever have dying, while you remained young. Eternal life must be a curse.

"Tess?"

She closed her eyes and averted her head. Maybe she could sense something from below. Almost as soon as she mentally envisioned the camp, she felt as if she were walking among the tents and shoddily built shelters, watching cold men gather around their fires, seeking heat and drinking ale to stave off the cold.

She saw men gambling with chicken knuckles and silver

coins changing hands. She saw prostitutes plying their wares and laughing with an edge when a soldier approached. She saw officers in their cups, gathered together around maps they no longer looked at, talking of home and the next time they would be allowed to leave this godforsaken frontier. She heard ugly things said about the Anari, and obscene things said about Anari women.

She heard one man brag about what he liked to do to young Anari boys.

At that her eyes snapped open, and her heart grew hard. "They are drinking and gaming," she told Archer. "Cold and miserable, and speaking the unspeakable."

"In short," he said, his voice as hard as stone, "soldiers passing the time, expecting no trouble."

She gave a jerky nod, not caring if he could see it.

"We'll take care of them at first light," he said, as if sensing her disgust.

"Aye," she answered quietly. "Aye." But the men below them were not all scum, she realized. Many were there for want of other choices. Many didn't care for what they were forced to do.

"The Bozandari," she said suddenly.

"Aye?" His voice gently questioned.

"They are not all scum."

"No, they are not," he agreed. He sidled his horse closer to her, until their knees touched, and he put his arm around her shoulders. "I am sorry, Tess, that you must be part of these things. I know how they offend my soul. I can only imagine how they must appall the soul of an Ilduin."

His touch was comforting, and she wanted to lean into it, to rely on his strength for just a few minutes, to feel the warmth of another human body close by.

But she dare not let herself give in to such things. Not with this man who seemed to be a primary player in the problems that had led the world to this pass. Not with this man whose own brother was the ultimate evil they would face.

A movement in the trees caught her eyes, and she drew a quick breath and stiffened.

"What is it?" he asked, his voice low.

"Something moves."

She cocked her head toward where she had seen the motion, and he followed with his eyes. Again a bush seemed to stir.

Then, causing her to gasp and hold her breath, the snow wolf emerged from the brush and trees, looking at her with those solemn golden eyes.

And this time she knew him, knew that somehow he was her totem, her protector, her friend.

For long moments they stared into each other's gaze, while Archer remained stock-still beside her. Then, regally, the wolf stretched out his front paws and bowed.

Tess drew another quick breath of amazement. She wanted to dismount and go to the creature, to touch him and rub his ears. But before she could make a move, he turned and melted back into the forest. Seconds later she heard him howl, then heard the answering howls of his pack, an eerie harmony she would never forget.

Then understanding struck her.

"Now," she said, turning quickly to Archer. "We must attack *now*."

"At night?" He didn't look as if he cared for the idea at all.

"Most of the men down there are drunk. Now."

"We could lose our forces to accidents," he argued. "The terrain is rough, and they won't be able to see except by starlight."

"Now," she repeated, certainty settling over her like a warm cloak. "The Anari see stone as brightly as you see fire. *Now*."

* * *

Cilla and Sara had both answered Tess's call and passed along the order. The army's movements began slowly, stealthily, working upward along protective ridges and down the far sides toward the camp. Everyone was as alert as they possibly could be, but no warning cries rang out, and no troops gathered in the camps below to meet the onslaught.

With little more than the faint crunching of boots on talus and the whisper of disturbed brush, Giri's column began to descend toward the camp.

As they moved, the fires in the camp began to burn down. Men were falling asleep from their drink and fatigue. If guards had been posted, they were nowhere to be seen.

"It seems," Archer remarked to Tess, "that Bozandar thinks the Anari are no threat at all."

"Have they ever been before?"

He did not answer the question, for the answer was obvious. He and Tess stayed toward the rear of their advancing column, for the sounds of horses could not be silenced. When it was time, they would move forward.

To the eye, it seemed that a river of shadow was pouring down the ridge. Nothing caught the starlight to gleam and announce the presence of soldiers. Instead, night covered them with its sheltering cloak, and the mountains gave them cover.

Giri looked to his right and left. They were formed up, in position, as ready as they could be. Many of these, his brothers and cousins, would not see first light. But more of the Bozandari would fall. And when Archer and his column rode down upon their rear...the trap would be complete.

He offered a soft prayer, gathering his courage and hoping to share that courage with those to either side. They in turn would pass their courage on to the others. Or so Giri hoped. Finally, he nodded silently, opening his eyes to take a final scan of the terrain his column would cross en route to the camp. Level ground, denuded of the rocks that the mountains had given, made smooth for the Bozandari…and the attacking Anari.

Giri lifted his sword, taking a final glance up and down the line, making sure his lieutenants had duplicated his signal, making sure his men were ready to move. Giri's muscles tensed, legs preparing for the exertion, until he felt the comfortable burn that said his body was prepared.

"Anari…onward!"

Foremark Leesen Tantor woke at the first thin wavering cries of the Anari attack. Cursing himself for having slept, he crawled out of his tent, struggling into one boot before giving up on the other in the rush to grab his sword, helm and shield. The rest would have to wait.

Why, on this of all nights, had he allowed himself the luxury of sleep? For the past three months he had forced himself to check the lines on an hourly basis, even as his superiors dismissed his actions as alarmist. The Anari would never dare attack, his superiors had said. The Anari were a race of cows. The Anari lacked the will, the moral courage, to rise up. They were created to be slaves, as if the gods had recognized that the Bozandari would need a race of servants to take care of them.

Foolishness, Tantor had thought. Foolish delusions, borne of arrogance and laziness. Again and again, his instructors at the academy had hammered home the lesson: base your plans not upon your hopes nor upon your fears, but upon your enemy's capabilities. Perhaps his overmark had slept through those classes. Or perhaps years in the field had dimmed his memory. It mattered not, for on this night, the overmark would doubtless learn the lesson again…if he lived through it.

The time for recriminations would come later. For now, Tantor had work to do. He fought the temptation to rush into the line to the west, whence the Anari were coming. To wade into the battle would merely surrender the most important duty of a Bozandari officer: leadership. No, his first task was to assess the situation and then to organize his men. Bozandari tactics, honed over decades of campaigning, valued organization over brute force. It was organization that distinguished an army from a mob. And even if this army had been surprised through the arrogance of its leaders, if Tantor had anything to say in the matter, it would fight as an army and not a mob.

Judging from the sound, the battle lay solely along the western perimeter. That made sense. The Anari had no standing army, and it was unlikely that they could muster sufficient numbers for a pincer attack. Given their state of training, a single rush from one side would be the most manageable maneuver. That left the passes to the east and north open, should it come to that, though Tantor had no doubt that the camp could hold. Once leadership replaced the drunken brawl that now prevailed, the Bozandari army would once again demonstrate why no Bozandari encampment had fallen in six generations.

"Rouse!" Tantor yelled, kicking over tents with his one booted foot. He ignored the discomfort of rock pricking his other, naked, sole. "Rouse and form on me!"

Many of his men were sound asleep and awoke only when his boot thudded into their sides. Others were in drunken stupors, useless in this battle, to be disciplined in the morning when order returned. He would not forget those who had neglected their duties, regardless of their positions in the chain of command.

In just a few minutes he had formed as many of his men as were fit for battle, barely half his company, but they would have to do. He had used the time to gain a better sense of the dimensions of the battle. The Anari were pressing forward over a front of perhaps five hundred paces. Although the Anari had no standing army or tactical doctrine, Tantor estimated their number based on Bozandari doctrine: a four-company attack, each in three ranks of forty, likely with at least one and probably two lines in reserve…perhaps fifteen hundred attackers in total.

It was a larger force than the Bozandari had yet encountered in Anari lands, but if even half of the three thousand men in the encampment were battle worthy, the Bozandari had equal numbers, plus superior training, experience and leadership. Standard battle drill called for one force to resist the enemy at his front and thus force him to commit his reserves. Then a second force would strike at an exposed flank or, if none were available, strike en masse at the weakest point of the enemy line. Tantor's men, part of the legionary guard, would be in that counterattack force.

Once his men were formed up, he marshaled them into formation with the other three companies of the guard and presented his report to his still groggy overmark.

"Second Company, presented for duty with seventy strong, sir." First and Third companies were also forming up in about the same strength. The Guard Regiment was not at full strength, but they were all men who could be relied on in a fight.

"Yes, Tantor. Fine."

Tantor studied his overmark's face. The man was not in command of himself and had no grasp of the situation. Doubtless he had spent the night drinking and gaming again, as the smell of ale was thick on his breath.

"Sir, the enemy attack in the west only. So far, our lines hold, though from the sounds of battle we are sore pressed. I suggest the guard counterattack by the right flank. This will protect our trains and the passes, turn the enemy and set him in flight."

The overmark gave him a dark, barely focused glare. "Are you assuming command of my regiment, Foremark Tantor?"

The words came out in a slushy stream. Tantor knew he

faced a critical decision here. To step forward would be charged as mutiny, punishable by death. To leave the guard regiment in the hands of a drunken fool would be disaster. In the end, the decision turned on purely practical terms. Tantor felt he could trust the judgment of a military court more than he could trust the mercy of the Anari attackers.

"Yes, sir. You are in no condition to command these men, Overmark Jassen."

For a moment it seemed as if his commander were about to strike him. But finally the man nodded. "Yes, Tantor. I am sure you are fit to combat mere Anari. Now is the time to prove yourself—or prove yourself unworthy."

So it had come to that, Tantor thought. His commander would both avoid the responsibility for his drunkenness and put Tantor to the test. And if he failed, Tantor had no doubt of the consequences. So be it.

"Guard Regiment, on me!" he cried, stepping forward to take Jassen's place at the front of the unit. "Do not fear the Anari, but neither disdain them. We must turn them, drive them and destroy them. On my standard, march!"

Behind him, he heard two hundred twenty men step off in perfect unison. If there were any doubts as to his fitness for command, the men kept them to themselves. For now, there was a battle to be won. And he would do his best to win it.

Archer watched the battle below. Giri's initial assault had pushed the Bozandari back, but they had rallied and were now giving ground only slowly, and at great price. Archer had no doubt that there would be many Anari to bury on the morn, but he could not think about that just now.

In the open yard at the center of the camp, a new unit had formed. That would be the legionary guard regiment for this camp, the elite and feared shock troops of a Bozandari legion. They would seek a flank, according to the pattern of Bozandari tactics hammered out and refined over hundreds of battles.

Archer was turning their own tactics against them. He had no doubt that his enemy was better trained. And, he suspected, better led. He and Giri had had time for only the most rudimentary training. Anari spirit, and sheer will in defending their homeland, would have to carry the day or fail in the attempt.

Below him, the legionary guard stepped off, marching for the near flank of Giri's line. In minutes they would be committed, and the time to strike would be upon him. He turned to Tess, whose face was fixed with a grim, steely stare as she, too, observed the battle.

"Let Giri know his left flank will be under attack," Archer said. "He needn't move reserves, as we will be taking the Bozandari counterattack force in our attack."

She nodded and closed her eyes for a moment, as if in prayer, her face falling for a moment in sadness, before she finally looked at him.

"What is it?" he asked.

"Giri's men are sore pressed. They are doing what they can, but many have fallen. We must help them soon."

He nodded. "We will, but we must wait until that regiment makes contact with Giri's flank and engages. If we strike too soon, they will simply turn to face us, and our advantage is lost. He must hold for another ten minutes. Then we will be there."

Tess was not happy with his response. That much was evident in her face. But there was little to be done about that right now. Her concern was for the fallen. His concern was that the fallen not have died in vain. For that, he must fight the battle as best he knew how. And that meant waiting for the legionary guard to get caught up in its attack on Giri's flank.

With a precision borne of countless hours of training, the guard marched. Just a few more moments and they would make contact. Within minutes, both the men and, more importantly, their officers would be caught up in the moment of close, personal, deadly combat. That would leave them unable to respond to Archer's attack. If Giri could hold for just a few more minutes…

Cilla had relayed Archer's orders for Giri not to shift his reserves, even as she quailed at them. All around her, Anari lay moaning and crying, praying and dying. She now knew what Ratha had meant, felt the wellspring of the rage that had darkened his soul. The Anari had never known war. And many who had fought this night would never know it again.

Stepping gingerly to avoid a nearly severed arm, she tended to the wounded as best she could while awaiting more news from Tess. She could not do enough. Binding wounds was little more than a way to feel she was helping, when in fact she knew the truth. Most of these men would die, unless Tess could somehow intervene to spare them.

She knelt beside a man whom she did not recognize as a cousin until she wiped the blood and grime of battle from his face. The ugly wound in his belly was far beyond her skill, and he seemed to know that. His hand clasped hers, his breath ragged.

"Cilla," he said softly.

"Yes, Sehnar. It is me."

"I cannot…"

"No, you cannot," she said softly. "But you were brave, my cousin. Brave beyond all measure. Monabi-Tel will sing of you throughout all time."

"Let them not sing of loss," he said, his breath labored. "Let them sing of…our freedom."

"Our freedom," she echoed, looking into his eyes as they lost focus and glazed over. "Our freedom. If it may come."

Tantor halted the regiment and ordered them to dress lines. He had to shout to be heard above the din and cry of battle, a battle his decisions would soon turn to victory. The men responded to each command with swift, disciplined movements. These were the best of the best, hand-picked from the ranks of the line regiments, tested in battle, having never tasted defeat. They would not taste it this day, either.

"Honor the Crown!" he cried.

"Honor the Crown!" they responded in a single voice.

"Honor the Guard!"

"Honor the Guard!"

He turned and lifted his sword. "On my standard, march!"

The battle would be his, or he would die in it. For a Bozandari officer, a Foremark of the Guard, there were no other options. As they approached the Anari line, he lifted his voice in the age-old battle cry of the legionary guard.

"Glory or death!"

"Glory or death!" the men behind him cried, and surged forward as one into the Anari line.

"Now!" Archer cried to Ratha. "We strike!"

Ratha was already moving, his upheld sword dropping in signal to the column. They rose from the rocks and gullies they had clung to for cover, barely two hundred paces from the battle. They closed the distance at a silent, uniform run, having adapted The Run of the Stone as a unit tactic, for there had been no time to train them in anything unfamiliar. Only when they reached the Bozandari soldiers did they form into the threshing line that Archer and Giri had drilled for hour upon hour in the plains outside Anahar.

It was not the perfectly choreographed threshing that Archer and Giri and he had developed over the years. These men were unaccustomed to the swirling, scything movements, and even less accustomed to the bite of steel on flesh. But fight they would. And fight they did.

Ratha fought with fury, but it was no longer the fury of a man betrayed. It was the fury of a people enslaved, the fury of freedom denied, the fury of sisters made whores and brothers made mules. It was the fury of the Anari soul, the fury of the very mountains themselves, that drove him forward.

The Bozandari before him recoiled with shock and horror at the unexpected attack. Let them recoil, Ratha thought. Let them turn and run. Let them know the shame of loss and the pain of defeat.

His sword arced up as the swords of the men beside him sliced through the air, shielding him, before he brought his weapon down onto the shoulder of the Bozandari soldier before him. Sharpened steel, driven through the wide arc of the swing by a trained and disciplined arm, slashed through bone and sinew and muscle, through lung and heart, blood spewing and then flowing as the man's eyes turned to glass, his face frozen in a final scream of pain.

Ratha felt neither hatred nor sympathy for the dead man as he wrenched his sword loose and prepared to step forward to the next enemy. He felt nothing at all. This was war, and war was killing. It was not the Anari way. But it was the necessary way.

Tantor heard the screams to his right even as he fought the Anari to his front. Step with the left foot. Lift with the shield arm. Thrust with the sword arm. Withdraw the sword. Push with the shield. Step with the left foot. Again and again. But now the rhythm of his men faltered. The screams grew louder. Shock set in as Tantor realized the enemy had waited for his attack and struck him in turn.

He had done what he had been trained to do. He had served as he had been trained to serve. Now he would lead as he had been trained to lead, or die as he had been trained to die.

"Company Three, Guard Regiment! By the right standard, turn!"

It was the last option available. Turning his left flank to receive the attack. Dividing his force while in contact with the enemy, the most difficult maneuver in war. But it was his last chance to regain control.

Had the guard commander recognized the situation only a few minutes earlier, Archer thought, he might have saved the battle. But those were minutes the Bozandari officer could not take back. And those were the minutes that had doomed the Bozandari camp.

Now surprise turned to shock, then to panic, as Ratha's men surged into an opponent struggling to hear and respond in the din and confusion of battle. Some of the Bozandari executed the command, but not nearly enough, and with the unity and safety of drilled precision gone, the fighting turned into a massacre and then to a rout.

Archer watched as the trickle of men to the rear became a torrent, rolling down the Bozandari line, until the whole of the camp was in full retreat. With Ratha attacking from the north, the only escape route lay in the pass to the west, where Jenah's column lay waiting. There would be no last miracle, no salvation for the Bozandari below. There would be only surrender—or death.

Archer turned to Tess. "Tell Jenah they are coming."

She nodded stiffly, her eyes fixed on the carnage in the valley below.

"Lady Tess," he repeated. "Warn Jenah."

"I heard you," she said, shaking her head as fleeing forms were caught and slain from behind. "So ugly. So ugly we are."

He took her chin in his hand and turned his face to hers. "Lady Tess!"

Finally her eyes focused on his. "Yes, I must warn Jenah. And then I must do what I can for the fallen. All of them."

"Yes, m'Lady," he said. "That you must. But first, there is a battle to be completed."

"Men are dying now," she said.

"They are," he agreed, nodding. "And they will. That is the horror of war, the horror against which we tried to protect the Anari. Now they must know it. But if they must know war, let them know victory. Warn Jenah."

"Yes," she said, nodding slowly. "Yes."

* * *

After the din of battle, the world became surprisingly silent. Almost deafeningly silent. The fallen on the field occasionally cried out, but most seemed to have accepted their lot.

Tess moved among them, laying her hands on the wounds of the living, growing increasingly exhausted as she poured her power into them, trying to husband it, trying to do just enough to save life so that she would be able to help others.

But there were so many fallen! So many dead and dying and wounded. Her mind could not grasp the carnage she saw, yet…yet…

She was kneeling beside a Bozandari officer who wore only one boot. A mortal wound pierced his chest, but he was still breathing. When she touched him, his eyes flew open. "Waste not your time on me," he said, and coughed up blood. "Save my comrades, lady, I beg you."

A tear crept down Tess's cheek as she looked into his eyes and read his resolve. "May the gods bless you," she murmured.

"They already have," he answered. He closed his eyes as the first ray of the morning sun struck his face and never opened them again.

Her vision blurred with tears, Tess lifted her head to survey the scene yet again. It was then that a strange thing happened, so strange that she froze. It was as if she was seeing two images, one laid atop the other.

The first image, quite clear, was the battlefield on which she knelt in her bloodstained clothes. The second was also a battlefield, but different, so very different. The men who lay on this second battlefield wore blotchy uniforms of a sandy color and thick heavy boots. Some wore helmets. There were not as many as lay on the field before her, but their wounds were every bit as bad, bodies torn open, burned, limbs cast about like pieces of broken dolls, their moans every bit as haunting, and a distant voice muttering, "Suicide bomber…"

She blinked and the image was gone, but in an instant she knew she had glimpsed another piece of her past. Another world. Another time.

And the same ugly things happening.

Angry, she rose to her feet and called mentally to her sisters. She felt Cilla and Sara, felt their grief and horror as they worked among the fallen. But she felt others, too, the untainted who had not yet been found. Holding out her arms, she called her sisters together and begged them to share their power to heal.

Blue lightning flew from her hands. The power of the mountains and rocks around her? She knew not whence it came, but she felt the power of her sisters flowing into her. As she grew stronger with their power, the lightning flowing from her hands and began to arc across the field of battle, touching here and there, as if seeking out individuals.

In her mind, Cilla gave a murmur of awe. Sara whispered, "My sisters."

Those Ilduin were too far away to know more than they could see through the minds of the three Ilduin on the battlefield, but they stopped everything they were doing and poured their power into the circle of light.

Lightning flared everywhere, creating a dome over the field, a bubble of incredible power. Those who were unhurt and still moved on the field, froze and watched with awe. The sky seemed to crackle with energy.

Then, with a thunderclap, it was over. Tess, Cilla and Sara all collapsed unconscious. They never saw how many of the wounded rose with wonder and awe, completely healed.

Jenah captured many Bozandari and pursued those who fled, but by day's end he was certain that some had escaped for good. He turned his army back toward the outpost where they had battled in the wee hours, feeling no good could come of this.

Archer, meanwhile, had managed to discover the lone surviving officer, Overmark Jassen of the legionary guard. His men had little good to say about him, and no reluctance to turn over the man who had spent too much time drinking and gaming to lead his unit. Their foremark lay dead, having done all he could in the overmark's absence.

One survivor told Archer with raw bitterness that Foremark Tantor might even be alive now, but for the overmark. "He was a sloppy soldier," the man said. "But for his connections in the royal court, he never would have held his rank."

Archer nodded sympathetically. It seemed the Bozandari were incredibly willing to talk in the presence of Lady Tess, for many of them knew beyond any shadow of a doubt that they owed their lives to her.

Tess was still recovering from that and sat quietly in a chair, her eyes nearly closed, saying little or nothing. Her presence was enough.

Beside Archer sat Tom, who also said little. Archer had never understood how prophecy worked, but he could imagine Tom feeling out the skeins of reality as each new person passed before them.

As the hours passed, however, it became clear that there was no overarching plan among the Bozandari to deal with the Anari. The legion guarded the border almost as an afterthought and sent out raiders for slaves whenever ordered to do so. Many overmarks became wealthy selling Anari in Bozandar. Apparently it was their compensation for this duty.

As distasteful as Archer found that, he let nothing of it show on his face. Tom, too, remained silent, listening.

Finally they came face-to-face with Overmark Jassen, the man maligned by his own troops. If he had been drunk during the battle, he was no longer so.

He sat before Archer with all the arrogance of a king indulging a commoner. He wrapped his gilded cloak about himself with a practiced swirl, then sat, leaning back, looking down his nose.

"Well?" he said disdainfully.

One of the Anari said just loudly enough for the overmark to hear him, "He has no idea before whom he sits."

Archer quickly waved the man to silence, but not before a flash of concern had passed across the overmark's face.

"Well," said Archer, calmly. "We have defeated you. The question is what to do with our captives. Are you a man of your word, Overmark?"

"No," said Tess, speaking for the first time, her voice faint. "He will say anything he perceives to be necessary."

One corner of Archer's mouth lifted in a mirthless smile as

he addressed the overmark. "Then I guess I need question you no further."

The overmark shrugged. "That is your choice. But know this. We Bozandari plan for every turn of events."

At that moment Tess rose to her feet, her face turning ashen. "Anahar!"

The council of war was hastily convened as the Anari continued to search the camp, some collecting what could be of use to the army, others rounding up the Bozandari prisoners, and others burying the dead. Archer stood in what had been the Bozandari command tent, looking at what had been Bozandari maps, listening as Tess spoke.

"They will attack Anahar," she said.

Archer nodded, thinking through the Bozandari plans. The careful maneuvers he'd worked out depended on the other two Bozandari camps holding in place until relief forces arrived. But now he realized that of course they would not do that. It would be suicide, as would playing hit-and-run with the Anari in the mountains. No, that was exactly what they would do. Move on Anahar, knowing they would draw any Anari army to them, and fight on ground of their own choice. Just as he had planned to do.

Now his plans had to change.

"We return to Anahar," Jenah said. "We choose the battlefield and wait for them."

Archer shook his head. "I don't think so. Anahar was built as an open city, a ceremonial heart, not a fortress. There are too many avenues of approach to defend. If we established our entire force across one, the Bozandari would choose another. If we tried to defend all, they would defeat our detachments one by one. Have no doubt that they will bring overwhelming force to bear. And while our men fought bravely tonight, we fought

what was largely a sleeping, drunken enemy. I doubt the Bozandari will make that mistake again."

"We cannot simply let them take the city, Lord Archer," Giri
said. "Anahar is the soul of the Anari people, the legacy of the
Ilduin themselves."

"It is also our library," Tess said. "A living library in stone.
Sara, Cilla and I have much more to learn before we are ready
to confront the Enemy. Anahar cannot be razed, but it must not
be violated. It is holy ground."

"But neither can we defend it directly. Our army is simply
not large enough." Archer pointed to the symbols drawn on the
Bozandari map. "They have two full-strength legions at hand
in the southern lands of Bozandar. Have no doubt that both
would come to crush us. We could not stand against such
numbers, no matter the depth of Anari courage."

"What, then?" Ratha asked. "You started this campaign with
a plan, my Lord. Surely that plan is not wholly rubbish to be
cast aside. Consider, if you would—"

Ratha stepped forward and looked at the map for a few moments, then began to trace his fingers over the symbols.

"Your plan will still work, my Lord. We must make changes,
though. We know that the two remaining camps will march
for Anahar as soon as they hear of tonight's battle. Their hope
was to reach it before we knew of their movement, and force
us to attack them at a time and place of their choice. We
cannot do that, for all the reasons you have explained.
But…we *know* of their plans. Surely we could ambush them
in these passes, here and here. We can catch them on the
march and unprepared. It is as close to drunken and sleeping
as we can hope for."

"But what then?" Archer said. He had some sense of where
Ratha was going, but he wanted to hear the rest of the plan.

"My brother's force suffered the most tonight and will need

time to recover," Ratha said. He looked up at Giri. "Do not deny it, brother. Honesty counts for more than courage in this time."

"I do not deny it," Giri said. "But neither will my men want to be left behind. They have bloodied themselves on the altar of Anari freedom. They will accept no less now."

"Worry not, my brother," Ratha said. "It was not my design to take you out of the battle. Far from it. Lord Archer, what I propose is this. Jenah's column was the least engaged in to-night's battle. They are the strongest among us. We send them to the east, to catch the Bozandari from the coastal camp here, in this pass. My column will head west, to intercept the Bozandari coming down from the mountains. We must move quickly and strike them hard."

"And my men?" Giri asked.

"You will be our eyes and ears on the frontier," Ratha said. "You head north. Your job is to find the advancing Bozandari legions, shadow them and let us know by what route they advance. If possible, you will steer them onto a road of our own choosing. We must force them into a long, narrow canyon…this one here, or over here, would be ideal. Then they cannot bring their superior numbers to bear, Lord Archer. We trap them and fight them where Anari courage can turn the day."

Archer studied the map, calculating force, distance and time. When he glanced up, he saw that Jenah and Giri were doing likewise. It would be a close run thing, this plan. But he could find no better course.

"I agree," he said, nodding. "But we have not a moment to waste. All will depend on speed now. We must deploy our detachments quickly enough to concentrate along the enemy's line of march and prepare our defenses. Jenah and Ratha, form up your men, and get them fed and rested. They must leave on the morrow at first light. Giri, your men will finish securing this camp and whatever tools and weapons we can recover. You will also march the prisoners to the Bozandari frontier and release them. We cannot hold them, and to release them here in Anari lands, without food or water, would be a sentence of death."

"A sentence justly deserved," Giri said.

"One should not burn the bridge across which one may one day need to pass," Tom said, breaking his silence. "We may find need of Bozandari allies in the war against the Enemy. A gesture of humanity may do much to ease the way of that alliance. A massacre, on the other hand…"

"Yes," Giri said. "Of course."

"Be at peace, my brother," Ratha said. "Justice may be served in many ways."

"Oh, it will be served," Giri said, his face bearing the apparent memory of the men who had been slain under his command. "It will be served."

After the council had broken up, the two brothers remained. Giri had not been able to spend a moment with his brother since before the murder of their cousin. Now he felt as if he were looking at the face of a changed man.

"You have become quite the commander," Giri said. "It is a good plan."

"You would have thought of it a moment later if I had not," Ratha said.

"Perhaps," Giri said. "My thoughts at the time were for my own column, however, and those who had fallen. I fear I was too angry to think clearly."

"Of that burden, at least, I have been relieved," Ratha said. "The stones spoke to me. They told me of the countless years they have spent watching over our people. They have shepherded us, in their own way, guiding us to their inner beauty, sharing it with us, giving us shelter, participating in our art and our music. Never have they needed rage or hate in that service. Neither do we."

"Battle breeds rage, brother," Giri said, still seeing his cousins fall around him in the dark. "There can be no other way. We are not stones. Would that we had their strength, but we do not."

"But we do," Ratha said, putting a hand on his brother's shoulder. "We are Anari, born of the stones, shaped by them, living among them, with them. Their songs run in our souls. Their strength runs in our blood. We are their children. We must find their heart within ours. For it is the heart of stone that can defend our people and win our freedom without sacrificing our dignity."

Giri considered his words. There was truth in his brother's voice, but his brother had not spent these last weeks training the men. He had not lived with them, admonished them, pushed them, corrected them, drilled them hour upon hour. And, in the process, come to love them. He had spent his time in the desert, a spiritual retreat, and not on the training grounds. And while Giri had no doubt of his valor, nor of his skill, he knew his brother was not yet fully absorbed into the face of war, killing and death. He wished that he could agree, but the words were not there.

"Tell me more of this after your next battle," Giri said. "For myself, I cannot have a heart of stone. My heart is with my men, and I will bury too many of them in the coming days. In the end, my brother, I fight not for freedom or truth or the light of the Ilduin. I fight for them, the men whom I have trained, the men with whom I will march and stand, and die if need be. Freedom may be the battle cry. May the gods will that freedom is our legacy. But I fight for my men, and they for me."

Ratha watched his brother turn and walk from the tent. He could not chide Giri for his words. He would have said the same upon his arrival in Anahar. Perhaps his brother needed a time of purification. There was no time for it now, but after the war, he would suggest it. No, he would insist upon it. For he knew his brother's true heart, his brother's true strength. His brother would find it again. And again they would laugh.

"Your face would make a woman weep," Cilla said, standing in the doorway to the tent.

Ratha smiled. "Weep not for me, cousin. How have the days fared you?"

"Long and hard," she said. "I still feel I have so much to learn and too little time. And now…the war is upon us. The time for learning must wait."

"You and Giri work well together," he said. "It is good that my brother has wise counsel at his side."

"Wise counsel?" She smiled. "I do not feel like that. I know little of your strategies and maneuvers. And what I know of battle, I would rather not have learned. My role is to listen to my sisters, report what they tell me and tell them of what I see. Beyond that…I can do little but watch my people suffer."

"Their suffering is not in vain," he said. "Pale words, I know, but true words nonetheless. We must live in the present, my cousin, but we must not forget the flicker of hope that guides us. Hope of seeing our people free again, and whole. Too long has it been since the Tel gathered without sons and daughters gone away in slavery. Soon we will be whole again. And then a day of celebration will be ours, a day unlike any before. Anahar will sing again, but there will be no sadness in her voice. She will sing in joy, her family finally home."

"But for those who have fallen," Cilla said. "And I fear the sadness of their passing may overshadow the joy of our liberation."

She took a breath and looked down. After a moment, she met his eyes again. "Listen to me. You speak of hope and the heart of our people. I speak of little but ill and suffering. Our roles, it seems, have been reversed."

"Ahh," Ratha said, "but I know of your heart, my cousin. Ilduin blood runs in your veins, pure and bright. Your heart will sing again. And perhaps then…"

His voice trailed off, unwilling to give words to the hope that had come to beat within his breast. For in this woman he could see the light of his own future, and in her eyes the glistening eyes of his children.

"Yes," Cilla said. "And perhaps then. For now, however, we are bound to the fate of battle. And your brother needs my help in preparing his men."

He took her hand gently and lifted it to his lips. "Go to him, then, and offer what guidance you may. For his heart is burdened, and he will need the light that comes from within you."

"I am not sure what light I can share," she replied, letting him hold her hand for a moment longer. "But I will do what I can. Farewell, Ratha. May the gods bless your march and protect you in the days to come."

"And you, my cousin. And you."

27

The day was beginning to wane, and with the lowering of the sun behind the western Panthos Mountains, the breeze began to bite as cold air poured down from the mountains onto the arid lands on which the battle had raged.

Men had labored to bury the dead in soil that had not been cleaved in human memory, but as the chill grew, the job was nearly finished. The stench of death had begun to give way to the smell of turned earth. The Anari burned piles of fragrant bush from the mountainside to carry the souls of the dead to the gods. The Bozandari prisoners helped gather the aromatic branches and leaves as if they, too, shared their captors' beliefs.

As the chill grew, Tess huddled inside the tent and wished the memories of the battle would stop hammering at her brain as if they were trying to pound open some securely sealed door. The vision she had had early that morning stayed with her, too, telling her that her past was no more peaceful than her present, and leaving her with a sense of internal sickness.

Cilla stopped in the tent to check on her and make sure she would be able to accompany Archer on the morrow.

"I will do what I must," Tess told her.

Cilla nodded. "I see the steel in your gaze, sister. But I feel the weakness in your body and heart."

"I will be fine. Please, don't worry about me. But take care of Giri. I worry about him."

"So do I. Perhaps I should have sent him into the mountains along with Ratha."

Tess nodded slowly. "Ratha is a healed man. Whatever happened to him, I wish he could share it with his brother."

Cilla smiled. "I will work on that."

Tess managed a smile of her own. "I will keep an eye on Ratha for you."

Cilla blushed. "My thanks."

"Love is all we have, Cilla. We must cherish every nugget of it."

Then, once again, Tess was alone, wondering how she could find the love in herself, for surely it could not be as blackened and withered as it felt at this moment.

"Tom!"

Tom had been standing alone as the last of the burials were completed, staring at the changing face of the mountains as the sun set ever farther behind them. His mind seem to be dancing on silvery strings, going this way and that, seeking something he would know only when he saw it.

But at the sound of Sara's voice, all that faded. She came riding up, still wearing the dust and dirt of the march, then slid from the saddle in one smooth movement.

His arms were ready for her, clutching her to him as if he would never let go.

"Oh, Tom," she sighed, clinging as tightly as he while the rest of her went soft as yearning was answered. "Oh, Tom."

He caught her face between his hands and showered it with

kisses, leaving no spot untouched. "Sara," he breathed again and again. "Sara…"

Minutes, hours, it would not matter. The universe itself did not hold enough time for their yearning to be satisfied. Until the stars fell from the sky, they would still long for one another.

"You come with me tomorrow," she whispered urgently. "I cannot bear to have you out of my sight. I have worried since we left Anahar."

He lifted his head, searching her face in the waning light, and finally a small smile lifted the corners of his mouth. "Yet you would have left me behind."

"That was different. I thought you would be safe there."

He kissed her again, this time on the mouth, sealing his love for her. Then, "No."

She stiffened and opened her eyes. "No?"

He shook his head. "I must stay with Archer."

"But… But if you see something, I can pass the information instantly to Tess."

"It matters not. I am called to stay with Archer." He brushed her cheek lightly with his thumb. "It is not my choice."

"Not your choice?" She pulled away from him, anger and despair both crumpling her face. "It *is* your choice. Say you will come with me and it will be so."

"I cannot." His voice broke on the words, as his breath seemed to lock in his throat.

"You cannot. You *cannot?* Who says you cannot?"

He reached for her again, but she stepped away.

"Answer me, Tom. Who commands you?"

"Something greater than any of us. I would it were not so."

Her hands clenched—her entire body shook—as she stared at him. "I could *make* you come with me."

He shook his head. "But you will not."

For long seconds she stood rigid, as if in the grip of a power she fought to restrain. Then she began to crumble.

He caught her and held her close, murmuring endearments, stroking her hair gently.

She spoke brokenly, tears streaming down her cheeks. "I have seen so much horror this day. How am I to part from you?"

"You have also done much good this day," he reminded her gently. "You saved many lives."

"All I did was help Tess. Tess is the focus of it all."

"I know. I know. But without you, she would have been too weak."

He kissed her again, and slowly her sobs eased. "We must follow the path the gods have set for us," he said when she had calmed. "We must do what is required. For now I must go with Archer."

At long last she nodded. A quivering sigh escaped her as she burrowed into his shoulder.

Night fell completely while they stood there, clinging to one another as if to life itself.

Archer joined Tess just as the last of the light was fading from the sky.

"We march at first light, Lady. Will you be able?"

"Aye. I am weary now, but recovering. I shall be able to ride on the morrow."

He crossed the small dirt floor of the tent and fell to one knee in front of her. Gently he took her hands and turned them over, as if he could read her strength there.

"You must eat," he said. "You are fading to nothing, Tess. You will burn yourself out."

"I feel no hunger."

"Hungry or not, I will have a bowl of stew brought to you. 'Tis actually quite tasty. The Anari know how to cook."

He went to the door of the tent and said something to a guard. "There. A few minutes, and hot food will fill you. If you don't feed yourself, I will feed you myself. You cannot keep exercising your power without replenishing yourself."

"It was the power of many."

"And you were the focal point. I know how it works." He pointed to the cot on the far side of the tent. "Some Bozandari was kind enough to leave that for you. After you eat, you will sleep. A guard will watch throughout the night."

"Those who fought must be even more tired than I."

"I did not say who would be the guard." For an instant, a puckish smile lit his face, and in spite of herself she smiled in answer.

An Anari soldier appeared bearing a large stone pot full of steaming stew. "My Lord, there is a Bozandari prisoner who would speak to Lady Tess. He claims it is urgent."

He set the stew and eating utensils on a folding table and awaited the answer.

Archer looked at Tess. "I leave it to you. I doubt anything ill is planned, but if it is, I will be here, and so will Freesah."

The soldier thus named stood a little taller. "I will protect the Lady Tess with my life."

Tess smiled. "Thank you, Freesah. Let us hope that does not become necessary, for I would like to hold your grandchild someday."

Freesah grinned. "I would, too. Shall I get the prisoner?"

"Send one of the others for him," Archer said. "I would keep you close, Freesah."

The man was positively beaming as he stepped outside again.

"A good man," Archer remarked.

"I love the Anari people," Tess answered. "I feel I could learn so much from them."

"As could we all."

Together they began eating the stew. As she lifted the first mouthful to her lips, Tess didn't think she could eat, but the instant it found her stomach with warmth, her appetite reappeared and she ate heartily. She and Archer dipped into the same pot, but it seemed he was eating only to encourage her to, for she ate most of what was there.

By the time she was done, she felt strength flowing to every part of her body. She gave Archer a grateful smile and was relieved when he didn't remind her that he had been right.

The flap of the tent drew back, and two Anari entered with an unarmed Bozandari soldier. His uniform was tattered, and his skin showed the nicks and bruises of the battle he had survived, but he was whole.

He bowed deeply to Archer, then fell to his knees before Tess.

"My Lady, I beg you to hear me."

"I am listening."

"I am Rearmark Otteda of the Legionary Guard. Today I saw many of my comrades felled, including my foremark, Tantor. But today I also saw something else. I saw the healing of those who had fallen around me. I saw men I thought must die regain their feet whole and healthy. We are now prisoners, but we know we owe our lives to you."

"No thanks are necessary, Rearmark. We Ilduin healed as many as we possibly could on both sides. Nor was I the only one involved."

He bowed his head, accepting her word. But then he looked up at her again. "My Lady, we saw from whose hands the lightning flowed. We know where we must give our thanks. There are among us thirty who wish to swear fealty to you. There are among us thirty who wish to accompany you as your personal guard."

Tess drew a sharp breath. Archer stiffened.

"But…" Tess hesitated. "But you might have to fight others of your comrades, Rearmark. Will that not trouble you?"

"Aye, 'twill trouble me. But it has troubled me my whole life long that my duty has involved snatching slaves from among innocent people. I have followed my orders and swallowed my conscience. I will do so no more. I owe you my life, and my life I give you. The others feel the same. We will protect you with our last breaths, and we will fight beside you for Anari freedom."

Slowly Tess reached out and touched the man's shoulder. She could feel no deception in him. Finally she said, "I accept your service, Rearmark, with gratitude. But I must meet the others individually, also."

Rearmark Otteda rose to his feet and bowed. "My thanks, my Lady. Will you have me bring them to you?"

Tess looked at Archer.

"I think," said Archer, "that 'twere best if we go to them." He nodded to the rearmark. "Let these soldiers take you back to your comrades. Gather together those who wish to serve Lady Tess. I will bring her to you shortly."

The rearmark bowed his way out of the tent as if he were in the presence of royalty. Tess looked at Archer. "Why do we not go immediately?"

"Because I have a small gift for you."

Opening the tent flap once again, he said something. A minute later a huge tub of water was carried in, along with a length of towel and some soap. The next man carried Tess's spare clothes, and from the scent, they had been washed that very day.

Archer smiled at her as he waved the soldiers out. "I shall be at the door if you need anything, my Lady." Then he, too, vanished, pausing only to tie the flap behind him.

The unexpected caring, the unexpected luxury, brought the

sting of tears to Tess's eyes. That Archer had thought so of her comfort at the end of a day like this…

She sat for a while, struggling with huge waves of emotion: gratitude, sorrow, relief and dread. But finally she rose and stripped and slipped into the steamy tub, where the heat almost immediately relaxed the tension from her body.

Except for the time in Anahar, she had grown used to bathing in icy streams, sometimes settling for a hurried sponge bath. This was a comfort beyond description after the past harsh days. Some Bozandari officer had left her not only a tent and a cot, but a tub, as well. She hoped he had survived the battle.

Images of another world began to float into her mind again. *Damn, I thought I'd never be clean again,* a voice said. *I don't think I'll ever wash all the sand out of my skin.* She felt herself standing under a stinging torrent of hot water, feeling it scrub away sand and blood, wishing it could scrub away the memories. Too many dead. But worse, too many wounded, cries of *Corpsman!* cutting through the din of battle. One shattered body after another, an endless stream of hands reaching for bandages, applying medicine, injecting morphine, working until her body and her soul were numb with the hopelessness of it all. Until finally, finally…a hot shower.

She returned to the present wondering what "morphine" was, knowing it was a memory she ought to recognize as she let herself settle into the depths of the tub. Small mercies, she thought, when at last she toweled dry and dressed in her white leather riding pants and white wool overtunic. Her dirty clothes she left on the cot, assuming they might not be clean again for a long time. But for now she felt fresh and revived.

She pulled up the hood of her cloak, for her blonde hair, growing steadily longer, was still damp, and the night was chilly. Then she stepped forth, and found Archer and Freesah awaiting her.

"Thank you," she said simply, knowing no amount of words could possibly suffice for the gift she had just been given.

"My pleasure, my Lady," Archer said, smiling. "Freesah has found someone who will wash your other garments tonight."

Freesah bowed, smiling proudly. "Where can your clothes be found, my Lady?"

"On the cot."

"Thank you," he said, and waved to two soldiers a few feet away. At once they entered the tent to collect the garments.

"And now," said Archer, "the three of us will go to see Rear-mark Otteda and his fellows." He paused, then smiled once again. "At times I feel hope that the world can really change."

28

The world had changed during the course of the day. Tess was both astonished and relieved to see how few signs of the battle remained now. The Anari had gathered around campfires, quietly talking, some even managing to laugh. Fragrant *sistren* burned on every fire, filling the night with its pleasant scent, mingling with the aromas of food recently cooked. The remains of the Bozandari camp were being fully used for shelter and comfort.

Only the Bozandari prisoners themselves stood separate and cold in a stockade that some of them had surely helped build. Anari stood guard all around them as they huddled together in the center of their prison for warmth.

The walk to the stockade took several minutes.

"The Bozandari are now held in pens they created to hold slaves," Freesah remarked.

Instinctively Tess reached out and gripped Freesah's forearm. "I am sorry, Freesah."

He shook his head. "There is no further cause. We struck our first blow for freedom today. Soon no more of our kin will be carried away to such places."

"'Tis to be hoped."

Freesah smiled at her. "I am certain of it, my Lady."

When they reached the stockade, Archer was immediately unhappy with what he saw. He called to the guards, "Have these men been fed? Why are there not fires to warm them? They are not animals to be treated thus."

One of the guards, sullen-faced, answered, "They stole my brothers and my sisters. *They* were kept here without food or water or heat. Why should I treat their captors any better?"

"Because," Freesah answered before Archer could say a word, "we are not animals! See to it, Tenna. But build the fires outside the stockade."

The Anari were not soldiers by nature, but they were accustomed to discipline and good conduct. Tenna might have objected, but the other Anari moved swiftly to take care of their prisoners. After a few minutes, even Tenna grudgingly joined in.

"Not all hearts are pure," Archer murmured to Tess.

"They are just people. When people have been hurt, they want to strike back. 'Tis normal."

He looked at her as if she had just said something remarkably brilliant. Finally she flushed. "Can we see the rearmark now?"

"Rearmark Otteda," Archer called. "Bring forth your chosen to speak with the lady."

At once a group detached itself from the huddle and formed up, marching toward Archer and Tess. They were at least thirty strong, with Otteda in their lead. Others of the prisoners drew back from them and spat at them, muttering words Tess could not quite hear. The marching group ignored their fellows, however.

When they reached the gate where Archer and Tess stood, Otteda called them to a halt. Archer scanned the group, his eyes narrowed, then stood back from the gate. "Allow these men to step out of the pen," he said.

Several Anari, spears and swords at the ready, leaped to obey his command. Otteda marched his company out the gate and formed them in two ranks to face Tess and Archer.

"My Lady," he said, putting his hand to his heart. "These men wish to swear their fealty to you and enter into your service."

At once the two ranks knelt and bowed their heads. "We do," they said as one.

"I am so touched," Tess said quietly to them. "But I must move among you and touch each of you before I can accept your oath."

"Lady…" Archer began.

Sensing his concern that not all the men before her might be honest in their intentions, she smiled at him. "I am Ilduin," she said gently.

He nodded and stepped back a pace to allow her to move among the men, but his hand gripped his sword hilt, and she was sure he could have drawn it in the merest blink of an eye if the need arose.

She began at one end of the front row of men, touching each one's shoulder. Closing her eyes, she sensed the truth of each man's oath, and only then did she say she accepted it. As she passed among them, a good feeling seemed to swell around the group, as if they were touched by something holier than the mere human heart. Each man seemed to regain his pride and purpose at her touch.

Even the watching Anari guards seemed moved by the aura that filled the air.

Until at last, near the end of the thirty, Tess found one she could not read. With her hand on his shoulder, she opened her eyes and looked into his, reading her death there.

Before she could react, he pulled a small dagger from within his clothes and drove it toward her. In the distance she heard cries, saw the men on either side of him move to protect her, felt as if time slowed to a crawl, every split second etched clearly in her mind.

As the dagger plunged toward her, she reached out swiftly with her hand and grabbed the blade, barely feeling the hammering pain as it gashed her palm. At once her hand began to bleed, and as her blood fell on the soldier's skin, it burned him like molten fire.

He screamed and dropped the dagger, falling backward as his former comrades wrestled him away from Tess.

She did not move. Perhaps it was shock. But she stared at her sliced palm, watching her blood fall. As it hit the ground it sizzled for a moment; then, from its dampness, small purple flowers sprang out of the soil.

The man she had burned was still screaming in pain as he was hauled away and hurled by his fellows back into the stockade.

"Judgment is upon him," Tess murmured.

Archer reached her side. "My Lady! Your hand."

"Hush." Her tone of voice surprised even herself. She held up her hand, and, right before their eyes, the wound closed. The scar, however, remained.

Slowly she turned and looked at the men whose fealty she had accepted. They gazed at her with awe approaching fear. "I heal willingly," she said, a quiet intensity almost crackling in the air. "I would heal the entire world if I could. But my blood burns those who are filled with shadow."

Then she turned and began to walk back to her tent. Behind her, twenty-nine Bozandari leapt to their feet and followed her in tight formation. It gave her no comfort.

She had become a monster.

* * *

Archer paused at the entrance to the tent, deciding whether to follow her. Ten from her guard formed a perimeter around the tent, two at each corner and two at the door, while the others set to work retrieving their belongings and establishing a separate living area for themselves. When he heard her sobbing, he could wait no longer. Nodding to the guards, he slipped through the opening of the tent and went to her.

"Lady Tess," he said, sitting beside her bed.

"Would you please stop calling me that?" she replied, opening her eyes. "I'm just Tess. 'Lady Tess' is a woman you and the gods have created. 'Lady Tess' is a monster."

He shook his head. "Not a monster, Tess. An Ilduin, yes. And Ilduin blood judges. But you are no monster."

"Do you know why I am Ilduin?" she asked, anger rising in her voice.

"It is in your bloodline," Archer said. "Beyond that, there are mysteries the Ilduin never revealed, even to we of the Firstborn."

"Bloodline," she said, almost spitting out the word. "Yes, that word fits. I became an Ilduin when I was bathed in my mother's blood, just as Sara's talents only fully emerged after she watched her mother die."

"No," he said. "I saw her at the Eshkar. A blue-white light shimmered around her. It destroyed the hive attackers sent by Glassidor."

"And have you seen blue-white light flash around her since?" Tess asked. "No, you haven't. That wasn't her, Archer. It was me. The Eshkar…transmitted her prayer to me. I was on the back of a horse, headed to Lorense, thinking of a way to escape, when I heard her words. The stones at my throat burned, and I felt the power drain from me. I awoke in Glassidor's cell."

"No, Sara's mother had to die for her Ilduin gifts to emerge.

Just as my mother had to die. And, like Sara, I held my dying mother in my arms. Bloodline? Oh yes. There is too much blood on my line."

"You are remembering your past?"

"Only damnably tiny fragments," Tess said. "Or perhaps I am fortunate that they are so few. For that which I remember is not pleasant. I knew war before I came to your world, Archer. War and screaming and death. It seems that death has been my life-long companion. And now, I cannot be touched. For if there be any evil in he who touches me, that evil will be met with judgment. And who among us has no evil?"

"Your sisters touch you," he said. Then, pausing, he reached out and took her hand in hers. "I touch you. I am far from per-fect, Tess. There is blood on my hands, also. The blood of bat-tle, more than you can imagine. And yet I fear not to touch you. For there is ordinary wrong, Tess, and then there are those who have given their hearts over to the Shadow that blights this world. It is on their choice that your blood passes judgment. And good that it does, else we would not know whom among us to trust."

"Choice?" she asked. "Do you believe any of us has a choice? My choices were made for me before I left my mother's womb. She made a contract with Elanor, a contract to die that I might become…who I am. I did not choose to be in this world, your world. I was taken here, dropped into that caravan, naked and covered in the blood of those who were slain around me. Those who were doubtless slain because the Enemy sought to slay me. I was destined to be in this place, at this time, Archer. But des-tiny is not a choice. It is a sentence upon my soul."

"Perhaps," he said. "But…"

"And if I am here as a pawn of destiny," she said, cutting him off, "then who are we to say that Lantav Glassidor was no less a pawn? Or that man whose hand will bear my scar forever?

The gods create and scheme amongst themselves, and we are but pieces to be shifted about in the sands of their games. Choices? I have none, Archer. Nor, I suspect, do you."

Her anger was painful to watch, and yet he understood its source. She spoke words that he himself had spoken more than once in his sojourns. The cruel hand of the gods lay upon him and always had. That was his birthright, his curse. He had learned to accept it and to make of it the best that he could. But only after long years—more years than the sands of the desert, it seemed—spent wandering. And most of that time he had spent alone, not for lack of those who would accompany him, but for the same reason that Tess herself now sought safety behind her wall of anger. To touch another meant daring to hurt another, to inflict upon them the cruel hands that had steered his life.

Aye, he knew her anger. He had spent countless years nearly consumed by it. But she could not afford such a lonely pilgrimage as he had taken. Time and events would not permit it. At first light they would ride into the next phase of the war for Anari freedom. And doubtless then they would ride on the Enemy himself. The gods had not given her the time that he had been granted. And he would need to ask much of her in the days to come.

"Tess," he said, "if we step back far enough, none of us has any choices. We are born not of our own design but that of our parents. We live not because we want to, but because instinct rebels at death. And in the end, the fortunate among us die, no matter how hard we seek to avoid it. Those of us who do not die suffer a worse fate, to wander increasingly alone among those who cannot share our days. All the rest merely fills in the time between birth and death.

"And yet," he continued, squeezing her hand gently, "it is that filler that gives our lives meaning. If prophecies have placed you here, among us, in this place, in this time, the gods have left to you the choice of how to give those prophecies life. If you fear yourself, you can be but a shadow of that prophecy. But if you accept who you are, you can be its beacon. And we will all have need of that beacon in the days to come."

"Was it hard?" she asked, as if peering into his soul. "To come to terms with those who set you upon this path?"

"I raged, Tess. When I permit it, I rage still. Against the gods. Against myself. Against all that I have lost, all I have yet to lose. But that is a luxury I cannot afford in this time. Nor can you."

"No," she said. A strength was building in her eyes. "I cannot. Not for long. Tomorrow we march. But for this night, let me rage."

Slowly, he nodded. "Yes, m'Lady. I will let you be."

"Thank you," she said, for the first time returning the squeeze of his hand. "I will be better tomorrow."

"I understand," he said. "As for me, I must make the last preparations for our march. We will move quickly."

He just hoped they could move quickly enough.

29

The march began at first light, before the sun had risen over the eastern horizon. Jenah's group marched to the southwest, toward a pass along the road from the Bozandari encampment in the mountain, to Anahar. For Jenah, it would be something of a homecoming, returning to the lands of Gewindi-Tel.

Giri remained behind with the prisoners, taking a few extra days to reorganize his battered column before marching north to the frontier to release the prisoners and deploy patrols along the likely routes of march for the Bozandari reinforcements that would doubtless come. He did not like the idea of releasing the prisoners, but the simple fact was that he did not have enough men to guard them and retain a fighting force. Archer would not let him put them to the sword. All that was left was to set them free. His would be a dangerous job, for until he was certain of their route of approach, he could not concentrate his own force to help steer them in the direction Archer needed them to go.

Ratha, at the head of Archer's group, led his small army toward the shores of the Great South Sea to intercept the Bozandari column moving along that route.

Tess, Archer and Tom rode with them. Tess was surrounded by a very determined phalanx of Bozandari, who seemed unwilling to let anyone near her. Archer raised a finger to his forehead in a kind of salute; then he and Tom rode a little ahead.

Tess would need to talk with Otteda about this. She could not spend the rest of the march separated from her companions. She felt alone enough as it was. She signaled to him, and he rode over to her.

"Your courage and fealty are beyond question," she said. "But I am no glass doll, and I have need to speak with my friends. They are no less vital to our mission than I, and much is our wisdom increased by the sharing of our thoughts. Please make arrangements that they can ride with me."

"Of course, my Lady," he said, dipping his head. "I will see to it at once."

True to his word, he worked through the column and retrieved Archer, Tom and Ratha, spreading the guard around them all, at a respectful distance that permitted them privacy to talk. Tom's face bore a look of worry.

"You are troubled," she said.

"It is three days' march to the Bozandari camp," Tom said, "and yet already they ride for Anahar. Apparently the servant of the darkness, he whom Lady Tess touched, was part of an enemy hive."

"What do they know of our plans?" Tess asked. "If they know we march—and where—our plans of ambush are a shambles. It will be we who march into ambush."

"Our plans are our own," Tom said. "At least for the present. Who knows what Giri may let slip to his lieutenants, and they in turn to their men, and thence to the Bozandari prisoners among them. If word gets back to the spy, then yes, the Enemy will know."

"Then we must see that word does not get back to him," Archer said. "Tess, you can tell Cilla to warn Giri, yes?"

"I already have," Tess said. "But it strikes me that if this spy can betray our intentions, perhaps he may also be useful to us."

"Yes," Archer said, immediately understanding her intent. "For the Enemy cannot see more than this spy sees and cannot know more than he knows. If the spy cannot judge the truth of what he hears, then he is helpless to warn the Enemy of a lie."

"And if my brother lets slip only what we want the spy to know," Ratha said, "then we may increase the Enemy's disorder at the moment of battle."

Tess nodded. A fleeting snippet of her mother's voice passed through her conscious: *make lemonade.* She let her thoughts go silent while she listened for the rest of the echo, but it was nowhere to be found. Doubtless the words were part of one of her mother's proverbs. Tess had only a vague memory of the wisdom that had lain in the countless such sayings her mother had repeated to her in childhood. It was one thing to lose one's mother. But to lose even the memory of her…

She will come back in time, sister. The voice was Sara's, now fully a day's march away. *I did not mean to pry. Your thoughts shifted quickly.*

Tess agreed. She had grown accustomed to the presence of her sisters in her thoughts. More and more often they had taken to conversing this way, even when they were in each others' presence, with no movement beyond a knowing look or a quiet smile.

Thank you for calling Tom over, Sara continued. *If I cannot look upon him with my own eyes, at least I can with yours, and know he is safe.*

For a time, yes, Tess thought. The cruel twist, of course, was that when the danger was greatest, Tess would be least able to keep an eye on Tom and Sara least able to pause to look at him. This war had cleaved so many.

'Tis but a passing time, Cilla thought, joining in the conversation. *Let Ratha worry not for his brother. I will look after him. I would that it were Ratha with whom I rode, but if I can look after his brother, perhaps I serve him in the best way I can.*

Oh, really? Tess thought. She had barely noticed the sparks between Cilla and Ratha, or had been too busy with her own thoughts to pay attention to them.

Yes, sister, Sara thought. *You had worries enough of your own, and that troubles us. You bear not this burden alone. All of us have lost much to become who we are. Perhaps that is the way of things for everyone. But know, sister, that we stand beside you.*

Tess knew that, and felt selfish for her moment of rage last night. But neither would her sisters permit that, for both quickly scolded her back into the present. For better or for worse, she had done last night what she thought she had needed to do at the time. That time was past, and in the present there were plans to be made, battles to be fought and countless leagues of dry, dusty marching to be done. And two sisters who would doubtless keep watch over her darkest thoughts, lest such thoughts distract her at a critical moment.

Of course, Sara thought. *You would do no less for us.*

All too soon, Sara watched in horror as the battle unfolded beneath her. The past three days had been a flurry of perpetual motion, for Jenah had barely given his men time to eat in his haste to cut off the Bozandari column. Events had proved him right, for they had barely caught the column before it emerged into the rolling foothills, where the Bozandari tactics might have given them a hope of victory. They were no match for the Anari in the jagged mountain crevasses, however, and the issue had been decided almost from the moment of contact.

Of course, in the way of armies, this fact alone was not enough to end the carnage. Instead, it was proved out through blood and death. Anari archers had struck the first blows, arrows whistling through the air to strike the breasts and backs and throats of leaders first, and then to rain upon the surprised troops. Many had fallen in the first moments, yet still those who remained insisted on doing their duty. That their duty was only to die under a remorseless Anari threshing line, with no hope of turning the battle to their favor, meant nothing. Courage and honor demanded the final sacrifice, and the Bozandari troops had both those awful virtues in abundance, even if their leaders did not.

The Anari, too, had learned those virtues and were further buoyed by the prospect of victory, of winning their homeland. So they, too, obliged the gods of war, killing and dying in a battle that could have but one outcome. Perhaps in a more civilized time, in a more mature world, men would not need to rend limbs and shed blood in so futile an exercise. But in this world, in this time, what she could see as obvious had yet to be worked out in the minds that drove the surging, swirling, screaming mass below. Only blood could say *so be it*.

And so blood was shed, and she began to move among the wounded, doing what she could for those who could be spared, crying for those who could not, wishing she could do more and wishing there were no more to do.

Men deserved better than this. Perhaps, someday, they would demand it.

It was a nice thought, Tess agreed, although if the fragments of her past were any sign, it seemed unlikely that men would ever learn the folly of war. In the plain before her, with the sparkling emerald waters of the Great South Sea beyond, the Bozandari were setting up camp in an open field dotted with scrub sage. Soon their cooking fires would start, and soon after that the songs of home and love, hope and despair. One by one they would fall asleep, some in their tents, others preferring the sandy shore, where they would listen to the waves roll in and slip away into dreams.

And once they had, the Anari would fall upon them. Ratha had split his column into two strike forces. One would engage them from the south, the other from the north. His soldiers had unloaded all their belongings save for their swords, the faster to move through the camp and perform the business of slaughter.

Tess felt a pang of sorrow for the Bozandari column. Men who had done no wrong save to swear fealty to their king, in the manner of young men everywhere, would die in their sleep or wake to the horror of a sword plunging toward them. Yet she permitted herself only a moment to indulge that sorrow, for while the bulk of these men had done no more than follow the orders of their officers, those orders had included the abduction of Anari boys and girls, the murder of Anari men and women. And those Anari had been no less innocent.

It was the way of the world that young men's lives should be sacrificed in the pursuit of old men's ambitions. And if that be so, Tess thought, then let it be Bozandari lives that were sacrificed on this night, not Anari.

They had already paid enough in stolen lives for the battles to come.

Giri moved his column earlier than planned. Cilla was keeping him apprised of Jenah's battle and Ratha's approach to the final Bozandari encampment. He felt it was absolutely necessary for him to cut around behind Ratha's northern wing to prevent it from being attacked from the rear, and to be sure of that, he marched early.

Cilla cautioned him. "The man whom Lady Tess burned is part of the Enemy's hive. We must be careful what we say of our movements and intentions, for whatever he hears, the Enemy will know."

She stared at the scrubby desert before them, noting how the shadows deepened and lengthened with the late afternoon. In those shadows nearly anything could be hiding, so she cast her senses out as far as she could, seeking any threat.

There seemed to be none. But the world was full of threats, and at some level, even as she turned her attention elsewhere, she kept seeking a hint of shadow.

After speaking with his lieutenants about the need for secrecy, Giri again fell in beside Cilla. "Why is Archer so certain about a spy?"

Cilla quickly related the incident with the Bozandari, and what Tom had told Tess on the march.

"Likely there is more than one, then," he agreed.

Cilla was quiet for a while as they continued riding northeast into the deepening evening. Blue shadows became reddish, then darkened almost to black.

"Giri?"

"Aye, cousin?"

"Ratha spoke to you of his retreat?"

"Aye." He sounded reluctant, as if he did not wish to continue in this direction.

"Then you know he has set aside his anger."

"Aye." This time his answer was short.

Cilla looked at him. "My beloved cousin, while the shadow does not sit in you the way it did in Ratha, your anger gives it a place to enter and lodge. You must find a way to let it go."

He snorted. "You were not enslaved, cousin. You did not see what I saw, nor endure what I endured. My anger gives me the fire to do what must be done."

"Anger is not necessary for this fight. Love of your fellow Anari alone should be enough."

Giri fell silent. The evening deepened into night, and still he kept his troop moving, as if the stars alone were enough to guide him. And perhaps they were.

Cilla sighed deeply, sensing her cousin's desperate need for peace and healing but unable to force it upon him.

They were miles farther along their way before Giri addressed her again. "I understand," he said, "the concern you and my brother hold for me. Do not think I am ungrateful."

"Never would I have thought such a thing, cousin."

"I am aware of the dangers of which you speak. But I need my anger, cousin. I need it to hone myself to steel. I need to remember the things that make this march and these battles necessary. Nor do I fear the shadow or the hives. I know their evil and will not fall before it."

"I know your strength, too, Giri Monabi," she said. "But I think you misunderstand something."

"What is that?"

"The way the sorcerers draw their hives to them. I do not believe they force these people to become their minions. I think they find a weakness that works to their advantage and use it to gain control."

Again Giri rode in silence for a long time. "Then I must be more on guard."

Cilla nearly sighed aloud, for she loved her cousin and feared for his soul. "Do nothing out of blind anger, Giri," she said finally. "But most of all, do nothing out of hatred."

"I feel no hatred," he said firmly. "None at all. But I *will* free my people."

She believed that he would free his people. She wished she were nearly so certain about his lack of hatred.

"The waiting is always the worst part," Archer remarked to Ratha. They sat behind a dune together with Tom and Tess, hiding from view of any alert scout or sentry. They were still quite a distance from the camp, but as they drew closer to the Great South Sea, cover grew sparser. There were still pockets of brush and even trees in some places, but this side of the sea was a desert for the most part. Foothills and, closer to the water, dunes provided most of the cover they could find.

In theory the Bozandari would not be looking for attacks from the north and south, but from the west and the direction of the Anari capital. If they looked for an attack at all. The difficulty was that they had no idea if this encampment had received word of the attack a few days past. Archer assumed they must have and thus would expect the Anari to come directly from the field of battle. In that expectation they would be disappointed.

Suddenly Tess stiffened. Archer turned at once. "Is something wrong?"

She shook her head. "I just heard from Sara. Jenah has defeated the Bozandari at the pass."

"Then why do you stiffen?" Ratha asked.

"Because I feel my sister's pain. She tries to heal all, but many are past saving."

With that she edged away from them and put her head on her knees. There would be more, she thought. There would be more, and she did not know how much of this dying she could bear.

30

As the night deepened, Archer and Ratha split up. Archer went to lead the southern column in its attack and Ratha to lead the northern column. Tess, Tom and her new bodyguards stayed to the west, presumably safely out of harm's way, but ready to report instantly if the Bozandari attempted to escape the pincers by running to the west.

Since the west held only Anahar and the Anari, it would probably be the last direction in which they would choose to flee. But Archer's plan had taken all that into account, and still he was prepared to block any western movement.

The soldiers guarding Tess and Tom, among them a handful of Anari, grew restive as they waited. Finally Tess spoke to Otteda. "Your companions are worried."

He shook his head. "We know what we have pledged to you. It is only the warrior's restlessness when he is forbidden to take part in the battle."

"But you would not wish to fight this battle—against your fellows."

He looked at her, his face stern. "They are no longer our fellows. We have made that choice."

Tess nodded. "I still puzzle over that, Otteda."

He looked around, as if making sure that all was well; then he sat beside her on a rock. "When I was young, my father bought a young Anari slave girl. She was to look after me and be something of a companion, for my parents were busy with their duties. She was a gentle girl, kind to me at all times, and I tried to be as kind to her."

Tess nodded, listening.

"I don't know what happened, but as I grew older and thought about it, I decided my mother must have feared my attachment to the girl, for one day she ordered the girl to be killed. And made me watch her death."

"How awful!"

"When I complained to my mother and tried to prevent the killing, my mother said, 'It is only a slave. I will buy you a better one.'"

Otteda looked up at the stars. "Everyone around me held the same attitude, so I was forced to accept it. But I never forgot…and… Frankly, my Lady, the older I get the more it troubles me. Bozandari treat curs as well as slaves. And Luca, my young friend, taught me something very important: even slaves have families and friends. And feelings. They are not dogs. They are human beings, just like us."

"So these years with the army must have troubled you."

"More and more with the passage of time. When I was on the northern frontier, my duties made sense to me. But here, on this duty…no. It makes no sense. I finally sickened enough of it that I had requested a new post, not something a rearmark should do if he wishes to advance. I am glad you came along, lady. Perhaps before all is done I will be able to atone and regain my self-respect."

Impulsively Tess reached out to touch his shoulder and willed him to feel better. "You are a good man, Rearmark."

"Not yet. But at last I have the chance to become one."

The night finally grew so still and deep that the susurration of the waves on the beaches of the Great South Sea carried across miles of desert, bringing the scent of water and the scent of the shore. The air grew soft with the moisture from the sea until it felt almost like a lover's caress. Tess drew deep lungfuls of it, enjoying the relief from the parched days just past.

"Nothing smells quite like the sea," Otteda remarked. "It always seems to call to me."

"I have never smelled it before," Tom said. "It is wonderful."

Tess knew she had smelled it before, and for an instant the coppery tang of blood seemed to mingle with it, nearly jarring free yet another memory. But the moment passed, and only the gentle, moist breeze remained.

She looked up at the stars, gauging the hour as Archer had been teaching her. "Soon."

"Aye," Tom said. "Blood will flow heavily this night, and the waters of the sea will turn red near the shore. But out of this will grow a new rose...."

His voice trailed off as if he were seeing something, and Tess waited patiently for his next words. In the meantime she could sense from Cilla that Giri was on the move, hoping to protect Ratha's rear to the north. And Jenah was marching down toward them, seeking any others who might attempt to approach Anahar.

So far, so good. If such a night could be called good.

The attacks fell like twin hammer blows, first with arrows whistling down out of the night, then with the deep hiss of the Anari battle cry and the thunder of footfalls across hard ground.

Soon that, too, was swallowed into the clang of metal upon metal, and the screams of wounded and dying men. Tom could see it in his mind as if the armies were groups of pebbles being pushed around on a table. From the north, Ratha's men were pushing relentlessly into the Bozandari lines, fissures turning to fractures and then into gaping holes to be exploited. From the south, Archer's column kept a slow, steady pace, not allowing the Bozandari before him to turn and move to the aid of their shattered comrades. It was a ruthless, brutal, efficient attack, and Tom once again found himself sickened by the thought that he could not do more for the Anari, for his companions, for Sara.

"Why do you feel the need to shed blood?" Tess asked, her voice almost silent against the sounds of battle.

He turned to her, wondering how she had gained access to his thoughts. She glanced down at his hand, which was clutching the hilt of the sword his father had given him. A sword he had raised only once.

"We are outnumbered," he said. "Every able-bodied hand should be at service."

"There are enough hands to shed blood," Tess said, "and too few eyes to see why. Your service is in your vision, Tom. Not in killing."

"I was given a sword, Lady Tess."

"And in time we will know why," she said. "There is no honor in killing, Tom. No glory. There is only pain and heartache and hatred and loss. There are no winners in battle. There are only the dead and the living. And even the living die a little."

For an instant he had a glimpse into the cacophony of her memory. An inhuman scream came down out of the sky and burst into flames, scattering men and parts of men around a desert town. Tess had to wipe blood from her eyes before she could go to the aid of those for whom hope remained.

"You did not choose this war, Lady Tess. Just as you did not choose the strange wars of your past. I do not know what evil mind could devise the weapons I see in your memories. Weapons that tear men apart without even having to see the victims. I do not know why you were drawn into those battles. But I know you, Lady, and you would not have chosen them of your free will."

"What did you see?" she asked.

He described the scene as best he could, although words failed him more than once. When he was finished, tears trickled from her eyes.

"I wish I had happy memories," she said.

"Are all of them thus, Lady?"

She sighed and nodded. "Most that I have been able to recover. It seems that I have spent my life in the company of death."

He sat in silence for a moment, watching her distant eyes grow even more distant. Sara would have known what to say to make her feel better. But Sara was not here, and he found himself at a loss for words.

Tess looked at her hands, then at him. "I have touched so much blood. My hands have been in parts of a body that no man was meant to touch. I've held a dying heart in my hand, squeezing gently, trying to wrest a last few minutes of life from it, hoping help would come in time. I've watched the light go out of so many eyes, Tom. So many eyes."

"And I would wager that you killed almost none of them," Tom said. "You were trying to heal them."

"Trying and failing, Tom. So many will die tonight, are dying right now. I will do what I can for as many as I can, but too many will die anyway. Too many mothers and fathers, sisters and brothers, will weep in the morning. I have spent my life watching it, it seems. Steeped in the blood of human hate and anger and distrust."

"You weren't just watching, Lady Tess. You were trying to heal. You were trying to find some tiny measure of humanity in the inhumanity of war. And if you have seen too many eyes fade into death, ask yourself this. How many of those dying men saw your kind eyes as their last memory? How many were eased into the arms of the gods by your kindness and compassion? How many felt cared for in their last moments, rather than lost and in pain, afraid and alone?"

She smiled stiffly. "You are a kind man, Tom Downey. If your heart were enough to heal the world, no man would ever make war again."

"But my heart is not," he said, grasping her hand so that she could not retreat into her own thoughts. "Yours is. I have watched you work miracles that men will tell of to the end of days. Perhaps they were born of Ilduin blood. But it was Ilduin blood that pumped through your heart, propelled by your kindness, by your love for us all, even the enemies who are dying out there on that field tonight. And if that love hurts you, Lady, know that it fills the rest of us with awe and wonder, and a belief that even we could be more than what we have been, love more than we have loved, give more than we have given, and trust more than we have trusted."

"I am no god," she said bitterly.

"No, you are not. If you were, your love would be easy to dismiss. We could simply tell a story, let the priests in the temples wave their arms and burn incense, and walk away knowing we are not gods and cannot expect so much of ourselves."

He squeezed her hand. "Instead we make camp with you. We watch you sleep. We see your tears. We see you slump in exhaustion at the end of a day's march. We see you live among us, facing the same aches and trials that we face. And yet you love—more than any of us would have imagined possible. And we cannot tell ourselves that it is impossible for us to love as you love. We can only try to be worthy of what we see in you."

Tess pulled her hand away. "Place me not on too high a pedestal, Tom. I will only disappoint you."

"Perhaps," he said. "Perhaps you will. But it is the journey that purifies us, not the destination. And if we are to walk this road, at least we are walking it with you. For better or for worse, we will walk as one. And if we fail, we will have failed trying for the best that was within us."

Tess smiled. "I shall never again call you Young Tom, for you are far too wise for such a name. And if you can find it in your heart to strengthen me in times like this, then your heart will heal this world as surely as mine."

He bowed his head. "It would be my honor, Lady."

For a moment she considered drawing him into a hug, for it felt wrong for him to bow to her. But then, seeing the eyes of her guards, she simply returned the gesture with a bow of her own.

"There will be honor enough in the morning, Tom," she said. "For now, let us do what we can to save the dying."

Ratha watched as his men moved among the wounded, offering water and comfort to friend and foe alike. The battle, such as it had been, was decided long before he or anyone caught up in it had known. Like a fire in dry desert tinder, it had burst into a roaring conflagration, and only slowly had died out. Now its last embers had been consumed, and what remained was the ash and ruin of human hatred.

Before his sojourn into the desert, he would have looked upon this scene with swelling pride, confident that he had dealt death to the deserving, confident that only their blood, flowing in rivers, could heal the wounds of his people.

Now he knew that it would not be Bozandari blood that healed his people. The men around him were acquiring scars that would haunt them in the night for years to come. It hurt to watch, even while Ratha realized that there was no other way. But while it was a necessary thing, that did not make it an easy one.

What they were doing now, tending to those whose lives could be saved, giving comfort, showing mercy...he hoped these would be the memories his men would carry long after the nightmares eased. For these actions were not merely necessary, they were *right,* and it was in doing them that the Anari would find healing and peace.

"We caught them by surprise," Archer said, walking beside him. "We were fortunate this time."

Ratha nodded. "There will be no more easy battles, Lord Archer. But the Anari were not born for easy things. We are a people of sand and stone and scrub ground that yields only what we need even in times of plenty. We are a strong people. Stronger than even our creators realized."

"It pains me to see your people fight," Archer said. "You were to be the ones who would never know war."

Ratha looked at him and nodded. "But those who do not know war also do not know peace, my Lord. And perhaps wiser minds than yours guided you in that time. My people will heal. And a thousand years from now, people will tell stories of these days and speak of them as the time in which the Anari were no longer children of the desert but men of the mountains."

"But at what cost?" Archer asked, looking at Lady Tess as she moved among the wounded.

Ratha, too, watched as she moved from one man to the next, closing her eyes and placing her hands over wounds that were beyond description, leaving healing and peace in her wake, but a mounting weight of fatigue in her face.

"The cost is grave, Lord," Ratha said. "But do we not owe this to the Anari who have suffered, to those whom we watched freeze and die in Derda, to the butchered traders in that caravan? If we bear not this cost, we shame their suffering. So let us bear it and make their sacrifices worthy of their courage."

Archer smiled and put a hand on Ratha's shoulder. "Perhaps I, too, should take a sojourn in the desert, my friend. I hardly know the man who stands with me, save to say I am grateful and honored to stand beside you."

"Then perhaps you should take that sojourn, my Lord," Ratha said, the faintest flicker of a smile in his eyes despite his exhaustion. "Perhaps if more of us spent time in the company of the stones and their songs, none of this would be necessary."

"It is a shame that only Anari women can be priests," Archer said, chuckling.

Ratha shook his head. "I am no priest. I am only a warrior who has learned that war must serve something greater than itself, lest we all become nothing but fodder in its hungry maw."

"And those," Archer said, "are words worthy of a priest. Perhaps when this war is over."

"I will worry about that time when it comes," Ratha said. "There is still much to be done."

Tess suddenly stood and walked up to them, her face pale and strained. "We must hurry. Giri has found the enemy. Even now they are nearing the frontier."

"But how?" Ratha asked. Not even the Bozandari, with all of their vaunted organization, could move this quickly. "We are not ready."

"Then we must get ready," Tess said. "And we must do it with haste. The Enemy's hive is among us, and we will get no pause from his evil."

31

Topmark Tuzza rode south at the head of his column, pushing the men past their daily limit in order to reach the side of the legion that was under attack by the Anari. He had been dispatched two days ago when a seer at the court had reported the defeat of the camp near Anahar. Now he was sure the camp at the Great South Sea would soon be under attack if it was not already.

Tuzza felt little fear. He knew his position in the world, scion of the titled house of Ousa, cousin to the royal Bozan family, twenty-second in line for the throne. He had been raised to fearlessness and a sense of duty that made it impossible for him to indulge himself in even the smallest of ways.

As he rode his large black horse, his heavy cloth-of-gold cloak hung neatly from his shoulders, announcing his rank, both among soldiers and in his society. It was a beacon intended to keep the attention of his legionnaires, to guide them through a fight and to keep them right behind him. It was for this reason he was known as the topmark. Into battle he always went first.

It was growing late in the day, and little light was left, but ignoring the suggestions of some of his rearmarks and fore-marks, he pressed on.

"Our comrades sorely need us," was his only response. Their encounter just the day before with prisoners who had been released by the Anari at the border had caused him mixed feelings. On the one hand, the prisoners had been well-treated and spoke of healing at the hands of Ilduin. On the other hand, they spoke of a savage battle that had defeated them.

The peaceful Anari, it seemed, had learned the ways of war. Bozandar could not tolerate this insurrection.

He had sent scouts ahead to alert him before they walked into the Anari army. Just as the last light was fading from the day, he came upon two of those scouts. They lay in the open, as if in warning, as if whoever had killed them wished to leave a message. And they had been brutally mutilated.

"Gods!" said one of his officers nearby. "Gods!"

It was not as if the Bozandari themselves had never done such a thing. Tuzza was no youth to believe in the purity of the hearts of soldiers. He recognized rage when he saw it.

But still, it sickened him and made him furious, the more so because one of the bodies belonged to his young cousin Xuro. His fists clenched around his reins and sword hilt, and breathing became difficult. If he ever found the Anari who had done this...

"Bury them," he said shortly, to conceal his feelings.

"But..."

He turned to the protesting overmark, controlling himself because he must. "We have no time to take the dead with us. More will die while we dally. Get to it!"

The overmark's lips compressed, but he nodded and passed the order along.

No need, thought Tuzza, for either of the slain men's families to know what had been done to them. Better to claim expedience and bury them here. But even as his trained mind clicked with well-oiled precision, the man in him felt a hot thirst for vengeance.

Overmark Thul drew his horse close and spoke in a low voice. "These people have always been peaceable. I would not have expected such from them."

Tuzza slowly turned his head and looked straight at the overmark. "Perhaps, Thul, generations of slavery change men. Perhaps it teaches them cruelty."

Thul frowned. "That could be interpreted as treason."

"Or as common sense."

As a rule, Tuzza ignored the entire issue of slavery, because it was out of his hands. But now he was facing the population that unwillingly provided those slaves, and he wasn't about to underestimate their rage or cunning. Underestimation was a commander's deadliest foe.

And right before him lay the evidence of the Anari rage. No, he would not underestimate them. Nor would he allow his own fury to overcome him. Instead, he would use their rage against them.

With a deliberate effort of will, he crushed his feelings to dust and forced his attention to the dangers those bodies might signify.

Giri looked out from behind the rocks and nodded. Good. Let that man be angry. Let him feel just the smallest inkling of the horrors that had been visited upon the Anari people. Then, when what passed for his soul went to meet its maker, perhaps he might understand why that god was angry.

And the gods were doubtless angry with men like this. Haughty, imperial men like that owned his brothers and sisters. Bought them. Sold them. Used them. Killed them. Well, now the circle turned. This man's own kin would be wary to venture into Anari lands and would pay in blood for every league of their advance. That would buy Archer and the rest time to plan the final ambush. But it might also slake the rage in Giri's soul.

"We go," he said, whispering to the Anari beside him. "It is a four-hour walk to our next ambush point."

They slid silently down the reverse slope of the ridge, slipping through the deepening shadows of falling night, negotiating the path of songs in the stones that led them back through Giri's own screen of scouts. Soon he had joined Cilla and his chief lieutenants at a low campfire, and gave his report.

"The Bozandari will grow more cautious now," he concluded. "They will need to send out larger teams of scouts, and their scout teams will have to be more careful about procedure. We will not get easy pickings again, but pick we must. What we harvest in blood here, our cousins will not face later."

Giri gave final instructions to his lieutenants, then made his way to his tent, contemplating the events of the day. His ambush had worked here, in the broken area of the frontier. Soon they would be into the low, rolling hills of the northern Anari lands, and there would be fewer ambush sites for a time. But he wouldn't be able to simply melt away and let the Bozandari column march unmolested. He had to steer them toward Archer's force and report on their progress.

Much would depend on the next two days, when he would gain a sense of how the arrogant Bozandari commander reacted to the pinpricks that Giri inflicted. If the man's response was to turn toward the ambushes, hoping to trap and destroy the Anari force, then Giri's task would be easier. He could simply strike and withdraw along the path he wanted the Bozandari to follow. But if the man's response was to seek the path of least resistance, Giri would have to keep his force dispersed, picking away at the flanks and channeling the Bozandari.

That was the other reason he had ordered the mutilation of the bodies. He wanted his enemy to be angry, vengeful. The angrier the Bozandari were, the more likely it was that their commander would decide to end the league-by-league bleeding and run his tormentors to ground. And the more he tried to do that, the more Giri would be free to concentrate his force along his chosen line, providing more security and fewer opportunities for confusion.

His thoughts were interrupted by Cilla's quiet cough at the entrance to his tent. He tried to conceal the impatience in his voice.

"Enter."

She came in and sat on a low stool. "I have told Lady Tess of their progress and their course."

"Excellent. And where will they meet us?"

"They have not yet decided," Cilla said. "Archer is still a day's march from meeting Jenah's column, and then they will need to find a suitable place for the battle."

"The sooner they decide," Giri said, "the sooner we can begin to lead these beasts to their slaughter."

"Pray, do not think that way, my cousin. They are our enemies now, yes, but Tom is sure that we will need them as allies in the future. What we do now will affect that."

Giri nodded. "That will be then. Right now, I need to make them angry enough to seek us out. Otherwise I will have to keep my men spread all over the desert and trust too much in my lieutenants. They are good men, and brave, but they lack experience. If something goes wrong, they may not know how to respond. I would be happier if they were where I could see them and guide them."

"I understand, my cousin." Her dark eyes were deep and earnest. "But will angry men not also fight harder?"

"Of course they will," he said, with a wave of his hand. "But already the Bozandari fight hard. What they have, what we lack, is discipline and training. Angry men may fight more fiercely, but they are less likely to fight with self-control. Bozandari gone berserk are less to be feared than Bozandari with ice in their veins."

"And what about the rage in your blood?" she asked.

He shook his head. Always it came back to this. It was doubtless his brother's doing. And while he understood Ratha's heart, this was not a time for kindness and mercy. This was a time to make war, and war was an ugly, bloody, deadly business.

"The rage in my blood is good for my men," he said. "They are not used to fighting. Even now, after thrice meeting the enemy, they hesitate at the moment of truth. That moment of hesitation can get them killed. We buried enough of them at the first camp and have buried more since. So long as they think of the Bozandari as men, that hesitation will continue and we will continue to bury too many who might otherwise have lived."

"But if the Bozandari enraged are less to be feared, might not the same be said of you, my cousin? Your rage can lead you to mistakes, just as theirs leads them. And your mistakes will kill Anari just as surely as their hesitation now does."

"What mistakes have I made, cousin?" he demanded. "Point them out to me, or slander not my efforts."

"I am no military commander," Cilla said softly.

"No, you are not!" he said. "So question not my efforts, nor my mind."

She leaned toward him, reaching out to touch his arm. "I question not your efforts, cousin, nor your mind. It is your soul for which I am concerned."

Giri snatched his arm away from her touch. "My soul is my own worry. The gods will judge if I have served my people well. Worry for your own soul, if worry you must, and for the dangers of Ilduin blood."

Cilla recoiled, her eyes wide. For a moment she seemed about to lash out at him, but then she took a long breath and rose to leave. Pausing at the entrance to the tent, she looked back at him.

"Be careful, my cousin. Be careful of who you are and who you may become. For Ilduin blood heals and cleanses, but Ilduin blood also judges. It would pain me if Ilduin blood were to judge you. For that judgment would not be my own, tempered by the mercy of my memories of our youth and my love for my cousin. Be careful, Giri. And cut me not."

She turned and left, the warning hanging in the stale air of the tent like an ominous cloud. Giri considered calling after her, to confront her, but decided against it. He considered a meal, then abandoned that idea, as well. Instead, he spread his map on the small table and looked for the next place from which to strike his enemies.

Tuzza watched as yet another sunset faded into dusty, golden-red shadows. For three days he had pursued this maddening band of Anari. For three nights he had cursed the gods as his men fought off one raid after another, each attack carried out with the stealth and savagery of a Deder panther. And each day's march, following what few tracks these Anari left of their passage, led Tuzza's men farther south, deeper into this bleak and forbidding land the Anari called home.

That part, at least, was progress. His objective was Anahar, where he would no longer have to follow scratches in the dirt and fight shadows in the night. But Anahar was still five days' march distant, and his men would have to traverse the narrow river crevasses and defiles that lay across their path. Doubtless there would be more ambushes waiting for him in those defiles.

"Damn this country," he muttered, looking at the forbidding peaks that loomed on the horizon like the shoulders of an angry bear.

The Anari land had not one thing to recommend itself. The soil was dry, stony, reddish, dotted only by the occasional small tree or patch of scrub grass. His horses could not find fodder along their route, and already many were showing their ribs and weakening in their traces. He had warned the royal court that he would need to bring hay wagons with him if he hoped to bring his cavalry to bear in the final battle. He had argued for extra water skins, and extra provisions for his men.

"You are not going to do battle," the king's military advisor had declared, "but to slay cattle. This is but a punitive expedition. March to Anahar, killing any who dare resist the Crown of Bozandar, and put down this rebellion."

Fools. The Anari were not cattle. And though they had no history of war, they were writing one now in Bozandari blood, league by miserable league. They fought with the fury of a boar in the sport ring, years of slavery their teasing lancets, blood in their eyes, death in their hearts. Already fear was spreading among his men, fear of the night and blue-black shadows that seemed to move through it like evil spirits on the wind.

It was not that his men were cowards. Far from it. They were brave men, disciplined and trained from years of service. But they were hungry, and tired. Their days were filled with dry marches under the hot southern sun, their nights with long watches and deadly patrols. Already his men were growing lax in those patrols, less willing to wander out into the night, to find the enemy before the enemy found them. Too many patrols had gone out and not come back, or come back in bloody parts flung into the camp by the silent wraiths that stalked his column.

Tuzza had sent out mounted patrols, but they were hopeless on this hard, stony ground. Horses made far too much noise, and the Anari avoided them with ease. Nor could his cavalry mount lightning raids at the gallop, for fear of their mounts being lamed in the darkness by the hard, uneven ground. So his horses remained in camp, their traveling fodder long since consumed, now having to share what little food remained for his men.

If he could but find this damned Anari shadowing force and destroy it, his men would be able to forage what little the land did offer. But it was too risky to send out supply parties when even his armed patrols were met with such ferocity. And so they parceled out the food that remained, the rations smaller each day, huddling in their nighttime camps, catching snatches of sleep when they could, and waiting—waiting for the next screams, the next sudden rush of nearly silent footsteps, the next comrade slain at their feet.

"The camp is ready, Topmark."

Tuzza turned and nodded to the young man beside him, studying his tired face, seeing his own thoughts mirrored in the man's eyes. "Very well, Overmark Onsala. And the patrol assignments?"

"Company strength, as ordered, sir. The men aren't happy about it, but they'll do it."

"They're not supposed to be happy," Tuzza said. "They're supposed to be soldiers. But do make sure that each patrol company gets an extra ration in the morning."

"Yes, sir," Onsala said.

Onsala saluted and returned to his duties, leaving Tuzza with the foreboding sense that too many of those men would not live to see that extra ration at dawn. Company strength or not, his patrols would be struck in the night. And more men would die in this miserable land.

32

The taste of victory was beginning to grow sweet in Giri's mouth. His men had inflicted enough damage during the past nights that he could now see and almost smell the fear among the Bozandari army.

And they were headed exactly where he wanted them. Archer's and Jenah's columns were now moving steadily northward, opening a maw between them for the Bozandari to march into. Then they would fall on the enemy's flanks, while Giri fell on their rear.

In his mind, when he closed his eyes, he could summon a bird's eye view of the battle to come, and he knew it would be victory.

But he had to make sure that the arrogant Topmark in his cloak of gold didn't change directions too soon. If they kept moving as they were now for at least another half day, the plan would work. If not…

He lay in the darkness, his men scattered all around the Bozandari encampment, awaiting the patrols that came every night to the slaughter.

He no longer needed to guide his troops, for they had learned the thrust, feint and parry of the silent, secret attack. They had learned to separate the patrols, to lead them into the darkness beyond help, and to deal with them.

Watching the camp form before him now, he sensed that something was going to be different tonight. Hissing in imitation of the sand viper, he caught the attention of one of his lieutenants.

"Get Cilla."

The lieutenant nodded and turned, sending a runner on silent feet off into the darkness.

Minutes ticked by, and Giri grew increasingly uneasy. Too many men were not settling down. Instead, they seemed to be getting ready for something.

At last Cilla arrived beside him. She had taken to wearing leathers like the rest of them, blending into the night, the leather oiled so that it made no sound.

"What's going on down there?" he asked her.

Without a word, she closed her eyes, shutting out distraction. Minutes passed before she spoke, her voice a whisper.

"They are sending out larger patrols. Many men. 'Twill be too much for your raiders to handle, cousin. You either need more men or you need to withdraw now."

Giri didn't need to think for long. Making the sand viper sounds in a preordained sequence, the word passed from group to group.

Silently, guided by the stones beneath their feet, they melted into the darkness and moved southwest to join their main body, which was positioning itself to swing like a trapdoor on the rear of the Bozandari army once it marched into the waiting maw.

Several hours later, the three Ilduin conferred. All were worried about Giri, but none knew what they could do to heal him before his anger took him too far.

Tess passed along the message that Archer was glad Giri had

decided to forgo the night's raids. He felt it would encourage the enemy to continue their southward march. Sara announced that Jenah agreed.

Military matters dealt with for the moment, the women huddled together mentally, offering one another comfort and strength. Offering it particularly to Cilla, who was so worried about Giri's state of mind that she could not cease thinking of it.

"Perhaps," said Tess after a long time had passed, "perhaps we *all* need to speak with Giri. Perhaps it is not enough that his cousin warns him."

"How can we do that?" Sara asked.

Silence passed among them for a timeless space. Then Tess spoke again in their minds. "Cilla, go to Giri. Sara and I will try to use you as a beacon so that our images can appear beside you and speak."

Cilla's answering thought was hesitant. "Do you…think it can work?"

Tess's reply was almost a laugh, but there seemed no humor in her thought. "We can only try."

"I have heard of such," Sara said, trying to feel sure. Her sisters heard her doubt anyway.

"Let us try," Cilla said finally.

She turned from the boulder on which she leaned and headed straight for Giri's tent. As usual, his oil lamp was lit and he was hard at work. She doubted he had slept much in days.

"What is it?" he asked irritably, looking up from his maps.

"Archer thinks it is good we do not raid tonight. He believes the absence of resistance will cause the Bozandari to make a swift push forward, right into the trap."

"Good. Good." He looked down again, obviously dismissing her, but she didn't leave.

Finally he looked up once more, annoyed words on his lips.

But then he caught his breath and his eyes widened, for before him stood all three Ilduin, Sara and Tess to either side of Cilla.

He blinked, doubting his eyes, but still he saw them. It was as if…no, Sara and Tess didn't seem quite solid, not as solid as Cilla, but solid enough to make the nape of his neck prickle atavistically.

"What…what are you doing?"

Tess's shade spoke. "We worry about you, Giri. The three of us are concerned. Your anger does not fade. It is not slaked by battle."

"My anger is necessary!" He slammed his palm on the table, but none of the women seemed disturbed.

Tess spoke again. "But your thirst for blood is not. And it grows by the hour. Examine yourself, Giri Monabi. Examine yourself and ask whether you want a drop of our blood to fall on you now."

At that, Cilla drew her dagger and made a small slash on her palm. Blood dripped to the rocky floor of the tent.

"Cilla!"

"Cousin, I would not judge you. But I fear for your soul. Ask yourself if you feel worthy to touch a drop of my blood."

Giri stared at the women, then at the glistening drops of blood that fell steadily from his cousin's hand. She held it out so he could see the droplets but made no move to approach.

"As a Monabi judge, I find you wanting," she said sadly. "Will you test the judgment over which I have no control?"

A struggle was visible on Giri's face, but finally, at long last, he stilled. When at last he looked at Cilla again, there was sorrow on his face.

"I will try, cousin," he said. "I will try."

As soon as he spoke, the wound on Cilla's hand healed and the blood stopped falling.

"Think about it, Giri," she said gently. "Think and try. For in these times we must guard our souls with every defense we have."

"Will you stay with me?"

"Aye."

Tess and Sara flickered out as if they were dying candle flames, and only Cilla remained.

She pulled up a camp stool beside Giri and took both of his dark hands in hers. "Try, cousin, for a single soul matters more than the lives of an entire race."

Giri nodded, but still Cilla could feel the anger in him, and her fear for her cousin deepened.

Finally he said, "I will go on retreat when this is over."

It was a hard concession for him to make, and she had to take what solace she could find in it. She only hoped his retreat would not come too late.

"The Enemy lurks," she reminded him, squeezing his hands. "Give him no room to enter."

At first light, Topmark Tuzza was an unhappy man. His men ate a cheerless and too-lean meal before starting to break camp. Tuzza found himself a high, rocky ridge from which he surveyed the surrounding country. Even his keen eye could pick out nothing unusual.

But the night had been too quiet. They had run a gauntlet of death for days now, but last night nothing had happened amiss. Perhaps the size of his patrols had scared off the raiders. He had no way of knowing.

What he *did* know when he looked at his men was that, given a choice, he would turn them right around and march back to the frontier. The legion that had been encamped here was already destroyed. Its commander had banked on the passivity of the Anari and dispersed his men into three camps, each of which had been crushed. Indeed, from the outset he had thought this mission dangerous foolery.

But he was a soldier, and he obeyed. *Save the camp and attack Anahar.*

Words easily spoken from the capital city of Bozandar. Easily spoken by men who sat in comfortable chairs while being waited on by slaves they considered passive and unthreatening.

A very different story for the army sent to achieve those goals, an army suffering from the speed of their march and the cut in their rations. An army that was being attacked nightly by unseen raiders who were apparently little more than shadows in the dark. An army that was discovering the Anari were not so passive after all.

There were no Bozandari camps left to save here. And to attack the Anari holy city? Had anyone asked him, Tuzza would have told them that was a folly beyond belief. Some indignities would not be borne, even by an enslaved people. He could capture Anahar, yes. He could try to raze it to the ground, though if the stories were to be believed, the city itself was beyond the destruction of man. But what then? Would that bring the Anari to heel? Hardly.

Not that Tuzza cared one way or the other about the Anari. His father had never owned a slave, believing that no slave could ever be truly trustworthy. Tuzza had felt the same. In his holdings, where matters of great importance to the empire were often discussed, he did not need to be wondering about the loyalty of those who moved silently among them serving choice tidbits of food and vessels of ale.

But now he wished he had troubled to know just *one* Anari. Even a slave. For he found himself blinded by his own inability to imagine how they might think.

Except that whoever led them seemed to be a good general.

Sighing, he scanned the rocky foothills and eyed the pass ahead. Was he being led into a trap? Had he already fallen into one?

But what did these questions matter? He had been sent on a mission, and he had no choice but to pursue it, though he and every man under his command might die in the process.

Retreat was not an option. Ever.

The mutilated body of his young cousin flashed before his eyes, and he hardened himself against all doubts. For that alone he would march his men into the jaws of death.

Tess, who had been distracted all night and unwilling to sleep, climbed to the rim of the canyon to watch the sun rise. The stars still wheeled above, but dawn was approaching. Soon the first gray light would appear in the east, the faint harbinger of a day she dreaded.

For she could sense the nearness of the enemy army. Below her, the Anari were furiously digging pits and lining their bases with sharp stones to further hamper the Bozandari who would soon attack. Archer had ordered them to build a series of defensive lines. The plan was to draw the attackers in, thinning them at each line, luring them deeper into the canyon. Only then would Giri fall upon their rear.

"It will be a battle of annihilation," Archer had said last night as he explained the plan.

Thinking back on those words, Tess found neither confidence nor peace. *Annihilation.* Yes, that was what would happen. The evil of men ladled out upon each other, imagination and intelligence and courage stewed together and then left to ferment into a deadly, bitter brew. Her heart already ached for what would happen.

Worse, everyone in the camp was on edge. Whether they concealed or displayed it, every heart felt fear. Fear of death. Fear of failure. It was palpable, like a blanket thrown over them, heavy and oppressive. That affected her concentration. She did not know how to block the miasma of feelings that filled the atmosphere.

I can teach you.

The voice, the one she had so long ago blocked, was back. Cold, oily fingers in her mind told her that *he* had found his way within her once more.

Come, my love, the voice said. *I can teach you many things.*

Squeezing her hands into fists until her nails bit into her palms, she shoved the presence away, then mentally squeezed it until, with a *pop,* it disappeared. With a last glance to the east, she descended to the valley floor.

Behind her, the gray light began to limn the mountain peaks, as if the earth itself was marking this day in stark relief.

Jenah's men had borne the brunt of the marching, up into and then down from the rugged Panthos Mountains. In the days since, they had dug, then dug some more, the pace brutal and unending as they prepared their positions for the assault. Two defensive belts, pits twice as deep as a man, their bottoms and sides lined with jagged rocks, now stretched across the valley floor. In each belt, there were two lines of pits, those in one line behind the gaps in the line in front, so there was no direct route to the Anari forces. Jenah's force lay behind the first belt and Archer's behind the second.

The plan was brutally simple. Jenah's men were to delay the Bozandari for as long as they could, showering them with arrows as they negotiated the pits, then meeting them in pockets as they emerged. Jenah had no doubt that his men would falter. Bravery counted for only so much in the face of utter exhaustion. But that, too, was part of the plan.

Once it became apparent that his men were spent, they would withdraw through the second belt, feigning a rout. The Bozandari would surge forward in pursuit and fall upon the second defensive line, both its pit traps and Archer's men, who would be carefully concealed. Shock and confusion would break down the Bozandaris' careful battle tactics, and the steep valley walls would prevent any flanking maneuvers.

The hope was to bleed the Bozandari legion white as it battered its way through the narrow valley. Then, at nightfall, Archer, too, would withdraw to re-form beside Jenah in a third line of fortifications at the southern mouth of the valley. In the morning, when the Bozandari pressed on, still hemmed in by the valley and unable to deploy in full, the Anari would meet them with overwhelming force. The trap would be completed when Giri's column, hiding in the hills, fell upon the enemy's rear.

It sounded so simple in the conversations at Archer's command tent. It looked so simple on the carefully drawn maps. Jenah knew it would be anything but. Somehow, amidst the chaos and confusion of close quarters combat, he would have to withdraw his men and feign a rout without it actually becoming the real thing. And he had no doubt as to the fate of those who were caught by the pursuing Bozandari. He would bleed the enemy, yes. But the enemy would also bleed him.

The earth seemed to rumble beneath his feet, its own heartbeat offset by the thudding of thousands of feet. Beyond a curve in the valley, dust rose high into the air. The Bozandari were coming. They were coming soon.

Tuzza watched the first rays of dawn strike fire from the mountain peaks around him. He and his army were moving sluggishly, tired and underfed, and facing the most difficult part of their march: the pass through those mountains.

There were other ways to Anahar, he knew, but from where he was, there were none that would not cost him at least a week's further marching. His men didn't have another week in them. Time and supplies commanded that he march through this valley. Below it, it was rumored, there were open fields and richer soil. That meant he could deploy his forces properly and perhaps even find some forage to slake his men's bellies before the final leg of his march on Anahar.

First, though, they had to survive this valley, with walls that loomed more forbiddingly with every step he took. Tuzza, a man of reason, a man of both letters and numbers, who took pride in dismissing the superstitious beliefs of others, felt as if those mountains were watching him. Brooding over him and his army. Threatening.

Yet they were just mountains, immobile, unchanging. Dead rock. So why did he feel *these* mountains were somehow different?

With no room to deploy, his legion was marching in a column, with only a single company frontage. He could, at most, put two companies forward in line. Thus the legion was spread out, a slender serpent crawling through a long pipe, vulnerable and unable to bring most of its force to bear. The horses, such as were left, hauled the remaining baggage trains.

It was a terrible formation in which to meet the enemy, and as the first reports rippled back from the advance scouts, he knew the enemy had planned for exactly this outcome. The Anari might be peaceful by nature, but they had all too quickly learned the wiles of war. And he had no choice but to press home the attack.

"Deploy your brigade with two regiments abreast in assault columns," he said to Overmark Gansar. "Break their lines, and make haste with it. I do not wish to be picked apart in this damned valley."

"At once, sir," Gansar said, snapping a salute. "It will be done."

It was mid-morning as Jenah watched the Bozandari approaching in two columns, each with three ranks of sixty men abreast. Forming from a single column into attack order had taken time, given the tight confines of the valley floor. Now they were ready, and their leaders sounded the advance. Within minutes, however, their smooth, orderly advance faltered as they came upon the first lines of pit traps. While only a few fell victim, the rest were forced to reorder and shift their lines of march toward the gaps. It was the moment Jenah had been waiting for.

"Archers, loose your arrows!" he cried.

With a rippling whistle, the arrows flew forth, arching over the heads of Jenah's front lines before plunging down onto the already discomfited Bozandari. Within seconds, all sense of order in the Bozandari ranks gave way as men staggered to avoid pits, scrambled to heft shields overhead, and pushed and shoved to find some measure of safety from the rain of death.

The few that surged forward did so in scattered groups, which became easy pickings for the whirling blades of Jenah's men. Confusion reigned, and for brief moments it appeared as if Jenah's men might halt the Bozandari attack in its tracks.

But then the Bozandari commander asserted his will on the battle, screaming and kicking at men, creating order from chaos. The enemy's archers, their skills honed by years of practice, rained down arrows on Jenah's men with an accuracy that was truly amazing to watch. The deadly storm became a shield behind which the Bozandari infantry could form, then burst into Jenah's lines as the clatter of plunging arrows finally gave way to the clang and bite and scream of close combat.

This commander knew his business, Jenah realized. Gone were the days of confused and terrified Bozandari falling to the flensing blades of the Anari. The step-and-thrust, step-and-thrust, of the Bozandari infantry was slowly pushing his men back upon themselves, and Jenah knew his forces had done as much as they could. Now it was time to trust Archer's battle plan.

"Sound retreat!" Jenah cried, praying that his men would retain their self-control.

"On them!" Gansar bellowed, as the Anari lines began to waver and then melt away. "On them now! Give them no quarter!"

It was the moment Gansar had waited for, the moment in which he could catch the Anari without their practiced threshing lines. Let them taste Bozandari steel now, when they were helpless to resist it.

He surged forward with his men, sword held high, driving them onward as they hacked and chopped into the faces of those who tried to stand, and the backs of those who turned and fled too late. Tuzza had ordered him to break their lines and make haste. Gansar had followed his orders to the letter. Now, truly, it would be done.

And then the earth opened beneath his feet.

Tuzza watched as the next line of Anari threw off the dust-covered tents beneath which they'd been lying and rose from the ground as if they were the spawn of the mountains themselves.

Already Gansar's brigade was falling victim to the damnable pit traps the Anari had dug. Those in the second and third regiments, unaware of what had befallen those in front, fueled by blood lust and the ephemeral scent of victory, were pushing hard against those ahead of them, sending even more tumbling into the concealed holes that seemed to open like angry mouths. A rain of arrows from the second line's archers added to the tumult, and now men began to push and shove with only one thought: personal survival. The screams of the wounded and dying rendered meaningless any commands their leaders might give.

His officers, those that survived, would sort it out, of course. But the attack was broken, and the sorting out process would take time. Worse, Tuzza could not send his second brigade forward until the remnants of Gansar's force had managed to make their way to the rear. It would be midafternoon, at the earliest, before Tuzza could organize another attack to breach this new line.

"This is madness," he said, turning to Overmark Thul. "They may have another line behind this one, and another behind that. Battering our way through this valley will leave us too weak to march on Anahar."

Thul simply nodded.

Tuzza turned and looked at him. "We must find a way around them, Thul. Take your brigade and do it. Crawl through these hills like goats, if you must, but find a way around to their rear. I will send the second brigade up to breach their line this afternoon and hold the Guard Brigade in reserve. If the Anari know their business, and apparently they do, their main defense line will be at the mouth of this valley. I will attack them there at dawn. I expect you to fall on their rear at the same time."

Thul looked up at the forbidding mountains, as if taking their measure and weighing it against that of his exhausted men. They would be marching all night, climbing, scrambling, making their way through terrain that would give a panther pause. But Topmark Tuzza was right. To simply attempt to bash their way through this valley, one line at a time, was suicide.

"Yes, sir," Thul said. "My men will run all night, if need be. But we will be formed up and ready for battle at dawn. You have my word."

"I had no need of your word," Tuzza said. "You are a Bozandari officer, and a fine one. Your obedience and loyalty are beyond question."

"Yes, sir."

Tuzza looked at him. "You are not sure we can beat these Anari, are you?"

"They are skilled warriors, sir," Thul replied. "Far beyond anything we expected. We are on their terrain, and I fear their raiding force has drawn us into precisely this trap at this time. Something binds them, unites the minds of their commanders, as if they have formed their own hive. That leaves me to fear for your safety, and the safety of my men. Their raiding force is still out there, somewhere in these hills, waiting for the moment to strike."

"You doubt my plan," Tuzza said. It was neither a question nor an accusation but merely a statement.

"I do not, sir," Thul said. "We cannot win the battle but by doing as you say. I ask only that you be wary of committing the Guard, sir. For once we do, the Anari hiding in these hills will descend on us. On you, sir. And I have no wish to carry your body back to Bozandar."

"Nor I yours, my friend," Tuzza said, reaching out to place a hand on Thul's shoulder. "Your words are well spoken and well received. I will withhold the Guard until your attack is well under way, until we are certain of breaking out of this valley. Then, if their raiders fall upon our rear, we can withdraw forward, into the fertile ground beyond."

"Withdraw forward, sir?" Thul asked, a smile forming on his face.

"You will not find that in the manuals, my friend," Tuzza replied. "But these Anari are not in the manuals, either. Before this is over, I expect we will all have much to learn."

"I must be off, sir," Thul said.

"Yes, yes," Tuzza replied. "Make haste, my friend, and I will see you at the dawn."

"At the dawn," Thul replied.

As Tuzza watched Thul make his preparations, he knew that Thul was right. The raiders who had dogged his steps at every league had been luring him along, leading him to this valley, to this battle, a battle they could fight and win. They were making the best possible use of an inferior force. They were outwitting him.

It was time to gather his own wits and turn the tables. He could not win their battle, but neither could they win his. Initiative was the key, and he meant to seize it.

"Tensanar!" he bellowed, calling for the commander of the Guard Brigade. "At once!"

Overmark Tensanar snapped to attention and marched over, stopping at the regulation two paces to salute.

"I want company strength patrols of the Guard in these hills tonight. Find that Anari raiding force. Do not give them battle, for I will need your men on the morrow. But find them. At the very least, I must know whence my enemy will come."

"Yes, sir," Tensanar said, his face betraying surprise, for Guardsmen were usually far too valuable to waste on patrol duty.

"I know, Overmark," Thul said. "But I have no one else to send."

"I will see to it, sir," Tensanar said.

Tuzza looked out at the valley, watching as the remnants of Gansar's brigade finally organized their withdrawal, carrying the shattered bodies of their fallen comrades. Tuzza would break through this valley. And he would ensure that his men did not die in vain.

But then he would return to Bozandar, and his report would not please the court. Let them be displeased. Let them know the scope of that which they had undertaken. Let them see the bodies of the fallen and weigh their worth.

Squeezing his fists in disgust, he set off to organize the next attack.

34

Tess knelt down by a wounded Anari, looking into his eyes. They seemed slow to focus and find her, which was not surprising, given the horrific gash that had laid open four ribs in his back, breaking three. She tried to focus her vision within him, to assess the internal damage, but her overtaxed mind rebelled at the attempt. She had given away a lot of herself on this day, and she knew she had few reserves left. The man tried to cough, and foamy blood appeared at his lips. The wound had cut a lung. There was little she could do for him, not if she were to have anything left for the dozens of others yet to be seen.

Tess looked up at the two Anari women beside her, with the faintest shake of her head. "Over there, please."

She would have expected tears in their eyes, or hers, at those words. She was pointing to the growing body of men who were beyond hope. But the women took it with stoic calm, shifting the man onto a makeshift litter and moving him as instructed. Tess shifted her attention to the next man as they moved away.

"So many," Sara said, placing a hand on Tess's shoulder. "You've saved so many. But you're tired, sister. You need rest."

Tess nodded. "I *am* tired, Sara. But no more so than these men who lie here. The Anari in the lines are not sleeping. They are digging, preparing. I will not rest until they rest."

"You're acting as if the war will end tomorrow, Tess, as if it's written in the stars that the Bozandari will press on with their hopeless attacks until we crush them. But Bozandar did not become a great empire by behaving in stupid ways. They will have a surprise for us on the morrow. And what if they force us to retreat to Anahar? This war may drag on for months, sister. Will you go without rest for months?"

Tess looked up into Sara's eyes. Gone were the almost passive, domestic eyes Tess had met in Whitewater. Sara had seen too much in their journey to remain that quiet innkeeper's daughter. Her eyes were not yet hardened, but her gaze was firm and unyielding.

She's right, Cilla thought, adding her voice to the conversation. *I feel your exhaustion, too, Tess. You must care for yourself, also, lest there be nothing in you left to care for others.*

Tess finally nodded. They were right. She'd been treating the wounded since the first casualties of Jenah's line had begun to arrive, hours earlier. While there had been breaks in the battle, there had been no respite in the cries of those whose bodies had been broken by it. Sara and Cilla had lent their energies, but even the combined life force of three Ilduin was inadequate in the face of so much suffering, especially when Archer had forbade them to create any disturbance in the fabric of reality. In the presence of the enemy, and doubtless the presence of the greater Enemy, any such display would attract piercing and potentially disastrous attention.

"Yes," Tess said. "I must eat, at least. And we must ensure that the wounded are fed and have water. And they must have blankets, all of them."

"I will see to it," Sara said. "Tom can help me. You rest. At least for an hour or two. Trust someone else to carry this burden for a while."

Tess nodded and rose, stretching her back, looking at the red-tinged clouds on the western horizon and back down at the red-spattered ground around her. Sara's Ilduin healing power might not rival hers, but Jenah's men spoke of her in reverent terms. She had cared for his wounded, often on her own, with healing herbs and caring touches. She knew what to do.

Otteda appeared at her side almost immediately, for he was never far from her. "You have worked wonders, Lady."

"And too many will still die," Tess said, exhaustion weighting every word. "Let us first go to Lord Archer, to tell him where I will be."

Otteda studied her face for a moment. "As you wish, Lady, though I can send a runner to tell him for you."

"That is very kind, Rearmark, but the walk will do me good. Doubtless there is news of the battle."

"Ratha's men held off the enemy until sunset," Otteda said. "The Bozandari withdrew at dusk rather than fight in the dark. Ratha's men are retiring to the main line now. So far, Lord Archer's plan is working."

"Why do I think you are attempting to keep me from visiting the command tent?" Tess asked, the faintest hint of a laugh in her words.

"My men and I have sworn ourselves to your protection," Otteda replied. "If in that we must protect you from yourself, then so be it."

"I have entirely too many keepers," Tess said.

"Or perhaps too few, judging by the manner in which you punish yourself, Lady."

She looked up at him, remembering the conversation with Tom after the battle near the sea. "You overheard."

"Yes, Lady. Perhaps it is not my place to speak."

"If you judge that to be so, then speak not," Tess replied, her voice betraying an anger she did not feel. She took a breath. "I am sorry."

"Think nothing of it, Lady," Otteda said, smiling. "I have heard far worse from far lesser men. And forgive my blunt words, for I am no prophet like Tom. I am merely a soldier, with a soldier's grasp of thought."

"Why do I fear I am to be chastised?" Tess asked.

"Because you are, Lady," Otteda said. "No one leaves the field of battle without guilt. You punish yourself as if you and you alone bear the sin of war. Not just this war, but of war itself. Do you think I hear not in the night the cries of those I have slain? Do you think the men you treated today feel not the shame of their wounds and of having yielded their place in the ranks? Do Jenah and Ratha and Lord Archer not carry the weight of their decisions upon their shoulders, decisions which they know will send men to their deaths?"

"Of course," Tess replied. "But..."

"There is no 'but,' Lady Tess," Otteda said, stepping in front of her, blocking her path. "We all ache for the wounded and grieve for the dead, none more so than those who have wounded and killed, or caused men to be wounded and killed. Your duty weighs heavy enough without adding to that the weight of guilt and, dare I say it, self pity.

"You have been a soldier, Lady, perhaps in a way and in a world I cannot understand, but a soldier regardless. And now you must behave as a soldier behaves. You must care for your body, as any soldier must care for his body. You must eat, and rest, as any soldier must eat and rest. We who serve beside you deserve no less."

"Ruck up, suck up and press on," Tess said, the words coming from a memory unbidden. And yet she knew they were true in her old life and no less true in this one. "You are right, Rearmark. In my quest to be selfless I have been selfish above all. I trust you will not let me repeat that mistake."

"Be assured that I will not," Otteda said. "For now, let us feed you and find you a place to rest. I will wake you at moonrise for the commanders' conference."

"Lead the way, my friend," Tess said.

Otteda smiled and ushered her toward the mess area.

Overmark Thul saw a movement in the darkness and held up his hand to halt his column. The movement materialized in the form of a man from his scout force, panting as he ran back to the main body.

"I think we have found a safe route, Overmark," the man said. He lifted an exhausted arm to point. "At the crest of that hill, you will see a gap in the mountains. The path bends to the west at first, but then back east. From the bend, I could see the plains beyond. It should lead us into the right rear of the enemy's line."

"You have done well, soldier," Thul said, patting the man's shoulder. "Perhaps this endless night will bring us to victory. Go forward now, with your company, and make certain the way is clear. I have no wish to walk into an ambush in this darkness."

"Yes, sir," the man said.

As the man jogged back up the hill, Thul passed the word down the column to the rest of his men. To the east, the moon was just creeping over the horizon. While only a half-moon, its pale light would at least ease his men's fears. He guessed that he had but four or five hours at most to get through these hills and form up his brigade in assault order. There was no time to waste.

He lifted his arm and pointed it forward, his tired legs rebelling as he willed them into motion. If his scout was right, there was perhaps one last steep climb before they began to descend. His legs could manage one more climb. He would accept nothing less.

* * *

Archer scratched at the stubble on his chin as Jenah and Ratha joined him in the command tent with Sara, Tom, Tess and now Otteda. Jenah had looked upon the Bozandari guards with dark skepticism at first but seemed to be adapting to the notion that they were committed to Tess and to the Anari cause. But this was the first time Otteda had joined their command conference, at Tess's insistence, and even Archer felt a prickle of tension at the back of his neck.

Or perhaps it was simple exhaustion. He had slept but three hours in the past two days, and while the gods had both blessed and cursed him to walk the earth without aging, they had not relieved him of the demands of bodily existence. He dipped his hands into a basin of water and splashed it over his face. While that did not equal a hot meal, a bath and a night's sleep, it would have to do.

"We fought well yesterday," he said. "The enemy will be much weaker at dawn than he was yesterday. But there is much hard fighting left to do."

"Yes, Lord," Jenah said. "And we, too, are weaker than we were at yesterdawn. I have but nine hundred men fit for battle today."

"And I but two hundred more than that," Ratha said.

Two thousand, Archer thought. Two weeks ago, each of their columns alone had numbered that. Losses in battle, and the inevitable fatigue and injuries from their forced marches, had cut their numbers by half.

"And Giri?" Archer said to Tess.

She closed her eyes for a moment, her lips moving in inaudible words that he knew only her fellow Ilduin could hear. "Cilla says there are perhaps one thousand who can fight today. Giri is right now directing his men against the Bozandari patrols that have crept into the hills since sunset. And the Bozandari they have captured this night are not men of the line. They are Guard."

"Topmark Tuzza is not a stupid man," Otteda said. "He knows that Giri's force still lurks in the background. He is anticipating Giri's attack. But the Guard Brigade…"

"What?" Archer asked.

"It is not our custom for the Guard to conduct routine patrols," Otteda said. "Those selected and trained for the Guard are too valuable to risk thus. Giri reported that the enemy's legion was four brigades strong, as is our standard. Three would be line brigades and the fourth the Overmark's Guard Brigade."

"Yes," Ratha said, impatience in his voice. "You told us this when Giri first made contact with them. And now?"

"Topmark Tuzza committed one brigade in the assault on Jenah yestermorn," Otteda said, "and a second against your lines in the afternoon. He has a third brigade from which to form patrols against Giri. And yet he sends men from the Guard. It leads me to wonder where his third brigade might be."

"Perhaps he is resting them for the attack in the morning," Jenah said.

Otteda shook his head. "If a brigade were to be rested, it would be the Guard. No, he has sent his third brigade on some other mission." He pointed to the map. "Are there any paths through these mountains to the west?"

"Jenah?" Archer asked. "This is the land of Gewindi-Tel. Are there paths there?"

Jenah stood in silence, staring at the map, as if trying to picture the terrain in his mind. "Yes, Lord, there is one. But the Bozandari would have to march all night over steep terrain, and march quickly. Even Anari would be pressed to do it in less than twelve hours."

"We are trained for nighttime quick marches," Otteda said. "It is common to Bozandari doctrine. 'Steal the night and carry the day.' Topmark Tuzza is a brave and resourceful leader. He would have known after the first attack yesterday that this valley was a death trap. He might well have given the marching orders then, before the second attack was joined. With an afternoon and a night to march, that brigade might even now be emerging from the mountains behind us, forming up, ready to fall upon our rear as Tuzza assails our front."

"That makes sense," Archer said, nodding. "It is what we had planned, after all. And if we can think of it…"

He had no need to finish the thought.

"We have no reserves, Lord," Ratha said. "If we turn any men to protect our rear, there will be too few to hold our front."

"I know," Archer said.

"You have one reserve, Lord," Otteda said. "My men. We doubled our strength from those who joined us after the battle at the sea."

"There are still but three score of you," Archer said. "Barely a company. How can you hold a brigade?"

"They can," Tom said, stepping forward, his hand on the hilt of his sword. "With this."

Sara shook her head. "Tom, you cannot kill. Your gift of prophecy counts for more than your sword."

"In my own hands, perhaps," Tom said. "But it was not for me to wield this blade, my love."

Tess felt his thought an instant before he said it and began to shake her head.

"Yes, Lady," Tom said, stepping to her. "This is the Weaver's Blade. Ask me not how I know it. Know only that I do, beyond all doubt. You must wield it, Lady Tess, and in your hands it will grow in might."

"No…no," Tess said, backing away.

"Yes, Lady," Otteda said. "You are a soldier. If the young prophet's words be true, and true they all have been, then now is the time for you to pledge to my men, as they have pledged to you."

"I cannot," Tess said, fear etched in her face.

"Prophecy has guided us thus far," Archer said, taking her hand. "Prophecy commands us."

"Yes," Sara said. "You know the truth of it, sister. As Cilla says, the freedom of a people is in your hands. The Anari swore themselves to you. Your guard swore themselves to you. Now you must bear their oath. I will join you, if I must."

"No," Tom said. "Your place will be with Lord Archer, that he may speak with Giri. This is a battle that Lady Tess must face herself, with those pledged at her side. Thus it must be."

"Thus it must be," Tess echoed softly.

"Then let it be," Archer said.

He squeezed her hands gently, looking into her eyes. What evil had the First Ones wrought in their arrogance? A people who had not known war now bore its burden, and hands made to heal must now kill.

"I am sorry, Lady," he said. "If I could take this burden from you…"

"If wishes were horses," Tess said with a bitter smile. Another memory, and no better than the rest. "Wish not for what cannot be, my friend. Wish only that needs be met in the breach. We have no time for other dreams."

Archer felt the strength return to her hands, though a cold strength it was. "Then we must prepare."

Tom removed the scabbard and offered it with outstretched hands. "Your blade, Lady Tess."

The hilt seemed to hum with white fire as Tess touched it, and for an instant she snatched her hand away. Then, once again, she grasped it. Archer felt his throat squeeze.

Only once before had he heard that music from a sword.

Tuzza watched as the sky began to lighten. It had been a quiet night by the standards he had come to expect in the Anari lands. His Guard patrols had found the enemy force lurking in the hills to the east, and while a few of his Guardsmen had been captured, at least now he knew whence to expect that attack.

Overmark Thul's brigade was poised to strike at the enemy's rear, of that Tuzza had no doubts. Thul was his most trusted officer. If Thul had said it would be done, then it had been done.

As Tuzza surveyed the main Anari line, he realized they had no idea of the danger that lurked behind them. Their entire force was facing forward, behind another array of their pit traps. The pits would channel Tuzza's troops, and there was little he could do about that. His men would simply have to negotiate the gaps between the traps, as they had done yesterday, at least until he had the enemy's full attention. Then Thul would strike.

At least here, at the mouth of the valley, he had more room to maneuver. The shattered pieces of Gansar's brigade had been collected into one regiment, which was attached to the second brigade. That brigade, with a fourth regiment at hand, could deploy in two waves, each consisting of two regiments abreast. Judging the enemy's strength by eye, Tuzza reasoned that he had the prescribed numerical superiority in second brigade alone, and he also had the Guard Brigade at his disposal, should second brigade falter.

It wasn't an ideal plan. The enemy had chosen his ground too well to permit an ideal plan. But it made the best use of Tuzza's forces and the options available. As the sun crept over the mountains, Tuzza turned to his bugler.

"Sound the attack."

Tess heard the thin, wavering strains of the bugle call behind her, but her concentration was on the troops emerging from the hills to her front. She and Otteda had been watching them for over an hour now, first in the dim light of the waning moon and then in the rising light of the early dawn.

"A full brigade," Otteda said.

"You were right," Tess replied. "We would have been destroyed, and yet may be. I do not know how a single company can stand against them."

"We can but do our best, Lady," Otteda said. "That is what duty demands. My men have faith in you."

"And I in them," Tess replied. "But it will take more than faith to prevail here."

"Perhaps," Otteda said. "But that is what we have."

Tess nodded. There was no fatalism in the Bozandari's words. It was simply a soldier's factual description of his situation.

And in the time she'd spent this morning, marching and deploying with Otteda's men, she'd come to appreciate their professionalism as men of arms. They had formed up into marching order and moved off within minutes after the command conference, moving at the double-quick for two hours, almost soundlessly, to arrive at the plain where the path descended from the hills. With mere hand signals from Otteda, they had deployed into battle order. They had sipped water from leather skins and passed bread among themselves, then settled into concealed positions, every eye and ear alert.

She had known men like this before, she realized. Men who understood the importance of even the tiniest details of soldiering. The Anari were brave, without doubt, and they had learned at least the basic tactics that Archer and Giri had taught them. But they were not yet soldiers like these men, soldiers who knew to inspect every boot strap, to wipe their sword hilts clean and dust their hands before taking up arms, to tighten loosened shield binders. In the chaos of battle, such details were often the difference between living and dying.

But that was scant comfort. Tess knew the men now descending from the path were equally well trained, equally disciplined, equally professional. And while they were doubtless exhausted from their trek through the hills, they outnumbered Otteda's men by over ten to one.

"We cannot stand here and wait for them to form battle order," she said. "Defense offers us no hope, for they are too many and we too few."

Otteda nodded. "Yes, Lady Tess. We must attack, and hope to catch them tired and ill-prepared."

"We must move now," she said in agreement.

The command to make ready was whispered down the lines. The bowmen notched their arrows, taking aim on the second rank of the enemy. Otteda lifted his sword, and the tiny force surged forward.

As Tess lifted her sword to follow, its hum swelled, and the world around her seemed to slow. It felt as if she and her companions were running through a twisting tunnel, the edges of her vision warping and dimming, the enemy before them seemingly frozen in place. Her sword cleaved the first man as if he were made of butter, biting into the right side of his neck and emerging at his left hip. She was hardly aware of the splash of blood upon her, nor had she time to question how her sword seemed to guide her arm to every weakness, every momentary hesitation. The battle had taken on a life of its own, both around and within her.

She was killing. And she felt nothing.

Archer stood on a small knoll behind his lines, watching the Bozandari advance. The enemy had adjusted his attacking columns to negotiate the gaps between the pits, the rain of arrows turning to a torrent as they emerged and fell into battle order. The Anari were holding fast so far, but this was no mere delaying action, as yesterday's battles had been. If this line broke, the Bozandari would flood through the gap and annihilate them.

In the distance, he saw Giri's force descend out of the hills, in trickles at first, taking advantage of any cover the rocks offered, moving into position for their attack. Much of Archer's plan lay on Giri's shoulders. There was no way Ratha's and Jenah's men could hold off the Bozandari indefinitely. Sooner or later they would be worn down, unless Giri's attack so distracted the enemy that panic became Archer's ally.

He had passed orders to Giri to hold his attack until the Bozandari commander committed his Guard, but so far there was little sign of that. The massive weight of the Bozandari was battering its way forward, step by bloody step, and right now it seemed unlikely that the tired and battered Anari would stop them.

"They begin to give way already," he said to Tom and Sara, who stood at his side. He turned to a young boy, a runner. "Tell Ratha and Giri to commit their reserves."

"Yes, Lord," the man said, scurrying away.

* * *

Overmark Thul screamed orders to his men, trying to shake them from their shock, even while his mind rebelled at what was happening around them. In the span between one heartbeat and the next, the enemy had materialized in the plain beneath him and surged into his lead column. These were not Anari but fellow Bozandari, marching at the side of a woman from whom death seemed to crackle and strike like lightning from a summer storm. She fought like a woman possessed, the blood of his men forming vivid red splashes on her white tunic and breeches.

Even from two hundred yards away, he felt as if he could see into her eyes, pale eyes that showed no feeling whatever but only the frenzy of battle. They were eyes that spread terror, and Thul had to steel himself against that terror.

The attackers were not flitting about from place to place in the blink of an eye, he knew. That could not happen. It was fear that made it seem thus, and he had to master that fear or he had no hope of commanding his men.

It was not possible that the pale-eyed woman was now only one hundred paces distant and in the next breath, only fifty. It was not possible that so tiny a force had already slain a third of Thul's brigade. It was not possible that the woman was now upon him, her blade rising and now descending in less time than he—a trained soldier of the Realm, with reflexes honed in a dozen years of battles—could lift his shield.

It was not possible that she was already past, leaving him on the ground, choking and coughing on his own blood as his life flowed away into the rocky soil.

It was not possible.

Ratha had ordered his reserves forward, and they brought a new energy among the Anari, a ferocity that Ratha had feared might wane in the critical moment. But now the low rumbling of their battle cry echoed in the valley.

As the Bozandari were driven back toward the pit traps, gaps began to form in their lines as men tumbled onto the sharp stones. Their agonized screams rose above the din of battle, worming their way into Ratha's soul, another memory that he would carry to his death.

He felt no joy at their suffering. He had not chosen this war, nor the enslavement that had sown the seeds of it. But the blood was still upon his hands, spattered across his chest and legs, bitter in his mouth. Blood for which he would have to atone someday.

He looked through one of the gaps, saw the enemy commander lower his arm and the enemy's Guard begin to move forward. This would be Giri's cue, and as if they were joined by a single mind, he saw Giri's force rise from the stones and begin their descent into the enemy's rear.

His brother was a brave soldier, and he and his men would fight well. Ratha could only hope that Giri fought not with rage but with the sober determination that Ratha himself had found. If not, Ratha knew, Giri could never find peace, even in the absence of war.

And what Ratha most wished for at that moment was peace. But that was, he knew, a wish that lay far downstream in the river of time. Ratha turned his attention from Giri to the men around him, and to the horrible business of war.

Giri's men rose around him as the Bozandari general was finally forced to commit his last reserve. The Anari battle cry boomed across the valley floor like a clap of thunder, and his men descended as if on bolts of lightning, surging into the flank of the enemy column, hewing men the way farmers harvested wheat.

Giri was neither surprised nor alarmed when the enemy pivoted to receive his attack. And while his forces lacked the cover of darkness that had cloaked their previous battles, they were men who had faced this enemy countless times in the past weeks and come away victorious every time. They fought with the courage of confidence and the rage of a people who for too long had felt the boot of Bozandar upon their necks.

Giri, too, felt that rage and unleashed it upon the man before him, looking into his eyes as he wrenched his sword free of his body and stepped over him to the next, and the next, and the next. Whatever Ratha and Cilla might say, battle was rage and hate and blood and death, and Giri knew the best he could hope for was that the enemy shed more blood than he. It was that which drove him, propelled him, hurled him into the Bozandari ranks with the fury of a storm wave crashing against the shore.

His men felt that fury in him, found it in themselves, and pressed forward beside him, turning the Bozandari before them into leaking shreds of human refuse, advancing with pitiless determination.

Tuzza saw the enemy force come down out of the hills, and he knew instinctively that this was the force that had stalked his men since he had crossed the frontier. The savagery with which they hacked into his lines left no doubt that these were the Anari who had butchered his cousin and the other dead who had lain mutilated in the wake of those nighttime raids.

These were not soldiers like the Anari pressing hard against his lines at the mouth of the valley. These were jackals, with a taste for blood, falling always upon the unsuspecting and devouring them with cruel relish.

Hate rose in Tuzza's belly, hate for these animals who were threshing his elite Guardsmen, hate for the man who led them, the man who had doubtless birthed their cruelty.

He saw that man now, yelling orders amidst the turmoil of battle, and felt his sword in his hand before he was aware of having drawn it. That one Anari became the object of his rage, his rage at the crown that had stolen these men as slaves, his rage at the council that had ordered him into this land, his rage at the grieving families whose sons would not return and whose lives were forfeit without victory or the hope of victory.

Tuzza could not win this battle, he knew. But he could slay that one Anari. He advanced on that Anari with an inhuman scream rising from his throat, a scream that pierced the air like an arrow, a scream against everything that had written the names of so many in blood on the ledger of Tuzza's soul.

Ratha heard a single scream pierce the valley and looked up to see the Bozandari commander riding hard upon a single man…Giri. The scream seemed to freeze everyone for an instant, silence falling over the battlefield like a wet woolen cloak. Even Giri hesitated for an instant. For an instant too long.

Giri heard the thunder of hooves in the echo of the scream, but by the time his eyes drew into focus, he knew it was too late. He looked up into the eyes of the enemy commander and saw reflected in them his own hate, his own pain, his own rage against the cruel scars that fate had carved into his heart.

As Giri tried to raise his sword, knowing it would be far too late, he knew the scars were not carved by fate but by his own dark thoughts, the anger that had driven him so savagely to this place.

As the enemy commander's sword arched down, Giri realized that Ratha had been right. Anger could not fill a soul. It could only consume one.

Tuzza saw the moment of realization in the Anari's eyes in the instant before his sword slashed into the man's throat, passing completely through to sever the head that now slowly fell and rolled on the bloody stones beneath his feet.

It was more than the acceptance of death. It was the acceptance of the life that had led to that death.

Tuzza's sword fell from his open hand, and he became aware that his horse was tumbling, some stone or sword having broken its stride and its leg, their terrified screams rising together as the rocks rose up to meet him and the world went black.

"Noooooooo!" Ratha screamed, seeing his brother fall, knowing even as he screamed the word that the depth of his scream could not undo what had happened. It was as if he could feel his brother's soul ripped from his own, leaving an emptiness he had never known. "Nooooooooooo!"

The world crystallized into that hollow in his heart. With another booming cry, he set upon the Bozandari in front of him. Their blood could not fill that hole within him. But he would try regardless.

Tess and Otteda too, had heard the scream, and now they and their men scrambled up the side of the mountain as if carried on the backs of panthers, effortlessly leaping from rock to crag to boulder, until she could see the horror laid out beneath her.

The battle had descended into a chaotic swirl, hundreds of individual life and death struggles. The Bozandari lines had collapsed, and the Anari were pressing them from front and rear, killing and maiming, an orgy of blood that made Tess's stomach roll.

She had been part of this orgy, she realized. The world around her no longer seemed to bend and flex with every breath, and in its wake, looking down at her blood-stained clothes, she realized what she had done.

Otteda and his companions had been at her side, but Tess

knew that she was responsible for the weakening screams and sobs that rose from the path behind. And, turning back to look at the battle in the valley, she knew that, too, lay upon her shoulders. She knew not why the gods had cruelly laden her with this burden. But the burden, and the blood, lay upon her, heavy, cloying, sickening her to the depths of her soul.

Her attention fell on a single Bozandari in the valley below, one man kneeling on the ground beside a dying comrade, holding the man's head in his lap. Time seemed to dim and flicker, and Tess saw herself in the street with her mother, holding her mother's head as she died. For an instant she heard the man's thoughts flicker through the shredded weave of consciousness and realized he was holding his dying brother, felt his shuddering sobs, felt the last light of hope flicker from his breast as his brother's eyes stilled.

She could bear no more. This madness must end.

She lifted her sword and her voice as one, feeling the sword hum once more in her hand, feeling the white hot stones against her breast beneath her tunic, and screamed.

"By Elanor, *enough!*"

Stillness swept across the valley like a gust of wind, and in its wake lay only the ragged gasps of the living and the ragged cries of the dying. Swords fell to the ground. Men stopped in their tracks, then fell to their knees, their chests heaving in exhaustion.

The battle was over.

The Anari had won.

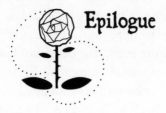 **Epilogue**

The funeral cortege wound through Anahar to the music of the city itself, which sang with grief for fallen Anari. If there lay within that the song of victory, Ratha could not hear it. He and Archer and Tom and Jenah carried a tightly wrapped form upon their shoulders, the body of his brother, borne through the city at the head of the column.

Ratha had no taste for this and would have quietly buried Giri among the other dead of Monabi-Tel, in what was now called the Valley of Victory. Giri deserved to lie in the company of the men with whom he had died, the men who had marched beside him and given their lives as willingly as Giri had given his. But the survivors of his column had insisted that he receive a hero's honors.

And Anahar agreed, for from the stones rose a low, haunting melody, drawing words from the people who lined the streets, a song of courage and honor, a song of struggle and loss, a song of the men whose blood had purchased their freedom.

As Ratha listened more closely, he realized that every family he passed spoke the name of their own fallen, for it seemed that every family had given at least one of its sons in that valley. The ceremony, Ratha realized, honored Giri as the symbol of every Anari who had fallen. His brother would not have wanted to be such a symbol.

In Ratha's eyes, Giri was still the laughing, jesting brother who had been Ratha's childhood partner in mischief and companion in life. Giri should live in their memory as the boy and the man who had laughed, not as the soldier who had died.

Ratha realized he was weeping and made no attempt to cover his face or wipe away the tears. Perhaps the tears could wash away the stain of those last moments in battle, when Ratha had once again become the man he loathed, a savage angel of death, thirsting for blood. Everything that he had become in the desert, everything that he had meditated upon, every enlightenment he had found, had fled in the instant he had watched his brother die.

Cilla had said that she had felt Giri's soul pass into light as he died, that in his last moments he had found the peace that she and Ratha had pressed upon him in their last days. Perhaps that was true. But Ratha had not felt it. He had felt only the wrenching, tearing loss as half of himself was ripped away forever.

He had not been able to look into Cilla's eyes since the day of the battle. Nor had he looked into the eyes of Tess, or Sara. If Ilduin blood had stirred the Anari, it was Anari blood that had bought the victory. The hearts of the gods might live in the Ilduin, but the bloody hands of the gods were the Anari themselves. Ratha's hands.

As they reached the dwellings of Monabi-Tel and the hole that had been dug near the telner, Ratha shut his eyes and let himself be guided by the movements of his companions. The Anari were children of the mountains, and to the roots of the mountains Giri would return. But Ratha could not bear to see it.

* * *

Cilla wept as she watched Ratha's pain. She stood beside Tess and Sara in the circle of Monabi priestesses who ringed the grave. Her heart grieved not for Giri, who now walked among the gods in peace. Her heart grieved for Ratha. He had borne so much in life, and now he bore the loss of his brother with grim silence. Cilla could not read his thoughts, but she could read his face. Anger and guilt in equal measure.

She had tried to talk to him, to comfort him, but he had rejected her every attempt. He was locked within a prison of his own heart now, and she felt his absence as palpably as he felt the loss of his brother. Giri had been her friend and cousin, and they had endured much together during the war. She would forever miss the sparkle that, even to the end, had flickered in Giri's eyes. And now, it seemed, she had lost Ratha, as well.

As she bowed her head and listened, she heard her thoughts echoed throughout Anahar. There had been no victory parade, for they had no doubt that the Bozandari would come again. There was only the grim satisfaction of this battle won, and the weight of grief.

Perhaps one day the Anari would celebrate their freedom. But this was not that day.

Cilla sang the funeral prayers with her sisters, Anari and Ilduin alike, and stooped to place a desert rose upon Giri's body before it was lowered into the grave. Tess spoke, saying that the brilliant desert roses would grow forever in this place, in honor of the thirst for freedom that had bloomed in the man who now lay here. The words might be true, but Cilla knew they were scant comfort for Ratha. And so long as Ratha's heart was darkened, she herself could feel no light.

Tuzza watched the procession wind past the compound where he and his captured men were held. His shoulder and hip ached, although the woman in white had mended the broken bones. She had not the strength to take away the memory of the fall, or that of the Anari soldiers falling upon him, ready to cut him to ribbons until the woman's voice had stilled the valley. She had not the strength to take away his shame, or his fear of what would happen if ever he were to return to Bozandar.

His career was ruined, of that he had no doubt. He knew he should have cared for that, worried for how he would be treated by a court of the council. Instead, he found himself counting the names of his fallen. He had brought eight thousand men into the Anari lands. Fewer than a quarter of that number now wandered with him in the prison compound, their faces clouded with confusion, their sleep shattered by the memories of that final day. He and his men moved as if in a daze, numbed by the totality of their defeat.

His officers, those who had survived, had taken roll and passed to him the names of those who now lay buried in Anari soil, never again to see their homeland. Tuzza had delegated to the surviving officers the duty of writing the letters to the families of the fallen. But he alone could sign them. One after another, and yet another, and yet another.

As the tail of the cortege passed, he numbly walked back to his tent, picked up the next stack of letters, dipped his quill in ink and began again the task that now filled his days. The last humanity his dead comrades would know. A commander's letter to their families, empty words of praise that would never fill the voids left behind.

Tuzza feared their eyes more than anything, their glares of anger if he were taken to execution. The death he deserved, even welcomed. But the specter of their eyes haunted every moment.

He had failed his men, their sons and brothers.

And that he could not forgive.

* * *

Archer watched Tom and Sara, and while he could not hear their words, he had no need to. They had found each other quickly after the formalities of the funeral dinner, and Tom had drawn her away from her Ilduin sisters. He had seen something, Archer knew, his heart tightening. There was more to come. The Bozandari had launched another column. Or his brother had felt the rift in the weave of the universe when Tess had lifted the Weaver's Blade. Or both. Regardless, there would be more fighting.

Tom rose to speak. "The Enemy is filled with wrath and seeks a way to destroy you. The Crown of Bozandar marches even now upon us. The Enemy will settle for nothing less than your blood, Lord Archer."

Archer nodded slowly. He had known this reckoning would come. He felt Tess beside him before she spoke.

"How can brother hate brother so?"

"None can hate as a brother," Archer said. "When the love of brothers is broken, that gulf must be filled with something. For my brother, there was nothing left."

"I am sorry," Tess said quietly.

"There is no reason for you to apologize," he replied. "You played no part in it."

"Perhaps," Tess said. "Or perhaps I did. The ways of the gods confound us all now, and the more I learn of their ways, the more confounded I find myself."

"That may be for the best," Archer said. "To know the ways of the gods is to know our destiny. And that must lie before us, unknown and unknowable, lest we think ourselves their equals."

"As you and the First Ones did," Tess said.

"Exactly," Archer said. "All that we have fought for thus far is but a step on the journey to repair what I and my kindred did in the First Age. And that journey is not yet complete."

"No, it is not," she said. "But we can but take each step as it is presented to us."

"Perhaps someday there will be a step that is not wet with blood and fire," Archer said.

But in his heart he knew that no such steps were near.

Later, alone, Archer went to the stockade and walked inside, unguarded, to the topmark's tent. Sullen eyes watched him, but none dared touch him. Too many Anari guards were about.

The flaps of Tuzza's tent were open, and from within came lamplight. Archer stepped inside and waited while the man scrawled something at the bottom of a piece of parchment.

When Tuzza looked up and saw who was standing there, his expression tightened. Then he rose to his feet. "I'm writing letters to the families of my slain."

Archer nodded. "I, too, grieve for all who fell on the field." He paused, then said wearily, "I am Annuvil."

For just an instant, Tuzza's face seemed blank; then recognition appeared. He hesitated, then dropped his quill and fell to one knee. "My lord."

Archer reached out and drew him to his feet. "Tuzza, we need to talk. For dark things stalk the land, and there will be more fighting ahead. We will need you, and your men, beside us."

"I will not fight Bozandar," Tuzza said.

Archer shook his head. "It is not Bozandar that we fear, my friend. There is another Enemy."

Tuzza's eyes widened. "No."

"Yes," Archer said. "And he stalks us all."

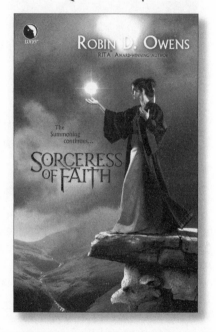

From the forest she will come...

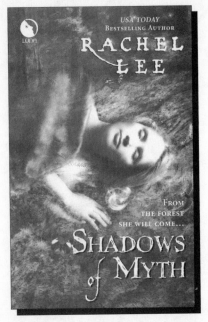

On the trail of Ilduin Bane, a gang of assassin mages whose blades drip poison and whose minds share a common purpose, Archer Blackcloak and his band come across something quite different—a woman named Tess Birdsong. With no memory, no future and only a white rose to identify her, Tess joins Archer and his band, bringing with her the will of one who has nothing to lose.

The road to freedom is long and twisted, but the band cannot turn back now that they have started—no matter how high the price to be paid....

Visit your local bookseller.

LUNA™